The Snowstorm

– UTE MANECKE –

THE SNOWSTORM

Copyright © 2018 Ute Manecke

All rights reserved.

ISBN: 978-0-244-97756-6

No part of this publication may be reproduced, distributed, or transmitted in any form or by any means, including photocopying, recording, or other electronic or mechanical methods, without the prior written permission of the publisher, except in the case of brief quotations embodied in critical reviews and certain other non-commercial uses permitted by copyright law.

This is a work of fiction. Names, characters, businesses, places, events, locales and incidents are either the products of the author's imagination or used in a fictitious manner. Any resemblance to actual persons, living or dead, or actual events is purely coincidental.

First published 2018 by Lulu Books

THE SNOWSTORM

Waking from his daze, he felt the oppressive atmosphere in the room sharply and distinctly. The people around him seemed enveloped in a deep silence avoiding eye contact with each other for the most part but casting suspicious glances at each other here and there.

He must have been unconscious, as he had no recollection of what had happened before, or why or how he had got here, or who these people who now shared the same space as he did were. He merely had a faint memory of people having handled him and tended to him and that there had been some words exchanged between them which sounded abrupt, commanding and harsh. At that point, he started to fully regain his consciousness finding himself lying on the hard stone floor in a stretched-out position with someone pummelling his right arm and tending to him in a simultaneously determined and concerned manner.

It was only after he had begun to move his limbs and to slowly emerge from his daze that the person working on him and the others who had been standing in a close circle around him dispersed and claimed their separate spaces in the room they shared. The atmosphere was becoming tenser.

Suddenly the heavy silence was interrupted by an almost aggressive outburst. 'For God's sake, are we going to continue pretending the others don't exist and give each other the silent treatment by trying to ignore each other? This is unbearable.'

The others flinched at this outburst but soon returned to their largely immobile positions and somehow vacant facial expressions that they had displayed before.

'Right, guys, let's do this differently,' the booming voice from a few moments ago bellowed. 'Why are you all here? Explain!'

The utterance resembled something that one might hear in court when the accused is asked to make a statement that might either exonerate them from the charge of having committed a major crime or prove their guilt. Again, the other people stirred uncomfortably for a few moments but did not react to the command in any other way.

The space surrounding him and the shadowy shapes around him now took on concrete forms, probably because his daze had vanished and his somehow blurred vision had restored itself. He could make out a relatively small interior that was suggestive of a barn with wooden boards for walls and a derelict roof that seemed barely supported by the wooden beams. It was obvious that the place was in a state of disrepair and showed many gaps and slits in the wooden structure that allowed an icy wind to blow in, which made the room very draughty as well as unpleasant to be in. The gaps in the wood were big enough to let some of the smaller snowflakes in. The interior was empty with the exception of a number of farming tools that were loosely stacked in one corner. He could see a rake, shovels, a bucket and a metal canister with a lid.

He slowly, and with great effort, got up on his feet and unsteadily walked a couple of steps towards a lighter area of the interior. Taking a look out of one of the milky-white, small window panes, he could just about discern the giant snowflakes that rushed, propelled by the force of a storm, to all sides and then down to earth. He believed that he had never seen anything quite like it. There was also a suggestion of ice crystals beginning to form on the glass of the window pane.

He felt faint and dizzy so he returned to the place he had been lying in before and sat down carefully. When he returned his gaze back to the room, it came to rest on a woman of middle age who stood a few metres away from him on the other side of the small barn. She stood there rigidly with her arms crossed in front of her in all-purple attire, which – despite consisting of thick snow boots and a padded winter jacket – evoked a touch of elegance although this might have mainly been the result of the alluring shine of her copper-coloured straight hair that was held up at the back of her head by a broad, dark brown clasp that just about managed to handle her hair's volume. The dark-purple suede trousers that she wore revealed the shape of slender but strong legs. Her face was devoid of any traces of make-up and her amber eyes looked straight in front of her appearing stern and distant, an expression that was mirrored by the rest of her features. Her thin lips were pinched and almost colourless next to her flaming red hair. Small wrinkles showed at the corners of her mouth.

To the right of the red-haired woman, a youngish woman of slight build sat on the ground as well. However, she was sitting further back and was leaning against the wall with a small handbag by her side. Her arms inside her white snow jacket were wrapped around her legs and her face was buried in her raspberry-coloured, long woollen dress where it touched her knees. Her feet, clad in brown snow boots, were firmly placed on the ground so that her knees formed the highest point of her legs. Her face and features could not be seen in this pose. A cascade of long, straight, strawberry-blonde hair fell around her knees. There was something beautiful and moving in her pose.

His eyes moved further to the left until they came to rest on a tall, male figure of muscly but not overly heavy appearance. The man was young, probably the youngest one amongst them and his physique seemed to exude strength and power. His hands were shoved deeply into the pockets of his light-brown suede coat that was lined with white woollen material on the inside and also on the collar. The coat was unbuttoned as if he did not feel, or did not mind, the cold in this barn, which was pervasive even if it felt less harsh in there due to the diminished force of the howling storm and the dense snowflakes.

Although his light brown hair was slightly dishevelled, it looked as if the original cut had been a modern and rather stylish one that must have displayed his curls that ended at his earlobes to best effect. His features seemed hostile and aggression was reflected in his hazelnut eyes. It was immediately obvious that the confrontational exclamations earlier must have been made by him. He moved his feet, which were clad in trainers, back and forth on the floor so that he never seemed to stand still for any length of time and seemed rather restless instead.

Their eyes met and in that instant, it was clear that the situation had to be defused. He directly and calmly addressed the young man. 'I'm Charles. Do you want to tell me your name?'

The young man was somewhat taken aback but, after a moment's hesitation, grumbled, 'Leo.'

Charles then fixed his eyes on the other people until they emerged from their withdrawn positions to equally introduce themselves.

'Karen,' the woman dressed in purple said calmly. Her voice did not betray any of her emotions and was without inflection.

'Lisa,' the woman sitting on the floor, hugging her legs, said very quietly. Her name was barely more than whispered, but she did lift her head and briefly looked at Charles when she spoke before lowering her gaze.

At the moment their eyes met, Charles was startled by the greenness of hers, which – he noticed even from this distance – showed small golden lines that accentuated the colour of the iris to best effect. Suddenly another image superimposed itself on Lisa's face of a young woman with greenish eyes interspersed with golden flecks. The young woman was laughing and twirling around and, for a moment, Charles forgot to breathe. The people who shared the same physical space with him once again receded into the background of his consciousness. Still transfixed by the image of the young woman dancing in front of his eyes, he asked, 'Where am I? How did I get here?'

The question seemed more aimed at himself than at the others, but after a few seconds, Karen responded, 'You had fainted in the snowstorm outside. We heard a heavy thud next to the door of this barn. When we saw you lying unconscious in the snow we lifted you and carried you inside. We checked your pulse and breathing, which we managed to detect, albeit both were faint, and placed you in a hopefully comfortable enough position for you to rest and recover. We also massaged your body to increase your blood flow and to wake you up.'

This account was precise and matter-of-fact, stripped of any unnecessary details. And there it was. Like a flash of lightning, he knew who the woman on Lisa's face was. It was Annie! Annie, the love of his life. Now he remembered why he had been out walking in the snowstorm. A yelp escaped him involuntarily followed by uncontrollable sobbing and shaking of his entire body. Tears started streaming down his face.

The others stirred uncomfortably, unsure how to react or what to do. When the sobbing continued unabated, Karen quickly stepped towards him and knelt down by his side.

'Please, sir, do not upset yourself so. Do tell us what it is that aggravates you to such an extent,' she urged him.

Charles, however, responded to this request with a violent shake of his head. 'No! No, I can't! It's tearing me apart! I can't... I can't speak about it!' he exclaimed.

Karen hesitated for a second. Her first instinct to his reaction was to peremptorily tell him off for speaking such nonsense and insist on an account that would explain his despair. She was used to being obeyed most of the time and was known in professional circles for her perseverance, insistence and fierce determination with which she approached any case she worked on. Her hesitation now was rather unusual and was in strong contrast to her assured approach in court. But it was precisely because she was not in court and did not have a legal case to deal with that she felt less certain of the next course of action she should take. She could not simply adopt the role of a High Court judge in this context. She took a somewhat different approach.
'You'll feel better afterwards.'

Charles did not respond to this reassurance but appeared inconsolable.

Everyone else was silent but unsettled and clearly at a loss as to what to do or say that might make a difference. After what seemed a rather long time but had probably just been a minute or two, Lisa mumbled something unintelligible.

Leo turned to her and asked loudly, 'What did you say?'

Lisa flinched when she heard his forceful voice.

'Listen, I don't bite,' Leo continued in what could be regarded as a patronising and slightly aggressive tone. However, after studying Lisa's face for a few moments, he adopted a kinder and more soft-spoken stance.

'Tell us, Lisa...' He instinctively guessed that what she had to say related to the state Charles found himself in. 'Is there anything else we can do?'

Lisa, who had collected herself again, felt more although not completely reassured by Leo's more gentle approach. She said quietly: 'He doesn't have to talk about what troubles him. He should talk though, talk about anything, but ideally tell us a story.'

She now had the attention of the others with the exception of Charles who still seemed to be imprisoned in his grief.

Leo frowned, not understanding the possible use of this suggestion. 'A story?' he asked incredulously.

Lisa nodded thoughtfully. 'Yes. Any story he wants to tell. *He* needs to make a choice, otherwise it won't work.'

Leo still eyed her sceptically, but when he heard another heart-breaking moan from Charles, he made a decision and walked up to him. He crouched down next to Charles and Karen, who had not moved from Charles's side since trying to console him. Bizarre as Lisa's idea sounded, Leo realised that they had nothing to lose if they took it seriously, particularly in the absence of any other constructive suggestions that might help Charles.

As a consequence, he now spoke to Charles calmly and seriously. 'Charles, it's fine. Don't talk about what upsets you if you don't want to. Just tell us a story. Talk about anything you want to talk about. Just speak to us. We need to hear a story from you.' He paused briefly and added, 'You can tell us a fairy-tale or a funny story from a telly programme. We just need to hear a story from you.'

Charles looked up at him for a moment before his head sank down.

Lisa, who had come up behind Leo and who had observed Leo's interaction with Charles, plucked up her courage and asked Charles: 'Can you tell us what has made you happiest in your life? Please, we do want to hear it.'

Charles lifted his head again and, exhausted from the crying and sobbing, looked at her pensively.

Lisa persevered: 'Anything, Charles. It might have been a book or a film, it might have been the early light of a beautiful summer's day or a life event or the radiant colours of the rainbow. What has happiness been for you?'

Charles finally looked too depleted of energy to continue crying. He spoke in a hoarse voice. 'When I met Annie and when our relationship continued to blossom.'

He then remembered again what had happened to Annie and was about to retreat into himself when Lisa, who noticed this, brought him back to the present moment by saying to him, 'It's fine. You're here now. You are not alone. Please, tell us about how you met Annie.'

Charles became calmer and more conscious of his environment again. For a moment, he had the fleeting thought of how odd it was for four strangers to be gathered in an old barn on New Year's Eve in the dwindling light of a winter's afternoon. His thoughts were then directed towards his first meeting with Annie. His surroundings faded and instead, a brightly-lit dance hall filled with animated music emerged.

Dances and Laughter

The swing music created a joyous, carefree atmosphere that made the young people in the dance hall itch to start dancing with the exuberance and recklessness of youth. The band was first class and knew how to bring the dance floor alive.

As soon as the majority of the young people had filed into the hall, the band started playing another lively, but more well-known, piece that served as the opening dance of the night. Each of the young men quickly scanned the space for a girl they wanted to dance with, then swiftly approached her and pulled her to the dance floor, as soon as the girl had blessed them with an encouraging smile.

Charles's eyes fell on a slight girl that stood close to some other girls who seemed to form a closely-knit group. She wore a green dress with some cream-coloured embroidery on it and matching shoes. The wide skirt ended at her knees as was the fashion at the time. However, more than her attire, it was her dazzling smile from her cherry-red lips and the mischievous shine of her unusually green eyes that caught his attention. Her curly hair was the colour of hazelnut and, by ending at the chin, framed her heart-shaped face in a very becoming way. He was immediately drawn to her and knew he had to walk up to her straight away before any of the other young men who had started moving towards the girls could get to her.

When she saw him approach, her smile instantly widened. He wore a casual-smart, cream-coloured suit and made a tall, handsome figure with his strong body and square jaw line. Even his somewhat dishevelled hair, which resembled hers in colour, looked endearing and his dark eyes showed depth and warmth. She was excited when he finally stood in front of her and asked her for the first dance, and she did nothing to conceal it. It was her first time in the dance hall and although she had heard her older sisters and brother speak about it, it was completely different to experience it all at last.

She had longed for her sixteenth birthday to come along for a while now, sixteen being the age that her parents considered their children to be old enough to go out dancing at the end of the week, provided some of their friends who were known to them, and considered reliable, went with them. She had quite a number of friends, as she was lively and vivacious and found it easy to connect with people.

Most of the friends who were with her on that evening were friends from school or her neighbourhood, but there were also a couple of girls who worked with her at the local hairdresser's where she had started work over a year ago. She had always been fascinated by the art of hairdressing. Although she didn't consider herself talented or suitable to go into hairdressing herself, she loved to watch hairdressers at work. Therefore, when she had seen an advert in the local paper for a receptionist at her hairdresser's, she wasted no time in applying for it. Her parents had already asked her what she wanted to do, as compulsory schooling had been about to come to an end, and she had not been able to decide on a trade or kind of job until then. The advert had thus appeared at the right time and she was delighted when she was asked to attend for an interview. She had borrowed one of her sister's beige blouses and brown skirts, polished her rather old shoes as much as she could, borrowed a stylish brown hat from one of her friends and had gone to the interview with a deep determination to get this job. It must have been a mixture of her determination, her open manner, cheerfulness and her ability to communicate freely without any shyness or inhibition in the office of the hairdresser's owner that convinced him and the other receptionist, who worked there part-time, that she would be the right choice.

She was elated when she was offered the job as a result and her joy had continued undiminished ever since she had started her work there. She enjoyed welcoming the clients and learning about the hairstyle they wanted and, after a while, she remembered which hairdresser each of the clients came to see and what they wanted to have done. She loved communicating with them and established a good rapport even with the most difficult of clients. And then there were the moments when the reception went quiet and she managed to spend a few moments watching the hairdressers engaged in their craft, which was sheer bliss to her. Only reluctantly did she then pull herself away from the scene in front of her in which the ladies' hair was set in curls or waves after being washed or long tresses were cut fashionably short. During these moments, the sound of the doorbell or the telephone was an unwelcome interruption in her immersion in the spectacle in front of her. The hairdressers laughed good-naturedly at her fascination with their trade and soon became good friends with her, often exchanging a joke with her when walking past the reception area. It was on such occasions or when they were closing the salon in the evening that she talked about her impending birthday and the prospect of going on dances. And when a couple of the young hairdressers told her that they had never been dancing, she asked them to join her. They started to attend classes for a few weeks on Friday evenings before then going to the Saturday evening open dance events with live music.

Her excitement and anticipation were high on that first Saturday evening in the dance hall when she met Charles. She had enjoyed her dance lessons but had all the time mostly looked forward to the more spontaneous and less formalised way Saturday night dancing was conducted. She was curious what boy or man would first ask her to dance and hoped for a tall, attractive and excellent dancer.

She was not disappointed when Charles led her to the dance floor. She loved his masculine build and, once they started dancing to the swing music, realised that he was a confident dancer who led well and quickly covered up any mistakes she made and brought her back into position with ease. During that evening, they danced another couple of times with each other, which was equally enjoyable as it had been the first time around. They adapted their way of dancing in terms of speed and synchronicity of their moves, and at the end of the night they appeared a well-matched dance couple. Between the dances that they shared, they danced with other partners. She was popular among the men and relished it. She could not stop laughing and smiling and the call announcing the last dance came rather unexpectedly and far too soon. It was hard to believe that it was nearly eleven o'clock and that she had spent the better part of three hours in the dance hall and, mainly, on the dance floor.

After finishing the evening's last dance with a skinny blond boy, she and her friends moved to the dance hall's exit. Just when she was about to step outside, Charles, who must have waited for her at the door, stepped forward, took her hand and said with a big smile and a twinkle in his eyes, 'Good bye, Annie.'

They had introduced themselves before embarking on their first dance.

'It has been a pleasure to meet you and to dance with you.'

Annie smiled at him and shook his hand for a few seconds before releasing it whilst her friends paused and watched the exchange.

'May I?' Charles indicated the downward step from the doorway and offered his arm to her in a slightly clumsy but, at the same time, most charming fashion.

Annie, who was not used to such gentlemanly behaviour, blushed and hesitated for a moment before taking his arm and walking down the step.

Her friends behind her looked at each other and had a hard time suppressing their giggles.

Charles turned around to face Annie again and said, 'I hope you will come back.'

He paused and seemed to want to add something but reconsidered and walked away with rapid steps.

Annie, looking somewhat stunned, knew she would be teased by her friends but did not mind that at all after such a dazzling night.

From then on, she went to the dance hall every Saturday evening and danced her heart out. Although she had many admirers she and Charles always managed to dance some dances together and started looking for each other as soon as they had separately entered the dance hall.

Soon they began to talk more between the dances and at the end of the evening, and after a couple of months Charles asked her whether she was free the following Sunday and would like to go for a walk and a picnic with him.

She nodded excitedly and answered, 'Yes, that would be lovely, Charles.'

True to his word, Charles came to her house the next Sunday in his father's old, but well-maintained, car in flared trousers, a chequered vest and matching cap.

Annie's mother opened the door for him. She was a small woman whose features were recognisably reflected in her daughter and whose eyes and hair were of the same shade as her daughter's, although the strong colour of her hair was interlaced with silvery threads. She asked Charles into their modest but clean and tidy abode. On her request, he followed her into the living-room where two young boys of about eight and ten were playing with a model railway on the coarse carpet that covered the entire living room floor space. She asked them in a tone that discouraged any attempts at disobedience to stand up and say 'hello' to Charles.

They did as they were told and introduced themselves as Seb and Joe, which really – so they explained – were short but much preferred versions of Sebastian and Joseph.

Their mother laughingly shook her head and tousled their blond hair that was beautifully contrasted by their expressive brown eyes. She then turned her attention towards three people who were standing near the window and had been talking to each other, and beckoned them to come over to meet their guest.

A young woman who looked hardly older than twenty offered him her hand first.

'I'm Elaine. It's very nice to meet you. Annie has mentioned you a lot.'

Charles would normally have felt embarrassed at hearing such words but something about Elaine made him immediately feel at ease. Her voice was warm and her smile was genuine. Moreover, she had Annie's golden-green eyes and her hair was also the colour of rich hazelnut although much longer than Annie's and draped around her head in thick plaits. She wore a simple blue dress that bulged around her midriff making it immediately obvious that she was in the late stage of pregnancy.

Charles gave her a warm handshake and returned her greeting before the young, dark-haired and slightly stocky man next to her added, 'I'm Tom, Elaine's husband. Pleased to meet you.'

Whilst his features looked rather coarse and his stocky build did not immediately appear attractive, Charles could quickly detect his warmth, and his eyes expressed humour and a gentle disposition, which must all have been attributes that Elaine had found appealing.

After exchanging greetings with him, Charles directed his attention to the third figure in that group, who – he guessed – must have been the father of the house. He was much taller than his wife and daughters and of a strong, muscular body build that suggested being used to hard work outside. Charles learned later that he was the right-hand to the farmer who lived around the corner, where he did the hard work on the field as well as having a supervisor's function over the other two members of staff and helping out with the accounts. He was an indispensable part of the farm and had been asked several times over the years to move into one part of the farmhouse with his family, which was currently mostly empty and only used for guests. He had repeatedly declined this offer though, as he valued the privacy of his own home, modest as it was. He knew that if he moved into the farmhouse he would probably be called upon all the time whenever there was an issue that had to be resolved and, as it was, he already spent a considerable amount of time at work almost every day and often struggled to find enough time for his family, which was very dear to him.

He now shook Charles's hand with a firm grip and welcomed him in a simple but friendly manner. His short hair was mainly grey but still showed some blond streaks, which were the colour of his sons' hair. His blue eyes looked at Charles directly and inquisitively.

'Annie is getting ready and should be down in a minute. Why don't you take a seat in the meantime?' He gestured to one of the dining chairs at the end of the room.

When Charles approached the chair he noticed that, already curled up on it, was a well-nourished cat whose dense, black fur had been rendered almost invisible by having seemingly merged with the dark chair cover.

When Annie's father saw Charles's hesitation and spotted the cat, he shooed it off the chair telling it, 'Molly, get off. We have a guest. Go and find Deirdre. Ah, look, there she is.' He pointed to one of the window-sills where a ginger tabby was stretched out in deep slumber. Molly ignored her though and walked out of the room in a sulk.

Charles took a seat feeling a bit awkward, as he was now the only person in the room sitting. Annie's father offered him a hot toddy or grog, but remembered before Charles had an opportunity to answer that Charles had a car with him and would be driving.

'What about tea or coffee then?' Annie's father asked.

Again, there was no opportunity for Charles to reply, as Annie now entered the room after she must have run down the stairs judging from the sound of quick footsteps he had heard a second ago. She looked absolutely radiant as she stood near the doorway and Charles was conscious of a sharp intake of breath on his part. She wore a sea-blue dress with white dots, white sandals without heels and a straw hat with a blue ribbon. Her lips were again bright red and her cheeks looked flushed. Her hair looked springy and voluminous.

'I'm here,' she announced unnecessarily. 'Are you ready to go, Charles?'

Charles nodded and somehow shyly walked towards her whilst being fully aware of the other family members around them.

When they said their good byes, Annie's father said to him, 'You must come for a proper visit soon, Charles.'

Annie's mother added, 'Come for Sunday lunch soon. You'll meet the whole family. Elaine and Tom are always here and so are Marisa and Andrew. Matthew, who works with his father at the farm, comes whenever he is not needed there on a Sunday and brings Maria along. Sunday is an important day for the family when we go to Church, prepare the food and spend time in each other's company.'

'Although,' she continued with a frown on her face, 'the work at the farm doesn't always allow for it. Jacob barely manages to spend the entire Sunday with us anymore.'

Her husband was about to protest, but Annie's mother was having none of it. 'It's true, Jacob. I know you're trying, but I think they take advantage of your work ethic, dedication and sense of duty at the farm. They can't expect you to be there every day and you have to learn to say 'no'!'

'Helen,' Jacob interjected. 'It's not quite like that.'

'It is and you know it,' Helen retorted. 'I grant you that you have made more of an effort lately, but whenever you've been here on a Sunday, you can guarantee that Matthew is called out there. Tell me, when do I ever have the whole family gathered here?'

On that note, Annie and Charles said 'good bye' to everyone in the room and made their way out. When they walked along the stone path next to the small front garden with its wild plants, flowers and an apple tree, Annie said laughingly to Charles, 'Welcome to the McKenzie family.'

Charles smiled, opened the car and held the door open for Annie so that she could lower herself into the vehicle with its low seats. After he got in on the other side, he asked, 'Are the other family members your mother mentioned all siblings of yours?'

Annie, who was visibly excited to sit in that car with Charles, replied, 'Marisa is my sister. She's eighteen and got married and moved to a place of her own with her husband Andrew five months ago. She doesn't live far though. None of my siblings have moved out of town and you know that this town is not that big. Matthew is my older brother. He's twenty and got married to Maria, my sister-in-law, about a year ago. As you have heard, he helps father with the farm. Well, I should probably say that he works for the farmer. He's very dedicated to his work and loves being in the open air and working with the earth. He thrives on physical labour. And Elaine you've just met. She is twenty-one and the eldest. She and Tom married two years ago. They had already been sweethearts at school so Tom had been part of the family for a long time. He's like a brother to me. He's so much fun.'

Annie laughed, obviously remembering some of the fun times they had had together. 'You've seen that Elaine is expecting a baby. It's due in four weeks' time and we are all hugely excited. I'm very close to her and I can't wait to welcome a little nephew or niece to this world.'

They had left the outskirts of town behind by now. Charles was amused by Annie's carefree chatter and liveliness. He had initially worried a little whether there might be awkwardness or embarrassment on their first outing together, but he realised now that his worries had been unfounded.

It was a truly glorious day. The May sun was shining brightly in the light-blue sky lighting up the patchwork of undulating green meadows and well-tended fields of the mid-Devonshire landscape. They drove past homesteads and a couple of small villages until they stopped at the top of a hill.

'We're here,' Charles said to Annie, getting out of the car and opening her door on the other side. 'This is what I wanted to show you.' He pointed to the landscape below them that stretched like a beautiful, colourful, shiny carpet to the far horizon.

Annie stepped out of the car and followed his gaze. A breeze nearly swept away her straw hat but she grabbed it just in time and kept holding it firmly down on her head. She was clearly impressed by the natural beauty all around them.

'Charles, this is so beautiful. It reminds me of our family's Sunday trips in the past when the whole family spent the day in a beautiful spot like this one. We just haven't done that for so long now that my older siblings don't live at home any longer and my father often goes to the farm at some point on a Sunday.'

Charles smiled and stepped close to her. 'I'm glad you like it. Do you want to walk for a bit?'

Annie tore her gaze away from the landscape below, turned to Charles and nodded eagerly. 'Yes, let's go for a walk.'

He offered her his arm, which she took trustingly and without any hesitation and they strolled happily along with the sun warming their bare arms and faces. After about an hour they returned to their car and Charles took a red-and-white chequered blanket and basket out of the boot. His mother had prepared the picnic basket, as he hadn't been sure what to put into it. She had prepared a range of sandwiches using wholesome rye bread, had added some carrots and radishes, apples, lemonade and some slices of the Victoria sponge Sunday cake that she had made the previous evening. Charles had told Annie that he would arrange the picnic so she should not bring anything along.

Annie's eyes shone when she saw the lovingly prepared contents of the picnic basket and exclaimed, 'Oh, Charles, this is such a lovely picnic!'

Charles smiled, gave her a paper plate and a plastic cup and then started to distribute the contents of the picnic basket. After finishing the food and drink they both stretched out on the grass next to each other, feeling satiated and happy, listening to the hum of the bees around them.

After a while, Charles propped himself up on his elbows and turned to Annie, who was lying on the grass to his right with her eyes closed and a contented smile on her face, and asked her, 'What makes you happiest in life, Annie? What do you most want or wish for?'

Annie briefly opened her eyes but quickly closed them again when she was blinded by the sunlight. She answered promptly. 'This is pretty good, you know. Many things make me happy. Being with my family, dancing and walking and picnicking in the countryside are all bliss.'

'Yes, but is there anything specifically that you want in the future?' Charles insisted.

Annie thought for a moment and then replied: 'I would love to keep all the pleasures that I currently enjoy but, of course, I also want a family – ideally, a big family like the one I have grown up in. What about you, Charles?'

'I like the idea of a family very much. I am an only child and always had to find some playmates outside of home. I find this sense of community that you seem to get in a big family appealing.' Charles thought for a second and then asked: 'But did you always get on? Were there no character clashes or arguments?'

Annie laughed at what appeared to her to be rather naïve questions. 'Of course, we have argued and still do sometimes. We are all different personalities with our own ideas, beliefs and thoughts. But we are all rather close as well so that any differences don't really matter. There is too much fondness and common ground between us all for that to happen.'

It was late in the afternoon when they started to pack up the picnic things and got themselves ready to get back into the car to drive home. When Annie was about to get into the car again, Charles followed an impulse, took her hand and pulled her close to him. Her face was now only a few centimetres away from his and her eyes looked seriously into his. Charles swallowed and said in a hoarse, quiet voice, 'Annie, I'm so glad I have met you.' He then pulled her even closer and his lips found hers, initially just resting on them, but then opening them and inserting his tongue between her lips.

Annie didn't do anything at first but then put her arms around him and responded to the kiss, moving her lips and exploring his tongue with hers. She felt heat suffuse her entire body.

Charles held her close and started to perspire heavily. He had only kissed a couple of girls before Annie, so this was still new and exciting, and he knew that he had never been as much in love with a girl before as he now was with Annie.

It seemed a long time until they stopped holding each other and got into the car and drove back in silence. It was not necessary to speak. When they said 'good bye' outside Annie's family home, they kissed again, albeit briefly, as they were somehow shy about being observed. They both felt a warmth and elation inside themselves that was new to them and that they treasured experiencing.

From then on, they went on walks and picnics together most weekends and it certainly helped that late spring and summer showed themselves from their most dazzling and finest sides delighting them with their high temperatures and long hours of sunshine. Charles soon became part of the McKenzie's traditional Sunday lunches, which were always convivial occasions filled with laughter, teasing and much chatter. Charles found that he got on with the family very well and established a particularly good rapport with Annie's younger brothers, Seb and Joe, who adored Charles as he made them laugh and played with them and was genuinely interested in what they did. When Annie and Charles joined the Sunday lunches they would go out together later or they would occasionally go on a Saturday trip when they did not have to help out that much at home.

On Friday evenings, they started going to the local picture house together. Charles loved films and introduced Annie to the big screen, all the time chuckling at her sense of wonder and excitement whenever they watched a movie together. Charles couldn't think of anything better than sitting in the back row of the cinema with Annie, holding her hand tightly whilst the room was steeped in darkness and barely illuminated by the moving pictures in the front. Sometimes, when they watched a particularly moving or poignant scene, they would slightly turn to look at each other, and Charles then usually took Annie's face into his hands and gave her a long, lingering kiss.

He was also intrigued by how films on the big screen were projected and shown to the audience. When they once left the picture house together arm-in-arm after having watched a hilarious comedy together, he said to Annie, 'I want to learn how to project films, Annie. I do want to learn this skill. Just imagine what it must be like to make all these people in the audience happy, smile, weep or shudder with fright – to make them emotionally and mentally engage with something on a deeper level, to get involved in something that is outside their day-to-day experience and that opens worlds and horizons to them!'

His eyes sparkled as he continued, 'Just think of how wonderful it is to take people completely elsewhere and out of themselves. They go on an exciting journey with you.'

Annie loved his enthusiasm and suggested to him to speak to the projectionist next time they came again.

This was exactly what Charles did. The following week, Charles asked the member of staff at the door who checked their tickets whether it was possible to speak to the projectionist after the screening of the film and spoke of his interest to learn more about it.

The helpful staff member promised he would try to arrange this for Charles, asking him to wait outside the screening room once the film had ended and he would ask the projectionist to see him for a quick chat.

And this was how Charles met Tobias: After about twenty minutes of waiting outside the screening room whilst talking about and reliving some scenes with Annie, a small, elderly man with a hunchback, white hair and beard and clear blue eyes came walking towards them with quick footsteps. His eyes were inquisitive and suggested a sharp intellect and wit. He gave both Annie and Charles a firm handshake introducing himself and asking them for their names. He then ushered them into the projectionist's room, which was a relatively small space that did not only house the large projector made of silver metal but also a large array of film reels that were scattered all around the room. A couple of them were placed on the table right next to the projector, others were piled on a wall-to-wall counter at the back of the room, but the majority of them were sitting in wall shelf compartments that seemed to follow an alphabetical order system indicated by the letters of the alphabet at the bottom of some of the compartments. On the left-hand side of the door upon entering was a dark grey metal cupboard with some large drawers. One of the drawers was open when they entered the room and offered them a view of the index card system that was used to organise and manage the film reels. The room was dusty and the uneven stone floor nearly caused Annie to fall when she stumbled over a sudden elevation, which her shoes with their smooth soles and high heels struggled to cope with. Charles just managed to catch her in time to prevent her from injuring herself.

Tobias, who had seen Annie's stumble when he was turning around to them, told them, 'Be careful. This is very much a working environment that is not suited to a pretty lady's shoes.' He pointed to a couple of simple old chairs on the wall facing the door and asked them to take a seat. He sat on a wooden stool that was placed in front of the projector and studied them.

'Now what can I do for you, Annie and Charles? Paul said to me that you would like to know more about my work. Is there anything in particular that interests you? And what is it that evokes your curiosity about the work of a projectionist?'

Charles, who was full of excitement and who had been scanning the room until his attention was attracted by the large window in the wall facing the projector that allowed him a good view of the screen in the adjacent room, turned towards Tobias and almost stammered, 'I... I just want to learn everything about it. I'm fascinated by film and I want to know how all these wonderful moving images are being created, about how they can be safely stored in these film reels over there and then displayed in a big format to move the audience.'

Tobias had to smile at Charles's apparent excitement. 'The first aspect you mention is the responsibility of a cinematographer and therefore best not to be explained by me, but I can certainly explain how to store film reels safely and most of all the projection work itself. This might take some time though. Have you got the time for it now? I only have some tidying up to do but I can do that later.'

Charles was just about to nod vociferously when he realised that Annie might be less keen on learning about the technicalities of the projection process. He stopped himself from responding to Tobias's question straight away and addressed Annie instead, 'Annie, would that be alright with you?'

He considered asking the question of whether she would prefer going home instead but couldn't quite bring himself to do so as this would have meant letting this wonderful opportunity to learn more about what he was truly interested in slip.

Annie did indeed not particularly relish the prospect of listening to detailed explanations of how films were screened, but she was acutely aware of how much Charles was keen on precisely that experience. She therefore hesitated, unsure how to answer Charles's question and being torn between asserting her own wishes and granting Charles the fulfilment of his.

Tobias quickly understood what was going on and suggested, 'What about you coming in to see me another time, Charles? I can explain everything to you then, and tonight you and Annie can enjoy the rest of the evening together.'

Charles, still keen to learn everything there and then, but also guessing Annie's different preferences, said slowly, 'If this is fine with you, I'd love to. Would you really have time for that in the near future though?'

Tobias watched him with a sombre expression on his face before he replied, 'One thing you must know, Charles, is that I'm true to my word. If I say I will do something, I will do it.'

Charles was visibly embarrassed now and blushed deeply. 'I didn't mean to doubt your sincerity.'

Tobias cut him off with a twinkle in his eyes: 'Do you want to come and see me tomorrow? I have a matinee screening and an evening screening to do but I could see you either before the matinee film or between the two.'

Charles literally jumped at these proposals. 'I will have to help father in the workshop tomorrow morning but I can see you after the matinee screening. Thank you. Thank you so much!'

Tobias looked at him benignly. 'I'm here a lot and I like being here and take pleasure in speaking to people, especially – but not only – if they are interested in projection work as well. I love what I do but there don't always seem to be enough opportunities to engage verbally with people. And as I'm getting older and some of my friends and acquaintances are not around any longer, life can easily become a bit isolating. If it wasn't for Pete, I would probably constantly talk to myself. – Pete is my cat, you know,' he added when he became aware of the puzzled expressions on Charles and Annie's faces. 'He's a grumpy bugger, but I wouldn't swap him for the world. The two of us are a good team, independent and free-spirited and at the same time very curious.'

Annie laughed. 'I know what you mean. We have two cats at home, Molly and Deirdre, and they do whatever they feel like doing. They take pleasure in going wild and playing their little tricks, and are spoilt little brats. You won't believe how many things they have broken or scratched. But then, after creating all that turmoil, they curl up in front of the fireplace and nobody can be cross with them any longer. They purr and look ever so peaceful and ask to be adored.'

Tobias, taking pleasure in Annie's vivacious cheerfulness, agreed. 'I used to have a dog, Ada, a cocker spaniel that was my companion for thirteen years. I took her in when she was still a puppy and the neighbours who owned her mother couldn't keep all of the latter's litter. She was tiny then but already very inquisitive and full of energy. We went on walks together in the mornings and evenings and she definitely contributed her fair share to my reasonably good health and fitness during the time I had her. Whenever I had her off the leash she ran around as if she was determined to win a race. She was a loyal soul,' Tobias mused. 'Her death five years ago nearly broke my heart. I didn't think that I would ever provide a home for another animal again at first.'

Annie interjected. 'Didn't you consider having another dog?'

Tobias answered. 'That would have reminded me too much of Ada. I needed a new start with a very different being.' He laughed. 'And a very different being I got in Pete. He was a stray that I found on one of my walks hiding in a bush and in an obviously bad state. He was dirty, had lice, his fur was without shine and he must have been attacked by a bigger animal, as he had a wound on his left side that had become infected. When I picked him up he started to scratch and bite but I managed to calm him down and reassure him soon enough. I took him to the vet, who de-liced him and treated his wound, and then he moved in with me. He settled in fairly quickly despite his tough life so far as a stray and seems to be contented on the whole, despite his grumpy façade.'

Annie beamed.

Charles asked, 'What made you decide to become a projectionist?'

Tobias looked at him pensively. 'Well, I would be lying if I told you it was a childhood dream of mine for the simple reason that projectionists did not exist at that time. We didn't even have the wireless yet. The latter was only introduced when I reached young adulthood.' He paused and then resumed in a louder voice, 'But we talk and I haven't even offered you a drink. What would you like? Coffee or tea?'

'Coffee, please,' Charles answered.

'Tea, please, with milk but no sugar,' Annie replied.

Tobias excused himself for a moment and shuffled out of the room.

Whilst Annie and Charles were on their own they glanced at the items in the room more closely, especially the film reels in the wall shelf compartments. Charles couldn't resist the temptation to pull some of the reels out and read out the labels, which displayed the titles of the films. There were so many of them that Charles hadn't even heard of, and some of the titles sounded most intriguing and mysterious. He was just about to read out another such title when Tobias returned with a couple of chipped ceramic mugs of different shapes and colours and put them on the small table near the projector.

Charles wheeled around with the expression of a small child who had been caught doing something forbidden. 'I... I'm sorry, Tobias, I just wanted to see what films you have.' He looked rather contrite, unsure of how Tobias would react.

Tobias gave him a long, stern look before commenting drily, 'Curiosity killed the cat.'

Charles held his gaze uneasily and didn't know what to do or say until Tobias added, with a broad grin spreading across his face, 'But satisfaction brought it back.'

Charles realised with relief that Tobias wasn't angry at all and went back to him with Annie to take his coffee and Annie's tea before resuming his seat on one of the stools.

Tobias stood in front of them and explained: 'I think the roots to my enjoyment of cinema projection lie in my curiosity about people, their lives and stories. I've always watched people ever since my childhood. At that time, I not only asked my parents but also strangers many questions, which often focused not only on general or specific areas of knowledge but also on personal matters relevant to these people. I wanted to know why people acted in a certain way or why they would find themselves in particular situations. However, I soon learned that it wasn't always appropriate to ask these questions, and my parents would reprimand me if they thought I made people uncomfortable with my inquisitive nature. As a result, I asked fewer personal questions when I met people, but my curiosity about the world, and people in particular, was undiminished. I continued to closely observe my environment and drew my own conclusions. The moment I started working full-time at my uncle's convenience store and was in a position to interact with a range of different customers on a daily basis, I came into my own. I love seeing so many different personalities of all ages and backgrounds and I soon learned a lot about their lives.'

Annie, who had been listening intently, asked eagerly, 'Did your customers talk a lot about themselves to you? Would they just start talking or would you prompt them?'

Tobias replied, 'Sometimes they just referred to some circumstances at home in the context of their shopping activities, for example why they might suddenly buy a certain product that they normally don't buy. In these circumstances, I often learned that a fussy aunt or an old friend with unusual tastes had come to stay in my customers' homes. At other times, customers did in fact come to me after a while and tell me what they did or thought or felt on their own accord. But frequently I would just observe my customers and try to guess what was going on in their lives. Their moods, words and behaviour served as indicators.'

Charles grinned and said, 'You sound like Sherlock Holmes. Did you ever think of becoming a private detective and coming to fame and fortune in that way?'

Tobias smiled briefly but then became more serious again. 'I suppose that could have been a possibility. However, apart from my thirst for knowledge, I developed an interest in furthering people's enjoyment and appreciation of the world around them. I wanted to show them sunlight when they could only see darkness. I wanted to reveal the beauty of colours to them when they only perceived shades of black and white.' He paused for a moment, cleared his throat and then carried on. 'Don't get me wrong. I'm not a magician or better than anyone else. I could – and still can – however, often put myself into another person's shoes and feel what might come close to what they experienced. The many occasions on which I observed and studied people and reflected on what I saw certainly contributed to this deeper understanding of others. There have been numerous times when I saw a child's disappointment and frustration when they didn't get what they wanted, but when I showed them a toy that appealed to them, they soon started to smile again and managed to refocus. Or when a young person looked dejected because their parents appeared unreasonably strict in their opinion or they had been disappointed in their first love, but when I gave them a book that I thought might speak to them in their situation, they looked at it and then became immersed in something outside themselves that took them away from their present circumstances and lessened their pain and distress. On occasion, if there was nothing around that attracted their attention, I just told them a story that I thought might appeal to them. However, I found that most people were particularly susceptible to visual elements.

'Although I appreciated the introduction of the wireless with its many educational programmes as well as entertainment broadcasts, I always thought that there should be a visual equivalent. When at last the first films – silent films – were screened I knew that this was the start of something I had been waiting for for a long time and that this could be a powerful tool to reach out to people.' Tobias smiled thinking back to that time. 'I went to see every film I could possibly watch as far as time and pocket-money allowed. Initially that wasn't too difficult when the first few films appeared, but soon there was an explosion of new films and it was hard to keep up with all the new releases. After watching a film, I would always examine my friends or other cinema-goers to see what effect the film had had on them. There was usually an emotional reaction of some kind, be it smiles, laughter, tears or expressions of shock on their faces. When listening to them speak about the film, I noticed how individual their reactions were, how they took note of different aspects of it and how the same film meant completely different things to them.

'Eventually I spoke to the film theatre's projectionist, as you are doing now and asked him whether I could assist him in his work. He was hesitant at first but when he saw how keen I was to learn about it and how much films meant to me, he introduced me to the art of projection. From then on I assisted him whenever I could in my free time.'

Charles, who was excited by the parallels he saw in Tobias's and his love of film and its potential to move people and make a difference – at least momentarily – to their lives, eagerly asked, 'Did you not want to start working in the movie theatre full-time?'

Tobias replied that it would have been difficult to give up his job and be financially independent in a still relatively new area of work and, besides, the projectionist he worked with had no intention at the time of cutting down his hours or letting him work there any more hours than he already did, and the movie theatre could not afford to pay another salary.

'When did you start working here as the main projectionist then?' Charles asked, curiously.

Tobias frowned. 'The projectionist I worked with died suddenly of a stroke one day. It was a huge shock and a very sad occasion that then led to my progression to main projectionist. His will stated that he wanted me to step into his footsteps and I was delighted about his final wish. I was only a few years away from retirement anyway; the film business had been booming and had, without doubt, established itself exceedingly well so that it was not difficult to finish work at the store after having trained someone else up for it. Of course I sometimes missed my customers at first, but some of them now came to see the movies and I met up with many of those I had become close to. And I love this work and have never looked back,' he added.

Charles and Annie looked at Tobias with shiny eyes giving him their undivided attention. This made Tobias smile. 'But I've talked enough now. You've heard how I have become involved with the joys of projection. You should leave now and enjoy the rest of your evening together. I will tidy up for a bit.' With these words, he walked to the door and Annie and Charles followed his cue and did the same.

They shook hands at the door.

'I'll see you tomorrow, Charles,' Tobias reminded him.

Charles nodded keenly. 'Yes, see you tomorrow, Tobias.'

Then he and Annie left Tobias and the movie theatre.

When Charles finally returned home that evening, his parents were still up despite the late hour, his mother finishing her sewing in the living-room and his father reading one of his sports magazines. They had just decided to call it a day and retire to bed when an animated Charles entered the living-room ready to tell his parents about his encounter with Tobias.

His parents listened to what he told them.

His father, William, a stocky man of medium height and considerable physical strength, said in a booming voice that a stranger might have mistaken for a stern one but that really was teasing and jocular in nature, 'You're not running off to the movies now and leaving your old parents and the business behind, are you?'

Charles laughed light-heartedly, as he knew that his father only played at being severe and authoritarian. 'Of course not, father. I won't leave you alone with the business. But I want to learn everything about films while I'm off work. I'm passionate about it. One day, dad, I might become a projectionist myself.'

His mother, Ellen, was a tall, slender woman who was both practical as well as quietly intelligent. She formed an almost comical contrast to her husband both in appearance and in temperament. Unlike most of her female friends at the time, she had decided to undergo nursing training and work in the profession rather than stay at home after marrying young and bring up a large family. Although she got to know William through friends at a young age, she asked him to wait for marriage and children until she had actually worked as a nurse for a while. Waiting for marriage and children to focus on a career was a rather revolutionary act at the time and her attitude was initially sharply criticised. However, when she did not submit to the wishes of others, her family and William eventually accepted her decision and William, who was besotted with her, resigned himself to waiting for her. And this is how it had continued ever since: Although it appeared at first glance as if William was the dominant one in their relationship, nothing was really implemented without Ellen's seal of approval.

Ellen now said to Charles, 'As long as you know that the carpentry business is a reliable source of income and hold on to that, it doesn't do you any harm to pursue other interests. Will you still have enough time for Annie though?'

His parents had met Annie a few times as well by now as she sometimes came over for supper on a weekday or after they had been on a Sunday outing together and had seen her family first.

Charles had been a bit nervous about the first meeting between Annie and his parents. He knew that his father could be very direct and a bit brash and that this, sometimes, put people off who didn't perceive his good intentions.

However, he didn't need to worry about Annie. She and his father hit it off extremely well, probably because Annie was used to a direct approach at work and at home, and her personality found it easy to relate to it. She had been in the house for less than five minutes when she burst out laughing at one of his father's jokes and the rest of her stay there continued in the same vein.

His mother was more serious and reticent, but Charles knew that this was his mother's nature and was not related to her feelings towards Annie. And indeed, after Annie had left and he had a few moments on his own with his mother, she commented on what a lovely girl Annie appeared to be and that she was very happy for Charles. This concern for his happiness and her genuine liking of Annie was expressed in this question of hers about Charles's time planning and availability.

Charles brushed Ellen's concern aside though, telling her, 'I merely go there between leaving work on Saturday and meeting Annie to go dancing. Besides, I might only go there tomorrow if Tobias manages to explain everything to me then. There might not be any more Saturday meetings at the cinema to learn more after tomorrow.'

There would be more Saturday meetings with Tobias at the cinema, however.

True to his word, Tobias expounded the basics of his job to Charles, but asked him at the end of the afternoon whether Charles wanted to come back the following week to learn something about the history, which was quite recent, of cinema projection.

Naturally, Charles went back the following week and the following weeks when Tobias started to give him small tasks and let him help. Soon Charles went to the movie theatre to assist Charles when a film was actually screened on some weekday evenings. To Charles, it was a dream and he relished every moment of it. At the same time, he did not neglect Annie and spent all his remaining free time with her, and treasured his new relationship.

The months went by in this manner and the Christmas season arrived. It was a Saturday evening; Charles and Annie had left the dance hall and were on their way home using their usual shortcut through the park. As they entered the park, the scene in front of them was enchanting: The trees on both sides of their path were shimmering white and seemed to have been dusted with fine icing sugar that formed a soft layer on their branches and twigs. The ground was also covered in a thin blanket of snow, which was only interrupted by some footsteps that had walked across it earlier and after which it had not snowed any more. It had snowed for a while in the afternoon but it had stopped by early evening. The clouds had completely disappeared and instead, the light of the stars in the clear night sky lent a subtle illumination to the landscape in front of them that was heightened by the white of the snow. In fact, ice crystals were visible on the surface of the snow under the light of a lamp post next to a bench where Charles stopped. He and Annie had been walking arm-in-arm so that she was forced to stop as well when Charles came to a halt.

Annie looked at Charles and said, 'You don't want to sit down on this cold bench that is covered in snow, Charles, do you? I know this is all extremely pretty but I need to get home now.'

Charles knew that Annie was extremely busy with Christmas preparations at home, and it had taken some persuading to make Annie come out dancing with him. Not only had she helped to make advent wreaths and other seasonal decorations at home over the previous few weeks, she had also been busy knitting and crocheting winter jumpers, warm cardigans and woolly socks for her younger brothers and her five-month old nephew, James. Her mother couldn't possibly make all these new clothes herself whilst being still busy with darning old clothes, curtains and other items. Besides, Annie was good at these crafts. She and Elaine had spent past afternoons with their mother pursuing these activities and had both been quick to learn. Elaine was usually the more patient and focused one of them. Annie was easily distracted by physically more active pursuits such as running around with her younger brothers or playing interactive games with them. Their sister Marisa was out of the equation, as anything her mother had taught her fell on barren ground. She could just not replicate what she was shown to the extent that even buttons she'd sew on an item of clothing would be misaligned and come loose.

After years of trying to develop such skills in her, her mother had given up and decided that she had other talents that were valuable, such as establishing a great connection with animals, which she used in her work as a veterinary assistant in her husband's practice. Now that Elaine was very busy with James, it mainly fell to Annie and Helen to make and mend clothes and other items for the house that they could not always afford to buy. Before James was born, Helen had worked for months on a quilt for him on which he could lie, and had shown Annie the art of quilting and subsequently used her as her assistant. The end result was nothing short of stunning in both its colours and details: It showed sailing boats on the blue sea with its high waves crashing on the beach next to a meadow with flowers in all shapes and colours; tractors and other agricultural equipment tilling the fields; a forest with deer in it and squirrels playing between trees in a clearing. These were just some of the quilt's motifs. When it was given to Elaine after she had given birth to James, she was moved to tears and did not know how to thank her mother and Annie for it. But they brushed away her objections to having invested so much of their time in it. Elaine placed James on the quilt immediately after receiving it and James soon came to love his colourful and artistic baby quilt and didn't want to be without it.

Despite all the many festive preparations, Charles knew that he needed to spend this evening in Annie's company and had planned to speak to her at the spot they were standing in now. He addressed her: 'I know you need to go home but I want us to stay her for a minute and be quiet. Trust me.'

Annie looked questioningly at Charles. She didn't know what to make of it but slowly realised that Charles had something on his mind that he struggled to put into words. This was unusual for him. Annie waited patiently and eventually Charles spoke. 'Annie, I want to ask you something.'

With these words, he took a small black velvet box from the inside of his winter coat, snapped the box open whilst holding it out to her and asked her solemnly, 'Annie, do you want to become my wife?' His voice was hoarse and faded almost completely at the end.

Annie gazed in surprise, first at the slim, silver ring that was without adornments but had a pretty shine to it and then at Charles's nervous-looking features. Although she had hoped that Charles would ask her to marry him at some point, she had not foreseen that it would happen in the run-up to Christmas. Her eyes became moist and she was speechless for a few moments before she took the box in one hand and lifted the ring out of it with the other and put it admiringly on her left ring finger before finally answering Charles's question emotionally, 'Yes! Yes, of course I will, Charles!'

At this moment, she flung herself onto him, her arms around his neck and her little face pressed close to his. She showered his face with kisses and said, 'Oh, Charles. I'm so happy! This is the best Christmas present I could ever be given!'

Charles beamed at her response and enthusiasm. He had never proposed to anyone before and even though he was fairly sure of Annie's affection, he did not want to mess this up. He had worked many extra shifts, frequently even coming to work on a Sunday morning, to be able to afford this fine engagement ring. He knew he wanted to give her a ring that she would like, but couldn't afford one with inset stones, which meant that it took him a long time to find this slender, shiny, silvery one. He was therefore glad that Annie seemed delighted about it.

They agreed though that she would keep the ring hidden until he had spoken to Annie's father and asked him for her hand in marriage the following day. They remained standing under the lamp post a little bit longer to relish what had just come to pass. When they finally walked on through the park in the snow, they talked about all the exciting events that happened this year including little James's birth and Marisa and Andrew's announcement of the former expecting a child. They would now have their own piece of good news to contribute.

The next day, Charles arrived at the McKenzie house half-an-hour before lunch was served. Deirdre and Molly brushed past him at the front door without taking any notice of him. When he came in and found Jacob McKenzie in the living-room with Joe and Seb playing with colourful, wooden toy trains on the wooden jigsaw rail tracks that they had previously assembled, he was relieved that the remaining family members had not yet arrived. He cleared his throat and said, 'Mr McKenzie, may I speak to you for a moment?'

Jacob looked up in a startled fashion and then responded with a smile, 'Charles, hello. I didn't hear you come in.'

'Annie saw me from the kitchen window before I had a chance to ring the doorbell.'

Jacob kept smiling. 'People in love looking out for each other.'

Before Charles could think of a rejoinder, Jacob continued. 'Yes, of course you can speak to me. Any time, Charles.'

He got up, patted his trousers and informed the boys that he was taking a break from the game. He then waited for Charles to tell him what he had to say.

Charles was a little embarrassed. 'May I speak to you in private, sir?'

If Jacob was surprised by the request, he didn't show it and led Charles, after a moment's consideration, through the kitchen past a somewhat bewildered Helen and a blushing Annie into the small pantry where he swiftly closed the solid door to the kitchen.

'This kitchen will be busy all day today,' Jacob said with a glance at the door. 'Helen and Annie are planning to start the Christmas baking in the afternoon and the boys can help.'

Charles nodded. Annie had told him about their baking plans.

Jacob studied Charles's tense facial expression and prompted him, 'But what is it you want to speak to me about, Charles? You look very serious.'

Charles swallowed, let a couple of seconds pass and then plucked up his courage and verbalised what was on his mind: 'Mr McKenzie, I would like to ask you for Annie's hand in marriage.'

Silence followed this request and Charles's forehead showed beads of perspiration. This was not going well. He should have approached the topic gradually and carefully rather than come out with it all at once. He did not know how to make a retreat without completely losing face. He peeked at the door behind Jacob.

However, at just this moment, Jacob's inexpressive face transformed into a huge smile. He took a step towards Charles and took his hands into his. 'Charles! This is wonderful! I know how fond the two of you are of each other and you've become an important part of this family ever since you first came here.'

Charles's relief was palpable. 'So, you'd be happy with our marriage? I know Annie is still very young. I'm happy to wait longer.'

Jacob replied quickly, 'Annie will be seventeen next May. That's not too young, especially not if both parties are sure that they want this. Have you spoken to Annie?'

Charles answered the question in the affirmative.

Jacob opened the door to the kitchen and called out to his wife despite her only being a couple of yards away from him, 'Helen, come here! Come quickly!'

Helen, who had started washing the potatoes they would eat for lunch, gave her husband a startled look, before she interrupted her cooking, dried her hands, which were dripping wet, and hurried through the door to the pantry sensing the significance of whatever it was that was going on.

Once the door closed, leaving Annie by herself in the kitchen, Jacob related Charles's request.

Although there was another short delay, Helen was quicker at reacting to this plea than her husband earlier. She took Charles in her arms once the surprise had subsided and then spoke into his ear: 'Oh, Charles. This is so lovely. Of course, we will have you as a son-in-law. To us, you have already become part of the family and it will be wonderful to make it official.'

When they all joined Annie in the kitchen a few moments later, any nerves she had felt disappeared in an instant when she saw the three smiling faces in front of her. They all hugged each other and decided to announce their plans to the other family members over their Sunday roast and toast the young couple. Even the cats, having come back in from the cold outside, joined into the celebratory mood by meowing audibly and running excitedly around people's legs.

The next few months seemed busier than ever. Annie spent much of her time helping Elaine look after little James whom she adored. She informed Charles about every development that James underwent whether it was the emergence of his first teeth, being able to sit up or his first few steps when being held by Elaine or herself.

Whilst Charles wasn't as besotted with babies or small children as Annie was, he became fond of James as well when he saw him and was amused by Annie's excited accounts of his progress.

Charles had now become Tobias's right-hand man at the movie theatre and he loved the work there and the way Tobias and he fell into a quiet and pleasant way of working in tandem anticipating the other person's actions. Not only did Tobias teach Charles all the techniques of projection, he also conveyed to him how films had been made in the first place from the initial idea for a script over the casting decisions to the finished product, highlighting actors' preferences and dislikes during the process of filming. He was a fountain of knowledge and Charles asked him how he knew everything about so many films and actors.

Tobias smiled and said, 'If you're really involved with films, you don't just want to project them and thus do the bare minimum of what is required, you want to know everything about how they came into existence. Some people call this background information; I consider it deeper knowledge. You know and understand more about a film in this way than when you merely watch the pictures that are presented to you.'

William and Ellen Doyle were eventually pleased after Charles had told them that he wanted to marry Annie and promised that they would contribute to the wedding preparations as much as they could. William had become truly fond of Annie, and when he hadn't seen her for a while and they had spent much more time at her family's than at the Doyles's, he complained about it in his very own way:

'Where's your lass, boy? I haven't seen her for ages and you're always out and about. I need to see whether her smiles and laughter have changed so I can tell you how to treat her properly and make her truly happy. I know a thing or two about how to make a lass's heart beat faster.'

William gave Charles a mischievous wink and grin, which Charles laughed at with a bit of embarrassment mingled in.

Ellen gave William's arm a shove and retorted, 'William, leave the boy alone. You're a bad influence on him. You'll see Annie again soon enough.'

Ellen was fully aware that Charles had inherited his spark and zest for life from her husband. However, while William had been a bit of a bad boy in his youth, finding himself a number of girls in succession and sometimes simultaneously and being up for dares that sometimes involved minor criminal acts, such as thefts, Charles was not as wild as his father and 'better-behaved' as Ellen expressed it sometimes. She had been the stabilising influence in William's life from the time she first met him and had kept him on the straight and narrow ever since. She knew that William had initially thought that his son should enjoy life a bit longer as an unmarried man before tying the knot and not involve himself with all the responsibilities a marriage entailed just yet, but Ellen said that it would be good for Charles, knowing that William also didn't want Charles to move out of the parental home just yet. She and Charles had to reassure William that Charles would continue working with his father and share the business responsibilities after the wedding until William gradually started to entertain the idea of his son's wedding and acquiesced to it.

Ellen had established a better rapport with Annie since the latter asked her about nursing and many related aspects. Ellen found it easy to speak about topics she was knowledgeable in and passionate about so that their conversations about nursing and the profession soon started to flow. It was her who told Annie first how pleased they were for her and Charles and how they were very much looking forward to the wedding.

There was another major exciting event that occurred in mid-May, about a month before the wedding. Marisa went into labour three weeks before her due date. Andrew called Marisa's parents just before they left for the hospital in the next bigger town on a Saturday morning.

Annie, who couldn't sit still at home, ran to the Doyles's workshop and told Charles about the developments.

Her parents weren't ready to drive to the hospital just yet, as they expected a first birth to take many hours and they knew that they would all be much more nervous and restless once they were trapped at the hospital with nothing to do but wait for the child to be born.

This was certainly sensible but Annie felt already restless and over-excited as things were. She was also slightly worried for Marisa. Although her pregnancy had been a healthy one on the whole – disregarding a bout of morning sickness in the early stages – she didn't like the fact that the child would be premature. In a way it was unsurprising though, as Marisa had become big too quickly in her pregnancy. Although not as slender as her sisters, she wasn't normally a large person so everyone was surprised by her rapid weight increase. It seemed as if the baby was developing at a faster pace than usual. The midwife had reassured them that the baby was healthy and that its heartbeat was strong and regular.

Charles took the rest of the day off as his father saw that Annie could do with some reassurance and moral support from Charles.

The McKenzie family including Charles, but not Elaine and her small family, went to the hospital at lunchtime where they found a sweating and helpless Andrew on one of the chairs in the waiting area of the labour ward. They reassured him that it was normal for the first baby to take its time to emerge into the world, that Marisa was a healthy young woman and that the pregnancy had been without complications and that she was in the best hands on this ward.

Despite their own reassurances, they all felt tense as the hours went by without any news.

It was late afternoon when the door to the delivery room opened and the midwife approached them with a smile and asked them to come in and see Marisa but prepare themselves for a surprise.

Nobody quite knew how to interpret this announcement but decided that the news couldn't be so bad if the midwife was still able to smile.

They filed into the anteroom to the delivery suite where they immediately spotted an exhausted-looking but nevertheless smiling Marisa holding a tiny red-faced baby that was loosely wrapped in a white shawl. Its eyes were closed and its face scrunched up but everyone beamed and breathed a sigh of relief.

Andrew was the first one at her side, gave her a kiss and a hug whilst asking her how it had all gone and then gazed at the baby full of wonder and pride.

Marisa, overjoyed to see him and the rest of the family, smiled despite her apparent exhaustion and replied quietly, 'Long and very painful. But can I introduce you to Sara?'

Not knowing in advance whether they would have a baby boy or girl, they had already selected one for either eventuality.

When Andrew took Sara in his arms and started talking to his daughter, Marisa added, 'And Patrick. Say 'hello' to him, too.'

The midwife next to her was visibly amused by the visitors' confused facial expressions. She approached Jacob swiftly with a small white bundle in her arms that she handed to him.

Annie and Charles exclaimed at the same moment what everyone realised just then. 'Twins!'

It was an enormous surprise. Marisa's antenatal check-ups had not picked up on it and nobody had ever thought that she might have carried more than one baby, but of course her quickly-expanding belly and the premature labour and subsequent birth all made much more sense now.

It took everyone a few minutes to digest the news, but soon they all started laughing and chatting and handed Patrick and Sara around. That cheerfulness continued when Marisa and the babies were taken to a room in the labour ward in which other young mothers with their babies were spending their first few hours together.

Elaine and Tom were called and arrived shortly afterwards, with little James, to welcome the twins. Elaine had quickly packed any baby clothes or other items that James had outgrown so that Marisa and Andrew would have enough equipment for the second child that they had not prepared for to start with.

When Annie handed first Sara and then Patrick to Charles so that he could hold them as well, she leaned in on him and whispered into his ear: 'Aren't they wonderful? One day, we'll have such lovely babies as well!'

Charles, who handled the twins in a fairly clumsy way, nodded and fondly stroked her arm once he had passed the babies on to the person next to him.

And then the big day of the wedding finally arrived. It was a glorious day in June that saw the sun exude more heat than it had done in previous months. The landscape radiated a lush green, and the tiny rose buds announced the beginning of the summer season.

The local church was full to the last seat and the congregation waited expectantly for the bride to be walked in by her father whilst Charles was already positioned at the front with his parents just behind him. As the bells started to toll, Charles heard people starting to move and guessed that Annie and her father must have emerged in the door. He knew he was supposed not to turn his head until Annie was next to him and officially handed over to him by her father, but he couldn't help himself after the whispering and shuffling amongst the other members of the congregation. He turned around when Annie and her father were halfway up the aisle. The latter looked solemn but calm in his black suit with its thin white stripes. Annie, whose left hand rested on his right arm, was clad in a ravishing lace dress in a cream colour, which accentuated her warm brunette hair that was arranged in lavish curls today. Her long veil was carried by two young bridesmaids, who were neighbours of the McKenzies. They were followed by even younger flower girls, the younger sisters of the bridesmaids, who avidly took to their task of scattering flowers and petals behind the bride.

Charles couldn't take his eyes off the procession, especially Annie, until they arrived next to him and Jacob McKenzie handed Annie over to him with a nod and a hint of a smile.

Annie and Charles were somehow overwhelmed with the unprecedented situation they found themselves in, and felt self-conscious and a little embarrassed by the realisation that all eyes were upon them. They gave each other a nervous grin and then directed their attention to the vicar.

When it came to the part that involved the exchange of rings and making their vows, Charles could feel his heart beat so loudly that he thought the entire congregation would be talking about it afterwards. He suspected that Annie felt not much different from him and was relieved when everything went smoothly without any mishaps.

They both started to relax and enjoy themselves much more when food was served in the large community hall, and especially when the speeches were over and the dancing was about to start. Following tradition, Charles and Annie opened the dance floor with their wedding dance, a beautifully executed waltz that showed off their dancing skills that they had acquired over the last year.

Afterwards, other couples took to the floor and Annie made sure that everyone had a fantastic time by pulling children, self-conscious adolescents and single people onto the dance floor. She laughed so much and danced in such a carefree and happy manner that Charles was reminded of their early courtship and all the times they spent in the dance hall, dancing and speaking with each other, and of the laughter they shared with each other there and later in other places as well.

Later on, Annie followed the custom of throwing her bridal bouquet into the air across the floor, challenging the others to catch it so that they would then be the next in line to get married. There were a few girls in their town who hoped to get married soon although not all of them had boyfriends yet. Annie aimed her bridal bouquet at her best friend from school who had recently started dating a young lad who had not yet proposed to her though.

Her friend's eyes lit up when she saw the bouquet hurtling towards her and she stepped forward and stretched out her hands to catch it safely in her arms. But just as she was about to touch it, one of the children ran in front of her and made her trip so that she lost her balance and fell headlong on the floor. The bouquet landed on the floor without being caught as a result.

Annie emitted a scream of terror whose implications Charles couldn't fully comprehend at first. He later remembered how he had tried to laugh the incident off, as Annie's friend had not seriously hurt herself and he said that the latter would surely get married soon enough without the help of a caught bridal bouquet. He did not believe in such superstition, as he called it.

To his surprise, Annie vigorously and angrily shook her head and exclaimed with glowering eyes, 'But you don't understand! You don't understand, Charles! It's not just that. If the bridal bouquet hits the floor instead of being caught, it means bad luck is about to strike. Usually this affects the person who throws the bouquet. Something that should occur or is hoped to come about, is not going to happen now.'

Charles was taken aback by Annie's words and the vehemence in her voice. He wasn't sure whether what Annie had just told him was a widespread superstitious belief or whether she had invented it and it was her very personal superstition. Either way, he did not immediately manage to calm her down.

It was only after Annie had sat down next to her sister Marisa and gradually diverted her attention towards Sara and Patrick, who were in Marisa and Andrew's arms, that a smile slowly spread across her face again. When James, who had just started to walk on his own, tottered from Elaine to her and wanted to dance to the music, Annie's happiness appeared restored and her fright and worries, if not forgotten, were pushed into a distant corner of her mind for the time being.

⋆ ★ ⋆

There was total silence in the barn once Charles had finished putting the images and scenes in his mind into words. He had not been fully conscious that he had spoken aloud, so deeply was he immersed in the film that played itself out inside him. However, when he re-opened his eyes, which had been closed throughout his narrative, he saw how the other people in the barn were watching him attentively. He then understood that he must have spoken, possibly for quite some time, and started to feel self-conscious. He slowly got up from the floor and walked towards the window he had looked out of earlier in the hope that the weather might have improved to such a degree that he would be able to leave the barn and go on his way.

However, this hope was quickly dashed. The giant snowflakes were still coming down at great speed, pushed forward by the relentless power of the storm. The ice crystals on the window pane were now much more clearly formed and spreading out into a pattern of various shapes and lines. Daylight was clearly dwindling, which confirmed his assumption that a considerable length of time had passed since he had looked outside earlier.

A voice reached him. 'Thank you for sharing this with us, Charles. Are you feeling better now?'

He turned around and saw that it was Karen who had addressed him. Before he could give her an answer, Lisa said thoughtfully: 'I liked your story, Charles. You gave us so much more than merely the information of how you met Annie. I can see what your life was like at that time with the excitements of a new relationship and the passionate interest in cinema projection that you began to pursue.'

Charles blushed and muttered: 'I'm sorry. I didn't mean to speak for so long.'

Lisa shook her head. 'No, I'm glad you did. It took my mind off frightening and terrible things, too, which was vital.'

Karen nodded in assent, thus indicating that a burden she carried also appeared less present and overwhelming since she had listened to this rather happy account of a year in Charles's life as a young adult.

Charles's happy story of love and family bliss somehow grated on Leo though. It was too far removed from his own experiences of home life and relationships and he also felt uncomfortable with all the emotional content in it and the women's expressions of empathy.

He couldn't help himself but say flippantly, 'Well, it wasn't exactly a story of thrills and excitement. Not really my cup of tea but each to their own.'

Charles flinched and responded quietly, 'I didn't plan to tell an exciting story. I was asked to speak about a time in my life when I was happy. That's what I have done.'

Karen took a sharp intake of breath feeling defensive of Charles and his story and was angered by Leo's insensitive comments. 'What is an exciting story in your opinion then? What has to happen to make it more exciting?'

Leo didn't have to think about his answer. 'Action and adventure to start with.'

Karen challenged him: 'Then tell us such a story that you think is exciting. We will all be the judges of whether yours will be better.'

Lisa muttered something along the lines of different stories being valuable and interesting in their own right without having to be compared in order to make a quality statement, which was a sentiment that Charles, who had overheard her comments, shared.

Leo didn't immediately respond. Instead he joined Charles at the window apparently to gauge the weather situation. In reality, he also needed a few moments to think, as he needed a good story if he took and intended to win Karen's challenge. His throat was dry and hurt a little.

'No change out there,' he said in a croaky voice. 'We'll be here forever.' He cleared his throat. 'Does anyone have some water with them? I'm parched.'

It turned out that nobody had taken any liquids with them when leaving home.

Karen, still annoyed by Leo's dismissal of Charles's story, couldn't help but comment. 'So you can criticise someone else's story but you can't come up with your own narrative and show us what you consider a better story? This is poor, Leo. It's easy to criticise and leave it at that.'

Leo was riled by Karen's comment. Feverishly, he searched his mind for something he could tell them. Something about a revolution. Something about a rebellion against the status quo. An idea formed in his mind. He smiled before he returned to his previous spot and announced, 'Of course, I can tell you a gripping story. The question is whether you are ready for it,' he continued grandly.

Nobody objected to the prospect of listening to another story, and everybody settled back into a vaguely comfortable position. Not only were they aware of the pointlessness of attempting to venture out into the blizzard, they all felt calmer and more comfortable and less distraught after Charles had shared his story with them. Much of the tension in the room and the emotional pain that each of them carried with them and that had been palpable earlier in their silences seemed to have eased despite of Leo's ungenerous comments.

And thus Leo began his story.

The Island

'Many people had heard about the legend of an amazing island state in one of the Earth's oceans and not few of them were fascinated by it. According to the legend, the island didn't merely look stunning, it had all the features of an advanced civilization. There was no violent crime. In fact, there was no crime at all. People lived in harmony with nature, using its energy resources responsibly. They were said to have developed advanced technologies and products although it wasn't quite clear what they were. This uncertainty merely enhanced the island's mythical qualities. With few indicators of the island's location – if it did indeed exist – only a few intrepid adventurers and explorers set out on journeys to find it. Many of them returned without success; others did not come back, which meant that nobody who stayed behind could be certain of whether they had found the island and stayed there or whether the sea had claimed their lives.

'The island was, in fact, camouflaged very well and therefore – in conjunction with its remote location – hard to detect. If you approached it from above, all you could see was the deep blue sea with the crests of its waves prominently displayed. There did not appear to be a landmass at all. But it was a trick of the eye. Or maybe the island had a chameleon-like ability to change colours and patterns to blend in with its environment. Only when the viewer was a few metres away from it did the island reveal what it really looked like or what its true nature was. But maybe people just saw what they wanted to see or what they were capable of seeing at that moment.

'Anyway, let's take a closer look at what people who could see the island, when they got to a certain location in the ocean, found in front of them: There were vast stretches of sand that shimmered, both golden and silver with its different grains. Palm trees and other tropical plants formed an imposing image of lush, verdant scenery. Amongst the trees, colourful birds could be heard screeching and flapping their wings. The sun shone hotly on the exposed parts of land but there was enough shade between the vegetation to stay cool and enjoy a climate that was bearable, if not pleasant. The fertile earth was used to grow rice on several parts of the island and the rice paddies yielded much produce every year as a result of the hard work of the men tending to them. Other islanders collected the bark of trees to build furniture and implements for the home and some cut trees where the vegetation was dense. The trees were then used to build houses or huts as well as boats. The boats were employed as fishing boats. The sea surrounding the island was deep and rich in large varieties of fish and sea creatures of all imaginable shapes, colours and patterns. Most of them were edible and had delicious flavours when grilled over a fire. They – together with the rice – constituted the island's staple diet. It was complemented by fresh fruit such as mangoes, bananas and coconuts, which all grew on the island in abundance. The islanders were thus self-sufficient and lived seemingly in tune with nature as legend proclaimed. At first glance, the island looked like paradise on Earth.

'However, there was more to the island than this alluring image of natural beauty and ecological living. In the centre of the island there was a huge, extensive structure of shiny silver metal. It was a plant in both senses of the word; despite its industrial look that suggested productivity as a result of human labour where available technologies had been used, the natural world in its untouched and unspoilt form was evoked by the shape of it. The structure looked unusual with its tubes and curves that resembled branches with flower buds and petals at their ends. The base of the structure could be compared to a large tree trunk that was lying on the ground after it had been cut but many times bigger and higher.

'What happened inside the plant was not only kept secret from anyone without any dealings with the plant; it was to some extent not revealed to the plant's workers either. They were permitted to see a small part of it but forbidden to go outside a particular section of the trunk area of the plant. Their tasks there were limited to closely proscribed processes that made it almost impossible for them to guess what the final products of the plant's machinery would be. They knew that they were advancing technologies that placed them into a leading position worldwide, but they could only guess at their precise nature.

This information was kept in the offices situated in the buds and petals of the plant's branches, and the different technological parts that the workers produced were assembled in the part of the trunk that was strictly prohibited to the workers.

'At least this was what the workers suspected. As they were continuously monitored by their supervisors and a high number of surveillance cameras, they had not attempted to go to the areas that had been declared off-limits to them. They knew that doing so would mean risking their lives. They might only be cogs in a huge engine whose workings remained largely a mystery to them, which was especially well-expressed in their names consisting only of number-letter combinations such as A1 or D5, but they still tried to carve out a little privacy and a life away from their supervisors. This didn't only hold true for the plant workers but for any other people who were not part of the elite – as the supervisors were called –who ruled over them and who called the shots. They knew that surveillance was everywhere, but it seemed less obvious when they weren't at work so that they could at least imagine at times that they had a private sphere.

'One of the rice paddy workers, A3 – also called Mauros amongst his fellow workers – lived with his family in a simple hut near the paddies. On the path where he lived, there were many more huts of a similarly modest build that housed other rice paddy workers and their families. It was one of quite a few settlements on the island. The settlements were usually distinct and workers pursuing the same trade were members of the same settlement. Friendships and other social contacts didn't very often extend to relations between workers from different settlements. Neighbours tended to be civil and friendly with each other but, not infrequently, there was a certain wariness and caution present as well when they came across each other.

'On an evening in June when the sun was already low on the horizon and painted the sky above in stunning pink and orange shades, Mauros was walking home after having tended to the rice paddies all day. It was the end of a very hot day and beads of sweat were visible on his forehead. He wiped them off with his rough worker's hands. His short but strong body was slightly bent as a result of years of hard labour that had involved much stooping and crouching. His naturally dark skin had turned even darker than usual over the last month during which the intensity of the sun had noticeably increased. It was now of such a dark brown, it could hardly be distinguished from his thick, short, raven-black hair any longer. There were deep lines in his face, which were further emphasised by his frown and scowl he hadn't been able to get rid of. It had been one of these exceedingly aggravating days on which his supervisor had not only felt he had to be almost constantly present and watch over him but on which he had also kept chastising him over trifles and threatened him with various forms of punishment such as making it impossible for him to get hold of food at the market or depriving him of his share of timber to fix parts of his hut that had fallen into disrepair. Mauros knew his job and did not need to be supervised or managed in this fashion. But he knew that he couldn't simply contradict his supervisor or protest against his treatment. Whenever he or anyone else had tried this approach, severe punishment had been inflicted on them. As he approached his hut, he couldn't stifle a groan of frustration underneath his breath.

'A call and whistle from behind Mauros made him turn around. He saw Filippo whose name was frequently shortened to Fip walk down the path towards him with a smile on his face. They both lifted their hands in greeting. Mauros waited for Filippo to traverse the distance between them. Despite Filippo's smile, Mauros could see straightaway that something was amiss. His friend was a fisherman who often walked through the paddy workers' settlement because he felt he needed to walk on land for a while after having been on and near the water all day. He used to say that at the end of a long day one needed some firm ground under one's feet. By nature, Filippo was a happy man, cheerfully taking each day as it came. He loved to joke and laugh and tried not to take life too seriously. If there was some annoyance or a spot of bother coming his way, he normally quickly shrugged it off. However, today his tall, muscular figure did not approach Mauros with its usual swagger and his smile did not broaden into its characteristic, cheeky grin but remained faint.

'Like Mauros, his skin was dark and slightly wrinkled from the constant exposure to the sun despite not quite having reached middle-age. His hair was lighter than Mauros's. It was a deep shade of brown and fell in strong, thick curls around his face.

'When they stood in front of each other, neither of them were under any illusions about the other person's mood or frame of mind.

'Mauros, unaccustomed to seeing his friend like this, almost forgot his own troubles and asked his friend, "What's happened, Fip? Something is very wrong."

'His question was met with a deep frown on Filippo's part. "The elite," he snorted. "I could just..." he stopped mid-sentence because there was always the possibility they were overheard.

'Mauros nodded vigorously. He looked around to check for any potential elite staff or perfunctorily hidden listening devices but knew that it was unlikely at this spot to be overheard, as the huts were located a few metres away from where they stood and there were no trees in their immediate vicinity where devices could be hidden. He nevertheless lowered his voice when he replied to Filippo.

'"I know, Fip. Today I've been reminded of it again. Not that I need any reminding of the state of affairs. They have just given me so much grief." He paused for a moment before asking, "Was it the same for you? Unnecessary, constant surveillance and threats that – if carried out – could endanger your livelihood?"

'Filippo's facial expression darkened even more. "It was extreme. They made claims that I wasn't efficient enough, didn't bring back enough fish and shouldn't be rewarded for this. My provisions will be cut to a bare minimum and this will remain in place until my work output increases."

'Mauros cast a grim but simultaneously questioning glance at his friend. Although he knew that the elite didn't need much justification to mete out punishment, that particular reason of inefficiency they had given to Filippo lacked credibility altogether. Fip, for all his jocular and carefree manner, was a hard worker and was always ready to put in some extra time and effort. There was a standing joke at the market about Filippo 'out-fishing' everyone else both in the number of fish and the size and beauty of many of them. Everybody who knew him, liked him and the other fishermen relied on him for help and advice when their own work started to falter.

'"I have a family to provide for, Mauros. The little one is only three months old and the other three are still very young as well. I can't not bring home what they are so much in need of. Ellie already tries to make do with the little we have and divide it up fairly amongst all of us. But if they now carry out their threat of letting us have almost nothing, we might not cope. I'm very worried, Mauros, especially that the baby might get ill and die, but also that the other children become so malnourished that they become seriously sick." Worry and anger was written on Filippo's face.

'Mauros nodded. He had concerns not dissimilar to his friend's, having to provide for three children between the ages of two and eight. In a simultaneously angry and determined tone of voice he therefore declared, "This can't continue any longer! This is no life! We shouldn't have to put up with this and we won't any longer!" He realised that he had raised his voice upon which he forced himself to lower it to almost a whisper. It was an urgent, insistent whisper though that he maintained whilst watching Filippo's questioning, doubtful eyes. "We're going to rebel against this treatment. We want to fight for basic rights and fair, humane and respectful treatment. We're going to start a revolution and change the order of things!"

'Filippo heard Mauros out but did not show any sign of excitement about his friend's plans.

'"Mauros, this is silly. You know very well that we have no chance whatsoever in starting a revolution. The first sign of opposition and resistance on our part will result in harsh punishment. We don't stand a chance at changing even the tiniest thing in how this society is organised and ruled."

'It was most unusual for Filippo to be so negative and defeatist and discount an audacious idea as impossible to implement. Normally it was Fip who came up with some wild and crazy notions. But today he certainly wasn't his usual self.

'Mauros put his hand on Filippo's arm, making a concerted effort to convince him of the importance and feasibility of his plan. "Listen, Fip. This will be different. We're planning something really big. For this to work we'll need the help and support of the other workers – at least, those who are trustworthy and would not betray our secret plan to the elite. I think we know whose support we can count on. It is these people I want to bring together for a meeting during which we outline our plan. And then we can carry it out."

'Filippo couldn't help but notice how Mauros made consistent use of the first person plural when speaking about his plan and what he called the revolution as if the idea had not originated in him but was a shared, collective one. He didn't comment on it however.

'Mauros then gave his friend specific instructions to bring about such a meeting as he had in mind and Filippo listened and finally agreed to play along. After all, a meeting was only a meeting and if Mauros wasn't able to see sense now, he was likely to see it when the others would equally consider his goal impossible to reach and show him his foolishness. Fip had no energy left that day to argue with his friend.

'Thus, they parted ways, Mauros feeling more cheered by having a plan of action to work on that might indeed bring about a profound transformation of their social structure. At home, after the children had been tucked up in bed and fallen asleep, he sat down and worked some more on his plan.

'Two days later, the main settlement of the fishermen was busier than usual. The sun had just set and whilst this was the usual time for the fishermen to return home, there had also been other people entering the settlement earlier and now the number of people going into the huts seemed uncommonly large. Most of them disappeared into the huts that were encircled by huts that faced the sea or the island's interior. These outer huts were much more closely and easily watched by the elite and CCTV-recorded. This was the reason why the big meeting that Mauros had arranged was held in the inner huts.

'He and Filippo had contacted all the different types of workers on the island but had made sure that amongst those they only approached the workers who were very likely to sympathise with the call-for-action against the elite. Despite not being free to voice their sentiments and dissatisfactions, Mauros and Filippo had a fairly good idea who the workers were who would support them in their plan, especially the workers from their own communities. These made up the large majority of workers, probably about seventy-five percent of the total number.

'The messages about the meeting were mainly delivered orally when the opportunity arose, as written information could easily be intercepted. Within each of the communities, different sign and verbal languages had emerged over time for occasions when messages had to be communicated that should not be overheard by the elite. The mixture of words and signs that constituted each community's language was not highly advanced, as the constant surveillance the workers were kept under made them for the most part unwilling to communicate to anyone outside their hut. There was too much risk involved in being overheard by the elite or potentially being betrayed by someone they spoke to.

'Mauros and Filippo tried to further minimise both these risks for this meeting by asking the carefully chosen workers who had been invited to come to some of the fishermen's huts at different times so that it hopefully seemed less obvious that something big was being planned.

'Inside one of the huts, the first meeting was in full swing. The idea was to have a number of meetings in different huts throughout the late evening on that day, all covering the same ground and delivering the same plan. In order for that to go ahead a member of each community attended the first meeting. They, in turn, would then speak to invited members of their own communities in the different huts where they were in a position to use at least in part their own communal languages to decrease the likelihood even more that the elite would find out about their venture. The first meeting was therefore the riskiest one and Mauros was acutely aware of it. He and the other assembled workers had worked a very early shift and were therefore able to meet earlier than the others.

'The group consisted of Claudio, a tall and strongly built timber worker with a dense beard; Argos, a somewhat older machinist who had worked in the plant all his life and whose face was marked by years of toil; Paulo, a muscly carpenter with an almost golden skin tone; Filippo, who was – although still sceptical about an outright revolt – curious about the details of his friend's plan, and Mauros himself whose self-appointed task it was to outline and explain the rationale for his project and the course of action he had in mind.

'Not all communities were represented. For example, they hadn't invited any of the traders who took some of the respective communities' products to the marketplace where they traded them for other commodities and took these back to the communities in return. As they worked very closely with the elite who supervised them particularly intensely, many of the other workers didn't feel that they could trust them. More often than not they had the impression that the trading wasn't all above-board and that the traders either got an extra share for their work or, more likely, that the elite took away an unjustifiable amount of their wares, as the goods the workers received in return were usually ridiculously few in number. But then the elite didn't have to justify themselves or answer to anyone. Despite the likelihood of there being some honest traders who were not in league with the elite, the risk of betrayal was considered too high by the other workers to reveal their plan of action to them. They were therefore excluded from the meetings.

'The women had also not been invited although they had been informed about the gathering. They formed an important part of the island's population. Not only did they do their best to bring up the children and provide them with elementary home schooling, which was supplemented by the men teaching them other skills at home in the little time they were not at work, they also made clothes, did the cooking and made some of the smaller and finer tools that were used in the house. The rationale for letting them stay at home was simply a mixture of needing them to look after the children, not arousing more suspicion amongst the elite and potentially some uninvited workers, and not endangering the women unnecessarily. The women, for the most part, accepted this reasoning although some of them were not happy to be excluded from the gathering and, therefore, not be in a position to voice their opinions directly when it concerned such important matters as how their daily lives should be regulated and possibly fundamentally changed through bold intervention on the men's part. At least this was what the men had told them about the meeting's agenda.

'The space in the hut where the five men were sitting together in a circle felt small and cramped. There were two children sleeping in the alcove next to where the men were, and their mother was sitting next to them watching over them. The alcove was separated from the adjacent space by a bamboo curtain that rattled when one of the men accidentally brushed against it and when the woman had once briefly come out to them to make sure they had everything they needed.

'Earlier, after they had just assembled in the hut, Mauros had audibly cleared his throat, which served as a sign that the meeting was about to begin and had then tentatively outlined the reason for meeting and the plan he had devised. He was not used to giving speeches and certainly not to giving them to people from other communities. It took him a while to stop stumbling over his words and repeating himself, but finally, being encouraged by the calm faces of the others, he got into a flow and had now reached the point in his speech where he was expounding the details of the venture he had in mind.

'"Making it clear to the elite that we're not going to live and work like this any longer in a way that brings about change, requires an element of surprise and fear. You know that the elite would hardly just listen to and negotiate with us if we approached them at the end of our shifts. My suggestion therefore is that we go to the plant as a big group at night, infiltrate it and surprise them in their sleep."

'At this point, Paulo interrupted him. "How do you propose we are going to infiltrate the plant at night? Not only do they have guards; the plant is, of course, alarmed throughout and we would immediately be apprehended."

'Mauros resumed unperturbed. "The guards can easily be distracted if there are that many of us. With regards to the alarms, I want the plant workers..." and here he looked at Argos, "to find out how to disable them in the next few days."

'Argos looked at Mauros sceptically. "That's no mean feat, Mauros. Even if we do either distract or overwhelm the guards and enter the plant and get to the elite's sleeping quarters, how could we ever be a threat to them without any high-tech weapons or even any weapons at all?"

'Mauros patiently listened to Argos's objection before he replied. "That's exactly where we have to prepare ourselves. Yes, we don't have any high-tech weapons but we all use tools in our everyday work. Whether it's the axes and similar hard and sharp cutting tools handled by the timber workers..." here he directed his gaze at Claudio, "or the fishing rods with their sharp hooks of the fishermen, we can all equip ourselves with some tools that we can use as weapons. If we surprise the elite in their sleep and they haven't got the opportunity to make use of their technology at that time, it doesn't matter that our weapons are merely manual ones."

'Filippo, who had been following his friend's exhortations quietly, now spoke up to voice his reservation. "But you know very well, Mauros, that all our tools are locked away at the end of the day by the elite and that we have no access to them or to the keys."

'Mauros gave a brief nod. "I know. This is why we have to find a way to get hold of the keys and disable surveillance cameras near the storage boxes in which the keys are kept. Especially the plant workers will prove instrumental here."

'Argos lifted his eyebrows at Mauros's words. "You're placing an awful lot of responsibility on us, Mauros. Do you realise that? All this seems almost impossible to achieve."

'Claudio now spoke up for the first time. "And even if we overcome all the obstacles and threaten the elite that we would stop working for them if they did not agree to changed working and living conditions, which we outline in a document for them to sign, what would prevent them from forcing us back into the way of life, as we know it, on the next day when they are not at our mercy any longer? Or maybe the guards and some other members of the elite who had been elsewhere during our infiltration of the plant, might find and overwhelm us there and then! It sounds all unlikely to succeed."

'Suddenly, a shrill whistling sound could be heard, which sounded as if it was coming from a source nearby. The assembled workers looked at each other meaningfully and fearfully and went completely silent as well as rigid in their postures. They knew these whistles and their origin only too well: The elite regularly used them to communicate with each other across certain distances. The workers sometimes observed how the elite members paused in what they were doing when a whistle could be heard, seemingly to listen to it carefully.

'Moreover, the workers could tell that the whistles were of different lengths and duration and that their tunes were different in nature. Whistling seemed to constitute the elite's secret language that they employed when they didn't want the workers to overhear their conversations. It therefore came as a shock to make out such a whistle in close vicinity whilst they were holding this meeting. Were some of the elite members calling some of their fellows over in order to then barge into their meeting and punish them severely for plotting to overthrow the current order of things? Was Mauros's plan already falling apart before he had fully explained it? The assembled men were so shell-shocked that they trembled with fear.

'This fear was founded on observations as well as experiences of what happened if any of the workers had committed what the elite regarded as a very serious offence. Such an offence usually involved some form of challenge to the current order of things or to the elite's actions or orders, and cutting provisions was not considered sufficient punishment. Perpetrators were detained in an unknown location – although it was highly suspected that it must be somewhere in the plant – and when they were released again they were physically and mentally broken. They would refuse to speak about the ordeal they must have suffered because they were afraid of what would further be inflicted upon them if they revealed anything about their imprisonment. They had clearly been threatened to keep quiet.

'Sometimes detainees were not released at all. There were rumours that these workers were probably not detained indefinitely but killed in an excruciatingly slow and painful process. Although these suspicions had not been verified, the state in which the detainees who did return, as well as occasional outbursts of violence amongst the overseers towards the workers when the latter were pursuing their assigned tasks did justify the assumptions that the elite would not stop short of using methods of torture.

'At the sudden rattling of the bamboo curtain, the men flinched and emitted an audible gasp. When the woman they had met earlier in the hut appeared, they felt some momentary relief but there was still the underlying tension as a result of the whistle they had heard.

'The woman, who was about to cross the small space they were sitting in to go to the screened-off part of the hut that functioned as a basic kitchen, stopped in her tracks when she took note of the alarmed faces of the silent men. She immediately asked them what was amiss and Filippo told her about the whistle and their fear that their conversation might have been overheard.

'The woman listened calmly and then vigorously shook her head, sending her thick, black curls flying from side to side. "No, don't worry. I heard that whistle as well but it's not coming from anywhere close. We hear the elite's whistles here a lot and, admittedly, they sound as if their source is only a few metres away, but this is not the case. Due to the way the huts are arranged in particular formations and how the air currents from the sea and in-land come together here, we get odd sound effects. It's often hard to locate where the sounds originate from and, for the most part, they appear amplified and the source seems much nearer than it really is."

'At this point, another loud whistle could be heard, which made the men flinch again. Giving the woman's words some thought though and regarding it unlikely that she lied to them and was in league with the elite – a possibility that always had to be taken into consideration at least – they relaxed a bit more. Filippo commented that he had heard of these odd sound effects in his settlement but had never experienced them, an observation to which the woman responded that he lived too far inland and therefore just outside the area where he would come across this phenomenon.

'After the woman had gone to the kitchen area to fetch something to drink for herself and then retired to the children's sleeping quarters behind the bamboo curtain, the men resumed their conversation but in lower voices than before.

'Mauros addressed Claudio, whose earlier remark he had not had a chance to address, due to the whistling incident: "I know that we don't have any guarantees for this to succeed but it really is our best chance, believe me."

'Filippo retorted, "There is another option, Mauros. I know that the elite metes out terrible punishment to those who disobey, but what could they do if we all stopped working at once? We would be on the river or amongst the trees or in the plant and just put our tools down at the same moment. Would they really arrest and severely punish all of us and be left without workers? They would not get very far without us."

'Mauros shook his head. "That wouldn't work, Filippo. The elite in the different places would not know that a general strike was in force because they would – before even thinking of communicating with each other by whistling – just follow their gut instinct and immediately intervene in what was going on before their eyes. If we overwhelm them all in their quarters however, they are aware that this is serious, that we're prepared to stop working for them under these conditions and that they can't afford to lose the majority of their workers. Their world of business and high-tech would just disintegrate with the majority of their workforce being absent."

'Argos's gaze rested on Mauros when he remarked, "And what gives you the confidence to say that it will be the majority of the workers that will be staging this strike? Just because you invited the majority of us doesn't mean that everyone invited to the meeting will go ahead with the implementation of your plan."

'Mauros swallowed hard, knowing that Argos had a point here. "I'm confident that enough of us will go ahead with this simply because our frustration and anger have reached their limit and because we strongly feel the need for substantial social change."

"'They can always make one of their fancy trips abroad and recruit new workers from far-away places," Paulo replied.

'Mauros had expected this objection. "Yes, but the lengthy vetting procedures would still mean that for a while they would not have enough workers to run the plant."

'Everyone in the hut knew that this was true. Some of the elite members sometimes disappeared for what could be anything between a few days and a few weeks at a time. At times, these trips were made to make and reinforce business deals – at least this was what they were told – but on other occasions foreigners were brought back. It usually took several weeks until any of the workers outside the newcomers' community was able to catch a glimpse of them, as they were initially kept separate from anyone but their immediate fellow workers during the training they received. During that time, they were almost certainly indoctrinated into the island's ethos of obedience and blind submission. By the time they were allowed to settle into the respective community of workers they operated in, any potential for rebellion amongst them had been clearly undermined and their spirits had been, if not broken, then certainly violated.

'Mauros's voice was sombre. "Are there any other concerns or suggestions any of you would like to make?"

'The others were looking both serious and doubtful but did not say anything.

'"Can I then count on you to be allies and co-organisers in this venture?" Mauros went on.

'There was no immediate response to his question but some hesitation instead. Each of the men now considered the plan carefully by themselves.

'Claudio saw a vision of his brother, Kiro, appear in front of his eyes. He was standing on a ladder next to a pile of logs, which he tried to secure with a rope so that it could then be loaded onto one of their vehicles and driven to the timber workers' settlement where the timber would be scrutinised and – if considered to be of good enough quality – worked on. He was exhausted. It was evening and he had been busy with the logs all day. He should have finished the shift at least an hour ago, but one of the particularly sadistic supervisors had decided that his work quota was not high enough and forced him to keep working. Kiro suppressed a curse knowing it would be no good remonstrating and tried to focus on the task at hand. Beads of sweat were visible on his forehead.

'Claudio had just come out to check where his brother was, after his sister-in-law had come over looking for her husband, having prepared their food at home. He saw how Kiro stepped off the ladder and onto a pile of logs and grabbed the rope whose ends were loosely resting on the top log. He bent lower to tie the ends of the rope together so that his final load would be ready for transport, and this was when it happened. It might have been due to a combination of fatigue, heat and rapid movement that he lost his balance and fell backwards. He was still holding on to the end of the rope, which then received a sudden pull and caused, in turn, some of the logs to dislodge and follow Kiro's descent to the ground.

'Claudio shuddered when he heard a loud bang as well as a simultaneous cracking sound when Kiro's head hit one of the lower-lying logs. It was that terrible moment of impact that knocked Kiro out and possibly killed him. But even if he wasn't dead then, he had no chance of survival, as the logs that he had involuntarily dislodged now tumbled onto him with all their mighty weight and buried him underneath.

'Claudio still remembered his scream and his sprint towards the logs that had buried his brother as if it had happened yesterday and not three years ago. It were these images that were instrumental to his decision now. He nodded at Mauros to let him know that he could count on him.

'Argos, meanwhile, had his own scenes being played out like parts of a film in front of his eyes: There were some of his fellow workers being shouted at for not having worked neatly or fast enough; others, who had accidentally dropped something or had made a minor mistake, were humiliated in front of the others by being verbally abused and declared weaklings and not man enough to do this work in the plant; and then there was the incident when one of the plant workers had made a bigger mistake and the overseer was so enraged that he punched him there and then, squeezed his genitals and laughed at their size before he pushed him out of the shared space to undoubtedly inflict an even more atrocious punishment.

'The latter incident had especially shocked Argos, who had witnessed it, because most of the time such brute force and sexual assault were not openly displayed, but in this instance the overseer had obviously lost his composure and possibly also wanted to deter the other workers from making similar mistakes in this way. Argos and the other plant workers never saw this fellow worker again.

'It was incidents like these that strengthened Argos's conviction that he had harboured for a long time that something in the order of things needed to fundamentally change. Both careful and thoughtful by nature, he wouldn't have used terms like revolt, rebellion, revolution or uprising, which Mauros employed, but he principally agreed not only with Mauros's criticism of the elite but also with his call for mass action. His concern about the difficulties and feasibility of this venture had not been completely allayed but he couldn't see a better alternative. Moreover, he had become increasingly aggrieved by the total lack of action on the workers' part.

'He therefore now said pensively, "Yes, I'll support that action plan, hazardous and tricky as it is. We'll have to make sure, though, that we receive enough support from the other workers. A great part of our strength lies in numbers."

'Paulo didn't take long to give his answer. It was well-known both among his fellow workers and among the elite that he was 'rebel material'. He was outspoken about the injustices they suffered and had challenged the elite repeatedly about how little of what they produced they were actually allowed to keep. He had pointed out that they should at least be adequately rewarded for their labour and had demanded more rights. Unfortunately, his rebellious behaviour had had devastating repercussions. Not only had he been detained and undergone both harsh physical and mental punishment, he had returned home after his release to find his wife to be radically changed.

'By nature, a vivacious and direct woman who wore her heart on her sleeve, she had morphed into a fearful, reticent person who increasingly shied away from human contact and who had suddenly lost either the ability or the will to speak. Although she never fully clarified what had happened in Paulo's absence, it was not difficult for Paulo to guess that his wife, who was an admired beauty with her almond-shaped eyes, her symmetrical features, her glossy black hair and her slender yet curvy figure, had been sexually assaulted. She had always been someone who embraced her sexuality and enjoyed a very fulfilling sex life with her husband but that had suddenly changed. It was obvious that she tensed up before they had sex now and she never initiated intercourse any longer or actively participated in it as she used to do. Paulo was alarmed by this change in her but couldn't get any information out of her. In view of how traumatised she appeared, he feared something as horrendous as repeated gang rape might have taken place.

'His reservations about the feasibility of Mauros's plan therefore dwindled into insignificance when faced with the enormity of what had befallen his wife. In fact, he wanted more than justice. For him, the time was right to exact revenge, but he would, at least for the moment, keep this intention to himself. "Let's go ahead with it," he said with determination.

'At the end of the night, after all the meetings of small groups of workers had taken place, between half and two thirds of the workers had given their word to be part of the venture. They equally felt that the way their lives were largely determined from the outside with its almost constant surveillance, lack of freedom and coercion was unacceptable and shouldn't last forever. The workers who didn't give their promise to participate in the uprising saw these issues as well but believed that the proposed course of action was too hazardous and that they couldn't take such a risk when they had families to provide for at home. Some of them wished the workers who were willing to act the best of luck and openly admired them for their courage, others warned them not to go ahead with the plan, as they would almost certainly lose their battle and probably pay with their lives. All of them, however, promised loyalty insofar as they gave their word not to reveal the plan to the elite.

'In the following weeks, preparations were in full swing. The plant workers eventually located the boxes with the keys to the tool sheds for the different worker groups. Finding out where the mechanism was to disable the alarms proved much harder, but after about four weeks during which some of the plant workers took turns in snooping around as inconspicuously as they could, they believed that they knew where they had to go to switch the alarms off. Of course, that would have to be done before the last one of them left the building in the evening so they hatched a careful plan that would enable them to do just that.

'Kairos, a plant worker who worked with machinery and technology that was the furthest inside the plant that workers were allowed to go to and who had one of the technologically most involved jobs of them all, due to his expertise, was key to its implementation.

'Finally, the day of their planned adventure arrived. It was evening and about half an hour before the end of the work day. Kairos approached one of the overseers who stood a few metres away from him next to some intricate machinery. He had a serious expression on his face.

'"Excuse me," he said. "I'm concerned about the plant's alarm system. It keeps making these high-pitched sounds in irregular intervals as if the batteries are coming to the end of their life span."

'The overseer looked puzzled and was about to respond when Kairos stopped him in his tracks by resuming, "I know it probably can't be the batteries because they were recharged not long ago, as we were told, and they normally last a long time. But there is something not right with the alarms. I suspect a defect of some sort and I'm happy to look into it and fix if it is possible. You know that this is one of my areas of expertise."

'The overseer scrutinised Kairos's face for any sign of deception. Although he couldn't detect any, his tone of voice betrayed his suspicions as much as his words expressed them. "I don't know what you're talking about, E8. I haven't heard any shrill or unusual sounds from the alarm system at all. Everything is fine."

'Kairos calmly and steadfastly faced the overseer. "I beg to differ, sir." His tone was humble. "You live in the plant and I know that the constant exposure to its noise can cause a certain degree of hearing loss."

'When the overseer wanted to angrily object to this suggestion, Kairos put both his hands up in supplication and said quietly, "We all suffer from this, sir. It's just that by some lucky coincidence I seem to have maintained most of my hearing and am still able to make out sounds of certain frequencies that most others can't hear any longer. This is apparent now, for example, with the noise of the defective alarm."

'The supervisor looked at him doubtfully and considered the possibly veracity of Kairos's words.

'"Please, come with me if you wish, and we can look at the alarms together. I just think we have to act quickly if we don't want to risk the alarm shutting down completely."

'The two men looked at each other for a few long seconds before the overseer agreed.

'"Alright. Let's have a look at the system and fix it."

'With these words, he walked further into the belly of the plant and Kairos followed him on his heels until they arrived in a small control room with many switchboards on the walls. The overseer hesitantly walked Kairos to the alarm system.

'Kairos explained that he believed that it was the external alarm that was malfunctioning, as he heard the sounds also when he approached the plant in the mornings and when he entered the plant.

'Again, the overseer hesitated for a moment, as the workers were not supposed to know where the alarms were and especially not what switch and electrical circuit were linked to a particular alarm. However, he knew that Kairos had the edge in terms of expertise in these matters over not just the other plant workers but even over the elite. If he observed closely what Kairos did, everything should turn out well. If Kairos tried to do anything untoward, he hoped that he would spot it straightaway, as he should have enough knowledge for that. And besides, Kairos was a loyal and productive worker who had never caused any trouble.

'Just as Kairos was bending down over the electrical circuit that the overseer had pointed out to him, a din from outside the control room reached them, which consisted of shouts and officious exclamations that sounded like orders. This was followed by a whistle, which was obviously a request if not a command to congregate where the whistling came from. The overseer paused in alarm before he started walking towards the corridor on the other side of the control room. In the door, he turned back for a moment to instruct Kairos to do his job properly and added that he would be back in a moment. Then he walked out of the control room with rapid steps. He did not see the smile on Kairos's face, who was relieved that everything was going according to plan so far.

'The cause of the disturbance became apparent in one of the big machine halls. There, one of the machinists was writhing on the floor, his jerky movements being completely out of control. He was fitting and his eyes were rolled up whilst his mouth fell half open.

'Some of the other workers knelt next to him in an attempt to help him. One of them pointed to his exposed midriff that was – to the elite members' shock – covered in reddish-brown spots. Another one of the workers used the word infectious, which nearly pushed over the edge the elite staff who were already in the room or who were pouring in at that moment. They gave quick instructions to a couple of workers to take the sick worker out of the plant and to keep him isolated at home until the spots had disappeared. Under no circumstances was he – or his family – allowed to leave their hut until he had been given the all-clear.

'This, of course, was somehow futile, as they had no physician on the island who could make the professional judgement of whether he was still contagious or not. All the elite staff had gone down the technology and management route and the workers followed in their ancestors' footsteps and would not get a choice in the matter of vocation anyway, as the elite determined what trades were needed on the island.

'The workers barely received any education apart from what the women taught the children at home, which was fairly basic. Despite living in a high-tech island state, the workers didn't have access to the internet (or any form of telecommunications) that they might have used to learn something about the outside world or to educate themselves in some disciplines. All this was the privilege of the elite. They were clued up as to what was going on in other countries and on other continents, were continuously engaged in online trading and negotiations and had a couple of small planes as well as some boats on the island to get them to the next big landmass from where they then took their business flights to other parts of the world to secure their deals.

'When the two workers who had received the elite's command to carry the suffering worker home picked the latter up, his twitches and jerky movements seemed to settle and eventually stop, which of course made it much easier for the workers to move him around. When they were safely outside the plant and were approaching their huts, they grinned at each other and the previously seemingly badly ailing worker was told how well he had done and how convincing his charade had been.

'Kairos, in the meantime, knew he had to act swiftly, as the longer he was working on the alarm controls, the more suspicious the overseers were likely to become and were probably more inclined to check what he was doing. As he had earlier found out by sheer fluke when he overheard a conversation between some overseers who believed themselves to be alone that the interior alarms could only be manually triggered and time was of the essence, he did not bother to disable them but focused on putting the outer alarm of the plant out of action and then went in search of the surveillance cameras with the intention to turn them off. He reasoned that they were probably not far from the alarm controls and that he would recognise them for what they were once he saw them, as there would be monitors next to them displaying the live camera images. And he was right with this theory. It took him only a few seconds to find an adjoining, bigger space with numerous monitors hoisted on top of some shelves. It took a little while, which certainly caused him some worry, to find the specific monitors displaying the images directly outside as well as inside the plant, but when he saw them he worked swiftly and turned them off in no time. This had been extremely risky and he knew that one of the elite staff could enter the room any second and he was in no doubt that this would be the end of him. But he had succeeded in his actions almost against the odds.

'He then produced an equally convincing performance as his fellow worker when he came into the machine room by putting on a surprised and confused look at the commotion. Moreover, when asked later about the alarm by the elite member who had shown him where it was so that he could fix it, he said calmly and without batting an eyelid that he had repaired it and that everything should be working fine again now.

'The moon was a silver crescent in the sky, which provided a small source of light without fully illuminating the landscape. They had come to the plant in small groups and were now gathered there, mostly leaning against its wall in the hope that this would make it harder to be spotted.

'One of the workers had managed to discover the locking mechanism of the door outside, which was based on biometric data. Again, it was Kairos, with his expertise in technology who found a way of overcoming this obstacle. He had developed an instrument that overwrote the biometric system and unlocked the door mechanism.

'This was how the workers now gained entry to the plant. Filippo, whose big form was closely behind Kairos, tapped the latter on the shoulder once they were inside the plant and gestured to him asking how he had been able to develop such technological know-how when he and the other workers were only taught highly selective processes and facts, and books as well as the free use of the internet or any ICT devices were forbidden. Although Kairos didn't understand the fisherman's sign language completely, he got the gist of what he was being asked. Shrugging his shoulders, he explained that he observed a lot that was going on around him unobtrusively so that the elite didn't notice that they were watched in their actions. He added in a factual tone of voice that was devoid of bragging that he picked things up pretty quickly. His observations usually triggered long thought processes and this was how he came to understand phenomena and processes especially of a technological nature that he had never been taught and about which he should have no knowledge.

'Filippo nodded slowly after having finally made sense of the plant worker's gestures. He was impressed by Kairos's desire to learn and understand and by how he taught himself skills and increased his knowledge.

'Inside the plant, the workers were tiptoeing down the long, wide corridor trying not to make a sound. It was past two o'clock in the morning and there was almost complete silence in the plant with the exception of a low hum from some machinery. They entered and walked through one of the big machine rooms where the humming sound increased manifold in volume. Many of the plant workers were based here. They moved further along until they entered a large laboratory where some other workers toiled during the day.

'Glass vials were neatly placed at the end of each of the massive work tables. An array of other utensils was stored in the see-through overhead cupboards, which were firmly locked. The tall, white cupboards near the entrance stored chemicals, which the laboratory workers only got to handle under close supervision and whose names were kept hidden from them. The less the workers knew and understood about the bigger picture, the better for the elite.

'The laboratory was the last workroom the workers were allowed into. Behind that, they now discovered how the corridor sloped upwards and started the ascent. Shortly afterwards, they noticed smaller corridors branching off the main corridor they were in on both sides. Argos gestured to the others to stop for a second and then addressed them using only the signs of the plant workers' language.

'"I believe that we're now entering the living quarters of the elite. We have always suspected that they are located in the plant's branches and tendrils in its top half. It is now time for us to separate into the small groups we had decided on earlier and then pay a visit to each of the sleeping chambers simultaneously and surprise the elite there."

'Issuing a few brief instructions to the others, which were just a reminder of the next part in their action plan, he turned into the first corridor on his left and a few other workers promptly followed. The remaining workers walked further along the corridor, which continued to slope upwards, with the exception of a dozen workers who turned into the corridor to their right.

'When Mauros had reached the top end of the corridor he was slightly out of breath and felt his heart pound fast. He was somehow surprised by this, as his stamina and strength were usually well-developed from his long and laborious hours on the paddy-fields. He assumed that it was probably the result of the long and steady ascent, which posed different physiological challenges to those he encountered on a daily basis at his work, combined with the anxiety about how their venture would unfold when they entered the elite's bed chambers.

'He looked down at the tools he carried and which he was ready to use as weapons to defend himself if necessary. Presumably carrying them had contributed to his breathlessness and his fast heart rate. When he looked around, he saw that the other eleven workers with him were in a similar state so he gestured to them to stop for a minute to catch their breath.

'Then they split up into three groups of four to enter three short corridors that led to three doors at the end. It was now time to carry out the most important and most dangerous part of their mission. Mauros used another one of the instruments that Kairos had created in many long hours at night to open the doors in the plant. It took mere seconds for the door's locking mechanism to stop working and the door to move inwards. With a light, but determined push, Mauros opened the door wide and slipped in. He was closely followed by the other three workers in his group, who had also been at the initial meeting with him.

'Although it was the middle of the night, the apartment was steeped in a low yellow light, which emanated from one of the security lights that surrounded the plant and which shone through big windows at the other end of the room. This one was obviously fitted quite high up and now enabled the four workers in the apartment to make out the interior. They had expected to find small but nice and well-equipped flats in which their superiors lived and were unprepared for what they saw in front of them.

'The living-room, which was just behind the front door, was of such spacious dimensions that one would have been able to fit in more than the entire floor area of a worker's hut. Viewed from outside the plant these spaces resembled the buds of flowers and appeared rather small. This was, as the workers now discovered, deceptive and might have initially been set up in this way to keep workers' dissatisfaction low and productivity high.

'There was a large, white sofa set made of synthetic leather in front of them with a glass table in the middle and a huge television screen.

The walls were covered with abstract prints and paintings that showed black, white and maroon geometrical patterns. A fluffy white rug covered that area and had been put on top of the dark brown carpet. A dining area with a table and chairs made of light wood stood at the far end of the room near the windows. Paulo recognised the furniture that had been made by him and his fellow workers. He raised his eyebrows when he saw the luxury setting it had been put in.

'Claudio and Filippo, in the meantime, gaped at the grand hi-fi system, which didn't so much create the impression of the latest technology being used but was rather suggestive of something futuristic, something that should not have been invented yet. They wondered how much the plant worker technicians had contributed to its production. Probably a lot but it was unlikely that they had been allowed to see the final product.

'The apartment was too high up in the plant to get a good glimpse of it from outside. In addition, there were thick, opaque blinds that could be lowered when the room was being used by the elite family living in here to make completely sure that their home lives were kept a secret and their privacy was guarded.

'A small corridor near the TV screen led further into the flat. Mauros signalled to the others to follow him as he turned into the corridor. On the left, they came across a door that stood slightly ajar. Mauros looked back at the other workers and nodded. They grabbed their tools more firmly, held them up in front of themselves and got ready to wield them as weapons. Mauros gave the door a light but determined push with his hand, staring straight ahead. All he saw in the muted light were two small beds pushed to the walls at opposite ends of the room. He made out two heads with dishevelled, brown, curly hair on the pillow-cases. Their faces were turned towards the centre of the room, and it was clear that the children whom Mauros estimated to be about three or four were fast asleep. Their eyes were firmly closed, their mouths were open a little and their chests, under their blue pyjamas, moved up and down regularly, indicating their deep breathing. Their thin duvets only covered their legs, presumably because it was too warm to require full body cover despite the air conditioning that worked effectively in the apartment.

'Mauros turned around, shook his head and they tiptoed out of the children's room, venturing further down the corridor. The door at the very end of the corridor also stood slightly ajar. When Mauros carefully pushed it open without making any sound, he immediately spotted the double bed with its curtains of light, white fabric and the luxurious bedding in ruby-coloured silk that was intricately embroidered. Underneath, he made out the shapes of two figures who were lying on their sides and were closely pressed against each other, oblivious to the fact that their private space had just been invaded.

'He raised the rake that he was carrying with him so that its spikes pointed straight at the couple in bed whilst he held the rake's handle firmly in his sweating hands. He also carried a sickle with a sharp metal blade sheathed in a belt around his waist. Again, the others followed his example.

'Then Mauros raised his voice but just stopped short of shouting. "Wake up! We need to speak to you! Wake up!"

'A couple of seconds later, a woman's head jerked up from the pillow and her big, dark eyes gazed in confusion and fear at the four men standing all of a sudden in her bedroom. A piercing scream escaped her lips, its sound waves shattering the surrounding air. That, in turn, caused the head of the man lying next to her to rise up in an instant.

'Mauros immediately recognised one of the head overseers at the rice paddy fields he worked on. He was amongst the harshest and most cruel supervisors, used to making threats against the workers and known to frequently carry them out as well. Mauros nearly froze when he found himself so close to him but looking at his startled face he reminded himself that the power relationship was – at least for the moment – reversed.

'He shouted above the woman's voice. "Stop it! Stop screaming! We will not harm you if you stay quiet, listen to us and agree to our plan."

'The woman stopped screaming but trembled badly and held on to her husband's arm with a firm grip. The latter paid no attention to her. He was clearly flabbergasted, struggling to believe that some workers had managed to break into his apartment in the middle of the night. He could therefore not come up with any kind of response and remained silent.

'Mauros resumed in a less voluble but still fiercely determined voice. "Shouting won't help you anyway. There are workers in every single one of your apartments so that alerting your comrades would be a futile act."

He had now gained much in confidence and started to enjoy the role reversal that was being played out there.

'The other three stood slightly back, a bit closer to the door, but their own raised work tools and their grim expressions left no doubt that they meant business and formed a united front.

"'Wh... what do you want? H... how did you get in here?"

'The overseer was only a shadow of the person they knew him to be. The transformation was mind-blowing.

'Mauros took a deep breath: "We're here to tell you that this can't go on like this. You have treated us appallingly. We're nothing but irksome items to you that you think you can pick up and manipulate the way you like, disregarding our needs as human beings. We are constantly watched, oppressed and punished without good reason and have no freedom. Instead, we demand some essential rights, which will change everything, and we can then live as a happier and better society."

'The overseer started to slowly emerge from his state of shock and repeated with a certain amount of derision albeit without his usual force and conviction Mauros's words, "A happier and better society? We're developing our technology, expertise and products all the time so that we do continuously become better. Happiness doesn't come into this. Your happiness is not required to develop excellence, A3!"

'And, after a moment's pause, he added, "Nor does it require yours, D4, B9 and C5."

'Despite not dealing much directly with workers other than the rice paddy workers, he knew – like every elite member – about every worker; he was able to match their appearances to their letter-number designations and their whereabouts due to constant surveillance mechanisms that were in place for all workers and monitored by all of the elite at different times. This address was again a sharp reminder of being more or less constantly visible to the elite.

'Not taking the bait, Mauros rejoined, "You keep telling us how our civilization is praised as a model for others to emulate when you go abroad, but really, it is nothing like it. You completely misrepresent our reality here for the sake of building a reputation and forming more and stronger trade connections. All you create is an illusion."

'He paused for a moment, amazing himself by his ability to articulate himself in this way and by how forceful he sounded. It was all the pent-up anger and the long-held feeling of injustice he had harboured that now made him speak in such a decisive and resolute manner.

'"Every individual should have the right to being treated fairly and to have their personal freedom guaranteed as long as they do not harm others."

'The overseer, still uncomfortable and out of his depth in view of the armed and determined workers gathered at the foot of his bed, tried to regain his authority, quietly berating himself that the workers would never be capable of being violent towards him, his family or members of the elite. He therefore attempted to adopt his typical, scornful stance.

'"Individual? You aren't an individual, A3. You are merely a worker. What do you think a worker like you is entitled to?"

'"This is not what a civilization should be like though. We refuse to continue to work for you under these conditions. We won't resume work until we have agreed on the conditions and particulars of the Work and Social Contract we have drawn up here."

'With these words, he put down his sickle and pulled a roll of paper out of the back pocket of his trousers. Claudio stepped in and used his one free hand to help Mauros unroll two large, strong sheets of paper whilst holding onto his axe in the other hand. They then threw one of the densely written papers to the overseer and asked him to read it and to sign at the bottom before returning it to them. He would then receive the second sheet, which was a copy of the first one, which he was also required to sign but could keep.

'The overseer didn't make a move to pick up the paper that was now lying on the silk bedding in front of him.

'Mauros went on to read out the contract, which stipulated the demand for reduced working hours and more rewards including food, better housing and more goods, freedom from the excessive surveillance that was currently being used, opportunities to learn and study and to travel, and generally the freedom to say or do what they wanted if they didn't harm anybody without being punished for it.

'The overseer did not react to these demands but merely watched the workers in disbelief, marvelling at the audacity of their performance.

'In response to the overseer's lack of action, Mauros pointed out, "The work won't get done if you don't sign the contract, and you can't do without us. Productivity will drop drastically and you won't be able to make lucrative business deals any longer, invest in a major project or maintain your reputation abroad. As a result, you will not only stop being cutting-edge leaders in innovative technologies – technologies of whose nature you have never fully informed us – but you will also have to sacrifice many luxuries that you enjoy now. So, sign the contract!"

'The last sentence was added sharply. Both he and the other three moved closer to the bed, directing their work tools even more insistently at the couple. Their eyes expressed fierce resolve, which finally earned them a reaction from the overseer who gulped and said, "Hold on, hold on! Don't threaten me. We can talk about this calmly without using threats. You'll need to calm down first."

'"We're perfectly calm," Mauros replied. "If you think we're threatening you, this is because threats seem to be the only language you understand. Now sign the contract, otherwise you'll regret it!"

'Filippo had walked to the side of the double bed during this verbal exchange and was now only centimetres away from the overseer. He held his fishing hooks right in front of the overseer's face, which clearly frightened the latter.

'His wife shrieked and squeezed her husband's arm even harder, which made him pull it away from her. With both his arms and hands free now, he took the paper, which had rolled up, straightened it and seemed to look straight through it.

'Mauros, remembering that a pen was still in his pocket, handed the second sheet of paper over to Claudio, extracted the pen from his trousers and flung it across the bed where it landed next to the overseer's torso.

'The overseer briefly looked up at the workers and when he saw that they were deadly serious in their readiness to use force if he failed to sign the contract, he took the pen and signed at the bottom of the page. His face gave nothing away about his feelings.

'Filippo, who still held the fishing hooks close to the overseer and who had now positioned them next to his neck, took the document with one hand and passed it to Mauros, who in turn, was given the second sheet from Claudio, which he hurled towards the overseer.

'After the second sheet was signed, it was time for the workers to leave but not before sharply reminding the elite member to adhere to this 'binding' contract or face the disastrous consequences outlined before.

'They then made a quick retreat. They ran down the corridor, passing the children's bedroom from where they could now for the first time hear some wailing noises. It had been surprising that the children hadn't woken up and loudly complained earlier in view of some of the shouting in the bedroom. They now hoped that the distraught children would distract their parents long enough to let the workers make an escape from the plant unharmed.

'Having reached the door to the flat after briskly crossing the living-room, they could hear the sound of one of the adults getting out of bed. They lost no time and hurried out of the flat, raced to the end of the small corridor and then turned into the main corridor on the right and ran down its incline.

'They knew that the chances of a counter-attack were highest now that they were in the plant. The workers reckoned that once the overseers got over the first few moments of shock by this unsuspected invasion, they might easily react with outrage and try to take revenge as soon as the workers had left the apartments by triggering the plant's interior alarms and arming themselves with their own weapons, which couldn't take very long.

'In the apartments, all the workers had adhered to a previously agreed script to ensure not only that the contract whose content had been read out to the supervisors was signed but also that they left the apartments at roughly the same time and made their escape together, hoping to find safety and reassurance in numbers.

'Their calculation was that once they had all successfully left the plant, the elite would find it much harder to carry out a successful strike against them, as they would be dispersed in their respective settlements. It was unlikely, they reasoned, that the elite would blindly rush to the settlements and attack them, bearing in mind that they would have to distinguish between the workers that had infiltrated the plant and those that hadn't. Attacking the workers outside the plant most likely warranted an action plan. And by the time the elite had assembled to come up with such a plan, they would probably have considered the workers' threat of refusing to resume their work under the same conditions. The workers counted on the elite taking that threat seriously and on them realising the impact of what it meant for the majority of the workers to put down their work tools with regards to the island's productivity. Surely, the fact that the workers had dared to intrude into the plant in the middle of the night reflected the gravitas and determination on the workers' part to go ahead with their planned strike. They just needed to get out of the plant unharmed now to have some – even if only a small – chance of succeeding at least in part in having their demands met.

'They had only raced down the main corridor, where they were joined by other workers who had completed their mission in the elite's apartments, for a few seconds and had probably not traversed more than two or three dozen metres, when one of the interior alarms went off with an ear-shattering sound.

'They heard Argos shout in a voice whose volume surprised the workers, "Run! Everybody, run! You need to get out of here quickly!" They were all aware of that, but Argos's command added an additional urgency to their flight so that they moved even faster if that was at all possible, wondering fleetingly how Argos himself would fare in the rush to the outside considering that he wasn't the youngest and most nimble any longer.

'They could hear doors being thrown open and shouts of "After them!" or "Catch them!" echo along the walls of the corridor. They had to slow down a little at the door to the laboratory, as there were too many of them again by now to storm through it all at the same time.

'Just before entering the laboratory, Mauros caught the reflection of the bright beam emitted from a laser gun in the glass door in front of him. The beam's reach was not far behind him and he was in the middle of the moving crowd of workers, which meant there were workers behind him that might have been shot. He knew though that there was no point in checking on them, as they would all be stunned by the guns then. Mauros started to feel dizzy when he finally crossed the lab's threshold and nearly fell into one of the large cupboards. Although he managed to steady himself at the last moment, he felt like a man drunk on liquor, stumbling along blindly as the dark increasingly engulfed him, his ears buzzing and his heart pounding. He was barely conscious and later had no clear recollection of how he had moved through the machine room until he found himself outside at last.

'Maybe one of the other workers had helped and supported him when he was about to faint but he wasn't sure and nobody around him said anything to that effect. What he did know though was that he immediately revived after he had left the plant and deeply inhaled the warm, well-oxygenated air.

'The many workers near him were still hurrying on despite the effort it took to continue after having run through the plant as fast as they could. The adrenalin inside them pushed them on as did the knowledge that the elite would not remain impassive for much longer, that some of the elite had in fact already started to fight them if that laser beam was anything to go by and hadn't just been a figment of their feverish imagination.

'Any second now, the beams from the plant's outdoor lights would be shining brightly on them and illuminate them. They knew they had to get away while only a few night lights were on to save energy. They were lucky that the moon's crescent was now, quite unexpectedly, hidden behind the clouds so that it was darker than it had been before they went into the plant.

'Suddenly, Mauros became aware of Filippo's voice next to him. "We've done it, Mauros. We've stunned them into silence and have made our point."

'He paused to catch his breath, as they were still moving incredibly fast and were now not far from the rice paddy workers' settlement.

'"That's all that we can do for the moment. And at work later, we'll show them that we mean business if they do not respect our new contract and the conditions set out in it. Whatever happens now, we have tried our best to change the order of things."

'Mauros nodded but was too breathless to speak. They had now reached a fork in the path whose emerging trails led to the different settlements. Before the two friends went their separate ways, they gave each other a warm hug and a pat on the back that was as much congratulatory as it was encouraging and reassuring in nature.

'Shortly after, Mauros reached his hut, waving good-bye to the other paddy workers who hurried to their own huts. He had barely closed the door when his wife, Sana, approached him from their sleeping quarters without so much as making a sound in order not to wake the children. She had been worried about him, tossing and turning on her bamboo mat without a hope to fall asleep. They used to have a bed, which recently broke, and they hadn't been able to afford a new one from the market-place.

'Sana did not whole-heartedly approve of the men's plan to bring about positive change in the way Mauros had outlined. She believed that it was far too dangerous and that they would lose in this venture with terrifying consequences. Whilst she prayed every day and night to their god to make their lives easier, she did not think that the workers' plan could be successfully carried out. However, she did not have an alternative action plan to propose and realised that just waiting for their prayers to be answered was not enough for the men any longer. Seeing her husband return now whole and ostensibly uninjured even if panting, sweaty and exhausted, was such a relief that she had tears in her eyes.

'Mauros saw how overcome with emotion she was, fetched them both some water and sat down with her in their small living area. He described by the use of gestures and whispered words what they had achieved and smiled at the end of his narrative.

'Sana asked him whether the elite had shot and injured, or even killed, some of the workers behind him when they started firing laser guns and probably some other weapons.

'"I don't know, Sana," Mauros replied. "We couldn't just stop, you see; otherwise we would all have been hit and injured or worse. Let us hope that everyone is well and got away."

'They talked about how things might proceed when the men were back at work, especially about what they could realistically expect. Then they remained sitting next to each other in silence holding their hands and cherishing these moments of intimacy.

'It was still dark outside although there was a subtle change in the night's depth, which seemed to herald the early morning. Mauros got up to wash himself and then lie down for an hour before he had to face the new working day. But just as he walked into the hut's washing space, he heard footsteps and voices outside and a couple of seconds later, someone hammered against their door.

'Mauros stopped in his tracks and stood stock-still in front of the wash-basin. Instinctively, he knew that this did not bode well. His fellow workers were likely to shout out when knocking on the door at an unusual hour to quickly identify themselves, thus saving him from becoming alarmed. And even if they wanted to escape the attention of the elite, they would probably still have said a few words in their own language in a less voluble tone. The door made of palm wood and the bamboo wood that had been used to build most of the hut was far from sound-proof; Mauros often joked how he could hear the leaves of trees being stirred by the wind and the birds screech even at night. Sana, however, would just laugh at him when he said this, pointing out that his sleep was so deep that he would not even wake if a hurricane took the roof off their hut.

'In view of how easily sound was carried from outside to the inside of the house, Mauros was quite certain that no words had accompanied the rap on the door, not even quiet ones, and this was what alarmed him rather than the lateness of the hour, as this night of their big venture was unusual with regards to time anyway and he would expect the workers to report any developments he wasn't aware of. After all, he was both the instigator and one of the main organisers of this project.

'All of a sudden, he heard the door being forcibly opened and shuddered with fear. His wife shrieked in terror, which made her voice unusually high-pitched. As he was rushing back to their living area, his momentary inaction due to his shock gave way to his urge to protect his family at all cost.

'There, next to the now broken door stood two members of the elite pointing their laser guns at his wife! One of them heard him run in and before Mauros could dart towards them, this elite member directed his laser gun at him and fired a shot. Mauros's body collapsed within a second. Whilst his body was lifelessly slumped on the ground, his mind was still partially aware of what was going on around him albeit in a patchy, slow-motion and muffled kind of way. He heard his wife let out another scream, which now seemed to come from a great distance, followed by a laser beam that was followed by a thud.

'Even in his semi-conscious state, Mauros knew that this must have been his wife hitting the ground and he inwardly flinched. At the same time, his children wailed loudly and he could hear them get up and walk from their niche in the hut towards them. Mauros wanted to shout out to them to stay where they were but even his voice didn't obey him and he remained silent to his utmost frustration. Not being able to protect his family when they most needed him felt humiliating and emasculating and he sensed tears come to his eyes – one of the few physical reactions he still had. From the position he was in, he could not make out whether the children had come close enough to see them lie prone on the floor when more laser beams were fired, which were followed by heavy silence.

'It was useless telling himself that the laser guns the elite used would normally stun but not kill people; he was terrified of what had just happened to his family and he could not help fearing the worst.

After all, no sound came from any of them. Was that not confirmation of his dread having turned into reality? Of course, at that moment he was too afraid to think logically and reason that they, like him, were currently not able to speak due to the temporary paralysis brought about by the laser beam.

'The next thing he was aware of was that his surroundings had changed, that he was now enveloped by dark space, that he didn't seem to have firm ground underneath him any longer and that there was a light pressure around his shoulders and ankles. As he marginally lifted his head to look in front of him rather than just upwards, he briefly discerned the upper half of the head of one of the elite members who had confronted him in the hut earlier before his head fell backwards again. As he was still under the mentally numbing effect of the laser beam that had struck him, it took him some time to figure out that he was carried in a horizontal position through his settlement in the dark by afore-mentioned elite members.

'Clouds were still covering most of the sky and the few stars that peeked out between them did not shed enough light to make it easy for Mauros to get an idea of where they were going, which was not helped by the fact that he was still unable to lift his head for any length of time to have a good look at his surroundings. By now he had lost both his bearings and his sense of time.

'When he was finally lowered into a sitting position in which his back was supported by what felt like a wooden structure behind him, he realised that he was at the market square where all the trading took normally place. The structure he was leaning against must be the high platform as they called it, which was used for market stalls that offered the more valuable and coveted goods.

'Anyone who wanted any of the goods had to do the negotiating from below, which immediately put them into an inferior position. Besides, the rationale was that this arrangement made it more unlikely to have any of these goods stolen. The traders truly had their work cut out, particularly those that were not allowed to trade more than the most basic of goods to start with, necessary as they were for survival: It was hard, if not impossible, to acquire any necessities for their abodes such as new roofs or basic furniture if they had only a few fish to offer in exchange. The different traders both represented the various communities but also traded with these commodities that the communities had delivered to them for their own profit so whatever they managed to get after the trading had finished was both theirs and the respective communities'. Naturally, the traders selected their share when the market closed for the day first but not before the elite had taken what they considered themselves entitled to claim. The little that was left in the end barely met most workers' needs.

'Mauros was sharply reminded of the injustice when he was learning against the podium and his facial expression became hard and bitter. His mind was clearer now and sensation gradually returned to his body. He could now slowly turn his head and saw to his surprise that many other workers were sitting next to him on either side and that more workers were carried to the podium by other elite members, who came from different directions. What on earth was going on? What were they all here for after presumably all having been gunned down by laser beams?

'The square was getting increasingly busy, which felt completely unreal at this time in the morning when the first light of the day tried to tentatively stretch its feelers out far enough to soften the night's darkness over the island and announce the arrival of the new day.

'More workers were pushed against the podium and the overseers' voices increased in volume. Suddenly, one of the voices gained prominence and boomed – presumably with the aid of loudspeakers or other amplifiers – across the square.

'"Listen, workers who have been brought here! You committed a serious offence when you intruded into the plant, threatened us with your weapons and made us sign a ridiculous, worthless piece of paper. We won't suffer this. Only the severest punishment can be our response to what you have done and we're meting this out now!"

'The speaker's voice went up at the end of this proclamation and rang in Mauros's ears. The clearer his head became, the more fearful he became. Instinctively, he tried to get on his feet, but he had not regained sufficient strength and control of his legs to even make it into a crouching position. His upper body felt a bit more nimble and he leant forward to look down the row of sitting workers to his right. A second later, he caught his friend Filippo's startled look about ten to fifteen metres further down. Like Mauros, Fip had also searched for the reassuring presence of a friend or relative and relief was reflected in his face when he recognised his friend despite the words of foreboding the supervisor had just uttered. Mauros was also glad to know his friend was nearby, and his pounding heart slowed down to a somewhat slower beat.

'But any let-up in fear was only of short duration when the overseer cried, "You do not deserve to live and serve this civilization! You've broken the rules with your disobedience and, as a result, you will now be annihilated!"

'A loud gunshot followed his exclamations, which made the workers flinch in sheer terror. They stared at the speaker who was standing a few metres in front of those who sat, like Mauros, on one side along the platform. He held the barrel of the gun pointed towards the sky, which was where he had just shot the bullet. Other overseers were standing in regular intervals from each other on the same side, but also on the other three, surrounding the podium on the market square. Some of the workers attempted to stand up and run but, like Mauros earlier, still couldn't make much use of their legs; others just sat there completely stunned and were too shocked to even try to move a muscle. All of them were petrified. It was obvious that all the workers who had stormed the plant earlier had been brought together here. The elite had clearly remembered the workers who had intruded. The workers who had not participated in the attack did not seem to be present.

'The realisation struck Mauros that his family – although also attacked earlier – was not with him. Had the elite left them lying motionlessly in the hut? Mauros swallowed hard and did not fight back the tears that rose in his eyes when he thought of how they must feel when they emerged from unconsciousness and the following daze. He worried about them so much. What would happen to them if something should befall him now?

'Whilst the workers had briefly talked about this eventuality in the context of the intrusion into the plant and had promised to each other that the families of any potential victims – they did not dare to mention the word fatalities – would be taken care of by the other workers, they had not dwelled on this point at length. Now, however, this possibility looked likely to become reality if nothing short of a miracle did not occur quickly.

'But could the elite afford to get rid of the majority of their workers? Most of them had previously decided that they couldn't, as the loss in productivity, which meant everything to the elite, would be enormous, and Mauros remembered vividly how he had driven this point home to the others.

'However, suddenly Mauros was far from convinced by this assumption any longer. In the brief period that the elite had had since the workers had departed from the plant, they had sufficiently organised themselves to assemble them here and get themselves ready for an act of retaliation. Was this the tragic end to their rebellion? The end to their attempt to bring about change and a fairer society? The end to their strife for justice as well as the end to their own lives?

'Mauros couldn't stifle a sob. It was devastating. When he looked up next, he saw a handful of his community's fellow workers who had not taken part in the rebellion approach the market square with their eyes wide open in shock and horror at the scene that presented itself in front of them. They must have woken up from all the noise and, believing their fellow workers to be in danger, set out to check on them and help them if at all possible. Just because they hadn't agreed to take part in the rebellion didn't mean that they would leave their neighbours in the lurch now that they were back from their venture and needed their help. They stopped in their tracks though when they were almost at the square and became aware of the gravity of the situation. The now stood rooted to the spot.

'Sharp gasps from the workers next to him made Mauros shift his gaze back to the overseers in front of him, as he immediately guessed that the danger posed by them had become even more acute. He instantaneously identified the reason for the gasps when his eyes came to rest on the overseer furthest to his right, who had his gun pointed straight ahead as well as slightly lowered to a level where the head of one of the workers must be. From what he could see, from where he was sitting, the overseer's features were tense and showed great focus as he took aim. And fired. A gunshot. Nearly bursting Mauros's eardrums. Earth-shattering. Soul-destroying. Annihilating. Cruel. Harsh. Remorseless. Ice cold. Ruthless. Stopping Mauros's breath. Making his heart jump. Paralysing his body and mind.

'Reduced to rigidity, he heard more shots shatter the silence of the early morning, this time, he thought, from the other sides of the platform. The shots came in quick succession. Each one was a stab in his brain. Trying to blow his brain out. The pain so overpowering that sounds receded around him. Frantic cries and screams became increasingly indistinct. More shots. Closer now, he knew, despite of them sounding more muted to him. His brain was pulsating with waves of excruciating pain. His vision started to fade and everything around him turned to grey and black interspersed with flashes of colour. The last thing he heard was a shot parting the air right next to him that caused his whole body to vibrate.

'The mid-morning sun stood already high in the sky and illuminated the scenes of lively trading at the market square. Traders on and below the high platform were showing and praising their wares, intent on getting the best possible return. To all intent and purposes, it was a normal morning on which nothing appeared out of the ordinary. And yet – weren't there dark stains between the high platform and the stalls on the ground that hadn't been there the previous day? And weren't the trading transactions somehow more restrained in their execution today despite the obvious buzz and noise?

'The plant was strangely transformed. Many of its machines weren't working at full capacity, the laboratory was clearly understaffed and one of the bigger offices of the plant was used for a meeting by the elite that was grave and serious in nature judging from the assembled members' facial expressions.

'Amongst the palm trees, the timber workers went about their work more quietly with much less shouting between them than usual when they liaised about their work such as when some of them were up on the trees and others on the ground.

'The make-shift sheds that the carpenters used for their activities were half empty and the hammering and sawing that emanated from them was fainter in sound than ever.

'The rice paddy workers sweated in the unrelenting sun's heat, not being able to find any shade on the exposed paddies. The men seemed more spaced out this morning and, if one looked at their faces closely enough, one could detect a mixture of resignation and woe. Their movements lacked energy and resolve.

'Out at sea, a few fishermen had cast out their nets and stared gloomily at the water's surface waiting for some big fish to get caught in them. Their shoulders were hunched and their heads hung low.

'The island's birds were singing as joyfully and loudly as ever, their feathers' manifold colours shining brightly in the sun as did the skins of the bananas and mangoes on whose trees they were sitting.

'Hovering over the island, it was a wonderful image of colour and beauty to behold. It looked, in fact, truly paradisal. Moving further away from the island, however, all of a sudden, the island gave way to the deep blue sea. Not a trace of it was left where it had been only moments ago. All that could be seen were the choppy waves of the ocean glinting in the sunlight.'

⋆ ★ ⋆

The barn was now steeped into near-darkness. Only the bright white of the snow and the snow-illuminated sky allowed the four people in the barn to make out each other's shapes and hinted more at, than directly revealed, their facial expressions.

Leo, who had had his eyes closed during his narrative, now looked at the others with a triumphant smile on his face. He obviously waited for them to say something.

The other three people started stretching their limbs and one after the other got up from the floor to shed the stiffness they experienced after sitting for so long in one position on the cold floor and in the draughty air in the barn.

When Leo didn't get an immediate reaction to his story because the others were obviously still pondering it, he decided to give them some time, muttered that he had to go for a leak, walked to the door and opened it. As soon as the door stood open a couple of inches, the storm and snowflakes lashed against Leo's face, nearly throwing him backwards. The others gasped when being faced again with the force of the storm.

Leo threw the door quickly shut again when a voice behind him exclaimed, 'What do you think you are doing! For heaven's sake! Do not try to open this door again in these weather conditions! Why do you think we're all cooped up together in here?' Karen swore albeit in a sophisticated way if that was possible. It was apparent that she was really angry.

Leo turned towards her, amazed at her wrath, and snapped at her, 'I told you all that I need to go for a leak. It's a normal biological need that I have to fulfil if you can understand me better that way. We've been here forever. Shall I get my trousers wet or do you want me to piss in the corner in here?' His tone of voice mirrored the sarcasm in his words.

Karen took a deep breath, but before she could retort anything Charles expressed the same need in other words, too.

He added, 'We need to think of something. There is no toilet-like facility or another room here and I don't think it's a good idea to use one of the barn's corners for that purpose. If we slip out of the barn quickly, make it around the corner and are fast, we can relieve ourselves without freezing to death, being blown over or letting all the snow into the barn. But I suggest we don't go there alone. Leo and I can go together and check whether it's feasible, and then the women can go next. Is everyone happy to give that a go?'

After a few moments of considering this suggestion, they all agreed that that was probably the most acceptable approach considering the circumstances. Leo and Karen gave each other some vexed looks, but decided to let their disagreement go.

Charles opened the door very carefully until the gap was just wide enough to let him and Leo slip through. He pulled the door to behind him with a bang, which made Lisa flinch.

Lisa stood close to the window that Charles and Leo had looked out of earlier and gazed into the snow-lit darkness outside. Whilst she could make out the twirling snowflakes through part of the window-pane, big areas of the window could not be seen through any longer, as they were now covered in an extensive web of ice crystals. Lisa studied them in silent fascination. Impressed by their intricate shapes, she was carried away into a new land of wonders, beauty and magic.

Karen did not share Lisa's mood of silent contemplation. She was restless and agitated. It did not help that the other two had walked into the hostile conditions outside even if they were probably safe enough out there for a couple of minutes and in the company of each other. She wasn't used to being in one place without actively doing or working towards something. Although she had been too distressed and exhausted when she first reached the barn to even think of taking constructive action, she now seemed to recover some of her usual life spark and urge to busy herself with a purpose in mind. Looking at Lisa, she realised that there wasn't much point in discussing with her what they could possibly do to change their situation of being trapped in the barn. She paced up and down the barn feeling like an animal in a cage.

Then the door was abruptly pushed open and a coughing and rapidly blinking Leo stumbled in. 'For fuck's sake!' he cried out. 'I'm freezing my arse off out there. It's mental.'

Karen, who had stopped her pacing close to the door when Leo burst in, gave him a look that shot daggers at him.

Leo, who had nearly collided with Karen during his rush inside, saw her disapproving expression, guessing that it was probably partly due to his language.

Behind him, Charles stumbled inside and shut the door firmly behind him after everyone had been exposed to another strong gust of the storm. Although the two men had only been out for a few minutes, their hands and faces were bright red and wet and they looked most uncomfortable.

Karen looked at Charles questioningly and the latter said, 'Yes, we've managed to go to the toilet or whatever you want to call it, but it was difficult and the storm nearly made us fall over. You also have to be quick in the freezing temperatures. We only walked a couple of metres around the barn and kept an eye on each other disregarding the intimacies of toilet-related business.'

Karen nodded briefly and Charles went on.

'If you and Lisa need to go, I'd advise you to do the same. Although it's dark outside, the snow as well as the snow-clouded sky will give you enough light.'

Karen turned to Lisa, who was still standing near the window being deeply immersed in the contemplation of what must appear to her as the rich tapestry of ice crystals sprawling their filigree feelers across the window-pane.

'Lisa,' Karen called out to her.

When Lisa slowly turned and looked at her in confusion, Karen realised that she was only just emerging from her reverie, and felt compelled to repeat to her some of what Charles had just said in her usual concise way of summing up what had been mentioned or discussed.

Lisa nodded and Karen, who had found and extracted a couple of tissues from the pockets of her winter jacket, went outside with her, bracing herself for the icy cold and the tempest.

'I'd give anything for something hot inside myself now,' Leo commented while walking up and down the barn to warm up again and get the blood circulation going.

Charles was also moving around in the barn in the hope of getting at least marginally warmer. They were silent until the women returned after what seemed a rather long time.

Both women's faces were bright red from the exposure to the chilling temperature and wind and their hair was damp and thus looked darker than it had earlier. Lisa's hair seemed to have lost its blonde shine so that only the red hue in her hair was visible, which shed a warm glow, and Karen's flaming red hair was now a deep dark red colour, rich and heavy like wine in a decanter. Lisa was shivering and Karen kept rubbing her hands. Like the men, they were walking around in the barn for a few minutes before they became too tired and resumed their previous places in the barn, massaging their arms and legs that were aching from the cold.

Then they all heard a rumbling sound and looked at each other.

Leo lifted his eyebrows and remarked drily and not without a certain sarcasm in his voice, 'Don't worry, guys. It's not a bear or the big bad wolf. It's just my stomach complaining about its emptiness.'

Charles nodded and sat down on the floor again. 'We probably all feel a bit faint by now.'

That was certainly true. None of them had eaten anything for hours but the emotional turmoil they had been in and then the two stories they had listened to had deflected their attention from it.

Leo remembered something. His hands searched in the pockets of his suede jacket until he pulled out an opened packet of lemon sweets, extracted one with difficulty with his fingers that were almost stiff from the cold. Then he walked over to Charles, took a sweet out for him and put it into his hand. He hesitated for a moment before he said, 'I hope you didn't mind my comments earlier about your story. No hard feelings, yes, Charles?'

Charles took the sweet. 'No, of course not. Everyone is entitled to their opinion. Different stories speak to different people. Besides, I never thought that I would excite anyone with any part of my life story.'

After Leo had given the women a sweet each, he commented, 'It's not exactly food but it's something. What we need is water though. Actually, I have an idea what we could do. I just need to find…' He broke off there and walked along one of the barn's walls and tried to inspect the floor closely, which was difficult, as it was too dark to see clearly.

He stopped in the corner and rummaged around before holding something up in front of him and saying triumphantly, 'There. That's what I needed. A water canister. Quite logical to have this in a barn – even if it's an abandoned one like this one. I'm going outside again to fill the canister with snow and then try to warm the canister enough to make the snow melt.' Despite being far from keen on braving the storm again and still feeling half-frozen, he didn't hesitate but opened the door again and stepped outside. He knew that they needed water in whatever form it came. After having scooped snow into the water canister by using it simultaneously as a shovel and a container until it was almost filled to the brim, he screwed the lid back on and stepped inside. 'Right, my hands are nearly frozen, but we will have water to drink soon. It might be ice water but it's a start.' He wished he had gloves with him, as the water canister was now so cold in his hands that he felt his grip on it loosen. Attempting to strengthen his hold, he was surprised by the floor's irregularity, stumbled forward a few steps, caught himself and put the canister swiftly down before it could fall out of his hands.

A squeal right next to him reverberated in his ears. In confusion, he turned his head in the direction it come from and saw Karen's outline.

'My hand,' she gasped. 'My hand is being squashed.'

Leo realised that he had inadvertently lowered the canister onto her hand, which was trapped underneath. He quickly lifted it off.

Karen was shaking from the waves of intense pain that rolled through her. She held her right lower arm up with her left hand in order to restore blood circulation to her hand. The latter might well be broken. Right now she had to breathe through it in order not to lose consciousness.

Leo looked at her in shock and stood stock-still, uncertain of what to say. All he did utter in the end was, 'Are you okay?'

This rather foolish question was too much for Karen. With tears of pain in her eyes, she yelled at Leo, 'Am I okay? Are you bloody kidding me? You have squashed my hand! Of course, I'm not okay! Do you want to kill me?'

Leo hated to be shouted at, but his response to Karen's reaction was measured as he was fully aware that he had inflicted an injury on her. 'I didn't do it on purpose, you know. It was an accident.'

Karen was enraged. 'Accident? If you weren't such an idiot this wouldn't have happened. There are people who sue anyone responsible for such accidents.'

These comments pushed Leo over the edge. He would not let Karen call him an idiot and he would most certainly not let her threaten him!

'Fucking hell. You are not calling me an idiot! And your threat is ridiculous and you know it!'

Karen dismissed his words with a wave of her hand but did not respond. She was trying to assess the damage of her hand by moving her fingers carefully. Relieved that she managed to move them albeit with effort, she concluded that the hand or fingers might not be broken after all. She knew that eventually the pain would subside.

Realising that Karen did not want to continue the exchange and that there was nothing else he could do to improve the situation, Leo decided to change the topic.

'What do you think of my story then?'

Lisa, who was still shivering from the cold and was hugging herself for warmth and possibly for comfort, too, said slowly and thoughtfully, 'I like the solidarity amongst the workers. They bond so well and form wonderful friendships within and across the different settlements.'

Charles said thoughtfully, 'I guess it would have been too much to ask for the workers to be victorious at the end.'

Leo nodded and responded, 'It wasn't very likely from the start that this enterprise would be successful. Remember the valid concerns some of the workers voiced at their first meeting.'

'I know what you mean. You use social realism in this story and have planned it as a dystopia.'

Leo added sarcastically, 'Yep. It shows that life isn't usually that great and trying to change the status quo more often than not fails miserably. You are left with woe, misery and death, and things are much worse than before.'

Lisa flinched at these words and her eyes filled with tears. She changed her sitting position so that she once again hugged her legs and let her forehead sink down to her knees, which made her long hair fall around her legs like a semi-circular curtain.

Charles also seemed to shrink into himself.

Karen, who had looked up after Leo's stark words, watched Lisa and Charles revert to their desperate and hopeless states and knew that something had to be done.

Before she could say something though Leo pointed out, 'There was definitely a lot of action in my story. That's the prerogative of fiction. There is always a lot more action in fictitious stories than in real-life stories. Real life doesn't have much in store in terms of exciting adventures.'

Karen, feeling the pain ease a little, shook her head in disagreement. 'This is not necessarily true. I can tell you a story that will show you that adventures with a lot of action can very well happen in real life. This is a story that is based on my own life. I'll be telling you about an adventure I had when I was quite a bit younger.'

Leo gave her a look of scepticism. 'I doubt that an awful lot will be happening in it.'

Karen shrugged her shoulders, not taking the bait. 'Let's see,' she said, trying to ignore the pain in her hand. 'Let's put it to the test.'

She looked around and asked, 'Is everybody ready for my story?'

Charles and Lisa nodded almost imperceptibly.

Karen was hoping that by telling her story she would not only make her point about action in real life to Leo, but that Charles and Lisa would emerge again from their desolation and the heaviness in the atmosphere would lift. Besides, it might distract her from the physical discomfort that was still considerable.

Leo, who had still been standing, quietly sat down not noticing that he too retook his earlier place on the floor to the right of Lisa. He took off his jacket and wrapped the water canister filled with snow inside it, hoping that this would make the snow melt.

Karen cleared her throat, took a deep breath and then began her narrative.

The Dare

'I had turned thirteen in April before going to summer camp. I had been at the camp during the two previous summers and had loved it so I was keenly anticipating that year's camp experience: Two weeks of freedom, adventure, activities and physical challenges, camp fires and the company of other people my age. What could be better?

'Summer camp involved sleeping in tents although there was a nearby hostel in case it became too rainy. We had our own provisions, but if we fancied preparing a meal indoors we could use the hostel's kitchen. Sometimes we went to one of the nearby villages to buy some fresh, warm bakery products.

'The place where we camped was along the river Tamar, on the border between Devon and Cornwall. It was a World Heritage site and had been declared an area of outstanding beauty. We were surrounded by ancient woodland, which was a habitat for birds, butterflies and some rare plants, which we saw on our discovery trips on which we were asked to document the flora and fauna we discovered in order to later report on it to the others. On other trips through the woodland we had to do some orienteering and compass activities, which followed typical scout challenges. At other times, we went kayaking in our orange swimming vests on the river, before the tide came in and had much fun racing each other after everyone had been shown the ropes. We were only allowed to swim or splash near the embankment, as the river where we camped was deep and wide and often wild and tumultuous even when it wasn't high tide.

'These activities were all very much to my liking and I suppose in a way I treasured the beauty of the area in my own way without consciously acknowledging its important status though. We also went on trips to study the medieval stone arch bridges and pay a visit to the Stone and Bronze Age settlements. We found these trips less exciting, as there was a lot more standing or walking slowly around and much less fast-moving through wild territory. However, we still managed to have some sort of fun at the settlements: When the supervisors weren't watching, we enacted battles and scenes of gruesome punishment for whoever we considered a traitor amongst us. We often behaved like wolves in a pack that followed its alpha animal until a new leader established themselves.

'One way of testing our courage was through dares. As most of us didn't know one another, as there were many newcomers that year, we didn't know how we stood with each other and needed some kind of group organisation. I was used to dares and taking risks. It was what I had engaged in at school and in the neighbourhood and how I had gained respect amongst my peers as well as made new friends. The dare that I accepted on this occasion was made by one of the boys who was about a year older than me and who had been teasing me about my red hair. He kept calling me a 'redhead' until I lost my rag and shouted at him not only to stop it but also that he was a coward and that I would be able to compete with him and win on a physical challenge of his choosing. It was clear that if I won a contest against him, nobody would listen to him any longer and his words would cease to have any traction amongst his mates who had joined him in his tease.

'The boy whose name was George merely laughed at me and made his mates snicker, too. I was deadly serious though and adopted a fighting stance and stared at him with the fiercest facial expression that I could muster.

'George saw that and said, with tears of laughter in his eyes, "Okay then. Let's swim across the Tamar. We start at the embankment over there. Whoever reaches the embankment on the other side first is the winner."

'The boys surrounding George burst into uncontrollable laughter obviously thinking that this would shut me up and put me in my place. They clearly didn't know me at all.

'"Okay," I said matter-of-factly and with a slight nod of my head. "I accept. Let's do it. I'll put my swimsuit on and then I'll see you in fifteen minutes down at the embankment next to the big tree where we usually go swimming." With these words, I rapidly walked to my tent to get changed.

'George and the boys gaped at me and then shook their heads at what they must have thought of as my foolishness. George grinned and sauntered to his own tent.

'It was barely mid-morning and it was one of these rare mornings on which we were free to do what we wanted to do although the supervisors recommended we get on with our project work that involved more analysis and classification of the plants we had found the previous day in our self-created plant booklets. Of course, the majority of us had taken no notice of this recommendation and had immediately gone outside after breakfast. Not even the promise of a prize for the best and most creative work project could entice any of us to stay in and work on it, as we thought that the prize probably involved something rather boring and merely educational rather than enjoyable anyway and couldn't possibly compensate for the sacrifice of a fun-packed morning of games outside.

'And what a glorious morning it was: The sun was already high up in the sky, the air was gradually warming up and leaving the chill of the night behind. There was a breeze, which felt refreshing.

'Some of the girls who had witnessed my exchange with George were following me trying to persuade me into changing my mind, telling me that the river was wild and treacherous and that it was crazy to accept such a challenge. They added that it was too far to the embankment and that I would spend too much time in the cold water. Such a long and challenging swim couldn't be compared to our splashes and the handful of strokes that we had taken in the last couple of days since we had arrived at camp.

'I ignored their warnings and kept marching towards my tent undeterred. When I got there, I ducked to enter it and immediately located my blue swimsuit with a silver zigzag pattern. Just when I was starting to undress, Lottie, the girl who I shared the tent with came in and exclaimed, "Karen, you're not really going to swim across the river! You know that they have warned us about going further out. You don't want to drown because of a silly dare you want to emerge victoriously from!"

'I turned to look at her briefly and noticed the anxious expression on her face. I laughed off her concern though and resumed undressing myself. "Don't be ridiculous, Lottie. I'm not going to drown. I'm a pretty good swimmer, you know. I've been in swimming clubs and have worked as a volunteer at the local pool for a while. Do you want to see my course certificates and the medals my club has won in some regional competitions? Besides, I have often swum in the sea, as well as rivers, during holidays and am used to their different conditions. If anyone is qualified to step up to this challenge, it's me," I announced confidently. I had now taken off my clothes and put my swimsuit on, which hugged my developing female body.

"But what's the point?" Lottie insisted. "Can't you ask for another challenge? Something less risky."

'I was becoming unnerved by Lottie's scaremongering. I pulled the straps of my swimsuit up and slipped them over my shoulders with a snap and told Lottie in a rather impatient tone of voice, "It's not *that* dangerous. And besides, what's the point of a dare if there's no risk involved!" With these words I left the tent, grabbing a large towel on my way out.

'I knew Lottie from the summer camp we had both been to the previous two years and had become good friends with her during that time. We were both vivacious, up for a laugh and could easily become the centre of attention in a group of peers. At the same time, there was sometimes an air of carefulness about her when it came to serious physical challenges, which was something I couldn't fully understand and found disappointing in her. There was nothing gained without some daring.

'A few minutes later I reached the embankment where we usually went bathing. The group of girls that had followed me to my tent earlier walked behind me again still trying to dissuade me from swimming across the Tamar. They must have noticed my resolve though as their attempts at changing my mind became increasingly feeble.

'George already stood at the embankment wearing some red swimming trunks. He grinned and whistled when he saw me appear in my blue swimsuit.

'I was conscious of my well-toned, sportive body that was showing some fine female curves. My hair had already been gathered in a ponytail and then fastened close to my head with a large hairclip after I had got up in the morning. This was done less in an attempt to hide my red hair away from view to forestall any more teasing than for practical reasons: It reached below my shoulders and always bothered me when it came to games and adventures outside, as it would fall into my face and partially obstruct my field of vision.

'The other boys were standing around George and also had a grin on their faces when they saw me. They couldn't help themselves from commenting, "Hey, hot chick, are you trying to show George the ropes?" and "Don't swim too close to each other – you don't want to feel each other up in the middle of the river and be swept away with the water!"

'There was roaring laughter after this comment, which of course triggered a series of further comments such as "What a union that would be!" and "The winner, of course, will have the choice of what to do with the loser and we can imagine what that will be, so just wait for the grand union until you have reached the opposite embankment!" More laughter followed these comments.

'I barely batted an eyelid in response, knowing very well what boys in groups were like at that age. I merely retorted in a no-nonsense manner, "This is about recognition and respect. There are no other perks attached to the outcome of this competition."

'The boys were just about to make some lewd comments again but the disdainful look I gave them made them hold back this time and I only heard the odd saucy remark and snicker.

'I turned to George whose masculine and strong body would have made a bigger impression on me if we had met in other circumstances. I said to him, "So then. What's the deal? We start from this point and whoever reaches the other side first will be the winner? No cheating allowed, of course, by hanging on to a passing boat. Who does the countdown?"

'The girls shrieked at these words, realising that it became serious.

'One of George's rather mouthy mates, who was called Andy, quickly volunteered to do the countdown. George and I went to the edge of the embankment, keeping a distance of about ten metres from each other to avoid an immediate collision in the water. After all, it was hard to keep swimming in a straight line without any demarcations. Where we stood, the ground's earthiness gave way to pebbles. I knew that the first couple of metres into the river constituted a gradual transition from shallow into deeper water and after a few more metres we wouldn't be able to stand any longer.

'My heart beat fast. I was raring to go, conscious of the adrenalin rushing through my body. I felt the cold of the wind at the water's edge.

I looked at Andy, who had positioned himself directly between George and me. His arms were spread wide to both sides.

'He then shouted, "Ready".

'Everyone around us had gone quiet.

'A couple of seconds later he lifted his arms from their horizontal position by another forty-five degrees yelling, "Steady!"

'I now swayed back and forth on the top of my toes, barely able to contain my impatience until I heard what I had been waiting for. "Go!"

'The shout seemed to reverberate across the river. It went through my body like an electric current and my body responded instantaneously. It was propelled forwards and after a few quick steps into the river I kicked off when the water level was just below my hips. It came as a physical shock when I immersed my body in the cold water. It made me gasp and almost stop moving for a second but I pulled myself together quickly and managed to stifle a yelp. I could hear George a few metres from me dive into the river and thought I heard a squeal when he came up spurting out water that had ended up in his nose and mouth. I was trying to adjust to the cold water conditions as quickly as I could and took my first powerful strokes with fierce determination, kicking my legs as strongly as I could. I knew I would soon get warmer if I could just keep up the energy to move quickly until the end. What I hadn't taken sufficiently into account was the current of the river though.

'After barely a few strokes I started getting out of breath, as I had to fight against the current, which was trying to push me to the right, in order to maintain a straight course. Normally, water was the element I felt most confident in but the lack of swimming practice in tidal water in recent months now made itself felt. Suddenly I became aware of the difficulty of this challenge. But there was no way back now. I had to trust in the strength and resilience of my body and if this wasn't enough then I would hold on to the saying 'mind over matter'.

'I focused totally on my movement in the water. I co-ordinated my head movements to the side together with my breathing pattern in a way that they were aligned to my arm movements as you would expect from a proper crawl. Nothing around me was important any longer. It was just me and the water and the emerging rhythm, which created in turn the semblance of a harmonious whole even if I had to work hard to sustain that harmony. I carried on swimming one stroke at a time. I was barely conscious of how much my arm and shoulder and to some extent my leg muscles were hurting as a result of fighting against the current. My concentration was such that my pain merely drifted through my awareness. At one point, I thought I could hear a shout or scream to my left, but my head wasn't out of the water long enough to be certain. There were other sounds I thought I could make out for the second one of my ears was above the water's surface: It might have been the engine of a motorboat and the shouts and laughter of children but, again, I wasn't sure. I had almost lost my sense of direction and had no idea how far across the river I had got to.

'By now I felt as if I had been swimming for hours and should have reached the other embankment a long time ago. Had I allowed the current to push me to one side despite my concerted efforts to swim across in a straight line? Suddenly the pain in my arms and shoulders couldn't be ignored any longer. They were screaming at me to stop. I was clearly pushing them to the very limit. But I had to. There was nothing else I could do. I realised that I needed to halt my crawl for a second to get my bearings. I needed to know whether I was still going in the right direction and how far away I was from land. I therefore stopped my crawl and merely moved my legs. The rest of my body was upright and my head was above the water. Just before the current began to push me to the side, I discerned the other embankment. It was straight ahead of me, but there was still a longish stretch of water to be crossed. It looked as if I had only just traversed half of the river's width. This was a frightening recognition. For the first time during this challenge I felt in real danger and doubtful whether I was able to complete it.

'Now the current had swept me a few metres sideways and there was the peril of being completely carried away by it if I didn't start swimming again using the little energy I had left. And this was what I did. The few seconds of respite my arms and shoulder muscles had received were undoubtedly not enough to fully invigorate them again, but the strokes I took now that I resumed my crawl felt slightly more manageable than the ones I had taken before I stopped. However, that feeling didn't last very long. I don't think I had even managed ten strokes before my arms hurt so much that I cried out and had to stop moving them. I tried to be in an upright position in the water again before the current took me further along to the side. I had managed to glance at the distance to the embankment from there and noticed that it had barely diminished. I knew that now was really the point where my mind had to outwit my exhausted body by steering it safely across.

'Without warning I sensed the cold of the water again, probably because I didn't move enough to keep warm. Knowing the importance to take action, I emitted a brief but piercing scream and used all my willpower to move my arms and legs to carry my body forward. Amazingly, it worked for a few metres and I felt a grim sense of momentary relief.

'But then it happened. My shoulders seemed to lock and my arms went rigid just when I was attempting the next stroke. I went under water and instead of fresh air I gulped in river water. The current rapidly pushed me to the side but I was still under water and with my arms now being useless appeared unable to reach the surface of the water again. Panic spread through me, a panic that I had never experienced before. My lungs tightened and everything inside me felt constricted. Was this how it would all end? Would I drown? The end of the contest and the end of my life? And George would be the winner. Surely, a bitter-sweet win when I was dead. Such were the thoughts that were passing through my mind until the current turned my body slightly and propelled me upwards at the same time. My legs automatically started kicking strongly again and a moment later my head broke through the surface of the water. I instantaneously sucked in as much air as my lungs could cope with and spat out some of the water I had breathed and gulped in earlier. It was just enough to relieve the pressure of my lungs before I was pulled down again. I managed to kick my feet and legs strongly though and let myself instinctively fall backwards, trying to get into a position in which I could float on my back even if my arms were out of action.

'Having adopted this position, I quickly realised how difficult it was to maintain it with the current pushing my body and the river water washing over my face. I reassured myself that if I kept paddling firmly with my legs, I would still be moving towards the other side of the embankment and not just downstream so I kept kicking my aching legs. Having moved onto my back also seemed to have released some of the tension and rigour in my arms so that I could use them a little again at least. My shoulders still felt largely immobile so that any attempts at doing backstroke were in vain. Still hoping that I was slowly approaching the other shore, I nevertheless felt like a rudderless boat floating along. By now, my mind started to drift after having concentrated on every move I made for so long. I became aware of the iciness of the water that rapidly spread through my body. A deep fatigue descended on me and I struggled to keep my eyes open. The bright light of the mid-morning sun gave way to darkness, but it was a pleasant, comforting darkness. I entered a cave now that gave me shelter and protected me from the current. I smiled. I had made it. I had left the current behind and was safe. With this thought I tumbled into unconsciousness.

'When I opened my eyes again I was almost blinded by the force of the sun on my face. I blinked and when my eyes gradually adjusted to the brightness I found myself not in a cave as I had wrongly believed earlier but lying just outside a small cove on a sandy beach. Waves were lapping languidly against the sand but fell a couple of metres short of reaching me. Sea gulls screeched in the background and a light breeze stirred and caressed my sun-warmed skin. I felt utterly at peace. I hadn't felt such tranquillity for a long time and had, in the past, not much appreciated it. Unlike now. Something was stroking my face but I couldn't see anything that might have explained it. The stroking sensation then changed into an actual scratching sensation as if someone ran their long fingernails over my epidermis.

'Just when the sensation of pleasure was giving way to discomfort and pain and I was about to cry out and sit up, I heard voices close to me but could not identify what they said. They were talking over each other and became more voluble. Instead of jumping up or crying out, I found myself unable to move or make a sound. At the same time, everything went dark before my eyes and I couldn't discern anything any longer. I was trapped and completely at the mercy of whoever was descending on me.

'The voices were now shouting into my ears but remained indistinct until I, all of a sudden, understood what was articulated by a voice close to me. "Can you hear me?"'

'"Can you hear me?" The voice, which was deep and male, insisted.

'And now I saw my surroundings again after I must have had my eyes closed for a while. However, this time, there was no sandy beach or a cove. There were no seagulls either. Instead, I found myself entwined in twigs and branches that were growing from a tree near the riverbed. My lower body was immersed in shallow water and my upper body was almost upright and supported by a man in uniform, presumably the man who had just addressed me. A river, which was rather choppy, was directly in front of me and I was surrounded by more men in uniform. I didn't really understand what was going on any longer. Nothing made sense – neither the beach and the sea earlier, nor the river and the men in uniform now. Was this real? Where was I?

'A voice interrupted my confused thoughts. "Can you talk to us? What's your name?"

'The question came from an officer who stood next to the one that was propping me up. I understood what he was asking me but my brain was all jumbled up and I couldn't come up with an answer.

'"Are you Karen? Is your name Karen Renshaw?"

'A jolt of recognition went through me and I nodded almost automatically. Then the officer's voice next to me resumed. "Listen, Karen. We're rescue services staff. An ambulance is just about to arrive, which will take you to the nearest hospital to get you checked out. Do you think you can walk up to the road with our support?"

'I looked down at my body and noticed that I was wearing a big waterproof jacket, which one of the men must have draped over my shoulders. It looked identical to the jackets the men wore. I nodded again, not thinking that walking might pose a problem. But just as I was trying to stand up, I realised that I couldn't feel my body. This sent me into a panic and I screamed – or at least I thought I screamed in my partial confusion – but I later learned that I only whispered, "I can't move! I can't feel my body! Everything is wrong!"

'At that point, I heard a siren close by. The uniformed man who had supported me so far spoke quietly and reassuringly, wiping the tears that were running over my face.

'"Karen, it's fine. It will all be fine. You have hypothermia, which means your body has become very cold. In order to preserve life-sustaining functions, it has slowed down your body processes and this also affects your mobility. You'll be warmed up and will get better very soon."

'He had barely finished his sentence when some ambulancemen came, did what I assumed must have been a quick assessment, and then lifted me carefully onto a stretcher, secured me to it after drying my skin with towels and covering me with some strange, silver material and then carried me up the slope and into the ambulance, which was standing on the side of the road.

'Once I was in it, a great tiredness engulfed me. The last thing I was still aware of, before drifting into unconsciousness, was the quick movement of the ambulance as we set off and a calm voice speaking to me.'

'I don't know how much time had passed by the time I woke up again and found myself – to my utter amazement – wrapped in foil. That couldn't be true. Not even for Christmas would I dress up like that. I therefore closed my eyes and opened them again, hoping that they would resume their normal function. The result was the same however. The lower part of my body was hidden under a white duvet and I was lying in a bed that I didn't recognise. Nor did I recognise the white, sterile-looking room with its bare walls that contained no other furniture than a small, but high, table on wheels whose top looked as if it could be slid in and out and which sat on a storage compartment whose door stood ajar. The odd-looking table was positioned to the right of my bed.

'Trying not to panic, I endeavoured to make sense of both my highly unusual attire and my surroundings. Was I still asleep and dreaming all this? Or was I hallucinating? I was sure I hadn't taken any drugs. I also didn't seem to have much body sensation. Surely, all this silver foil that covered me should leave a cold but smooth sensation. I shook my head, uncertain what to do. Maybe it wasn't enough to close and open my eyes to return to reality. Perhaps I needed to go back to sleep and when I woke up later everything would be fine.

'I was therefore just closing my eyes when the door facing my bed was suddenly opened and I saw an unfamiliar figure in light-blue clothing emerge. When she approached my bed, I made out the name-tag that identified her as a nurse named Lizzie. That was the moment when I realised that I was in hospital and my surroundings started to make sense. I didn't have much time to ponder this though as Nurse Lizzie exclaimed with a beam on her face. "Karen! You're awake! That's great! How are you feeling?"

'I shook my head, as I didn't feel that I was in a position to provide a satisfactory answer to this question. Physically, I still felt next to nothing and mentally I was only just leaving behind the sense of disorientation that I had woken up with.

'Lizzie, who was now standing on my left side, gave me a friendly smile and asked, "Do you remember what happened, Karen?"

'I indicated to her that I didn't and started to get seriously worried. I had never been a worrier but this situation was unchartered territory for me. Not feeling my body any longer and not remembering the sequence of events leading up to my hospitalisation made me feel disembodied and out of control.

'Then the door opened again and a small group of people walked in. The woman who first entered the room looked familiar but I couldn't place her. Behind her, my parents walked up to my bed. When they found me conscious, they let out screams of delight and hugged and kissed me. I felt relieved to have finally recognised someone.

'Nurse Lizzie stood there still smiling and said, "She just woke up. I was about to get you. Karen might still feel a little disorientated but you may speak to her if you don't ask her too many questions. In the meantime, can I bring you a cup of tea, Karen? You'll get some proper food in a short while. After all, you haven't had anything since before you arrived here more than eight hours ago."

'I nodded at the suggestion of having some tea. Having usually made fun of the British predilection for tea, I could now see why it served as a means to comfort and restore one's equilibrium in difficult and confusing situations. When Lizzie left I thought about the length of time I must have been unconscious.

'My parents and the other woman in the room pulled some chairs, which I hadn't noticed before, to my bedside and filled me in on what they had been told had happened before I was taken to hospital. The other woman in the room was one of the camp supervisors whom I remembered now. Things fell into place and I gradually recalled having been at camp and then the events leading up to being found at the river.

'Rose, the camp supervisor, explained how some of the other young people had run to her and the other adults in a rather frantic state and reported to them the incident in the river. They had seen George splashing about and going under before he had reached the mid-way point of the river's width and knew that he was in danger.

'"We all ran to the riverbank and when we spotted how far out George was already, one of us ran quickly into the hostel and made an urgent phone call to the rescue services. They were quick in coming but it nevertheless seemed as if we were too late, as between our phone call and their arrival we had lost sight of George, who must have already been pulled below the surface of the water. Ben even went into the water and started swimming out to where we had last seen George.'

'I looked at Rose wide-eyed, recalling how I thought that I had heard a scream at one point at my side. Could that have been George shouting for help? An icy shiver ran down my spine. I wasn't sure whether I wanted to hear the end of that story. And, to make it worse, Ben, another one of our supervisors, might have come to harm as well when attempting to rescue George! I shut my eyes for a second but opened them again when Rose resumed her account of what had happened.

'"At the same time, some of your mates shouted how you were drifting down the river, being pulled along by its strong current. We weren't sure whether that was really the case or whether they imagined this because you were just a speck in the distance at best, but we alerted the rescue services by phone about these potential developments regardless and asked them to have some of their staff sent further downriver on the other side.

'"A couple of minutes later, the rescue services arrived at our side with all their equipment including a motorboat that they carried in their trailer. As soon as their boat was on the river they set off at high speed, overtaking Ben and shouting at him to turn back, which fortunately he did, probably because he had quickly become aware of the challenges the current posed to him. We couldn't hear or see clearly what happened then but we knew that a couple of rescue workers, who were clad in their full diving attire, had dived into the river. All we could do now was to be sensible and wait. Waiting for them to find George and pull him out of the river alive and waiting for the other rescue staff on the opposite embankment to find and save you. These were terrible moments and they seemed to stretch out endlessly until we finally saw the divers come up carrying what looked like a human figure. A murmuring went through the crowd.

'"It seemed to take an eternity until the motorboat returned. To our horror, we saw how the rescue staff were trying to resuscitate George, who must have gone into respiratory and cardiac arrest, as he was moved from the motorboat into the ambulance. Ben tried to keep his panic in check to find out which hospital they were taking George to and what would happen next.

'"One of the members of the rescue team answered quickly and added at the end whilst pointing towards the motorboat that was now going back out on the river: "The staff on the boat are going downriver in order to support the services on the other side in finding and helping Karen."

'At this point in Rose's narrative, I started shaking and fought off tears that were threatening to well in my eyes. Was that the outcome of the dare into which we had thrown ourselves with total abandon?

'Rose didn't seem to notice my distress however and continued, "Whilst Ben went off to contact George's parents; we were still waiting for news about you. This time, the wait seemed to last a very long time indeed, but it could not have been more than half an hour before a message came through that they had found you on the other embankment entangled in some low-lying branches of a tree. Fortunately, you weren't wholly submerged in water.

'"You had gained consciousness quickly after having been found and an ambulance was about to arrive to take you into hospital. A sigh of relief ran through our group that at least you had been found on time. We then went all back to the campsite and I contacted your parents."

'Rose glanced at my parents and my mother took up the narrative, working hard albeit with limited success not to betray the emotional turmoil in her voice. "I was at work when my phone rang. I was between meetings so it was lucky that I was able to take the call. When I heard that you had had an accident in the river and that rescue services had pulled you out of the water, I was stunned. I barely kept it together, called your father, who – as luck would have it – also managed to pick up the phone immediately, summarised what had happened and then left the office after having briefly informed my boss.

'"Half an hour later, your dad and I threw a few clothes and toiletries into a case at home, then jumped into the car and sped down the motorway."

'I had to smile at the thought of my mother throwing anything around, as it totally jarred with her meticulous, tidy PA manner, which she never fully put aside even outside her workplace. Her statement therefore had to be taken with a pinch of salt.

'"The hour and forty minutes that it took us to reach this hospital where you were admitted were the longest hour and forty minutes in our lives. Although we had been told that you were stable when you were taken into the ambulance, we had not received any information on how critical your condition was or might become. I believe that had been unclear at the time the phone call was made."

'Rose nodded, thus confirming my mother's assumption that no information had been withheld from my parents and that they had all had to wait for news from the medical staff at the hospital.

'My mum continued, "When we finally arrived here, you had already been assessed. The doctor treating you told us that you weren't in immediate danger but were unconscious after your ordeal and were being treated for hypothermia. Since then, we have been waiting for you to regain consciousness and we're so glad we can talk to you now."

'I indicated that I had listened and understood everything, but my thoughts returned to George and his fate. I needed to find out even if the news was devastating. My voice was barely under my control but I managed to croak, "George? What about George?"

'Rose's eyes met mine reassuringly. "He's doing alright. They've managed to resuscitate him and he's stable now but is being closely monitored. He has asked about you and sends his best wishes. In fact, when he heard that the rescue services found you on the other embankment he smiled and asked me to congratulate you on winning the dare."

'Added to my initial relief at the good news was now a sense of achievement and being recognised for it. I must have beamed a little too broadly though, as my father couldn't help himself but come out with: "For God's sake, Karen, what were you thinking! Trying to cross a tidal river with its cold, unpredictable water! This is madness."

'My mother put a restraining hand on my dad's arm, thus signalling that now was not a good time to have a word with me after I had only just become conscious again.

'I could have argued my case for accepting the dare but realised that it would also have been an inopportune moment for me to defend my actions, as my parents were still too emotional and my energy was depleted. I therefore changed my topic, focusing on something else that was on my mind. "I can't really feel my body. What does this mean?"

'My parents exchanged worried looks and Rose eyed me, her concern being clearly written on her face. My dad suggested that this might be a result of the hours I had spent in a state of unconsciousness or of the cold water I had been exposed to earlier, but it was clear that he didn't really know and was just trying to spread optimism. When the rest of us didn't react to the possible explanations he came up with, he said he would check and rang the nurse's bell next to my bed.

'Lizzie entered the room shortly afterwards. Before any of us had a chance to tell her why we rang for her, she exclaimed, "Oh, I'm sorry. I was going to bring you some tea. I haven't forgotten but I was called away to another patient after leaving your room and have only just finished there. I'll bring it to you right away." With these words, she bustled out of the room.

'She returned a couple of minutes later with the tea, which she put on the table-top next to me. I tried to move my hand and fingers to take the cup in my hand and drink from it but to no avail. My body still didn't move and panic was rising in me. Was I paralysed from the neck down? I shuddered in horror at the mere thought of it.

'I heard my dad's concerned voice addressing Nurse Lizzie. "My daughter says that she can't feel her body. What does this mean?"

'Lizzie looked from my father to me and responded, "I wouldn't worry about it at this stage. I expect that sensation will return to her body tomorrow, but we will continuously monitor her through the night. Don't worry, please."

'We signalled our acknowledgement in an attempt at taking her words at face value and staying positive.

'I asked her, "What's happening then? Can I go back to camp when I'm better?" I loved camp and especially now that I had won the swimming race I knew I would be in a position to lead and call the shots and be well respected amongst my peers. I wanted to enjoy this status. However, my hopes were immediately quashed when I became aware of four faces that looked aghast.

'Lizzie replied whilst shaking her head, "No, Karen. You'll be here until at least tomorrow afternoon and then it will be for the doctor to judge how your treatment continues. Even if you're discharged by the end of tomorrow, you'll need to be kept extremely warm and have some bed rest. In the next couple of weeks, you can't go on any adventures outside, I'm afraid. You're also extremely prone to infections at the moment so we'll have to take this into account as well during your period of convalescence."

'I turned my head towards my cup of tea, which was waiting to be drunk but was out of reach for me. Lizzie picked up on it, adjusted the upper part of my bed so that I reached a more upright position and then carefully put the cup to my slightly opening lips and tilted it slowly, which made the hot liquid run through my mouth and throat. The warm sensation inside me was reassuring. I felt less disembodied now. I couldn't take more than a couple of sips though, before I had to cough. Lizzie put the cup down again and said that she had deliberately left it to cool down a bit before she wanted to give it to me. She hoped it hadn't been too hot for me now.

'I shook my head, which felt a bit dizzy now that I was in a more upright position.

'Soon afterwards, Rose left, shaking hands with my parents and saying that she would be in touch the next day.

'My parents stayed with me until it was time for them to go to the nearby hotel where they had booked a room for the night. When they were gone I asked Lizzie to let George know that I was glad that he was getting better. My words felt inadequate to fully express the relief I felt about George being alive and that he had probably not suffered any lasting damage. Lizzie knew how I felt and promised to pass on the message immediately.

'In the late afternoon on the following day, I was discharged and, shortly afterwards, so was George. I had no occasion to see him, though, as neither of us was allowed to leave our rooms before the discharge. I had more body sensation again, which was positive. I now just felt totally exhausted.

'The doctor in charge and the nurses on the ward would have preferred to keep me in for another night or two to ensure that I was recovering well and not developing any infections, but they let me go in the end after having given my parents explicit instructions for my ongoing care, which involved being alert to any signs of further sickness. I believe that they discharged me early because of my protestations to let me go, guessing that the home environment would be instrumental to my convalescence. They also seemed to appreciate that we lived quite far away from the hospital and that they couldn't expect my parents to stay in a hotel and pay for it any longer than necessary.

'I was glad when I was back home. As much as I enjoyed being away and liked Nurse Lizzie, I didn't have any of my home entertainment such as videos or my favourite magazines with me at the hospital and when I couldn't go outside and be with others, I missed these as well as some simple home comforts such as my favourite meals. As it turned out however I didn't have much opportunity to fully enjoy these things: When we arrived at home in the evening, I was wrapped up in bed and fell asleep straight away. The next morning,

I was running a fever, coughed a lot and had almost completely lost my voice. I was taken to our local hospital and admitted. Later that day, I was diagnosed with severe pneumonia.

'The days that followed were spent in a haze. My fever didn't go down for a long time despite antibiotic treatment. Much of the time I was asleep but, before I woke up, my sleep would become disturbed and my dreams would turn sour and nightmarish. I was put on a different antibiotic twice before the last one finally started to work.

'After two weeks in hospital, during which I was in grave danger of succumbing to my illness and leaving this world, I was recuperating at last. I spent another week in hospital being treated and monitored until I could finally go home. It must have been an extremely worrying time for my parents. I remember the relief written on their faces when we walked out of the hospital entrance together, me being supported by them on either side.

'And I also vividly recall what it was like to feel the warm sunlight on my face on our way to the car. It was a feeling of utter bliss and I knew that life was a beautiful gift.

⋆ ★ ⋆

Karen felt, rather than saw, the others look at her in the faintly illuminated darkness in which she could make out the others' shapes, but couldn't clearly see their faces or their facial expressions. She knew, though, that she had held their attention throughout her narrative, which was initially received in silence. The latter, however, was soon punctuated with exclamations of shock and concern on the part of Lisa and Charles.

'You nearly died, Karen,' she heard Charles say, trying to be calm. 'I guess if you had known what consequences this dare would have, you'd never have accepted the challenge.' He continued pensively, 'The benefit of hindsight.'

Karen looked at Charles's outline thoughtfully before she remarked, 'I don't know, Charles. I'm not sure about that.' She could feel Charles's incomprehension at what she had just uttered. 'I mean, I probably would have just put this knowledge to one side and focused on what was there to be achieved. That's what mattered at the time. Anything else was secondary and was not to be contemplated at length.'

Lisa's voice made itself heard now with a slight, fearful quiver. 'Was it that important to achieve this river crossing? Just to prove to the others what you can do and that boys are not necessarily better at physical competitions than girls? Did you feel a lot of peer pressure?'

Karen answered slowly. 'The gender issue certainly came into it and the wish to be proven and accepted as a leader by others. But that's not all it was: I also needed to prove to myself that I can tackle a challenging task or activity, see it through and accomplish it in the end. There's nothing wrong with that notion. This is the only way we can eventually change something in society that isn't just or acceptable. Admittedly, in that instance, I didn't have social justice foremost in my mind, but the principle of setting and pursuing a goal until it is fulfilled on which I acted can be applied to such greater ends.'

'Big words,' Leo sneered, and once again, Karen's gaze hurled daggers at him, but she chose to otherwise ignore his comment.

'And besides,' she resumed, 'the idea was to tell you a real-life adventure story. There, you've heard it now.' Her voice had taken on a defensive tone that was tinged with triumph. Turning towards Leo, she added in way that turned her question into a declaration, 'Have I made my point?'

Ignoring Karen's last comment, Leo looked at her in a less confrontational but more thoughtful manner now. 'But what is the point in fighting for a cause if it's more likely than not that it kills you? Causes are important but when is it worth pursuing them and when would we better not fight for them because the risks are too high and nobody is helped in the end if the people who take up this struggle die and they can't complete their mission? There would only be loss but no gain. Many similar stories probably end in a far less positive way than yours.'

'But we must still try, Leo. We can't just not do something we truly believe in because the risks are high.' Karen's conviction was obvious. 'I know you are thinking of your story in which the workers died. But there are so many instances when fighting for a cause has changed the status quo and circumstances have improved.'

Leo looked at her doubtfully, but did not respond.

Everyone else appeared to be silently pondering Karen's words.

Leo remembered something. He unwrapped the water canister from his jacket and brought it to his mouth after having opened the lid. He flinched when his lips and tongue came into contact with the ice water. 'It's freezing cold water with icy parts in it but it's not quite snow any longer and you can drink it,' he announced to the others. He took it over to let first Charles and then Karen drink from it, both of whom struggled to even sip the water.

Karen indicated to Leo to leave the water with her for a second, as she needed time getting some more water down her throat. After a few minutes, she walked over to Lisa to let her drink as well. However, lifting and carrying the water canister for only a few metres caused her excruciating pain. During the time she had told her story, the pain had been reduced to a dull ache that she barely noticed any longer, but now it was acutely present again. She needed Lisa to take the water canister quickly if she wanted to avoid dropping it.

Lisa though initially didn't react to Karen's entreaty at all, and when the latter touched her lightly on the shoulder, she jumped before lifting her head slightly, turning it to Karen and hissing, 'Leave me alone! Just leave me alone! Get away from me!' The last few words were uttered in a whining tone.

Leo turned his gaze towards Lisa in surprise at her sudden anger. None of the previous interactions had prepared him for this violent, emotional outburst. He wondered what else she kept hidden from them that might erupt unexpectedly at some point.

Karen was also taken aback for a moment by Lisa's reaction but composed herself quickly. 'Lisa, you'll feel better once you've drunk some water. You're probably a bit dehydrated and faint from not having had much to eat and you look tired. I just want to help, Lisa, and alleviate any discomfort.'

Despite the intense pain in her injured hand, she tried again to make Lisa drink by holding the water canister directly in front of Lisa's face, which was turned down towards the floor. Despite the downward turn of Lisa's face, Karen could see tears starting to run down her cheeks and her body tremble. Lisa's anger had transformed into the deep sorrow and despair she had previously exhibited. Through gritted teeth, Karen kept holding out the water canister for her to grab, and persevered in urging her to drink from it.

Reluctantly, Lisa took the water container, but when she tried to swallow some water she spat some of it out again because her sobbing made it impossible to drink normally.

Satisfied for the time being with her partial success, Karen carried the container back to Leo with great effort who, after having lubricated his mouth, sipped the water that was left.

Leo could see – despite his distance to the window they had looked out of before – that the window-pane across from him was now fully covered in what had turned out as several webs of ice flowers. The web that had first formed and whose development they had observed was thicker and more firmly delineated as well as more intricate than the smaller and fainter webs that were still very much in the making. At the same time, the webs – although distinctive – started to interlace and form a more complex pattern whose future appearance was difficult if not impossible to predict. Leo sometimes surprised himself by the clarity of his vision, which had made ophthalmologists nod enthusiastically whenever he went to see one of them as a child and adolescent, or later, as a young adult, when his employer at the time had requested him and the other employees to get their eyes checked to ensure that they were fit to carry out their work. Apart from not wearing any vision-correcting aids, he didn't see how this ability had had any real, positive impact on his life or those of others, which was why he usually didn't pay much attention to it. It was just there.

He was briefly contemplating whether he should walk over to the window to see whether he would then be able to catch a glimpse of the outside world or not, thus ascertaining whether they still needed to stay in the barn or whether they might now be in a position to venture out and leave the barn behind them. He decided against it though.

Although a little time had elapsed since they had last checked the weather conditions, during which Karen had told her story, he thought it was unlikely that the snowstorm had abated to a degree sufficient enough for them to walk out of there safely and continue their respective journeys. Besides, he realised that he didn't have that much of an inclination to leave the barn – at least not in a hurry. Similarly, the others didn't make a move towards the window or door either. In fact, it looked as though leaving the barn wasn't on their minds, or at least not their top priority.

Karen, in the meantime, knew that Lisa was in need of being comforted. Despite being aware of the possibility of another explosion, Karen once again touched Lisa's left shoulder to attract her attention. Did Lisa almost imperceptibly move away from Karen when she felt the touch? Karen wasn't sure. She wasn't normally quick at hugging strangers, especially when she didn't think an embrace would be welcome on the receiving end, but she realised that she might have to try different approaches to bring about some change in Lisa's current emotional state. Karen therefore sat down right next to Lisa and put her arm around her whilst resting her left hand lightly on Lisa's left forearm. When Lisa didn't pull away, Karen felt encouraged and started to gently stroke her arm. She didn't feel especially adept at this but she knew that this more often than not had a calming effect on people and she sensed that this would be the case for Lisa as well.

Sitting next to each other like this, Lisa lifted her head, turned to Karen and then let her head rest on Karen's right shoulder. Karen was surprised by this move but also relieved that Lisa's tears started to abate and that she obviously started to feel comforted. She sensed that now was the right time to redirect Lisa's focus. Reassuring her first with the words, 'It's alright, Lisa. It's alright. You are not alone,' she followed this up with 'Please tell us a story. We need to hear something from you.'

She could hear Lisa whisper, 'I don't know what I can tell you. I don't know.'

Karen looked up at the others for the first time since she had sat down next to Lisa and watched their faces searchingly for an answer about what kind of story Lisa could tell them. If she had hoped for an answer to her questioning look, she was disappointed: Charles was again in a world of his own and did not appear to pay any attention to what was going on around him. Leo, who had followed the interaction between Lisa and Karen, showed embarrassment when Karen met his eyes, probably because he was unsure about how to react to such a scene that was very emotional and intimate. He once again shifted his gaze to the window out of which he couldn't see anything.

Karen, realising that she would not receive any suggestions from the other two, decided that anything that came to her mind that could be turned into a story would be better than nothing and hopefully give Lisa the impetus to get started with a narrative. She thus said, 'A mystery, Lisa. This will keep our minds engaged as we try to guess what is going on.' With a glimpse at a dejected Charles she added, 'And add a romantic element to it. Make it a romantic mystery. Can you do that, Lisa?' She paused to give Lisa the chance to reply. When she still didn't receive a response from Lisa, she was just starting to say, 'If that's too difficult...' when she heard Lisa's voice close to her.

'Yes. I can do that.'

Karen, elated to have finally got through to her and finding Lisa ready to tell them another story that could potentially improve the current mood of doom and hopelessness, expressed her joy by giving Lisa a squeeze.

'Oh, Lisa. That's brilliant! Do you need help to come up with one or more characters for it or with a setting?'

Lisa, feeling visibly reassured and comforted by Karen, spoke more calmly now that she was able to gather her thoughts again and her mind wasn't reduced to a single focal point. 'No, I'm fine. I can tell you a romantic mystery.' It was clear how Lisa's attention was shifting towards the task at hand. She lifted her head off Karen's shoulder, closed her eyes, even though it was fairly dark, and readjusted herself to assume a cross-legged posture.

Karen let go of Lisa and moved back to her place sensing that Lisa would no longer need her to keep holding her, as the story would claim all her attention and divert if not dispel the dark, heavy cloud that had oppressively hung over her.

And thus, Lisa commenced at first very quietly but increasingly with a more assured voice and more confidence to tell another story.

The Card

'Lara was looking out of the large windows, which stretched almost from floor to ceiling on one side on the upper floor of the big bookshop where its café was located. Outside, she could see people scurrying along the alley where not only the bookshop, but also many other shops, could be found and that led to the entrance to the top floor of the shopping centre where one could easily lose oneself in browsing the range of pretty wares that were sold at various prices. She didn't usually spend much time there looking at the goods with the exception of a couple of shops that she was very fond of, one selling decorative, small things for the home and the other paperbacks and art materials at reduced prices.

'Lara enjoyed watching the hustle and bustle in the alleys and streets from her vantage point at the end of her work day. It made her feel part of something bigger, of belonging to a place together with others. She didn't often have this sensation in other settings.

'Working in a small art gallery that was tucked away in one of the city's insignificant-looking side streets, she saw relatively few visitors on week days, and they tended to merely take a look before exiting the gallery again. Lara knew that the pictures weren't to everybody's taste, but she was fond of them. They were vibrant in colour and had happy motifs such as smiling cats or a bicycle surrounded by flowers and plants in a lush garden. They were all part of the so-called naïve art movement, which many artists and art lovers alike rejected for its apparent lack of complexity and the absence of formal training and expertise in these artists.

'Lara, on the other hand, liked the openness of the art form inviting everyone who wanted to paint to try their hand at it. There was something to be said for the non-elitist nature of it and she loved pointing this out to visitors when they were eager to learn more about this manner of painting. She herself enjoyed painting and drawing in her free time but had only ever attended a couple of short courses and was otherwise self-taught. Rather than working on her art continuously though, she delved into her creativity in spurts that were separated from each other by periods of artistic inactivity.

'Living in a medium-sized, two-bedroom, ground-floor flat, she used the second bedroom as a workroom or atelier where she kept her materials. The room was east-facing and in the morning the early light of the day shone into the room through the glass door and window front, which formed the entire fourth wall of the room and offered a view of the garden. The latter looked a bit wild, as Lara was not very good at mowing the lawn and, finding it hard work, avoided it whenever she could get away with it. Nevertheless, the garden had a picturesque look about it in its natural beauty that showed off colourful wild flowers. A wooden bench and table with a small cherry tree next to them were located slightly to the left of the garden's centre point. This was where Lara usually spent her evenings.

'Even during the times that she pursued her artistic inclinations, she wouldn't use the atelier late in the day as it became too dark in the evenings to make good use of it. Artificial light was not conducive to achieve satisfactory results for the painting and drawing that she did. Not even during the long summer evenings was the light bright enough to lead to best effects in her atelier. This certainly was the drawback of living in a ground floor flat. On the other hand, it always stayed nice and cool there and, of course, she had the garden to enjoy. Regardless of the season, Lara loved spending her free time there. In the summer and when the weather was favourable, she might do some sketches; in the autumn, she absorbed the smell and vibrant colours of the tree; in winter, she embraced the invigorating freshness and cold of the air, and in spring, she deeply inhaled the scent of the blossoms and flowers around her. More often than not, no matter what time of the year if was, she would just sit there, immerse herself in her surroundings and do nothing else. Sometimes, she would get carried away in a daydream. She was largely content with her independent life in which she was free to do what she wanted and with which nobody interfered. She appreciated the peace and quiet she found at home and, to some extent, in the gallery she worked at, but at the same time needed the brief spells of exposure to more people she could observe and feel part of that she found in her after-work visits to the bookshop. Most of the café staff and some of the booksellers knew her so that she felt recognised and acknowledged, which meant a lot to her.

'Today, she had just picked up her Earl Grey tea and set it on a small table near the window before she fetched a couple of art books, the art section being fortuitously closest to the café, and returned with them. She had draped her light denim jacket over the soft, upholstered chair in earth colours to make it clear to everyone that the seat was already taken. She put the art books on the other side of the dark brown wood table, sat down and eagerly took a sip of her tea. When she had come earlier there had been a queue, and instead of standing in there, she had sat down and watched the passers-by outside whilst waiting for the queue to dissolve. She was very thirsty by now though. It was a mild day in May and she felt somewhat dehydrated. The sensation of the aromatic tea on her tongue made her close her eyes in appreciation. A feeling of profound wellbeing suffused her.

'The café was unusually busy right now. She realised that this was probably the case because it was a Thursday, when many people decided to do some late shopping, making use of the longer opening hours and others chose to go out with their friends, treating Thursdays almost like Fridays. The bookshop café at this time served as an interlude where they could rest and refuel for a short while before joining the crowds in the stores or meeting their friends who might finish work a little later for an evening of laughter and entertainment.

'She was just about to put down her tea cup and pick up one of the art books that detailed a number of pencil sketching techniques when she noticed a postcard lying right next to her saucer. It was an art card, possibly bought at a gallery shop, and showed Franz Marc's famous painting *Blue Horses*.

'The painting's bold colours stood out and directed the viewer's gaze in almost hypnotic fashion to the three blue horses at the centre of the picture. The curved lines and shapes gave the picture a strong sense of dynamism and movement, whilst the muscular physique of the blue horses with their black manes exuded strength and power. Lara loved the boldness of the composition and was also intrigued by the sense of disquiet she had when she looked at the dark lines that denoted the eyes of the horse on the left. Another point of fascination to her was how the horses simultaneously stood out against and blended in with the undulating colourful landscape surrounding them.

Only the previous week had she perused an art book that presented Franz Marc's works and had studied this picture in particular. She remembered clearly how she had sat at the same table in the bookshop whilst studying this and some of his other pictures and reading up about the Blaue Reiter movement Marc belonged to. How strange to now find this postcard with the image on her table in front of her.

'Maybe someone was advertising an upcoming exhibition of Marc's paintings by putting art cards on the café's tables. After all, the bookshop itself had an exhibition and installation space on its top floor, which she sometimes visited. She had a quick glance at the other tables but could not see such a postcard on any of them. There was always the possibility though that the other visitors had already deposited them in their bags. She couldn't see any cards on the only two free tables. She turned the card over and what she saw astonished her even more.

'This entire side of the card was covered in a beautifully detailed, coloured pencil drawing of a park with dense leafy trees, which were interspersed with beds of roses that gave way to a circular space with dark green benches along its outline and a fountain with a stone heron that was spewing water from its beak in the centre. Despite the card's small dimensions, the image felt alive and very real and Lara could easily see herself walk between the roses towards the fountain where she stopped to look deeply into the heron's attentive eyes. The air was permeated with the scent of the roses and the pollen of the trees and she inhaled slowly for a long time until her lungs had reached their capacity and she exhaled for an even longer time and became increasingly part of her surroundings.

'A sudden tug at her arm made her flinch and brought her back to her whereabouts. A little girl was standing next to her, stretching her neck to get a proper view of the card that Lara was holding in front of her and gazed at with great focus. Lara had no time, though, to react to the girl's curiosity. A woman of resolute demeanour, who was, judging by the similarity between her and the child, the girl's mother, pulled the girl away and admonished her to leave other people alone.

'Lara looked at mother and child for a moment before directing her attention back to the card. She had the strong feeling that she knew the park depicted on the card and that this familiarity with what she saw had contributed to her getting so quickly transported to this place and losing herself in it. The talent of the artist in their creation was thus only one factor that led to her quick, mental immersion in the pictured scene. Was it one of the city's parks or a park she had visited elsewhere? She wasn't altogether sure. Letting her eyes scan the picture once again, she spotted what she had initially taken for the artist's signature in the bottom right hand corner but that in fact revealed itself to be a small but legible sequence of numbers and letters.

'At first, she believed it to be the number or code given to that sketch. Just as her eyes were about to focus again on the centre of the picture, she was struck by another idea: The number-letter combination looked like a date so presumably the artist had dated their work once it was finished. The combination read 21JUN161445. For a moment she felt excited by the fact that this was a brand-new sketch done this very year until she noticed something odd. The sketch couldn't possibly have been completed on the twenty-first of June 2016 because they were only in May of that year! How very strange. Was there an event scheduled on which the picture was going to be exhibited on that day? And if so, where would that be? It wasn't usually the case that an artist would leave the date of their picture's exhibition at the bottom of the picture. Also, if she had read the first part of the letter-number combination correctly, what did the last four numbers represent? 1445. She started to wonder whether she had misread it all and maybe the code referred to a postcode – although it didn't look like British postcode – or a license plate number. She wasn't confounded for long however, as she realised that the four digits might refer to the time as expressed by the twenty-four hour clock format. A slightly odd time. On the whole, events tended to commence at the full hour or half hour.

'Lara's curiosity was piqued. She was an inherently inquisitive person, which wasn't always immediately apparent to others due to her quiet nature and the relatively low number of questions she asked others. She rather learned about things by observation and by following up information on her own accord. Unsurprisingly, she loved mysteries and puzzles, and at that moment she was delighted to be confronted with what appeared like one of them. This time, she chose to ask questions, as she felt that the knowledge of others might be of much use to solve this puzzle.

'Considering it likely that the artist had left the date and time of their upcoming exhibition next month, she might get confirmation of this assumption by asking the city's other gallery owners. Working in a gallery herself, she was usually well-informed about current and upcoming exhibitions throughout the city. Her gallery normally received promotional material and she always read the local arts and events section in the local paper and on the main website that featured the city's art events. However, if this was going to be a very small exhibition by an unknown artist in a rather unknown venue, this might have been missed by the arts and culture correspondents and other artists, gallery staff or other people working in the industry. She decided to try her luck by asking staff in the event space of the bookshop upstairs if they knew anything more about this. She was keen on seeing more sketches and possibly other artistic works by that artist having enjoyed the detailed depiction of the beautiful park.

'Impatient to start with her enquiries, she didn't even finish her tea that she would normally have relished until there wasn't even a drop of it left in the cup. Uncharacteristically for her, she didn't put the sketch books that she had earlier picked up back on the shelf either. Instead, she quickly put on her denim jacket, slipped the strap of her colourful fabric bag with its quirky patchwork design over her left shoulder, picked the card that she had briefly put on the table up with her right hand and made her way upstairs to the store's event space.

'On the escalator, she pondered the drawing again, especially the familiarity of its motif. And just as she reached the top floor and stepped off the escalator, she suddenly knew where the setting in the picture was. It was one of the parks in the very north of the city that she had visited a couple of times. Due to its remote location in relation to the city centre and its lack of a playground or similar interactive attractions to families, it wasn't that well-known or sought after. Its charm was quiet and understated and in an era of speed, excitement and instant gratification, a large part of the population was more attracted to locations that offered thrills and adventures. It was mainly people living locally who frequented it or sometimes someone who happened to be in that area on a particular day and chanced upon it.

'When Lara had been there before she had appreciated the serene beauty of the place but hadn't made an effort since then to make the journey, due to the many stops en route on the relatively long journey by bus, which was then followed by a strenuous walk up the hill. She now thought though that it would be a lovely thing to do at a weekend and made a resolution to go back there at the end of the week.

'Having arrived on the top floor, she approached a member of staff who was moving some installations around. "Excuse me, I wonder whether you can help me with this."

'She waited until she had the young man's attention and he had put down what looked like a huge piece of lighting equipment. He had a lithe body with unobtrusive but well-defined arm muscles. Lara held out her hand with the drawing on the side she showed the employee.

'"Do you know anything about the artist who made this drawing? Are they going to exhibit their works here?"

'The man looked a bit puzzled at first, but collected himself quickly. He studied the sketch pensively for a few moments. He then shook his head and responded, "No, I'm not aware of this artist and don't think I have seen this picture before. There's certainly no exhibition planned for this kind of art in the near future. We mainly deal with conceptual art up here."

'After a moment's hesitation, he added, "You might be luckier if you ask at some of the city's art galleries. I'm afraid I can't help you any further with this."

'With these words, he picked up his equipment again and moved to the back of the gallery space whilst Lara nodded almost imperceptibly and made her way downstairs.'

'On the next morning, as soon as she had entered the gallery, she switched on one of the office computers, brought up one of the pages that was saved on the favourites bar and started to eyeball the information on it. The site she was on displayed information about all the city's current art exhibitions and art events provided that they had been brought to the council's attention. She and her colleagues usually looked at it most days. Not only was it important to know what else was out there for their exhibition planning and marketing, it was also imperative to have some knowledge and awareness of other exhibitions when they spoke to their visitors who often mentioned what else they had seen in other galleries and sometimes expected them to comment on these other exhibitions. The gallery team therefore didn't only read up on the artists' works currently made available to the public but also went to as many galleries and exhibition venues as possible. Another reason for doing so was that they, at times, got some inspiration from the arrangements of the art works and installations, especially in terms of how to make best use of available space.

'All of the gallery staff very much enjoyed art and were always keen to explore something new or, sometimes, to re-visit the old masters so that the process of information gathering, including the trips to different art venues was not an arduous one or considered a chore at all, but was instead experienced as a pleasure.

'Whilst she was intently scrolling through the webpage, opening links to exhibitions that sounded vaguely as if they might feature a picture like the one on her postcard, she relished the peace and quiet in the gallery as not even her colleagues had arrived yet. Lara was more often than not the first one to come in in the mornings, as she treasured the moments of silence, which were only interrupted by the jubilant sounds of bird song, filling the office once she had opened the window. On this morning, though, she hadn't even taken the time to open the office window so driven was she to find out more about the drawing. However, like in the bookshop previously, she drew a blank. Any exhibition link that had at the beginning looked as if it might lead her to success in finding something by or about the anonymous artist turned out to be a red herring or maybe just proof of her misplaced expectations and hopes. She stared in frustration at her computer screen, unwilling to concede defeat until Joshua's voice interrupted her musings and brought her back to her immediate surroundings.

'"Hey, Lara. Sorry if I've made you jump. What have you been pondering? You've been away with the fairies." He laughed at his own joke – if it could be considered that – and brushed one of his golden locks out of his face. He was proud of his thick, shiny hair, which framed his classic features. It was obvious that he knew what impression he made on others not least thanks to his muscular, tall stature and the deep tan he enjoyed to display. Lara was convinced that he spent quite a bit of his money on hair styling and skin products and frequently visited a tanning studio. Of course, Joshua denied such claims, pretending to always appear exactly as nature had created him without a helping hand. Lara inwardly just giggled whilst keeping a straight face in these situations.

'Admittedly, his looks and playful charm had worked on her, too, when she first met him nine months ago when he joined them in the gallery. He had initially come to them on a short-term contract to carry out some painting and decorating work on the new extension to the gallery that had just been built. They didn't have much left in funds after the building work was completed, which led to the decision to put an advert in the local paper rather than approach an established company, which would undoubtedly have charged a lot more for their work. The extension had been considered crucial by Ben, the gallery manager, as – he explained – more exhibition space meant more art works to look at, which in turn would attract more visitors to the gallery and, almost inevitably, more sales of art works or items such as art postcards, art prints and some stationery with the very same art motifs on them.

'Lara remembered clearly how Joshua had turned up on his first day on the job: He was dressed in white dungarees, and his blond mane was loosely tied together with a red band at the nape of his neck. Even his eyes had a golden shine. In hindsight, she realised that they were amber rather than golden but on that day, with the sunlight illuminating them, she felt as if she was having an angelic vision. It took her a few weeks to recover from her enchantment with him, but his many quirks, behavioural tics and idiosyncratic speech patterns including his unusual sense of humour in the end let her regard him more as a mate and amusing colleague rather than as a romantic possibility. Besides, they soon learned that Joshua was – albeit currently single – gay, so that any initial hopes on Lara's part of a romantic liaison between her and him were dashed anyway.

'As things were, Joshua didn't only do an excellent job painting and decorating the extension, he also came up with some interesting ideas regarding the arrangement of displays. It was obvious that he had a good eye for art and the presentation of art works and was keen to get more involved with this part of gallery work. Ben recognised his talent as well as his interest in art and the gallery and decided once Joshua's temporary decorating contract job had been completed to take him on as a gallery assistant for a couple of days a week and the occasional Saturday to help out even if he could only offer Joshua a low-paid salary.

'He so far hadn't seen hiring more staff as a necessity: The gallery only consisted of one main room and during the last two years since he had opened it, he and Lara had managed quite well on their own and at the weekend Marianne came in. Marianne was an elderly but very fit and active woman who used to work as an art school teacher, which she had truly loved. After retiring, she quickly noticed that the life of a pensioner wasn't for her and she started looking around for some part-time work. She was therefore excited when she came across the newspaper ad recruiting for both a full-time and a weekend gallery assistant. When she went for her interview, she easily won the gallery manager's approval with her lively and engaging personality, and was overjoyed when she was offered the weekend post.

'Ben had worked as an event manager in a community space and subsequently as an assistant gallery manager in a nearby town. Although he had enjoyed the work involved in these positions, he was looking for a new challenge that allowed him to be more innovative as well as to be his own boss. Opening a gallery suggested itself to him and soon he became obsessed with the idea, voraciously reading some of the literature about start-up businesses and ventures and how to make them a success.

'To him, it wasn't just a strategic business idea though. His passion for art was an important factor in his decision to open a new gallery. He wanted the city's population, as well as people from further afield, to have an even greater range of art to look at and appreciate and hoped to find a niche in the market. He liked much of the Expressionists' artistic output and was a big fan of Cubism and Surrealism, but he knew that these art forms were widely represented and sold. Browsing catalogues in the previous gallery he worked in, he came across some of Henri Rousseau's exotic landscapes and decided there and then that the public should have more opportunities to explore naïve art and what it stood for. Having made this decision, he unfortunately lacked the funds to implement his plans. It was only when his grandfather died fifteen months later and he inherited a large sum of money that he could start carrying out his ideas.

'He found an empty space for sale that he could afford and had it refurbished and made fit for purpose whilst simultaneously looking for paintings to buy. Once he had enough paintings and the gallery space was done up in the way he wanted it to be, he resigned from his previous position and advertised for a couple of staff positions after calculating the costs carefully. For a very small gallery that was tucked away in the back streets and had just opened, he quite rightly guessed that it could probably, at least initially, run on skeleton staff.

'Hiring Lara for the full-time position, he divided the tasks fairly between them. Whilst he was in full control of the finances and sought to create close relationships with artists who created naïve art, Lara was mainly greeting visitors, answering their questions, selling art works and was also tasked with keeping the gallery neat and presentable. Ben, moreover, worked on a viable marketing strategy, which could easily mean the difference between success and failure for the gallery project.

'As it was, it had been a rather slow start after they opened the gallery. Although Ben had advertised their presence on the local art and community websites and had also placed an advert in the local paper, they initially saw very few people enter their gallery. After over a year of very low visitor figures and increasing financial pressures, he decided on investing one more time to have the extension built.

'When Joshua did the decorating work, he came up with some valuable marketing suggestions as well as ideas of how they could best use the extension space: He picked up that Ben hadn't made much use of social media in his marketing approach, which were in his opinion vital to reach a big enough number of people to make the gallery financially viable so he suggested not only to use some key platforms like Facebook and Twitter but to create links between them and bring these links together on their own website on which he was keen to change the branding to make it more memorable. Moreover, he proposed that they didn't just display pictures from other art styles in the extension but that they tried to do temporary exhibitions that were themed.

'Ben was impressed by some of Joshua's ideas, which added further justification to his decision to hire him permanently. He wasn't totally convinced of the financial feasibility of some of Joshua's plans, but he realised – correctly, as it turned out – that his own financial business acumen joined with Ben's innovative approach would work to the gallery's benefit.

'Although they were currently running a loss, it was obvious that more visitors came to the gallery since Ben's joined-up social media marketing campaign and that their sales figures – albeit still modest – were on the rise. They were therefore very optimistic about the gallery's future and felt encouraged by the positive comments in their visitors' book and on their social media sites.

'Joshua predicted that they wouldn't run a loss for long even if they currently struggled to regularly set up differently themed exhibitions in the new extension, as it was hard to find enough artists who had enough work on a particular theme that they were ready to exhibit in their gallery. Many of the artists that would have been suitable had already got arrangements with other galleries and therefore declined.

'Nevertheless, Joshua's extensive networks and his untiring commitment to art and their gallery enabled them to host a lovely exhibition on anything related to cats. All the visitors loved the pictures and sculptures of varying sizes as well as the Japanese-style prints. It took a few months until they managed to have another exhibition, this time on life in cities. That exhibition was still on but they were avidly planning a new one, which was about nature in its different aspects. Joshua had realised that they needed to start by focusing on very broad themes in order to receive enough pieces. He firmly believed though that once they had established some relationships of trust with more artists, they would be able to choose more specific themes for their temporary exhibitions.

'Lara enjoyed being part of this new gallery venture and seeing it develop. Having studied art history and having then worked at a shop that sold art materials for quite a few years, she was overjoyed to now be given the opportunity to work in a gallery setting in which she could share her love for art with her colleagues and visitors.

'"Wow, even the window is still closed. That's so unlike you." Joshua stepped towards the window and opened it marginally. "Are you ill or is whatever you're reading on the computer so absorbing that you dare to neglect your morning routine?"

'He frequently teased her about her habit of opening the office window as soon as she entered in the morning. He did not share her love of fresh air and her affinity to nature. Instead, he got rather annoyed by the havoc the elements wreaked on his carefully styled hair and on his meticulously arranged clothes. Walking over to Lara, he looked over her shoulder to see what she was so engulfed in.

'Without answering him directly, Lara took the card out of her bag on the floor, turned it upside down so that only the drawing of the park was visible and held it out to Joshua. "Do you recognise this drawing? Do you know the artist?"

'Joshua took the card, studied it for a few moments with intense concentration and turned it over to look at the other side before he replied with a shake of his head.

'"No, I've never seen the drawing before, I think, although something about it looks familiar." He brushed one of his curls out of his face before emitting a quick laugh. 'The other picture, however, is all the more familiar. I've always liked Marc's *Blue Horses*."

'Lara nodded briefly, turned back to the computer screen, which she quickly scanned before deciding that it was time to set up the gallery for the day.

'Joshua, who had hung up his white and blue denim jacket with its frayed ends and a collection of badges pinned to it, switched on the other office computer and enquired, "Why do you ask? Where did you find the drawing and why is it so important to you?"

'Lara shrugged her shoulders in response to both his questions. Wasn't the answer obvious? What else but her interest in art as well as her natural curiosity and her eagerness to solve puzzles could have led her to her current preoccupation with the drawing? She told Joshua how and where she had come across it and about the number-letter combination, which she believed to be a date and time.

'At that point, Joshua looked at her attentively and said in an unusually pensive tone of voice, "Now that is interesting."

'Lara studied his face questioningly for any clues that might shed some light on the meaning of his words.

'Joshua, who just opened the online catalogues, database and websites he most frequently used for their work, still kept looking at her intently and resumed. "Well, what if this isn't about art first and foremost? I mean, yes, we deal with an art card here and have a well-executed drawing on the other side; but that doesn't necessarily mean that the message conveyed is about art or an art exhibition."

'Lara asked eagerly, "But what is the message then? What can it all possibly mean?"

'Joshua couldn't hide a smile at her continued drive to find an explanation to what she obviously perceived as a puzzle. He held up a hand to slow her down a bit. "I wouldn't know for sure, of course. But the drawing might have been done to point out the place of an event that is about to happen there and – what you assume to be – the date and time informs you when this is about to take place. It might be worth checking the local event websites and social media for such open-air park events."

'Then he added, "Of course it would be easier to find that information if we knew what park we're dealing with here."

'Lara eagerly interjected. "Oh, but I know what park it is. I've figured it out." She told him the name of the park that she believed was portrayed in the drawing. She knew she had to really start setting the gallery up for visitors now so she had to control her impulse to carry out this search straight away.

'Joshua was aware of how much Lara wanted to get on with this search so he told her to pursue her investigations a bit further whilst he would get everything ready and open up. He also reminded her that Ben would be coming in late that morning as he still had an appointment to attend before work.

'Lara sighed with relief and gratitude and immediately directed her attention towards the computer.

'When Joshua returned to the office about fifteen minutes later, Lara turned to him and shook her head. "Nothing. Absolutely no events or planned performances at this park for the date in question. In fact, it looks as if there won't be any advertised events at all in the near future, which ties in with my memory of it as a beautiful, but quiet and understated, location that is unlikely to attract crowds or many families that don't live in the vicinity due to its lack of playground features or fun rides."

'She continued disappointedly and with a frown on her face. "The mystery of the card remains then. I'm no closer to solving it. Maybe someone had merely enjoyed drawing that park, scribbled a random number-letter combination that they liked at the bottom of it and then either forgot it on the café table or left it there deliberately, hoping other bookshop café visitors would enjoy their creation."

'She paused for a moment before she reiterated emphatically as if trying to convince herself of the likelihood of the scenario that she had just described. "Yes. That's the explanation. As simple as that. No great mystery at all. My imagination has just run a bit wild."

'With these words, she tried to laugh the whole matter off, expecting Joshua to break into hearty laughter and to tease her relentlessly about her very vivid imagination as he often did. However, the reaction she expected did surprisingly not materialise, possibly because he had also made speculations of his own, which had turned out to be unfounded as well.

'Instead, Joshua gave her that direct look again that she often failed to hold, as it activated the shy and self-conscious part of her personality. Today, however, she did not avert her eyes, as her desire to understand the meaning of the picture was stronger than her timidity, and she sensed that Joshua had another thought on the significance of the picture. And she was right.

'Joshua said to her with a smile on his face, "Maybe it's not about an advertised event at all. This might be a personal message, Lara. It might be a personal invitation."

'Lara blinked uncomprehendingly. "I don't understand. What is that supposed to mean?"

'Joshua's eyes glinted mischievously and his smile became broader. "It's very simple, Lara. This might be a personal invitation for you to meet up with someone in this park at the given date and time. Basically, this could be an attempt at setting up a rendezvous with you."

'Had Lara not been absolutely flabbergasted by this explanation, she would have smiled about Joshua's uncharacteristically archaic language, which he obviously used in order to tease her. As it was, she merely gaped at him for a few seconds and then said quietly, "You're making fun of me now."

'Joshua shook his head and sent his curls flying. "No, Lisa. I'm quite serious even if I don't look it. I've only grinned because it was so easy to anticipate your reaction. You never seem to believe that someone would ask you out but always doubt yourself in this regard."

'Lara felt herself blush. Joshua was always very direct and would talk about his sharp observations even if he sometimes embarrassed others with them. It was true that Lara didn't have much faith in meeting someone special when it came to it, as she didn't consider herself confident enough. Having reached her early thirties and having only had fleeting romantic encounters, if they could be called that at all, she did not feel that she had any justification in believing this rendezvous explanation that Joshua had just put forward. This wouldn't be something that could realistically happen to her. She now also felt uncomfortable and self-conscious after Joshua had pointed out her fairly low self-esteem.

'Lara was desperate to change the topic but for want of coming up with a new one, she merely said quietly, "There is no reason why this idea should have any foundation in reality. There is no evidence that substantiates it."

'Joshua realised that Lara was trying to depersonalise their conversation by taking the issue at stake into the realm of ideas, logic and probability. He was willing to continue their conversation on that level but he would not let the topic drop altogether.

'"Look, Lara," he resumed. "It is rather odd that you have found the only card with that drawing on *your* table. If the card had been used to advertise an exhibition or a specific event, you would expect to find many of them in the café for people to take away. And when you asked the bookshop staff, they didn't know about the drawing or what it was about at all. Normally, if you distribute marketing material, you have to be given permission by the staff who run, or at least work at, the establishment you want to leave it in. Also, you told me that you only noticed the card after you had briefly left the table you had been sitting at, to fetch some art books. Chances are that the person in question watched you and placed the card on the table whilst you were briefly away. The café staff or customers might have seen him leave his encrypted message to you."

'Lara shook her head, trying to reason with Joshua. "That makes no sense. If someone really wanted to say something to me or…" and here she blushed and lowered her voice, "ask me out, why would they not just come over and approach me directly? And if they prefer to take an indirect approach for whatever reason, why make everything so ambiguous and difficult to decipher, leaving much room for misinterpretation?"

'Again, Joshua couldn't suppress a smile. "He might be shy, too, so he would find it hard to just walk up to you and start a conversation."

'Seeing that Lara once again looked awkward, he continued undeterred, "But do you know what I really think?"

'Lara wasn't sure she did but, undoubtedly, she was about to learn about it whether she wanted to or not. She therefore didn't react to what she considered to be a rhetorical question on his part and just waited, resigned to hear whatever was going to be said.

'"Just think for a moment." Joshua was gesturing now to add emphasis to his words. "You would have shrunk away from a direct approach, Lara. You would have tried to escape and that would have been the end of it. That other person must have recognised this and has therefore taken another line of action. He must also have known or guessed that you love mysteries and enjoy doing a bit of detective work, and this is why the message hasn't been a straightforward one."

'Lara still appeared doubtful albeit simultaneously intrigued. "But who would that be? I cannot possibly think of someone who might have done that."

'Joshua shrugged his shoulders. "Well, I guess someone in the bookshop who has observed you, possibly on many occasions. He has also observed that you appreciate art so that he chose to use his artistic talents to appeal to you and pique your curiosity."

'Lara gave him a sceptical glance until her gaze came to rest on the clock above their computers. "Gosh, it's late!" she exclaimed. "We should have opened almost ten minutes ago."

'With these words, she dashed out of the office to open the front door of the gallery trying to focus on the work that needed to be done next.

'At the end of the working day, Lara left the gallery quickly and made the normally ten-minute-long walk to the bookshop in a record time of eight minutes. She was slightly out of breath but still hurried up to the café on the third floor. At the top of the stairs she stopped for a couple of seconds to catch her breath before walking up to the café and queuing behind a woman with a toddler and a baby in a pushchair. The woman in front of her was just placing her order, which gave Lara the chance to cast her eyes over the seating area and get an idea of how busy the café was. It was less busy than on the previous day but there were some people sipping their teas, coffees and hot chocolates and Lara tried to take a good look at them. Although she had quickly dismissed Joshua's theory of a mysterious admirer of hers sending her cryptic messages in the bookshop, some questions lingered in her mind about whether there might not be at least some partial truth in what Joshua suspected. It was probably just some unrealistic hope that had been kindled, but ever since Joshua had outlined his thoughts she had wondered which one of the café visitors could have left that card for her.

'She couldn't remember all of the previous day's café visitors but hoped to jog her memory by possibly detecting some repeat visitors today. This expectation was not too far-fetched, as there were some regular customers like her who came here several times a week. In fact, she only recognised one of them: a man of advanced middle age with short salt-and-pepper hair, broad-rimmed, dark glasses, black jeans and a shirt whose two top buttons were unfastened. He had been a café regular for at least as long as she had been, which meant for at least a year.

'After a few months of seeing each other there regularly, they had started nodding to each other in greeting and eventually started exchanging some friendly words about the weather, the coffee and the books they perused at their individual tables. She learned that he was a science lecturer and writer. Frequently, he had some astronomy books with him, some of them being his own, others belonging to the bookshop. The latter tended to be massive tomes, which didn't appear easy to handle or carry. The man usually had at least one large notebook with him, which was the receptacle of his ideas.

'He now looked up from one of his books, turned his face towards Lara, who was still waiting near the counter to be served, and lifted his hand in greeting. Lara nodded hesitantly. Whilst she didn't mind having the odd little chat with him, she recently got the impression that he was actively looking for her and was keen to deepen their acquaintance, and she wasn't very eager to do so, especially because she treasured her time in the café and didn't want to be disturbed.

'Then it came to her like a bolt out of the blue: What if he had left the card for her? What if he had sent her the message that Joshua believed to have successfully deciphered? Could he have put the card on her table when she went to the shelves to fetch the art books? He had certainly been present yesterday, sitting at the lower end of the café where the toilets were located and she had been at a nearby window table. But had he only been there when she had first come in or had he still been at his table when she had returned with the books? She couldn't remember.

'Disappointment, mixed with shock, rapidly spread through her. He was certainly not anybody she fancied or was willing to associate with more closely. He was nice enough, but Lara found him also quite odd without being able to say exactly why that was. She found nothing remotely romantic in the notion of him attempting to draw her attention towards him in this way. Provided Joshua had been right with his interpretation of the card lying on her table, she was about to laugh to simultaneously dispel her discomfort and to give voice to the irony that something exciting was finally happening in her life but with entirely the wrong person being involved.

'At this moment, she was brought back to what was directly in front of her by an insistent, but clearly amused voice that was filled with laughter. "Hello! How can I help? Any drinks?"

'Lara shifted her attention to the barista in front of her, who gave her a huge grin. She blushed in response. She knew the café staff and the handsome – even if a bit short – young barista with his Mediterranean looks and the jet-black curls and tanned skin was one of her favourites. She loved his laughter, his slightly cheeky comments and his sunny disposition. He looked incredibly young though. She guessed that he was even younger than Joshua, who was in his late twenties. This dark Adonis might not even have reached his mid-twenties.

'Lara's initial inclination to laugh at the thought of the scientist leaving a secretive missive for her, gave way to an embarrassed smile. "Oh, sorry," she apologised, having no idea how long ago the woman in front of her had finished with her order. "I..." and then she was interrupted by the still broadly grinning barista whose name was Giovanni.

'"You were away with the fairies, weren't you?"

'Wow. The same teasing statement twice in a day, first from Joshua and now from Giovanni. This affair with the card had seriously distracted her. That much was clear. She needed to either find an explanation and then be a functioning actor in the real world again or forget about it all, which would also bring her back to her surroundings.

'Before she could retort anything, Giovanni saved her from her embarrassment by stating rather than asking, "The usual?"

'Laura nodded and caught a glimpse of the barista who had handled the coffee machine and whose name was Simon. He had obviously overheard their exchange and she thought she saw a smile play around the corners of his mouth before his face turned more serious again and he turned back to prepare Lara's tea. He, like Giovanni, had dark hair, but his was wavy rather than curly, and he was taller and probably a bit older than his fellow barista. He had served her a lot of the time, too, and whilst he was always friendly and had a nice smile, he was far less exuberant and extroverted than Giovanni and she had talked to him much less. Like Giovanni though, he evidently remembered that her usual order consisted of an Earl Grey tea.

'She paid Giovanni, whose eyes still twinkled with mirth, and took her tea from Simon, who only briefly looked at her after making sure that the cup was now safely placed in her hands. Then she entered the seating area, carrying her tea and looking out for a free seat, ideally by a window.

'There was just one window seat available, which was closest to the art books. The scientist hadn't been able to get his usual seat near the toilets either but was sitting surrounded by some empty tables in the middle of the café instead. Lara deliberately didn't give him another look, as she was determined not to offer him any encouragement in his potential interest in her. In fact, she felt that she needed to find a way to actively discourage him from communicating with her if he had deeper interests invested in her. Whether ignoring him or at least acting in an aloof manner was enough to put him off in his pursuit – if her suspicion proved to be correct – remained to be seen, but it was worth the attempt. At the same time, she knew that it could have easily been another café visitor who had mysteriously and indirectly approached her. She studied the other customers carefully after sitting down and letting the subtle bergamot flavour of her drink unfold in her mouth, gently activating her taste buds.

'At the adjacent table alongside the windows, two teenagers were perching on their chairs, holding their iPhones out to each other across the table, presumably to show each other some photos, something funny or exciting on a website or progress made in a game. They were dressed in black with some buttons attached to their bomber jackets, their straight hair dyed pitch-black and held back in slick pony-tails. Both of them wore a number of small silver rings and studs on one of their eyebrows and noses and one on their lips. It took her a second to differentiate between them and identify one of them as a boy and the other as a girl. They then leaned further forward and kissed, which might easily have developed into a snog had it not been so difficult to bring their faces together whilst still perching on their chairs. They also reached out to each other with their hands, still holding their phones with one hand and touching each other with the remaining hand.

'Lara's eyes wandered to the table behind the young teenage couple, having satisfied herself that neither of them would have approached her, absorbed as they were in each other and their phones. Besides, she didn't think she had seen them before. In order to get a good view of the people further along the window, Lara had to direct her gaze slightly towards the right, keeping her head so close to the window that she was almost leaning against it.

'At the table behind the teenage couple, she could see a young Asian family that she had spotted in the bookshop café a few times before. She always enjoyed watching them, as the couple was absolutely wonderful in how they tended to their small children. The older of them was a boy of two or three who was always very lively and demanded much of his parents' attention, especially when the parents were busy looking after the baby. The father, in particular, made sure that their eldest wasn't running around too wildly and disturbing the other customers, by endlessly coming up with new games he played with him that held the boy's attention for a while. Sometimes, he visited the bookshops without his partner, taking either both his children or just his eldest with him. On these occasions, Lara had sometimes watched him hold his son close and either moved a toy in front of his face or just talked to him and both of them laughed happily.

'Lara loved to witness such a close parent-child bond. Her intrigue could partly be explained by having lost her own parents when she was still young. Although she had spent her remaining childhood and adolescence under the care of a loving aunt and uncle, it wasn't quite the same, she believed, as being cared for by the same people from the time you were born.

'She and this amazing father had sometimes exchanged glances and smiles; Lara couldn't stop herself from smiling whenever she observed the father and son interact and the man appreciated Lara's friendliness. Another shiver – although this time not an unpleasant one – ran down Lara's spine. Could it be that this loving father and lovely man had left the card on her table? No. Impossible! It was easy to see how fond the couple were of each other. The woman just said something to her partner whilst holding the baby and smiled at him, and he reciprocated her smile with a ravishing one on his part. Surely, he wouldn't send her a message with romantic intentions! Or would he?

'Lara was now visibly confused and focused on the other visitors. At the table nearest to the toilets where normally the scientist sat, she saw a young guy, possibly a student, listen to the sounds through his headphones whilst watching something on his iPad that he had propped up on the table in front of him. Lara assumed that he was watching a film or video clips, as he was leaning back on his chair and did not seem to interact with whatever appeared on the screen. She had noticed him in the café several times before and every time he had been completely absorbed in his iPad, like now, or his iPhone. He didn't seem to acknowledge the others with as much as a glance. Lara thought that he would be the last person to leave a message on a card for her. Joshua might say that this could all just be camouflage and that she shouldn't be deceived by appearances, but she dismissed this minor objection in her head as extremely far-fetched.

'Next to the student, a middle-aged couple were having a leisurely conversation whilst drinking tea. She had seen the couple once before. Both of them were dressed in smart office attire – she in a dark-blue shirt and trouser suit and he in a classic, black suit with a light-blue shirt underneath. His hair was very short and displayed different shades of grey, whereas hers was the colour of mahogany and probably dyed to achieve that radiant shine.

'Ruling the businessman out as the mysterious stranger as well, she turned her head to the left, past the scientist, who was – as she noticed with discomfort – gazing at her, until her eyes came to rest on an elderly couple at the table to her left, which was the only remaining table that was occupied.

They were familiar to her and she always enjoyed seeing them. The elderly woman with her silver hair, that she wore in short waves, used a walking stick and she was hunched over and her gait was unsteady. Her husband always walked with her, lending his arm for support on her free side. He would also get in the queue and then carefully carry a tray with a large pot of tea and, more often than not, a couple of tea cakes back to their table. Frequently, one of the baristas, like Simon, or one of the girls took the tray over for them. Sometimes, the couple talked but mostly they would sit there in what felt like a comfortable silence, drink their tea and relish their tea cakes. At times, they would read the paper or look at a magazine together. Whatever they did, there was this sense of loving care and tenderness towards each other, which was underlying all their interactions. Lara loved watching them together for this reason and they had all exchanged a smile and a few friendly words on occasion.

'Of course, it was unthinkable that the elderly man would leave a card with a drawing for her. At least not if the message had romantic connotations. The age difference between them and his unmistakable devotion to his wife made the mere thought of it seem ludicrous. There was, however, a niggling voice at the back of her mind telling her that it's often the scenarios we rule out as impossible ones that were worth investigating from a different angle. Wasn't it possible that the message and intention of the card were quite different in nature from what Joshua had suggested or she had thought of so far? And then, maybe the elderly man could have left his card for her. It might be unlikely that he had done the drawing himself with his slightly shaky hands, but he could have asked someone else to do a drawing for him based on his instructions.

'Laura shrugged her shoulders. She was confused and didn't know how to get any more clarity in this matter.'

'In the following days and weeks, Lara tried to put the issue of the card out of her mind and just concentrate on her daily tasks and on her art in the long evenings she spent in the garden. But, of course, her intrigue didn't just go away and her curiosity surfaced at regular intervals. Even if she managed to stave it off when she was at the gallery, as soon as she approached the bookshop café, she looked out for the person who might have been the messenger. However, there were no further clues as to the person's identity and she dismissed most regular café visitors as unlikely candidates. Still the most probably person was the scientist and Lara remained unhappy about that and tried to put him off by behaving in an increasingly distant way.

'On Friday, the twentieth of June, she arrived at the gallery early as usual and was surprised to find Joshua already browsing various art-related websites on the computer. He gave the impression of having been in for quite a while. They exchanged greetings and once Lara had started up the other computer and settled into the office chair in front of it, Joshua turned, swivelled around to her and came straight to the point that was on his mind. "So, I take it that you'll be going to the park tomorrow?"

'The question in itself seemed to be nothing more than the usual, polite enquiry into a colleague's weekend plans. In fact, Lara didn't suspect a reference to anything else behind the question and was therefore a little confused to be asked about plans for visiting a park being sure that she had never mentioned such an intention. She thus enquired with a somehow puzzled expression on her face, "The park? What park?"

'Joshua grinned. "Oh, come on, Lara, don't pretend you don't know what I'm talking about. Tomorrow is the day of the rendezvous with your mysterious admirer, of course. In the park that he depicted so prettily on the card. Don't pretend you have forgotten all about it because I won't believe you."

'Lara blushed. She certainly hadn't forgotten about it, but hadn't realised that this was what the question referred to. The closer the date – if it was a date – on the card came, the more frequently she engaged in an internal dialogue on what she should do. Eventually, she had talked it all through with a friend she had known from university, with whom she met up every few weeks. Despite being essentially a very private person who was disinclined to discuss her private matters even with people she knew reasonably well or very well, she felt that what she needed now was a sounding board to let her confused thoughts find an expression and put them to the test.

'Her friend Mel was good for this. Like Lara, she was inquisitive and also very much into art so that it had been easy for the two to find common ground. Mel was a lot more extroverted than Lara, which explained why the latter was not surprised when Mel decided to do her PGCE and go into teaching with a focus on teaching art at secondary school. Over the years, she had also established herself as an artist in her own right, having pictures exhibited in galleries and having created her own website on which she sold her paintings and put out more background information about herself and her art for her customers. She created abstract paintings in different media although her favourite one was acrylic. Lara enjoyed the colours and patterns her paintings displayed and was always curious to see what Mel's latest project was.

'Mel was excited by the mystery of the anonymous artist and the card. She had, like Lara, a very fertile imagination, which found abundant expression in her artistic outpourings. Any impressions she gathered could easily make it into her paintings even if in a totally new and transformed way that would have made it hard for anyone to point to the original impression or idea. Besides, her paintings tended to be a huge amalgam of perceptions, sensations, thoughts and ideas and it would have been almost impossible to extricate one from another after they had undergone less of a transformation from their original appearance. She often created pieces quickly and easily got into an artistic flow that at times bordered on frenzy. Lara, in contrast, worked in a more measured way that didn't reach the ecstatic climaxes Mel experienced on a regular basis. Nevertheless, she also had a sense of satisfaction and achievement both during and after the creative process. Their somehow similar but still different ways of working and creating were an expression of their temperaments and also of Lara's tendency to be more analytic and thoughtful whilst Mel was more intuitive and spontaneous.

'These tendencies clearly came to the forefront during their conversation about the card and Lara's hesitation about what she should do. Once Lara had finished telling Mel everything about the matter that she considered relevant, Mel called out with gleaming eyes and a huge smile on her heart-shaped face, which was beautifully framed by bright red curls, "But of course you'll go to that park on the twenty-first, Lara! What are you worrying about?"

'Lara explained to Mel that she absolutely didn't want to run into the scientist there and give him the wrong idea and that she strongly suspected that it was him who had left the postcard for her. At least he was the most likely candidate among all the bookshop visitors.

'Mel shook her head vigorously. "But you can't know that for sure, Lara. It's not always the most obvious person who turns out to have done or said something that you're curious about. For all we know, it could be your handsome colleague, Joshua, who has sent someone else to the bookshop to leave a message there for you."

'Lara rolled her eyes. "Why would he do that? To make fun of me and my curiosity? He might sometimes make fun of me at work and undoubtedly he would be the type to play tricks on people, but I don't think that he would do so when it comes to romantic matters even in jest."

'Mel retorted, "But he pointed out that this could be an invitation for a rendezvous. He might have tried to help you interpret the meaning of his message."

'It was now Lara's turn to shake her head. "Would he then have said something along the lines of how important it is that I believe in myself in the context of romance and relationships? Saying that as part of a prank that involves falsely claiming that someone was interested in a date with me would just be cruel. And Joshua isn't cruel. He might at times be a little annoying, but there is nothing cruel in him."

'Mel waited for a moment before she said, "Okay. But I'm not suggesting that he was playing a prank on you. He could have done the picture because he wants to meet you outside the gallery setting himself."

'Lara gave her friend a stern look. "Firstly, Joshua would never take this approach. He would always be direct. And secondly..." she didn't give Mel a chance to interrupt her, which the latter was just about to do, "he's gay. Have you forgotten about that?"

'Lara paused and when her friend didn't immediately react but appeared to consider Lara's word, she resumed, "To come back to the scientist, I still don't know what to do."

'Mel said, "I repeat that it might not be him you would meet there but for the sake of argument, let's consider the possibility. I don't think it matters if you came across him there."

'Lara was about to interject, but Mel didn't give her occasion to do so. "I mean, if you see him there you can just make it crystal clear that you're not interested in him. You don't even have to spell it out to him. You can just ignore him or remain aloof if he directly addresses you. I know you're telling me that you have already tried that in the bookshop, but he might have put your distant attitude down to embarrassment in front of other bookshop visitors. If you equally show no interest in the park when he approaches you, I think you'll get the message across."

'Lara put forward another consideration. "He might just think that I play hard to get."

'Mel shook her head. "No, not if you look determined. Just don't hesitate or look at him for too long."

'Lara was acutely aware of this precaution posing a potential difficulty for her. She didn't feel self-assured and confident enough to be convincing in her attitude of rejection.

'"And besides," Mel added, "maybe he's quite different in another environment. This park sounds as if it is a far less busy environment and even if there were quite a few other people there on the day, you can always easily leave them behind by walking on the grassy areas or on some of the less well-used paths."

'She instantly noticed Lara's facial expression though, which reflected strong doubts if not disbelief. As long as one of her arguments had worked with Lara and had convinced her that her reason for not going to the park on the specified day and time was not good enough to act on, Mel was satisfied.

'Thinking of how to respond to Joshua's comments now, Lara was conscious that her friend Mel's insistence on her going to the park had certainly worked on her. It might not have fully removed her trepidation of being confronted with the scientist there and of not dealing with that situation successfully, but it had given renewed impulse to her curiosity and her strong inclination to solve the mystery of the card. Nevertheless, in front of Joshua she felt she had to play down her excitement, as she would otherwise never hear the end of it and be unceasingly questioned and teased by him. She therefore just said that the theory he had come up with might be totally wrong and that it would be somewhat crazy to base her actions on a vague hunch.

'Joshua retorted that he didn't equate his thoughts with a vague hunch, but that this was probably not the point. He gazed at her without batting an eyelid and it was as if the sun radiated from his eyes.

'"What is the point then?" Lara asked, unnerved by Joshua's apparent refusal to drop the topic.

'"The point is…" he continued calmly without letting her out of his field of vision, "that you will never *know* whether I was right or not if you don't go there tomorrow." He let this statement sink in before adding, "And even if I was wrong – I'm not saying I am, of course – would it be so bad to find yourself in this park on your own where you can watch the water of the fountain dance and sparkle and where you can then sit on a bench and let the skin of your face be tickled by the warm rays of the early summer sun? There are worse ways of spending your time, surely."

'Lara had nothing to say to that rather convincing argument. With great effort, she pushed her thoughts about the park to one side for the next few hours and made herself useful, engaging with the visitors – they had more that day than on most other weekdays – and making sure the displays remained untouched. She surprised herself by how well she had shifted her focus to work-related tasks.

'Before closing time, Joshua, of course, couldn't help winking at her when he wished her a most lovely and successful weekend with a big grin on his face, before rushing out to get to the massage parlour, where he worked part-time as a masseur, on time. He was very much a jack of all trades.

'Ben's face registered surprise at hearing Joshua's rather excessive good wishes despite being, by now, used to Joshua's exuberance and eccentricities. Whilst both he and Lara were busy with the closing procedures, he asked, "Are you doing anything special this weekend?"

'Lara was relieved that she had her back turned towards him while switching off the office computers so that he couldn't see her blush. She let a few seconds go by before she mumbled, "Not really. Just the usual. And you?" she added.

'Ben and Lara didn't usually talk much about their private lives. Whilst getting on very well at work, they both kept a professional distance, which reflected their personalities, which were both marked by a strong need for privacy. Although Ben was personable, confident and didn't lack confidence or suffer from reserve as Lara did, Joshua found him frequently elusive. But then, this was hardly surprising considering that Joshua was like an open book and would, if encouraged, talk about anything and everything about his life down to the most intimate details.

'At the most, Lara and Ben might briefly chat about weekend plans or events, but these exchanges were of short duration. She knew that Ben was an avid runner and also engaged in abstract painting, having managed to sell some of his works online. Lara and Joshua had started to encourage him to exhibit his works in their extension, but Ben had rather compellingly argued that this would break with their practice of having themed exhibitions in that space, as his art wasn't particularly theme-focused. This answer had naturally just led to Joshua entreat Ben to create art works around a theme. Ben had simply replied that his art didn't work like this and had, since then, not participated in any further discussions around this subject.

'Now, Ben answered Lara's question without evasion however. "I want to get on with a painting that has been on my mind for the last few days. I just have to do it. My fingers are itching to put my brush to the empty canvas."

'Lara nodded even though she guessed that Ben wouldn't see this.

'When they had finally completed the closing procedures and stepped through the gallery door to lock up, something unexpected happened. Lara had just wished Ben a nice and productive weekend and was about to turn around and be on her way, when she saw Ben's face light up as she had rarely seen it light up before and, uncharacteristically, virtually beam at her. "And to you, too, Lara! Take care."

'Confused by this unusual leave-taking, she nodded briefly and walked away from the gallery with rapid steps.'

'The following day, she boarded a moderately busy bus in the city centre, which was travelling north. It was only just after eleven o' clock and thus far too early for going to the park and for checking out whether anyone she knew would be there. She had looked up how to get there in case she couldn't remember it from last time. The last thing she wanted to happen was to get lost.

'After about forty minutes, she got off at the bus stop mentioned on the map. From here, she carefully followed the blue line on the printout of the Google map she had downloaded, at the same time having her phone ready to help her navigate her way if needed. She initially walked along a busy road, which seemed to be an offshoot of the high street before taking a sharp turn to the left following a path that was steadily climbing up a hill. The path was narrow and steep but the fact that it was displayed as a route option on Google maps suggested that it was a viable option for walkers who wanted to reach an excellent viewpoint or the park more quickly.

'When she finally reached the top of the hill, she was out of breath and paused for a few moments before she walked past some trees at the edge of a small plateau. A detailed view emerged in front of her: Straight down and slightly to the left, the estate where she had got off was visible with its busy high street and its similarly busy offshoot that she had walked along earlier. Further in the background, she could make out residential areas, which were mainly made up of old, red-brick houses.

'However, a truly lovely view offered itself to her when she turned her head to the right. Down in the valley, at quite a distance from her, the city lay sprawled out like a toy town with its predominantly grey roofs glinting in the midday sun, which lent the place a silver aura from where Lara stood. She enjoyed the sight for a few moments before turning back to the path and following it further along, simultaneously checking the map to make sure that she was still on her way to the park, as there didn't appear to be any signposts.

'It took her less than five minutes until the park opened up in front of her. She stepped on a broader path that led her through areas of neatly trimmed grass on either side of it. The Parks' Trust did put a lot of effort into maintaining the green spaces of the city and its surroundings. The lawns here could be compared to the impeccably tended front lawns of middle-class, suburban England. On her way along the path, she admired the tall, healthy and powerfully built chestnut trees with their succulent leaves to her left. Soon, she recognised the fountain from the drawing. It was straight in front of her and was truly picturesque.

'Approaching the circular space around the fountain that had been captured so well in the drawing, she watched the equally well-portrayed, proud, stone heron spout clear water from the beak of its upturned head. The water drops glinted in the sunlight and when Lara stopped right in front of the fountain, she could see the whole spectrum of colours in every single drop: like a rainbow in miniature. A feeling of deep joy spread through her and she felt the nervousness and tension she had been under since early that morning subside. After all, being in such magical surroundings on a beautiful summer's day was bliss and she didn't feel that she needed any pleasant surprises added to it. In fact, whilst she was standing next to the fountain for what seemed like hours but was probably hardly more than fifteen minutes, she didn't care any longer about whether she met the artist of the drawing on the card and thus solved the mystery or not. She merely wanted to stay in this moment, relishing what was in front of and around her now. It was a trance-like experience, which she sometimes had when she felt deeply in harmony with her surroundings, usually with nature.

'The sounds of gravel being crushed by feet and wheels caused her to shift her gaze towards the path where a mother dressed in a pastel blue linen dress was pushing a buggy, in which Lara spotted a sturdy boy of about two years of age. The mother was obviously too hot: Beads of sweat stood on her forehead, which caused some wisps of her blonde, curly hair to dampen and turn darker in shade.

'When the woman had passed Lara, the latter felt her legs become heavy from standing rooted to one spot for a while and from the preceding climb up the hill. She therefore turned around and walked to one of the dark green benches onto which she lowered herself but not before admiringly taking in the fragrant, yellow roses in the flower bed behind it. It struck her that the roses had also been captured very realistically in the drawing even with regard to their exact location even though a month ago, when she had found the card, the roses couldn't have possibly been in bloom yet. Had the artist anticipated what that circular space around the fountain in the park would look like on the day of the summer solstice?

'Lara was astonished when she removed the card from her white fabric bag with the small, colourful beads and compared its details to the setting she was in now: Even the direction of the bend of the roses' heads seemed identical. She smoothed her short, white cotton dress with the lace pattern, which she loved to wear in the summer. The small trinkets on her silver bracelet jingled from the movement and for a few moments her lips, which were painted in a soft pink, changed into a carefree smile.

'She looked down at her hands and was pleased with the nail polish, which was of a similar shade of pink to her lipstick and which she had applied carefully first thing that morning. Lara loved lipstick, nail polish and accessories of all sorts and usually wore at least one of them, but that morning she had taken more care than usual with how she dressed, and the make-up she wore, although she would not have admitted to it. The sensation of the warm sun on her face and the exposed skin of her arms and legs from the knees down was utterly pleasant and she closed her eyes in deep satisfaction. Her absorption in the sensations triggered by her surroundings still staved off any worries or anxieties about a potential meeting with anyone there.

'She thought of Joshua and Marianne now being at work in the gallery whilst she was enjoying the sunshine outside. She didn't know how Joshua managed to juggle all his jobs and activities – his main job as a decorator, his work at the massage parlour, the gallery work and some modelling jobs – but somehow, he seemed to get on and cope with the demands very well and almost always appeared cheerful.

'Had it not been for his father, who ran his own business as a painter and decorator, he would possibly not have gone into that trade but would probably have dipped in and out of various jobs that took his fancy at the time, but his father was a firm believer in learning a proper trade and having a steady income. For a few years, he worked with his father before it became clear that they were unable to work together in an amicable way. Joshua hated the nine-to-five, five-days-a-week nature of the work, which didn't leave him enough time to go out and do other things in his opinion, so he frequently used short-cuts such as extended lunch-breaks and earlier finishes at work. This exasperated his father a lot and both of them were relieved when Joshua decided to advertise his decorating services independently, which allowed him to mainly work to his own timeline. This gave him the time to learn massage, explore other interests of his such as body art, and start doing some modelling. He had often been financially hard-up but despite that, he had not gone back to the financially easier and more straightforward path so fervently advocated by his father. He had put in extra hours at his different jobs when needed and never complained of anything. Lara had once asked him whether the financial insecurity that came along with this lifestyle wasn't too much of a risk to take. She remembered his response quite clearly, suggesting to her that taking risks was what it meant to be alive. Lara wasn't sure whether this was just recklessness or whether it was a fundamental truth that she had not fully discovered.

'Opening her eyes again, she thought that taking a risk was exactly what she was doing herself by having followed what she thought were the instructions on the card without knowing who – if anyone – would turn up for her in the park. She fought down her resurging tension, closed her eyes again, took some deep and slow breaths, and forced herself to relax.

'After a while, she became aware of a low-level humming sound behind her, which must have come from some insects that were attracted by the scent of the roses. In her mind's eye, they were circling and hovering over the open blossoms, getting ready to land on them and pollinate them. However, each time one of them was only millimetres away from the blossom, it shot back up high in the air as if hit by an electric current. There, the insect seemed to sway back and forth as if drunk after having reached a certain height. However, barely minutes later, it would take a slow and elegant dive down to the flowers in a new attempt to touch down on the surface of one of them. Still, the attempt was in vain. This spectacle kept repeating itself until Lara suddenly had an inkling that the next dive one of the insects took would turn out differently. She didn't know where this feeling came from, but it was undeniably strongly present. When she focused on the insect, it was as if she zoomed in on it with a camera lens. The insect, which she could now identify as a bee, was greatly magnified and, to Lara's amazement, its movements appeared to be in slow motion. This made it possible for her to follow it closely when it dived again. It headed through the air in a straight, downward line and Lara believed she could make out its determination to this time land on a flower's blossom. When it was only a few centimetres away from the blossom, it started to slow down slightly. When Lara saw it go beyond the point where it had previously always bounced back up and it was almost touching the flower, she smiled at the bee's imminent success. Just as she felt the insect being embraced by the rose's velvet petals, she heard a shout in front of her and almost jumped when she realised that it was her name that was being shouted. "Lara!"

'She opened her eyes, taking a few moments to shift her attention from the compelling images of the bee's descent as seen under a lens to what was in front of her. A few metres away from her, at the level of the fountain, a young man clad in smart, black jeans and a white, short-sleeved shirt approached her with measured but purposeful steps. Lara noticed immediately that he was a familiar figure.

'However, it took her a few moments during which she shook off the vestiges of her daze to recognise the tall, slender man with the dark hair. Only when he came to a stop in front of her did it dawn on her that it was Simon, the bookshop barista, who had called out to her and who now faced her. Somehow confused, she merely managed to stammer, "Wh-what are you doing here? And how do you know my name?"

'Simon smiled at her. "It's not that difficult, Lara. Giovanni uses your name a lot when we serve you. He asks all our regular customers for their names and then he makes a point of using them whenever they come in, thus trying to personalise the service."

'He paused, giving Lara time to acknowledge what he had said with a nod. "I'm really pleased that you understood my message and have come here today."

'So it was Simon who had left her the mysterious card. She didn't know what to do or say now. She hadn't prepared herself to meet him here. But then who had she prepared herself to meet here? Apart from considering the possibility of seeing the scientist here and having discussed ways of dealing with such an encounter with Mel, she hadn't really imagined anyone in particular to visit the park in order to meet her for any length of time.

'Simon's dark brown eyes emitted a warm shine and both his smile and his voice were reassuring as if he was trying to assuage Lara's obvious confusion and embarrassment. "Do you want to go on a walk through the park together, Lara?"

'Lara swallowed and, after a moment of trying hard to get the better of her self-consciousness, she nodded and replied in a slightly hoarse voice, "Yes, that would be nice." She saw his eyes light up even more at her words, which made her suddenly smile – even if a little nervously – in return. A moment later, she stood up from the bench, briefly smoothed her white dress down and joined Simon for a walk down the gravel path.

⋆ ★ ⋆

As Lisa emerged from her narrative and looked up, she became aware of the other people's gaze resting on her. Before she had any time to feel self-conscious, Leo commented, 'Well, I certainly wouldn't have guessed that it was Simon who left the card for Lara.'

Lisa returned his gaze and replied, 'It's usually bad mysteries that allow people to easily identify the person who has done something of central interest in the story.'

Leo retorted promptly, 'Yes, but Simon has barely been mentioned. We don't really know anything about him.'

Lisa shook her head. 'Detective stories often don't shed much light on the person responsible for the main event. Otherwise, telling the story would be pointless. The readers or listeners would soon be bored and switch off.'

She paused briefly before she resumed. 'As long as there are no internal inconsistencies, and I don't think there were any, it wasn't highly improbable that Simon was the one who left the card for Lisa. There was nothing to suggest that this would go against logic or that it would be in complete contradiction to his personality. It was merely not obvious to us because we didn't learn much about Simon and had more information about the scientist. As a result, our attention was directed to the scientist as the potential artist of that picture. This way of directing a reader's, or listener's, focus is an intentional and deliberate act on the part of the storyteller. This particularly comes to the fore in detective stories, which work through the use of red herrings. What you imagine to be the most likely scenario, or who you think is the most probable person to have done something, are often not the true scenario or the person who have committed a certain act. A good detective story is characterised by unpredictability.'

Lisa's explanations and defence of her story had revealed a more confident and more impassioned side of her.

Karen, who had been following the story and the ensuing thought exchange closely, expressed her agreement. 'Yes, life is full of unpredictability. Often, we would never have anticipated what turns our lives would take. And even though the story's ending wasn't improbable as you have explained, Lisa, in life even improbable events sometimes happen and scenarios we have previously considered surreal unfold. Improbable is not the same as impossible.'

Charles rested his gaze on Karen pensively before he commented, 'Isn't us being here a case in point?'

Leo, still pondering the ending of the story, shrugged his shoulders. 'I still wouldn't have selected Simon. The scientist would have been a better option.'

Karen pointed out, 'Lara wasn't interested in the scientist so I don't think she would have regarded him as a desirable option. Different people have different preferences.'

Leo objected, 'It would have been nice to have some tension. The scientist might not have been the person Lara thinks he is and that can be revealed when they get to know each other.'

Lisa said, 'Why do you not give the story a different ending in which Lara meets the scientist and they walk off together. There can be different versions of the story. There doesn't have to be one version that is absolute and true. We all bring different perspectives and views with us. Everything we see is filtered through a lens of subjectivity.'

Leo commented: 'I think I know what you mean.'

The others at first thought he agreed with Lisa on the validity of different possible versions of the story, but then realised that he referred to something different altogether when he regarded Charles and carried on.

'Us being here together seems the most unlikely of events to occur. What is the likelihood of four complete strangers being stuck in an old barn in the middle of the English countryside on New Year's Eve?'

Charles nodded solemnly. Leo had grasped the meaning of his words. 'It's too strange. It's too unlikely to be real. And if it is real, does all this have a deeper meaning that currently eludes us?'

Leo replied, thoughtfully, 'It is real, which shows that highly improbable events can and do occur, I guess. It just feels a bit mind-boggling when that happens.'

Studying Charles, he resumed, 'I don't think that there is a deeper meaning to all this though. Not in the religious sense or in the sense of this being our pre-destined fate.'

Charles shrugged his shoulders. 'I don't necessarily attribute a religious meaning to it. I just wonder…'. He broke off at this point.

Karen now commented, 'Whether it has been our choices, or circumstances, or chance, or almost certainly a combination of these factors that has brought us together here now is futile to discuss. More importantly, we should focus on what to do next. I'm going to take a look at the weather.'

Karen said this less out of a desire to leave the barn – it struck her how little interest they had all shown in getting out of their current abode and back home – but more in order to lighten the mood of introspection by becoming practical and proactive. She got up and stretched her legs, which felt cramped and stiff after sitting on the stone floor for such a long time. Walking towards the window behind Charles, she immediately realised that she wouldn't be able to see anything much outside through the pane. Even though the snowy night sky still let its soft light into the barn, it was hard to see through the dense web of ice flowers and get a good idea of the weather conditions outside. She therefore turned towards the door and pulled it open with a couple of strong pulling movements. At once, a gust of icy wind hit her in the face and she was nearly pushed backwards.

She had been ready for this, though, and after a couple of seconds during which she stood firmly still against the raging storm, she braced herself and took a few steps outside whilst simultaneously pulling the door close behind her with all her strength.

Outside the barn, the storm literally took her breath away and she had trouble not to be blown back into the wall of the barn. The snowfall also didn't appear to have let up. It now formed a deep layer on the ground and the snowflakes whipped against her face and dampened her suede trousers almost straight away. She was grateful for her snow boots and the winter jacket, which kept at least her feet – despite them having completely sunk into the deep snow cover – and torso dry. The snowflakes that lashed with great force into her face however caused her a kind of pain best compared to the sensation of sharp needles piercing the surface of her skin. A few moments later, she pushed the door open and was almost hurled into the barn by the howling blizzard.

Leo took one look at her before he commented, 'I guess it's needless to ask whether anyone fancies a stroll outside.'

Karen didn't reply to that. She was busy trying to dry her damp trousers with her hands although these efforts turned out not to be very successful. She eventually gave up these attempts and directed her attention to the others in the room: They all looked tired, hungry and worn out. Karen herself felt the same way. Her brief burst of energy during which she had ventured outside had not lasted long and she was not surprised by this.

The day had ended and they had barely eaten or drunk anything since the morning. When she asked Leo whether he had any lemon sweets left, it turned out that he had one left for each of them, which he then distributed. He also passed the canister of ice-water around again.

Karen thought that the best course of action was probably to lie down and go to sleep for a while and she now suggested this to the others, pointing out that the weather would probably change for the better overnight. After all, when did they ever have a long-lasting snowstorm in this part of the country?

Leo was on the verge of retorting that normally they didn't have a snowstorm to start with but that they were nevertheless in the middle of one at the moment, which meant that her reasoning couldn't be convincingly applied, but he thought better of it and kept quiet instead.

Everyone was so tired now that they followed Karen's suggestion and curled up on the floor and got ready to get some sleep.

Karen hoped that the romantic mystery that they had listened to as the most recent story would at least give their dreams a happy note despite their present circumstances. At least her hand had almost stopped hurting. For a moment, she thought about Lara and Simon walking down one of the park's gravel paths before she drifted into sleep.

★

Her body oozed youth, vigour and sexuality as she emerged from the sea dripping wet with cold water and rapidly moving her head to shake some of it off her heavy, thick hair. She sent the water droplets flying in all directions whilst they shimmered in all colours of the rainbow in the bright sunlight. Her feet left wet indentations in the warm sand.

When she walked up the few metres of beach to where they had left their towels and bags, she saw that he was already standing there, waiting for her. He wore his dark blue swimming briefs and had only just got back from the water himself as evidenced by his well-built torso glistening and his usually honey-coloured hair appearing several shades darker.

Once she had reached him, he quickly picked up one of the large towels and wrapped it around her, using one end to dry her face. He then tried to wrap it around both of them, but didn't manage to fasten it well enough so that it slipped to the ground when he pulled her even closer to him and held her in a tight embrace.

Instantly, waves of excitement rolled through her body as her breasts pressed against his strong torso. His hands slid down her back until they came to rest on the small of her back and he pulled her pelvis against his until she clearly felt the bulge of his groin. She could sense the changes in it as he became aroused and she experienced a kind of arousal herself that she had never experienced before.

It then all happened extremely fast. He removed her arms around his neck and expertly and confidently slid the straps of her swimsuit off her shoulders. Pulling it further down, he exposed her young but full breasts with their pert nipples and large areolas. For a second, he created a gap between their lower bodies to bend down, cup both her breasts in his warm hands and kiss them passionately. He sucked her nipples and bit them and the surrounding skin. Then he took her right breast into his mouth and licked as much of it as he could when he slowly released it.

She groaned. She knew she was about to come, but did not want to do so before, this time, having gone all the way and experienced everything. He pulled her down to the towel on the sand and then knelt above her. She anticipated his next move and lifted her pelvis so that he could pull her swimsuit further down her legs. She had barely any time to remove her swimsuit completely from her lower legs before he had taken his briefs off and she saw his long, big and erect member hover a few inches above her. Both of them were now in a frenzy. Neither of them could bear any delay. She pulled his torso down to her and he lowered himself, aiming for the area that was covered by her red pubic hair. She had her feet on the ground, her knees up in the air and her legs apart to make it easy for him. When he did enter her, she felt the pain instantaneously. It was as if her insides were hurt in an attack and she gasped.

He pulled back at her reaction without having been able to get all the way in. He had felt the tightness and didn't think he would have been in a position to get any further in even if he hadn't pulled back.

Despite having a tear in her eye, she urged him on. 'No, please, don't stop! It's fine. Keep going!'

And he did. He pushed hard to get further inside her, finding it difficult to widen her vagina sufficiently to do so but simultaneously becoming more aroused by the intense squeezing sensation on his penis.

She was in even more pain now, but she didn't care because she wanted to embrace the experience, and if pain was a major part of it, so be it.

It took him quite a few more forceful pushes until he had totally penetrated her.

She thought that her insides were about to tear and completely break apart and emitted a small sound of pain and a gasp, but after a few seconds adjusted to the sensation of pain and started to go along with the rhythm that his pushes had taken on.

He had nearly had an orgasm straight after entering her due to the strong squeeze, but he just about managed to hold it off with a fierce determination to be inside her for as long as possible, not wanting this to end in spite of – on some level – longing for the relief of the climax.

Despite the pain, she could feel the increase in her arousal, which became so strong that she clutched his back and, inadvertently, dug her nails into it, using them like claws until she came with a massive shudder of her body, which at the end made her sink deeply into the towel she was lying on. She felt completely wet down below and knew that she had discharged her own body fluids.

After some further thrusts, he shrieked and climaxed inside her before he collapsed on the sand next to her.

They knew that the towel would show stains of blood, semen and vaginal discharge but they did not look at it. Instead, they just lay next to each other, spent, red-faced, with beads of sweat on their faces, but with smiles of fulfilment and exhilaration, holding each other's hot and sweaty bodies close.

It was hot in the pub and smelled of spilled alcohol and the sweat of too many bodies being confined to an enclosed space. He took off his heavy, black, leather jacket and exposed a sleeveless black top with a big skull on its front. He wore silver chains of varying sizes around his neck and his long hair was loosely tied back with a black band. Taking a swig from the pint of beer in front of him, he then picked up his electric guitar, put its attached belt around his neck, started to check its strings by playing some chords and then readjusting them accordingly. The others were tuning their instruments in a similar fashion. He could feel the eyes of many of the pub visitors on them but tried not to let himself become distracted. After a few more minutes of tuning their instruments, the keyboard player did the count to three to get them all started together and they began to play.

Soon, he felt his surroundings retreat and became one with the music. The steady beat of the drums always helped him from the start to play the chords in time, which in turn enabled their singer to join in at the right point during their piece. The keyboard player at first played slowly and dreamily. They played a rock ballad they had composed together and, like so many other rock ballads, it started off relatively quietly and slowly but then changed its tempo and mood quite drastically after less than two minutes. When they reached that moment of change, he grabbed the guitar and the strings harder and picked up the pace and volume. He could feel the vibrations of the music from his own as well as the others' instruments and the singer's voice ripple through his body. Beads of sweat stood on his forehead. When he looked up in front of him, he could see people move to the rhythm of their music whilst many of them attentively watched him and the other players. He didn't feel any pressure as a result of being watched however. In fact, everything around him appeared rather unreal. He felt enveloped by a dense cloud of sound, which now reached a crescendo that made him close his eyes and almost scream out. It was intense, it was overpowering and it was life fully lived.

She stretched her arms and legs languidly whilst simultaneously pushing away the warm, white duvet she had been submerged under. The autumnal morning light stroked her face even through the window pane and gave her hair a deep red shine rather than show her hair's usual mixture of gold and bronze shades. Its colour now resembled that of the leaves on the trees outside the bedroom window. She brought her right hand down to her expanding belly and let it rest there. A smile of utter bliss appeared on her face. She had felt movements inside her once before and now waited for the kicks inside her to start again. The baby didn't play along, but she kept waiting until she dozed off.

The sound of the bedroom door being opened woke her. She blinked and saw him stand in the door in his light grey track suit, his black hair damp where it framed his face, his breath still heavy and rapid from the physical exertion of the run from which he had just returned. He smiled when he saw her lie there with the glow of her pregnancy painted on her cheeks, awaking from her slumber and her rounded stomach clearly outlined under her simple, white nightgown. She returned his smile sleepily but happily and stretched her arms out to him.

He walked over to her bedside, bent down to her and said, 'Hey, sleepy-head. You have fallen asleep again. I've already been on a morning run.'

Then he kissed her flushed cheeks before giving her a long, lingering kiss on the mouth. He then lowered himself onto the bed right next to her and before she could protest about coming to bed in his sweaty, unshowered state, he had swiftly pushed up her nightgown until the alabaster skin of her taut, curved stomach and her swollen breasts was exposed. He showered it with passionate kisses until she groaned and slightly arched her back. As he worked himself further down her body, she pressed her head deeply back into the pillows, experiencing the budding life inside her.

The sun shone relentlessly and lent the citadel an aura of pure gold. The desert heat was hard to bear and the makeshift canopy offered little respite to the children who were gathered underneath it. However, despite the beads of sweat on their faces, the children seemed to be rather unfazed by it all. They stared at a huge screen in front of them on which they saw images emerge that they had never conceived: Dense forests alternated with emerald and turquoise lakes, and mountain ranges whose peaks were covered with snow appeared on the horizon. They wondered about this land that was so different from the unceasing desert they lived in.

One of the boys turned to the man who was positioned behind his projector, and asked him full of amazement, 'Is all this real? This place doesn't exist, does it?'

He smiled at the boy, nodding emphatically. 'Oh, yes! It does. There is so much more in this world than what you see around you. Just listen and watch and you'll find out where this is.'

And so the children were introduced to a very large country called Canada where they watched families who lived near a lake that was surrounded by woodland and whose huts were called log cabins. They went fishing, collected wood and hunted and the children splashed in the lake with delight.

When the moving images came to a finish with a happy ending for the families that had faced many dangers in the beautiful Canadian wilderness, the children were silent for a few moments before begging him to let the images continue. He explained to them that this was the end of the film, but invited them to let the families in the film have other adventures.

When one of the boys asked him how they should do that, he smiled again and replied, 'Use your mind! It's a treasure trove. All you have to do is learn how to uncover its treasure. Try it and soon you will discover magic.'

The children's deep, brown eyes were watching him captivatedly, hanging on his every word, and he was filled with joy and love for them.

Their laughter didn't cease. Whenever one of them seemed to run out of steam, another one of them broke into new outbursts of hilarity, which in turn made the others join in with renewed vigour. They were dancing and twirling around on the station platform, the young women dressed in dark green and beige dresses and the men in trousers and shirts. At first glance, the movements seemed to be wild and random, but looking at it more closely, it became apparent that they danced in formations even if each of them displayed their very own, individual style.

When it was her turn to dance through the lines, the other dancers formed, she felt carried on a wave of lightness born out of camaraderie between them. Her voice, which was naturally that of an alto, was as clear and high as the sound of a tiny bell when she sang along to the sound of the music. It was unclear where the music came from, as there was no orchestra in sight nor was there an electronic device visible that might have produced it.

Wherever it came from, it came to a sudden stop at the sound of a whistle being blown and so ended their dancing. It took her a moment to understand that the sound of the whistle signalled the imminent departure of the train from their platform, but when all the other dancers quickly moved to get on the train, she swiftly tried to join the others getting on the train. But somehow, she couldn't. She was trying to squeeze in behind a fellow dancer, when she was pushed aside and elbowed out of the way by the people attempting to board the train.

Looking to the side, she saw that there were more people descending the staircase to the platform where they must have been standing earlier and watching their dancing. At first, some of her fellow dancers tried to pull her on the train when they saw her struggle, and some of them gestured from behind the nearest window to her to get in immediately. She now tried with the greatest urgency to climb onto the train, but whenever she was only a step away from the open door and lifted a foot to step inside, one or more people pushed past her and forced her aside. They didn't seem to have any vicious intent; it seemed rather that, for one reason or another, they saw her as an inanimate object without a will of her own.

She looked through the window of the carriage that she had attempted, unsuccessfully, to get into, to make it clear to her fellow dancers that she needed their help to join them. As she used signs and gestures to express her predicament, she felt her heart sink when the dancers' facial expressions quickly changed to express boredom and disinterest when looking at her and then turning away.

When she ran to the adjacent window to attract the attention of some other dancers, it was the same. The dancers with whom she had laughed and danced only a little while earlier, turned away from her, their faces no longer showing any concern for her but being turned towards each other, chatting and laughing. She was frantic now, running back to the open carriage door as the last passengers poured into the train. Her heart made a leap of joy when she saw that in a second, she would be able to finally enter as the last passenger, when she heard the second blow of the whistle and the train doors started closing. There was still a person in the door opening who only narrowly escaped being squashed between the automatic doors. She was only centimetres away from the doors when they shut completely and she screamed for them to be opened again. But her voice wasn't heard. Nobody heard her inside the train and she couldn't make out any railway staff on the platform. Instead, the train slowly began to move. She saw the laughing faces of both her fellow dancers and the other travellers passing and overtaking her as the train gained speed rapidly now.

Again, she screamed out, her upper body turned in the direction the train was taking, her arm outstretched and her hand trying to grab it to stop its ineluctable journey away from where she was standing, alone and left behind.

The music of the drums and the deep chanting reverberated in his ears. More and more men had entered the chamber and were dancing around in circles, their white bodies forming a painful contrast to the semi-darkness of the chamber that was only faintly illuminated by some torches attached to the chamber's circular walls. Their strong, pale bodies were completely naked. The muscles in their arms and legs were well-defined, their penises, even in their limp state, big and fleshy, their stomachs protruding. Their faces seemed squashed and their ice-blue eyes were cold and ruthless.

They danced around an elevated stone slab on which a young woman lay stretched out with her wrists and ankles bound to the slab and ropes around her torso, fastening her firmly to the stone. Her naked body shone in the firelight, displaying black painting on her milky-white skin. Her breasts were circled in black and there was a thick black line at the centre of her body that went all the way down to her pubic bone. Zigzag lines branched off that prominent central line to the sides of her body, sprawling over her ribcage. Her eyes were open but glassy and devoid of any expression. One might have easily come to the conclusion that she was dead if one missed the subtle rise and fall of her chest.

He could barely watch what was unfolding around him, but unless he shut his eyes, he didn't have a choice, as he was bound and shackled to an iron ring that was attached to the wall of rock behind him. This crouching position caused him some pain in his legs and back but the pain was the least of his concerns. Closing his eyes to avoid witnessing the scene in front of him was not a real option, as when he had briefly tried to do that, he had found that it just made matters worse: The drums that the big, naked men played and their singing became just more frightening and sinister when he couldn't see what was unfolding in front of him and his imagination ran amok, conjuring up the most terrible endings to the scenario in front of him.

The men were now moving around the stone slab in ever smaller circles so that he could barely make out the young woman any longer. Occasionally, they bent over her whilst beating the drums faster and louder. There was a progression to this development, and he thought his ear drums would burst.

With shock, he noticed that the men's members were stiffening until they had a full erection of a size that he had never seen before.

Surely, any sexual intercourse between a woman and one of these men would either be impossible or extremely painful. He had barely finished this thought when one of the men cried out, which made everyone stop in their movement around the stone slab but continue their now increasingly frenzied drumming. The men's chanting had turned into a repetitive shouting rhythm. And then he saw how the man whose cry had put a hold on the men's movements around the table had heaved himself onto the stone slab and was now lying on the almost lifeless woman underneath him.

He tore and pulled on his shackles in despair, trying to free himself in a last-ditch attempt to rescue the woman. But he couldn't liberate himself and the iron shackles dug deep into his flesh. He barely perceived how the man pushed himself off the slab to adjust his position before descending on the young woman at a different angle to penetrate her, as he was frantically fighting with the shackles that kept him in his place. Hot tears were streaming down his cheeks and his mouth was open to let out an almighty scream, which would, however, undoubtedly be drowned out by the drums and the men's shouting.

The sky's greyness was matched by the large, grey tombstone in front of him. It was overgrown with moss in many places and the inscription could not be made out any longer; merely faint, single letters were visible. He didn't need the writing to be legible, however. He knew every word of it by heart: *In fondest memory and love for our devoted wife, sister, aunt and grandaunt, Annie Doyle (née McKenzie) 1942-2008.* The words were deeply engraved in his heart.

Standing there in the cemetery, on a murky November afternoon, wrapped up in his thick felt coat and being exposed to the sharp autumnal wind, which made the dead leaves rise from the ground and dance, his spirits dropped even more than usual. He contemplated the weather-beaten tombstone for a long time until the grey light of that day turned, almost imperceptibly, into a shadowy twilight. All Hallows had only just passed and he had noticed on his way to the grave that there were more visitors than usual at the cemetery, despite the dull and depressing weather. Or maybe it was exactly because of the season's sombre mood that called out for the quiet contemplation or remembrance of the dead that people flocked to the cemetery and adorned the graves with the first poinsettias of the year. He had put some twigs with bright red berries on Annie's grave to reverse the deserted and neglected look the grave had.

He had been standing, completely still in front of the grave for a long time when he suddenly noticed how the gravestone's surface changed. The moss vanished and the stone looked younger and was in a condition comparable to when it was set on the grave. The inscription became easily legible, as the silver letters stood out from the dark grey stone.

He first thought he had been standing there for too long and thus had involuntarily made his eyesight go funny or that he had taken his contemplation too far and he now seemed to see a memory from the past. However, what happened next could not easily be explained by any of these factors, he realised. The tombstone's surface became all blurry until it formed the outline of a human face against a milky-white backdrop. The features became increasingly distinct until the recognised, with an audible gasp, Annie's face illuminated in the golden light in front of him. And what he could read in her face were woe and deep sadness, which made his heart sink to the bottom of the pit that lay inside him. He had barely had any time to collect himself when Annie's features unravelled, and after a few seconds all that was left was a stark white skull that glared at him out of its big, empty eye sockets.

A shudder ran through his entire body, which was followed by a sensation of sheer horror when he realised that the tombstone all of a sudden started moving from side to side until it left its spot on the grave and was now gliding just above the ground and moving straight towards him. In his state of shock, his legs gave way underneath him and he fell to his knees just as the tombstone ascended above him where it hovered in a horizontal position with the side that showed Annie's skull turned towards the top of his head.

When he looked up and registered what was happening, he emitted a groan from deep within his soul and trembled so hard that he felt like an epileptic who could not control his seizures. The gravestone now quickly lowered itself down so that he – even had he been in control of his limbs again – did not have a chance to move away in time. He felt the impact the heavy stone made with his head and he was aware of how he sank down on his stomach and sprawled out, before the tombstone pressed down on his entire body to squash him until he was dead.

She was falling at an incredible speed. The pull of gravity was enormous in a way that she had never experienced before. Her limbs felt leaden as if attached to some heavy weights. She felt increasingly light-headed and knew that she was about to lose consciousness. At the same time, she sensed that staying conscious was her only chance to potentially resist the force of this vortex despite being uncertain of how to do so.

What felt like only a moment later, she slowed down in her descent of the deep, black hole. Maybe that was an illusion though, as whenever she tried to focus on a spot on the damp, rugged wall surrounding her, that spot was already gone. Still, her light-headedness receded, the gravitational pull on her body appeared to lessen and, strangely enough, she felt more as if she was floating in the humid, oxygen-impoverished air.

Suddenly, her view of the wall was partially obscured by a massive, black spider whose dimensions were about twice the size of her head. Its body was thick and in places covered by some brown fur, which made it look somehow bloated. Its amber eyes were completely focused on her and seemed to pierce her head with sharp darts. She flinched in pain and shrank away as far as this was possible in that narrow tunnel-like hole.

To her horror, she saw the spider slowly bend its long, thin legs further, then stretch them and, by doing so, crawl towards her with the same stare in its eyes.

She tried to move back to the wall a little bit more, which was not an easy thing to do whilst falling, until she touched it with her hands stretched out behind her. But how could this possibly help her? The spider was now very close and it was likely that it might be able to touch her if it stretched out one of her many, spindly legs again. But then the spider stalled in her approach towards her. Was it reconsidering and now reluctant to attack her? Hope and relief surged through her. Maybe she was safe from the spider. As long as she survived that seemingly never-ending fall she would actually be alright.

Just at that second when she had convinced herself to adopt that rather positive outlook, the spider jumped at her. Before she fully understood what was happening, the creature had its legs wrapped around her neck, its head just below her own. Was it a snarl or a smirk or both she could make out on the giant arachnid's face? Was that even possible or did her fear play tricks on her mind?

There was no time to ponder this, however, as the spider tightened its grip on her neck and squeezed her throat with a strength that she wouldn't have thought the creature capable of mustering. She tried to look down on her neck. Immediately, it became clear to her why she experienced such a powerful squeeze. The spider's legs had transformed themselves into the huge tentacles of an octopus that were now pressing down on her windpipe. Her impulse was to scream, but of course she couldn't make a sound. The squeeze on her throat tightened further. She could now not inhale any air whatsoever. Her fear and panic were indescribable, but the adrenalin accompanying these sensations could still not be employed to use her limbs to fight the monster off. Her body was almost paralysed by the gravity of the shock she was experiencing. Her head turned dizzy and she knew she would lose consciousness any moment now and die.

⋆ ★ ⋆

Her scream pierced the cold air of the barn and made the others start with alarm, shaken up from their own dreams. Sitting up and trying to get their bearings, they sensed rather than saw in the relative darkness of the barn how Lisa was trembling violently with beads of sweat on her ashen face. Maybe they were imagining these details after their nightmares had shown them other images of distress. However, what they were definitely not inventing was the now-seated figure of Lisa sobbing loudly and making small but abrupt upper body movements. It took them a few moments to put their own dreams to one side and gather themselves before they were able to respond to Lisa's terror. When they did, they all talked at the same time.

'Lisa, it's alright, we're all here,' Karen tried to reassure her.

'What the fuck!' Leo grumbled.

'Lisa, was it a bad dream you had?' Charles asked.

When Lisa didn't respond to the questions but continued sobbing, Karen got up, stretched her stiff limbs and walked to her. Kneeling down next to her, she hesitated a few seconds before she put her arm around Lisa's shoulders, which felt quite natural by now.

'Lisa, you're safe. You're not in danger.' She felt idiotic as soon as the words were out. Of course, Lisa was in danger and so were the rest of them in the barn: in danger of not leaving the barn alive or of dying in the heavy, deep snow outside if they tried. What she meant, of course, was that it was unlikely that Lisa was in danger of whatever her nightmare had shown her.

Lisa, who had believed that she couldn't breathe properly any longer when she woke up from her dream, slowly realised that she could in fact inhale air as she usually did even if her breathing was going a bit faster. She became a little calmer, but continued crying.

Normally, Karen would have found the situation quite challenging, as – due to her profession – she was more used to being firm with people when they needed to be put in their place than to giving comfort to a very upset person. However, she had started to rediscover her empathic side in some of her previous interactions with Lisa and Charles. Waiting in vain for the others to intervene or say something that was helpful, she tried again. 'Lisa, do you want to tell us what it is that is distressing you so much? Once we know, we can try to help.'

Charles, still weighed down by the horror of his own dream, nodded slowly.

Leo, who couldn't shake off the dream scenario he had been part of earlier, didn't react, but that at least might mean that he wasn't opposed to listening to Lisa if she felt she wanted, or needed, to get something off her chest.

Lisa spoke agitatedly through her tears. 'I don't know whether you want to hear what I could tell you. The dream I had was horrible, but I realise now that it was just a dream. However, it's my life I cannot cope with.'

Charles retorted in a very quiet even if slightly distracted voice, 'Tell us, Lisa. Talk to us.' Despite his immersion in his own woe, he was still able to react to someone else's sorrow and emotional pain.

Normally, Lisa would have found it extremely difficult to reveal any of the difficult parts of her life, but she was so distraught that she was now beyond being self-conscious or worried what the others might think. The words just began to pour out of her.

Imprisoned

'I just can't bear it any longer. My life is like a prison and I can't go back to it. The place I live should be home, but what happens if home becomes unbearable?

'I have a room in the house, but that is all. I'm thirty-seven years old and I live with my mother in the same house I grew up in. I've never lived anywhere else. My mother is almost always at home and I don't see anyone else except when I'm at work.

'It's always been like this, even before she retired from her senior admin position at the solicitors' office. When I grew up, I would go to school – often reluctantly – and then go straight home from there. Not long afterwards, my mother would come home and want to know everything about my day. What was I to tell her? That I arrived at school, sat down in the classroom, listened or sometimes pretended to listen to what the teacher was telling us and then stayed at my desk during the break whilst the other pupils were chatting with each other excitedly outside? That the next lessons and short breaks were a repeat of the first one and that I was usually sitting on my own during the lunch break away from my classmates?

'You might want to know why. Well, that was just what it was like. The others all seemed so confident, so self-assured and lively, and I didn't know how to interact with them. Sometimes when I happened to sit next to them at lunch because there were no other seats available or in the classroom one of them might briefly say something to me or ask me a question, and all I could come up with was a vague, short reply in a squeaky voice, which would make them turn away from me again.

'I can't really blame them though. If I had been in their position, I would have probably done the same. What a weird, awkward person to have as a classmate! Hardly a mate really and rather difficult to understand how she ticked. Of course, we were young and the others probably hadn't experienced many weirdoes like me so how could I expect them to understand me and maybe even make me their friend? That was never really on the cards. Whilst I admired the strength of their personalities, I was also afraid of them. I just felt like a nobody in their midst. It wasn't that they weren't decent to me for the most part.

'Yes, my first year at secondary school was pretty tough and involved some bullying by some of them, which frequently took the form of taking my hat, scarf or gloves away from me and making me run through the school corridors or the schoolyard in pursuit of the person who currently had the items in question.

'Or, a few years later, some of the boys would ridicule me and make sexual innuendos that made me feel uncomfortable or even sometimes touch my behind and laugh, showing off in front of each other about what they could get away with, as I wouldn't dare say anything or hold them accountable.

'On a school trip, I was asked – or maybe told – to join them in a game of truth and dare. We took an overnight train to Scotland. At the time, flights would have been too expensive and the bus too slow. Well, the trains were also pretty slow then and we were scheduled to depart in the late evening and to arrive at our destination in Scotland early the following morning. We had sleeper cubicles for six people respectively and I had one of the middle bunk beds. A couple of classmates from another cubicle also were in ours, sitting cross-legged on one of the other beds. And then the game started.

'I was the first one being asked the question, 'Truth or dare?' I most certainly didn't want to play this game, but I didn't have a choice in that. The choice that I did get was to decide on one of the two options. The answer wasn't hard, I thought. I most certainly did not want to be forced into any acts that I might find upsetting. "Truth", I therefore said, hoping that my turn would be over soon. Then the question I now had to answer came: "What's your bra size?" One of the boys asked the question with a smirk on his face. Of course, I felt myself redden instantly. I mumbled an answer and then quickly made my descent from the bunk bed and hurried out of the cubicle.

'A couple of seconds later, the door to my train cubicle was closed and locked from the inside. I felt violated. It was nobody's business what my bra size was. They probably now thought that I wasn't only generally shy but also a prude. But that was just how I felt and thought. Was it so very wrong? I was sure they were having a laugh in there. I had offered them cause for hilarity right at the beginning of the game. In the meantime, I was leaning against the large window pane along the train's aisle trying to fight down my oncoming tears in the glare of the fluorescent light.

'Then I heard my teacher's voice next to me. "Lisa. Is everything alright?" he said. "The others didn't lock you out, I hope?" I vigorously shook my head. "No, of course not," I said. I explained that I had just needed to step outside for a few minutes, as I didn't like to be cooped up in there together with the others for so many hours. My teacher's eyes rested on me, probably wondering whether he should challenge my explanation. Instead, he shrugged his shoulders and said to me, "Alright, if you're sure. Try to get some sleep before we are back home. I'm going to sleep myself now."

'With those words, he left me standing in the aisle where I remained for what felt like a very long time. When I became too tired to stand any longer, I turned back to the door of my cubicle and tried to push it open. But it was evidently still locked. I knocked at the door of the cubicle – without success. My classmates wouldn't let me in. It was clear to me that I was, at best, a laughing-stock in their games and, at worst, a waste of space that nobody needed to be with. What I also knew was that I needed to sit or lie down and sleep right then.

'I therefore walked further down the aisle until I located a toilet whose floor space was bigger than average. I went inside, locked the door, lowered myself to the floor and then tried to adopt a bearable position by leaning my back against the wall. Then I closed my eyes, which felt as heavy as lead by then. I must have fallen asleep, as when I woke up again more than two hours had passed. My back hurt and it took a little while until some feeling returned to my numb legs and I was able to get up. Even then, they weren't entirely normal and I temporarily had pins-and-needles. I went back along to the corridor to my cubicle, which was still firmly closed, but now I was ready to stand and wait, staring into the night.

'Shortly before we arrived at our destination, the door to my cubicle opened and when one of the girls came out, I scurried inside to get my things together. Some of the girls gave me some looks, but they didn't talk to me and neither was I inclined to talk to them. I prayed silently that they would leave me alone and let me leave the train quietly, and fortunately that's what they did.

'Otherwise, they were decent to me, as I said. You can't exactly blame them for not understanding who I was. After all, I didn't comprehend it myself. I often wished I could be different and act differently, but this didn't seem possible. My character just seemed to be what it was and it appeared impossible to change it. I therefore also understood why the girl in my final year at school said what she did when we attended an optional course in literature together.

'At one point during the course, we were asked to find or write a poem or a phrase or saying that we thought would be meaningful or fitting to one of our fellow classmates. The whole thing resembled a 'Secret Santa' a little, but focused on words. We put our names, which we had previously written down on pieces of paper, into a hat and took one piece of paper out of it in exchange. If it was our own name, we had to put it back in and repeat the process. Interestingly enough, I can't remember at all whose name I drew. What I do remember though is how I overheard one of my classmates telling one of the others whose name she had drawn.

'She said, "Oh, you know, I've drawn the short straw – I got Lisa. Why do I have to end up with this nobody? Fuck!"'

'I flinched when I walked past them. I knew I wasn't popular in the least but this still hurt. At least it meant I could emotionally prepare myself for the session in which we would read the poems or phrases out loud that we had chosen for the person we had been assigned to. I recall vividly how my classmate read out what she had written about me:

'Who are you?
Nobody seems to know.
You seem but a shadow
Without substance
Or definition.
I can't grasp you.
Are you there at all?
Do *you* know who you are?'

'That was all. When she stood up and walked over to where I was sitting and gave me what she had written, I stammered a 'thank you', blushing and hoping that the ground would swallow me. In hindsight,

I can see why she had written this. I had clearly not shown much of my personality to her or rather, my personality was probably barely defined. Of course, that had put her into a difficult situation: How could she find or write anything befitting my character if there was no real character she could draw from? I understood. I could see how I must have appeared to her.

'I kept most of these things to myself even at my mother's insistent questioning about my days. However, at times, I would unburden myself to her, as I had nobody else to talk to. There was too much pain and confusion inside me and I felt so incredibly lonely.

'My mother would listen to me empathetically at first, but then shrug her shoulders when I had come to the end of telling her my troubles on a given day and say in a tone replete with resignation on my behalf, "Oh, Lisa, what shall I do with you?", implying that I was just too weak to handle my life successfully. She didn't give me any help or advice for interacting with others. I guess she didn't know how to do that.

'That wasn't the worst, however. It's one thing not to have a role model and mentor, it's another one if you have to deal with your mother's rapidly changing moods, attitudes and behaviour towards you. As I said, my mother could be empathetic and caring. She also had a tendency to keep me close to her to the extent that it felt suffocating. I often knew her thoughts and reactions before they manifested themselves and frequently I felt that I wasn't really a separate person but in a symbiosis with her, unable to function on my own. She meant well though when she was overprotective. I believe that she had my best interests at heart.

'What was really hard to bear was when her emotions got the better of her. Especially when I was a teenager, I was often quite angry and aggressive at home. Outside the home environment, I showed no anger and, in fact, almost no emotion at all, but at home I started banging doors and shouting at her. I guess I just needed to feel something and I wanted to ward her off and get a sense that I could be my own person. When she felt wobbly and I was like that, she let me know what a terrible child I was. She would then compare me to her friends' or acquaintances' children and it would always be an unfavourable comparison. She would sob and express her regret at ever having wanted a child and now being stuck with one like me. And having had to bring me up on her own was another one of her regrets as if that was my fault, too. It was my father, whom I had never met, who made the decision to leave her when she was pregnant for another woman he had fallen in love with.

'She would withdraw to her bedroom, lock herself in and I heard that endless sobbing from behind her door; nothing would comfort her for hours on end. After a long time, she might unlock the door from the inside and let me come in, and it would take me a considerable time to make her feel better and have my apologies for my behaviour accepted.

'Sometimes her emotions escalated even further and she would threaten to kill herself by taking the car and driving into a tree. I'm trying not to go back there because I can distinctly feel the terror again that comes over me when she left with words to that effect and in a terrible state. The fear that she would actually carry out her threat, which would ultimately make me responsible for her death, was so immense and my inner pain so great that I thought my head would explode and that would be the end of it all. After a few minutes of extreme distress, I would just go numb though and was left empty and devoid of feeling. I guess human beings can only stand a certain amount and intensity of pain before a kind of protective mechanism sets in. In my case, it was not feeling, which is probably comparable to being anaesthetised.

'Moreover, my mother threatened to make phone calls to the authorities several times when she was in one of her bad states. When I was little, it was never entirely clear who she was actually referring to, but I guessed it could be the police or anyone else who had the power to remove me from my home and take me away. She would give me a look of both, deep hurt but also intense aversion, go to the phone, tell me what she intended to do and pick up the receiver to make the dreaded call. In the meantime, I trembled like a thin leaf on the branch of a tree that was exposed to a violent storm, being in imminent danger of being blown off and hurled to the ground. I then started pleading with her in a whiny voice, promising that I would be good from now on, that she wouldn't have any more trouble with me and that I would be whoever she wanted me to be.

'But it wasn't always obvious who that would be: Whilst I could see that she wanted me to be less combative and aggressive with her, I couldn't get my head around the fact that I could be fairly even-tempered on one day and my mother was fine with that, and I was similarly calm and level-headed on another day and my mother couldn't cope with me. When the latter happened, it was always my fault according to her even though I had done nothing different from the day before when she had been perfectly happy with me and my behaviour. It was a conundrum and not one that I have been successful at resolving. I couldn't be who she wanted me to be because it was impossible to define that imaginary person and I started to suspect in the last few years that such a person could simply not exist.

'Home life has been an emotional rollercoaster that never stops moving up and down the tracks and goes around the loops at dizzyingly high speeds.

'Up to the age of fourteen, I had at least my grandparents to go to or see on an almost regular basis and that contact offered a welcome relief from the isolation at school and the emotional turmoil at home. It was a breathing space and refuge that I welcomed and embraced. My grandparents lived in the next town and came over quite a bit when I was a baby and a toddler to see me and to help out.

'When I became older, my mother would sometimes take me to them and pick me up after she had browsed some stores or met up with a friend for coffee. She would never stay. I wondered about the reasons for this at the time but when I asked her about it, she never gave a straightforward explanation. It was apparent, though, that she was not keen on being in her parents' company if she could help it. As I was quite happy to spend time with my grandparents away from my mother's stifling presence, I was not inclined to probe further into the matter.

'Only much later did I learn more about my mother's antagonistic stance towards them. Having grown up as the middle child of five children, my mother revealed to me in recent years when she was in a downcast or bitter mood that she more often than not felt that she had no place in the family. Her two older brothers were close in age and stuck together and so did her younger sisters. She felt as if she was in no-man's land. Her brothers soon started their studies to become a teacher and an accountant respectively and also brought home their girlfriends who were very much loved by her parents and seemed to be almost regarded as their own children. When she brought home a boyfriend, she did not think that he received the same warm welcome that her brothers' girlfriends had received, and she resented this.

'Even when they married and she told her parents that they were expecting a child together, her parents didn't seem enthused. As a result, she distanced herself more and more from both her parents and her siblings. She would have cut all ties with them had it not been for the financial predicament she found herself in after her husband had left her. Being reluctant to rely solely on state benefits, she accepted not only some financial support her parents offered her, but let them – albeit reluctantly – help out with me.

'My grandparents always denied the notion that they had not been welcoming to my mother's former husband. I don't use the word father here because I've never met him, he's never been in contact with me and could – for all intents and purposes – have been dead. My mother never heard anything from him again either after he had left and for a long time refused to speak about him. It appeared that he had just disappeared, as when she initially tried to contact him, she could not reach him or find him anywhere. However, she soon stopped searching for him and accepted her fate if that was what she considered it.

'On the occasions on which I spoke to my grandparents about him, they usually mentioned how they delighted in his humorous, fun-loving and cheerful personality. In fact, they told me how glad they were for my mother to be with someone of such a sunny disposition and how they hoped it would brighten her life and lighten her dark moods and her brooding and provide an antidote to her angry outbursts. When I mentioned this to my mother at one point to clear up what seemed to be a colossal misunderstanding between them, she shrieked violently and pointed out that I could now see how her parents thought of her and how she was quite obviously treated as the black sheep of the family – as someone who was expected to change and to be different from who she was in order to be fully accepted. After having elicited this reaction from her, I usually kept quiet about the conversations I had with my grandparents if they involved her.

'When I visited my grandparents, there was always some fun and laughter, which I so sorely missed anywhere else. There was always some music on and some of my best memories were when we all danced along to the 'Rivers of Babylon' in my grandparents' living-room. Sometimes, they would dress up in the style of the 1920s and 1930s and put their most cherished jazz records on and we all moved and tapped along to the beats of the music whilst smiling and laughing.

Grandma would try to ignore her arthritis as much as she could then even if she had to pay for it later with more pain and swelling. Her motto was though to seize the moment rather than wait for a tomorrow that might never come.

'We also played board games together, which was great fun. My grandparents had a great range of them and many of them used to be played by their children decades ago but had lost none of their appeal over time, at least not on me. My grandparents were the most fiercely competitive players you could think of. The games were thus always accompanied by a sense of dynamic energy and excitement.

'When the weather was good we would often go outside to one of the local parks to feed the ducks. We usually had a bit of a contest going who could throw the breadcrumbs the farthest and also made a point of aiming the crumbs at individual ducks, partly in order to let each of them have their fair share of crumbs and partly because we were working on our aiming skills.

'Mostly, I was the only one at my grandparents' when I visited, but occasionally some of my cousins were around as well. My mother's older brothers each had two boys who were a little older than me. They all had very busy schedules though, usually being engaged in one of their many sports activities. When one or the other of my cousins was around, we tended to go outside more and play more active games in the park or the playground. I usually felt too intimidated by their boisterous personalities to join them in any of their games on my own accord, but when my grandparents both took an active part in the games, they would always include me and make sure that my cousins played with me nicely. Sometimes, my grandfather would play with the boys for a while during which I enjoyed having my grandma to myself: She would tell me stories about what it was like for her to grow up in a household that was completely anti-establishment. Her mother incorporated the light and carefree nature of the jazz era as it had taken hold in 1920s and 1930s America. Although she loved much of it and developed a similar taste in music and joie de vivre as her mother, there were differences: Her parents were frequently absent due to their extremely busy social calendars that were filled with lunches, soirees and dinner invitations as well as parties that went on until deep into the night. She missed company, especially because she was a vivacious and outgoing person who felt only truly alive in the company of others. She would have loved to have siblings, but her parents clearly prioritised the liberties they had or took, which would have been nearly impossible to enjoy with a bigger family. It was then that she decided that she wanted to have a big family of her own when she was an adult.

'And she did. She and my grandfather had been school-friends for a very long time before their friendship blossomed into love during their adolescence. They were both free spirits and – according to their teachers – hard to tame and very individualistic. They married young and had the family they – especially my grandma – had so much wished for.

'I could listen to these stories forever and my impression was that my mother and her siblings grew up in a house full of laughter, liberalism and joy. I wish my mother were able to appreciate that rather than finding and possibly magnifying negatives. But I never managed to bring her closer to her parents. Instead, it came to an ultimate breach between her and my grandparents when I was fourteen years old, which also stopped almost all contact between my grandparents and myself.

'I only think back of it with deep sadness and – to this day – a certain amount of disbelief. It should never have come to this. I remember the day clearly when things came to a head. I had spent the afternoon with my grandparents after my mum had dropped me off there, which gave her the chance to spend some time by herself in town. Over the previous couple of years, I had taken to visiting my grandparents regularly on a Saturday by taking the bus. My mother had taken on some part-time work on Saturdays and wanted to be sure that I wouldn't be on my own all day so my enthusiastic suggestion of me spending the day at her parents' was – if not exactly welcomed – reluctantly approved. After all, her job was in the same town where her parents lived. That day, however, she had not gone to her Saturday job at the stationery shop but had taken the day off. I think she must have got tired with her busy PA job during the week and having worked on Saturdays for many months without a break. It was probably tiredness that contributed to the explosive way she reacted to her mother's words. That and her volatile nature.

'I had been quite down that day, as my mother had been angry and frustrated with me the evening before and, in the morning, she still kept reproaching me for the way I was and behaved. I was too dejected to hide my feelings during the visit until my grandma finally took me aside and said, "Lisa, what's going on? I can clearly see that you are very downcast. Why don't you tell me?"

'I shook my head at first, knowing that it was best not to talk about my mother in front of grandma in case the former learned about it and would then unleash her anger on me. However, I was so low that my need to talk about the situation won over the warning voice inside me to exercise caution. I told her not just about the previous night's scenario but also about many of the other occasions during which my mother had completely lost her composure and I had been at the mercy of her unchecked emotions. Whilst I had sometimes mentioned to her some of my mother's behaviour that disturbed me most, I had never gone into the full fallout of my mother's temper. During my narrative, my grandpa, who had been out in the garden for a little while, joined us and his facial expression became increasingly sombre. My nan's face, similarly, looked concerned and grim at the same time. When I finished talking, she said resolutely, "I will talk to her. This is no good."

'Fearing that this would be counter-productive, I begged them both not to mention what I had said, but I could see that my plea didn't sway them.

'When my mother came to pick me up, my nan asked her in, which she refused. Asking me to wait inside, both my grandparents then joined her outside and had – what I assume was – a serious conversation with her there. Although I was inside, I soon heard my mother's shouting and screaming in the neighbourhood through the open living-room window. After what seemed to take ages, my nan and grandpa came back inside and told me that I could go with my mum now if I was ready to. I wasn't ready, but I knew my mother would storm in any moment and make me come out if I didn't go to her straight away.

'She didn't say a word to me during the entire car journey but I could detect the deep hurt showing on her features and I just knew that this would have far-reaching repercussions.

'And it did indeed. The accusatory manner she showed towards me didn't last forever but from then on, I was not allowed to see my grandparents any longer. In fact, I only saw them on a few occasions until they died a few years later: my granddad of a sudden and fatal heart attack and my nan less than two years later of incurable lung cancer. Sometimes, I wondered afterwards whether I could have made more of an effort to see them, but it was extremely difficult, as I felt tightly controlled in my movements. Before school started in the morning, I didn't have enough time for a quick visit, as my mother would leave the house less than an hour before I had to, and when school finished it was a similar scenario. You might want to know why I didn't just make up an excuse for returning home later than usual, for example that I spent some time in town. To be honest, I was too scared my mother would find out that I lied and then home life would become even harder to bear. I couldn't put aside my emotional need to be accepted as I was and in what I did, and every time that need was unfulfilled, I crumbled and was devastated. Sometimes, a look from her would be enough to send me into a downward spiral. Maybe that explains to you why I didn't even try to visit my grandparents on Saturdays when I wasn't at school and my mother was at the stationery shop and therefore couldn't easily know what I did during that time unless I told her. Even though it wasn't very likely that my mother would find out my true whereabouts, I was terrified of the potential consequences if she did as long as that possibility existed. I could not risk seeing my grandparents.

'Of course, this loss – which is what the ending of those visits was – was extremely difficult to cope with. It felt as if the last haven of sanity and even joy and happiness had disappeared behind the horizon. Shortly after my mother had made it clear that I was not to have any more contact with my grandparents, I suffered a terrible migraine, which turned out to be only the first of many more to come. The migraines manifested themselves not only by a sharp, pulsating pain sensation in a certain location of my head that quickly spread across the surrounding areas of the brain, but also by visual disturbances and sickness: Sometimes the world around me just appeared blurred, people and objects becoming elongated or squashed in turn; colours I had identified with a certain environment were replaced by bolder, brighter and more striking colours; geometrical shapes overlaid everything, many of them resembling flashes of lightning. And then there was nausea rising up inside me, which could not be ignored for a long time and I was violently sick.

'At the end of such acute migraine episodes, I lay in total silence in my darkened bedroom with my eyes closed and not moving for a very long time, waiting for the terrible sensations to pass. Once I was better and up on my feet, I more often than not could see my mother's look of concern rest on me. Despite her emotional instability and her frequent outbursts of anger and her bouts of depression, she had always been capable of showing and expressing empathy. It was just usually unpredictable when it would happen although a pattern soon emerged in that it began to occur most frequently after my migraine episodes or when I looked particularly miserable on my return from school. When my mother felt solicitous, she would suggest we do a jigsaw together on an old folding table. We both loved jigsaws. My mother got them from the charity shops and bazaars. Initially, she suggested we put our finished jigsaws up as pictures on the wall after having glued them on cardboard, but she only ever followed through with this suggestion once, when she displayed a finished meadow with some hedgehogs in the kitchen. After that, it never happened again because we did not achieve to assemble another jigsaw without finding one or more pieces missing. Every time it happened, my mother would become incensed and when I suggested we buy a new jigsaw from a store she would have none of it and tell me that she would not pay such high, hugely inflated prices for a jigsaw. As a result, we continued assembling incomplete jigsaws and it seemed as if the number of missing pieces was continually going up.

'Much of the time though, I found my own ways of distracting myself from the difficulties and sorrows of everyday life and built my own world that I felt belonged to me alone and that could shut everyone else out. One way of achieving this was by keeping a notebook. I know that this is a rather unusual expression; people tend to keep diaries rather than notebooks. But writing regularly in a notebook and using it for more than merely to record events of or thoughts about one's daily life is the process I allude to when I use that phrase. Yes, sometimes I would write down things that happened at school or at home and feel somehow better for having given expression on paper to what had previously just been trapped in my head. Often, though, I would deal with my feelings by adopting the voice of poetry and transform real events into something new. Short prose also proved conducive to put into words what was on my mind. When I opened my notebook and started writing I felt I was in charge, a conviction that I sorely lacked in all other aspects of my life. It was I who determined what would go on the page and it was I who created the words. The act of doing so was wonderful. Although I only wrote down words in brief spells of creative flurry, these moments were special. Everything else receded from my mind and I became wholly absorbed in the moment of writing. I later learned that these moments are called flow and are often used in mindfulness to denote the full presence of mind one gives to something at that time. It was also a feeling of being truly alive, which might seem ironic as writing also offered me an escape from much of my life. However, I don't really consider this an irreconcilable contradiction. I was content to become absorbed by the process and by its restorative properties. Had it not been for this and also for my voracious reading, I would probably have gone insane or not survived.

'Reading worked in similar even if not identical ways on me: Books opened up new worlds to me, worlds that enriched me manifold and allowed me to visit times and places that I would otherwise never have been able to go to, feel pleasures and pains my protagonists went through and just simply take me beyond the confines of my unstable home. My mother and grandparents introduced me to books early in life and, without having enough money to buy all the books I wanted to read, I soon started to use the local library on a regular basis and took piles of library books home with me. At first, I just browsed the shelves of teen fiction and borrowed whatever took my fancy. Soon, I would go to the library with a specific author in mind, to whom I had been introduced at school or had heard mentioned somewhere, and would borrow their books. There were phases during which I would read nothing but works from that one author and during which I would try my hardest to get hold of all their available books. Then there were other times when I had a book of poetry that I might take to school with me and read during my breaks, a modern detective story I could immerse myself in after school and a Victorian classic I read in bed until I fell asleep. There was so much choice and variety; it was like a bottomless treasure trove. I borrowed the literature anthologies to give me an idea of what else there was to read and soon I started to widen my literary repertoire further, by focusing on more than just English works. I delved into post-colonial literatures, reading texts as different as Narayan's and Achebe's before moving to European literature, voraciously lapping up Hesse and Thomas Mann to be then taken on even more unfamiliar journeys by Pamuk and Shafak. These travels in the mind were always wondrous and intriguing. The hardest thing was to put the books down and be in this world again.

'Reading and writing sustained me and carried me through the emotional upheavals at home and the isolation I felt. Soon I didn't experience the same intensity of pain any longer when my mother had one of her outbursts and meltdowns. Instead, I became increasingly numb and the notion of unreality visited me then as if all this was nothing but a bad dream from which I would wake up any minute. However, I had to contend with the physical pain of the migraines, which raged inside me far too frequently and threatened to burn me up. My mother took me to various doctors but none of the specialists could find an organic cause for them even after innumerable tests. They gave me some liquid drops for them, which were meant to alleviate the pain but didn't really do very much at all, and they saw me on a regular basis to check on any progress.

'Finishing school after completing my A-levels should have been a milestone. In some ways it was, as I now left an environment in which I had felt first and foremost like an outsider and was free to have a new start elsewhere. In other ways, it wasn't, as I didn't leave home to have a similarly radical new start as many of my class-mates did. Many of them went to university and moved away from home for their course. Whilst I was an average student in most subjects and struggled quite a bit in maths, I was good at English. Moreover, I had a keen interest in pursuing literary studies, having loved the literature lessons at school and enjoyed writing exams about certain works. I loved exploring authors, texts and genres and had done much of this on my own initiative, but I knew that there was so much more out there that I wanted to be introduced to by people who had studied the works in order to get the most out of my reading experience and understand the historical and cultural background better.

However, this keen desire of mine could not be satisfied because we simply didn't have the money for me to attend university, especially if it involved moving away and renting a room elsewhere. There might have been enough government help available to do it, but my mother was reluctant to ask for it. The reasons she gave for not looking further into the financial options for paying for a university place were that she had already received enough support from the state and also that she didn't want me to start my working life after university with a debt. I always suspected though that the real reason for her dismissal to explore avenues I could potentially take to attend university was that she didn't want me to go and leave her behind. She needed me to be close to her.

'It's hard to understand how my mother functioned but from what I had heard from herself and my grandparents, her perception of being in some way redundant in the family set-up led her to a search for something she could call her own and that she could hold close to herself and that she didn't have to share with anyone else. And that something turned out to be me. Soon after my birth I had become her project into which she could pour her affections, her hopes and much of her identity. I was a vessel to be both shaped and filled by her.

'When I said earlier that my mother possessed empathy, this was true. There was love for me on her part and often she felt sad when I felt downhearted about something that had happened at school. Generally, she wanted me to be happy so that – I guess – rejecting my wish to go to university could not have been as easy for her as I have made it sound. The problem was that there was a conflict between her wish to see me happy and her need to keep me close in this instance and her own need gained the upper hand. Her love of me was a complicated love.

'On the few occasions I had talked to my grandparents at greater length about my mother's behaviour without revealing everything she did or said, my nan had become pensive and finally commented that she wasn't actually surprised about my mother's helplessness, vulnerability and depression, which was what her crying spells and her episodic hostility towards me amounted to, in her opinion. She recognised in retrospect that her wilfulness as a child and teenager, her dark moods and her anger had all been precursors of a path of emotional instability and ill health. She then pondered that anger and aggression towards others was sometimes too exhausting to maintain and that, as a result, this anger was then at least partly turned inwards. That was quite a realisation by a person to whom these emotions seemed quite alien for the most part and whose light-hearted, sunny and fun-loving disposition appeared diametrically opposed to my mum's. It was hard to believe that they were mother and daughter.

'The question for me now was what I would and could do instead. My mother asked me what I was most interested in and, probably unsurprisingly, I came up with the idea of applying for a job in a bookshop. There wasn't an immediate vacancy in our local, fairly small bookshop after I finished my A-levels, but they took me on as a volunteer for a few hours once a week in order for me to gain experience and to see whether I wanted to pursue this path. During the remainder of the week, I had a part-time job in the laundry section of one of our local nursing homes where I spent most of the time ironing and taking the ironed clothes up to the residents' rooms. After about eight months of doing that, a full-time vacancy at the bookshop where I volunteered became available and I was delighted when my application for it was successful. I had enjoyed the volunteering experience and was proud of now being a full member of staff, helping customers who came in to find what they wanted, placing orders on our system and creating displays. Every now and then, we had an author's evening there, which involved the author reading from their book and signing copies of it for whoever wanted to buy one. I loved these events. Whilst I was too shy to ask any questions in front of the rest of the audience, I listened carefully and sometimes would ask some questions when I had a copy of their book signed and it was just the author and myself. I was fascinated by the process of creation and what emerged by the use and arrangement of words.

'I was lucky that I had friendly and supportive colleagues who tried to boost my self-esteem by encouraging me and offering praise where it was appropriate. Most of them were laid-back and I didn't usually feel quite so much that I was the odd one out, the way I had always done at school. This was a welcome change and probably another factor why I was able to live in the claustrophobic setting with my mother until now. My colleagues included me in most of their work-related chats and I actually started making friends during that time. When I say friends, I don't mean that I was suddenly part of a big social group but I made single friends here and there. One of them worked with me in the bookshop for a few years and we would sometimes, after work, go for a walk and talk or go to a coffee-shop and spend time together. Having a friend was a new experience for me and I initially didn't know how to behave, but soon I would forget my awkwardness and just enjoy the company. This friend, Sina, was very artistic and literary and I learned a lot from her about different artists and styles of painting and got recommendations of authors and works she thought highly of. We went to art exhibitions in Exeter together, attended concerts and author events and would always have stimulating conversations. It was very sad to see her move to London a few years later to study art history and literature, but it didn't come as a surprise because it had always been clear that our small town had been too parochial for her and didn't give her the opportunities she needed to thrive.

'I made another friend, Kaitlyn, in a yoga class I attended once a week. She was a gregarious person who laughed a lot and was curious about anything one could think of in life. As a result, we shared many laughs but also explored different topics from the media to the environment, religion and relationships. In some ways, it was quite astounding to have Kaitlyn as a close friend because we were so different in temperament and self-confidence. She could be quite voluble whereas I was quiet; she was not afraid to voice her opinions even if they might be regarded as controversial by others whereas I would hold back; she had a boyfriend whereas I, of course, didn't. I think Kaitlyn appreciated my quietness, as it provided a counterbalance to her exuberance, which sometimes developed into overexcitement and agitation. I, on my part, was fascinated by her liveliness and her hunger for life and experiences. When she moved away with her boyfriend after getting married and becoming pregnant with her first child, I was devastated. After almost thirteen years of sharing a close friendship, it was heart-breaking when she told me that she would be moving to Leeds where her husband had just been offered a fantastic job in a well-known company that he couldn't turn down.

'My mother's view of and relationship with my friends was an interesting one and was shaped by her insight that it was important for me to have friends to function as a healthy and normal human being, but that the time spent with my friends would leave less time together for the two of us. She usually accepted when I spent time with them and was welcoming to them when I brought them home. At the same time, I wished she would stand back a bit more: When my friends were around, she would involve them in lengthy conversations and spend a considerable amount of time with us rather than leave us to it. After all, they were my friends and I needed spaces in my life that were unoccupied by her. In addition, whenever I had met one of my friends she would usually quiz me about them and when I was reluctant to share much information, she would say that I was such a strange person and ask me not to act so weirdly or secretively. Feeling emotionally dependent on her and fearing further strong disapproval on her part, I would tell her more about my friends than I had initially intended to tell her. Over time, a subliminal jealousy emerged: My mother didn't want me to spend too much time with my friends and, when I did, she wanted to share in these friendships. I, in turn, was jealous of the easy rapport she established with my friends. The situation was not helped by the fact that my mother had lost all of her own friends over the years. I'm sure that she alienated them when she was unable to contain her dark moods in front of them and turned whiny and reproachful towards them numerous times. My mother had involuntarily isolated herself, which made her cling on to me all the more firmly.

'And so the years passed and I endured the volatile home life as well as I could. After the few friends I had were gone, my life was once again – like during my adolescence – almost impossible to cope with, not least because my migraines increased in frequency and intensity. I was extremely sick a lot of the time and was now under very close medical supervision. Regular visits to the specialists were insufficient and were replaced by an in-patient stay at the hospital followed by scores of out-patient appointments during which they monitored me closely and tried new treatment regimes on me with varying levels of success. It was then that I met the consultant neurologist who turned my life upside down.

'When I first met him at his clinic, I was immediately impressed by his broad smile and his sparkling, blue eyes. He was tall and slender but simultaneously of muscular build. He looked young despite his silver hair, which lent elegance and distinction to his appearance. His features were well-defined and his teeth were the whitest I had ever seen. I don't think I had ever met anyone so warm and caring before and whenever I saw him I always felt his genuine concern for me. I guess I must have subconsciously yearned for such unconditional regard for a long time, as I had never had it when I was growing up. I believed that at last something wonderful was happening in my life: I had finally met someone with whom I shared moments of magic, a deep bond and an affection that was tender and playful. Although nothing happened outwardly between us, everything was expressed in a look, a smile, a handshake, a light touch of the arm and in our voices and in how we modulated our speech. I knew it was hard if not impossible for him to be more explicit than that and make a direct move, as he was my doctor and, ethically, he did not have the option of turning our professional relationship into a personal one. Not as long as I was under his care at least. That wouldn't be forever though so I believed that the best strategy now was to demonstrate my love of him. And love it was: I impatiently counted the days between our meetings, yearning for him and hurting from not seeing him during these intervals. When I did see him, I felt heat suffuse my body, my hands started to shake and my heart beat faster.

'All those years during which I had never been with anyone suddenly didn't matter any longer. Seeing so many people getting coupled up and starting their families, I had for a long time accepted this as the status quo – albeit in the last couple of years with a rising resentment – and not questioned my own situation too much. However, now all my longing for a romantic relationship and children of my own came to the fore with a force that surprised me. Being in my mid-thirties, it was certainly time for all this but fortunately not too late. I convinced myself that the long wait had been worthwhile, as I had now met the man I wanted to spend the rest of my life with. I therefore took action. I wanted to give and share with him something deeply personal and what else could that be but my writing. I remember the moment clearly when I first gave him a poem of mine at the end of a consultation session. It was handwritten and I had folded it twice so that the writing was hidden from view. After shaking hands with him, I held the paper out to him and when he gave me a questioning look I mumbled, "For you to read" and quickly disappeared after he had taken the folded paper. I couldn't watch him read the poem. It was a love poem and a declaration of my love to him.

'The next time I came for an appointment, he looked at me for what seemed like an eternity. It was a searching, puzzled and confused look and I can best describe it as a filmic moment during which everything was revealed and there was no place to hide. It was the moment when our souls were exposed. I was a little baffled by his confusion, as I thought my admission could not have come as a surprise, but I suppose he might not have expected me to put my feelings into poetic words in that way. After some time had elapsed, he started the consultation as matter-of-factly as he was able to do and referred in no way to my poem for the rest of it. To me, that was all the more reason to provide him with more encouragement to open up to me, hoping that he would ask me out when appointments came to an end. I therefore gave him a poem every time I saw him, writing each one of them out in my best handwriting. Sometimes they were my own poems, but at other times I wrote out other people's poems that I considered meaningful and deeply moving.

'There came a day when he did refer to my poems. It was when we said good-bye to each other again that he kept my hand longer than usual in his own and came out with, "You know, I like your poems, Lisa. A good effort."

'I recognised that this was also his way of thanking me for them. I could feel myself blush, stammered a "You're very welcome," and walked out of the door, elated by him having finally reacted to my efforts. I was a step closer to a wonderful relationship that I imagined in all its wonder and glory.

'I didn't tell my mother about anything related to my consultant. She must have wondered though about my dreamy facial expressions, my silly smiles and my absent-mindedness and asked me a couple of times what was the matter with me. When I shrugged my shoulders, she didn't enquire further however. After all, she knew that I was absent-minded at the best of times so why should she continue questioning my probably only marginally weirder behaviour now?

'The hospital appointments with my consultant and the special status I attributed to our relationship went back over the last two years. And then the fateful day came two weeks ago when everything changed.

'I was sitting in the chair opposite my consultant's desk, nervously waiting for him to enter the consultation room. The receptionist had already called me in and normally he would greet me there if he hadn't already asked me in himself. That day, he was obviously still held up elsewhere although expected to start his consultation with me imminently as the receptionist assured me. Sitting still in my chair proved to be tricky for me, as I felt quite fidgety. I therefore got up after a couple of minutes and walked around the desk to the large window behind it to look at the frost-covered trees outside. It was a cold day in mid-December, cold enough for the frost to remain on the trees and the rooftops of the surrounding buildings. I loved that wintery image and was ready to immerse myself in it thus alleviating my restlessness when I heard my consultant's voice next door. Realising that it might look slightly strange if he came across me standing behind his desk, I turned and was ready to walk back to my chair when my gaze fell on a framed picture on his desk. It showed him smiling happily with his arm around a tall, slender and well-proportioned, blonde woman about his age whose symmetrical features radiated sheer joy. Her make-up was expertly applied and further enhanced her beauty. While her radiant, blue eyes, which were tastefully framed by the strokes of a black eyeliner, and her deep red lips were facing the camera, her hand rested on the shoulder of a girl of about eight or nine who was standing in front of her. It was immediately clear that the girl was her daughter: She had the same blue eyes as her mother and her features were almost a miniature replica of her mother's. Like her mother, she wore a dress, but while her mother's was a soft white and black one with undulating, large shapes, her dress was made of dark-red, corduroy material and matched by a long-sleeved, striped top in different colours. A younger boy was standing next to her with a sombre expression on his face, which contrasted the girl's easy smile. He wore matching, dark-blue trousers and a jumper and his dark blond hair was combed into a neat side-parting. His father exuded elegance in his smart, black trousers and his pale pink shirt.

I had an almost instantaneous physical reaction on taking in the image in front of me. Blood shot through my body and into my head, I started trembling and then shaking violently, my breathing became more rapid and more abrupt and a few moments later tears were streaming down my face. I didn't have time to collect myself before my consultant entered and found me in a crumpled heap on the floor next to his desk. He helped me up and walked me to my chair, settled me in there with a glass of water and tissues and after trying unsuccessfully to calm me down, made the consultation as brief as he could to let me go and be alone with my shock and grief. His concern and solicitude and the touch of his arm around my shoulders made matters even worse and more difficult for me to cope with. At least he didn't insist on an explanation for my alarming behaviour, as he soon noticed that I was too choked up to give him one. I don't know whether he figured out the reason for my breakdown later after I had left or not and I will probably never know.

'I walked back to the bus station in something resembling a trance. He had a family! Of course he did. How could I ever believe a man like him would be free and available?

'But it had been believable: His smile, his touch, his manner and demeanour had all indicated it. The connection and special rapport between us! What about all that? Maybe he used to have a happy family scenario at home previously, but all that must surely be in the past now.

Yes, that was it. That was the explanation. But why would he still have the photograph on his desk facing him whenever he was sitting behind it and looked in front of him? Oh, that was simple. People find it hard to dispose of objects that remind them of happy moments and times. And he probably mainly kept it displayed on his desk because of his children. A separation from a partner didn't mean that one stopped being a parent.

'My thoughts were interrupted when my bus was pulling into Exeter bus station just when I got there. I picked up my pace a little out of habit rather than because I genuinely cared whether I got on the bus or not. Right then I cared for nothing but the discovery about my consultant. Everything else had become irrelevant and insignificant in equal measure. The world was changed and more disconcerting than ever.

'On the bus, I stared out of the window without seeing anything. My tears were still running down my cheeks and my body was still making small, involuntary movements. My head was spinning and new thoughts emerged that challenged the earlier ones on the walk to the station, the latter having attempted to provide me with some comfort and reassurance. The new thoughts dismissed the comforting ones mercilessly and spoke to me with insistence. "You have made yourself believe in whatever you wanted or needed to believe, Lisa. You had fallen in love and from that point everything resembled a plot in a novel that you wrote in your mind and added to on a daily basis. You saw signs of special affection where your doctor had merely been his friendly, smiling and personable self. You were convinced of a special bond between you when there was none in reality. What a fool you've been, Lisa, what a fool!"

'The words in my head sounded metallic and reverberated in my head until I became aware of the familiar, early signs of an oncoming migraine. By the time I had got off the bus and reached home after a twenty-minute walk, the throbbing pain in my head could not be ignored any longer. My gait had become unsteady and nausea spread through me. I was praying that I could just go up to my room quietly and unseen, but of course I had no such luck: As soon as I entered, my mother was in the corridor, calling out to me, "Lisa, you're back. How did your appointment go?"

'When she caught sight of me, she stopped in her tracks. Judging from her alarmed facial expression, I must have looked like death itself.

I knew my eyes must have been red and swollen and stood out against my pale complexion. All I managed to say was, "It was fine, mum. I'm just having a migraine right now and need to lie down."

'My mother responded rather irrationally. "But, Lisa," she said. "You're going to the specialist to get help with them, not to come back from such a visit with a full-blown migraine," as if it was the doctor's or my fault that I was still experiencing migraines.

'I went straight to my bedroom with my mother in tow. All I needed now was to be left alone, and had I had the energy for it, I would have screamed at her in desperation to leave me alone. As it was, my plea for being given time alone was barely more than a whiny whisper, as even my voice was failing me. I shook my head when I was asked whether I wanted anything to eat or drink, but my mother nevertheless brought me a glass of water and my migraine tablets, saying that I needed to take them unless the doctor today had suggested a different treatment. She looked at me quizzically, obviously wanting to be told absolutely everything about my hospital consultation. Again, I had the urge to shout at her to leave my room, but all I could muster was a shake of the head, take off my trousers, crawl into bed and turn my face away from her to the wall and close my eyes. My mother must have finally got the message and left the room but not before telling me to say something to her if I needed anything and adding that I needed to tell her about my consultation when I was feeling a little better.

'The migraine was one of the worst I had ever suffered and kept me in bed for three days whilst the curtains were drawn. During that time, I was barely aware of my mother coming in my room to bring me drinks, light food and to check on how I was doing. I also hardly took any notice of my GP attending to me. Due to the overwhelming pain and sickness I suffered, I wasn't even able to think about the discovery regarding my consultant's private life, which was just as well. Once these three days of hell had passed, I spent the weekend trying to regain my strength. Albeit physically weak after my ordeal, I went on short walks up and down the street mainly in order to come to grips with my rising mental agitation. Now that the physical pain was gone, the emotional suffering set in again. I had vividly imagined the moments my consultant and I would have together down to the most intimate details. In fact, I had envisioned our lives, and shared future, with such frequency that they had become the real thing. Now, however, all that had been revealed as nothing but a fantasy captured in a soap bubble that had finally burst and spilled its contents in a dying shriek of agony.

'I couldn't sit still in my room and relax due to the chaos in my mind so I did what I usually resorted to in situations of great distress. I sat down at my desk, grabbed a pen and my notebook and started to give voice to my tumultuous emotions and sensations by letting the words flow like the effervescent water of a wild river. I spent hours writing fervently, being carried off by my words as on a big wave towards the horizon that couldn't be clearly made out. My whole body was in a state of tension during the process and when I finally put down the pen late in the evening on both days, I almost collapsed from both physical and mental exhaustion before crawling into bed.

'I went back to work the following week but only coped there because I had started spinning another story in my mind that I entered and increasingly became part of, only this time it was set in a different world and everything functioned in a slightly different way. Having another world to go to was my way of warding off the worst of my despair, which could have so easily driven me to doing something stupid and giving up on everything. Nevertheless, it was a tenuous equilibrium I had established, which became painfully apparent less than a week later.

'It was earlier today that my new, fragile house of cards disintegrated dramatically, not even leaving the foundations intact. Today being a Saturday and thus a day I didn't have to go to work, I took myself on a walk after breakfast and immersed myself in the world I was mentally creating. I don't know how long I was out on this bitter cold and snowy last morning of the year, but in view of how everything had changed when I returned it felt like a very long time. When I entered our small house again, it was quiet. There was no sound at all, which was very unusual when my mother was in. Usually, she would call out to me when she heard me come in and ask me questions about where I had been and would try to elicit further details from me. Not this time. I knew she wasn't out, as her coats and shoes including her snow boots were all still near the front door. There was no sound from the bathroom or the toilet either, which made it unlikely that she was in there. After hanging up my coat and taking off my boots, I walked upstairs, trying not to be alarmed by the house's unexpected silence. When I reached the open door to my room, I came to an abrupt stop. My mother was sitting on my bed, slightly bent forwards and with my notebook lying open in her lap! She was reading it with a deep frown on her face.

'She must have heard my approach, as she then looked up and straight at me when I was standing stock-still in the doorway. The seconds that passed while our eyes met seemed to last an eternity. A powerful electric current was running through me and kept me under its control. I saw, in my mother's gaze, the recognition of my inner life, which I had guarded so carefully as I had presumed. All my secrets, my emotions and ideas had been exposed and I had nothing, absolutely nothing left that was unknown to or hidden from her. There was no space, not even a tiny niche, left for me to go to, which might offer me shelter from her prying hawk's eyes. I knew I had lost the last few vestiges of individuality or unique personhood right then. I would just completely merge with her.

'I was in too much of a state of shock to respond to the situation in any way, whereas my mother – after a few seconds of quietly staring at me – broke the silence. She said, "Lisa, what on earth is this? All these violent and strong feelings you express here!" She held the notebook out to me for a second so that I could see what she was referring to. It was a reflection on my stifling home environment, which toyed with the possibility of leaving it all behind and having a different life elsewhere – a place where I could finally be free. "Are you telling me you regard your home as a prison in which I am the warden who keeps you locked behind bars?" she demanded. "Is this your way of thanking me for all the years of looking after you on my own, Lisa? I can tell you that it wasn't a walk in the park. You wouldn't understand because you don't have children of your own. And you weren't exactly an easy child and adolescent; just never forget that. I had to make sacrifices and you have often been difficult to manage and not of a very sunny disposition." My mother now glared at me, pausing in her lamentation before resuming with tears in her eyes and anger in her voice. "Reading this makes me wonder what a fool I have been," she said. "I should have just led a more selfish life on my own! I should never have had you!" She now hurled her words at me with vehemence.

'I then started shaking and began to hug myself in an attempt to comfort myself, still unable to move from the doorway. "And then," my mother said, her voice extremely shrill now, "you're keeping other secrets from me! What is all this about that man you mention who's a doctor? Lisa, is this about the doctor you see in hospital about your migraines? Have you behaved inappropriately and made a fool of yourself? Lisa, you're so naïve! A doctor is bound by his code of ethics! Are you trying to make him violate that code and get banned from professional practice?"

'It was then that I became completely undone. I had to hold on to the doorframe to steady myself, as my legs almost gave way. I felt as if I was swallowed up and actually started dying. Still, I couldn't break my mother's stare. It was torture, but that perception wasn't just my own as I realised when my mother's voice screeched, "Get out of my sight, Lisa! Get out of my sight!" Her face was distorted into an ugly grimace and I reacted instinctively: I turned on my heels, ran down the stairs just about avoiding an awkward fall on the bottom step, grabbed my small handbag that was sitting on the sideboard near the front door, slipped it over my shoulder, quickly put on my brown snow boots without taking time to zip them up, snatched my white snow jacket from the wardrobe and dashed outside.

'Once back out in the cold again, I started running as fast as I could. The weakness in my legs had given way to an adrenaline-fuelled, physical strength and desperate energy that pushed me forwards. I didn't run to a particular place, but unwittingly found myself at the bus station just when I was starting to tire and slow down. There, a voice in my head commanded, "Get on a bus and leave, Lisa! Get out of here." I looked around searchingly and when I spotted a bus at the station that was just about to leave, I ran the few metres towards it, urgently knocked on the door that was almost closed until the driver saw me and reluctantly opened the door again and let me in.

'He said, "Good God, girl, can't you arrive here on time? If I let everyone on the bus who arrived late, I wouldn't be able to stick to the timetable at all." I was both too breathless and too upset to respond and when I just stood there slightly bent over and trying to get my breath back to normal, he continued, "Alright. You can sit down in a second. Where are you going to?"

'I looked at him blankly. I hadn't even checked where the bus was going when I boarded it. The destination didn't matter to me. The important thing was to get away. I just wanted it to go as far away as possible. When I didn't immediately reply, the bus driver's patience with me was visibly running out. Surprisingly, I had now gained the presence of mind to say, "Final stop, please," took my purse out of my handbag and put the money for the ticket he asked for into his hand before I hurried to an empty seat in the far back of the bus.

'Looking down on myself, I only then realised that I was wearing my woollen, raspberry-coloured dress that I was very fond of but that was completely unsuited for running. It was surprising that I had managed to run in it and the snow boots at all, but my agitation had made me oblivious to any physical inconveniences that had the potential to delay me in my endeavour to get away from home as quickly as possible. I was hugging myself tightly in my white snow jacket, attempting to hold the little bit of me that was still there together. I stared outside the window whilst tears were streaming down my face, barely seeing anything through my tears and the increasingly dense snow flurries. The bus driver, not used to such weather conditions, steered the bus carefully through villages and estates. I took barely any notice of people, who were clad in their warmest winter outfits, getting on and off the bus. At first, I recognised the places the bus went through, but eventually the roads became unfamiliar. The lanes were smaller and less easy to drive on, as the fast-falling snow hadn't been cleared there and there were occasional patches of black ice. The bus was crawling along now and I became increasingly restless. Having experienced some relief at having left any familiar environment behind earlier on the bus journey, I now felt disappointed that we didn't get much further more quickly. I pressed the stop button near me to get off and be able to move at a faster speed, walking or running. A few minutes later, the bus deposited me in the middle of a small estate that I had never been to. The bus driver shouted after me that this wasn't the final stop, obviously remembering what I had said to him when asking him for a ticket. But his words barely reached me. Having slung my small bag around my neck so that the strap was resting across my chest and the bag itself was touching my right hip, I started walking as fast as I could. The snow here was already quite deep on the pavements and the snow kept falling thick and fast. These conditions made it impossible to maintain the brisk pace I had adopted after getting off the bus and when I reached the end of the estate and continued along a path in the fields that was barely visible, it became a physical struggle to move forward whatsoever, no matter at what speed. The wind had increased in strength manifold and whipped the snowflakes against my face with great force but I barely flinched. To me, that battle with the elements felt right and appropriate as it seemed a manifestation of the battle that raged inside me. Being exposed to what had now turned into a raging snowstorm almost came as a kind of relief as I felt that the inner turmoil found an expression rather than just eating me up from the inside. I could barely see what was two metres ahead of me, the snow on the uncleared path reached up to my shins and after a few minutes I sensed exhaustion setting in. I didn't care about that.

'In fact, if anything, I was glad to let exhaustion take the place of the intense stabs of inner pain. The former might not have completely replaced the latter, but it certainly took the edge of things. Maybe this makes it more comprehensible to you why I didn't turn back and try to find refuge somewhere on the estate that I had just passed through, for example by knocking at someone's door or at the very least by trying to find an open shop, café or pub. Such a course of action wasn't on my mind. Instead, my mind was almost blank and I was propelled onwards by the urge to get far, far away rather than by a rational plan that involved heading to a specific destination. The further I left the inhabited world behind me, the more frequently did I experience bolts of warning as I call them: They were trying hard to make me aware of the danger I found myself in, offering me the briefest of glimpses at the potential causes of death that might await me if I continued walking but also if I stopped moving altogether: death by exhaustion, exposure or hypothermia or, most likely, a combination of the three. Although, these visions were faintly met by dull echoes of melancholy and regret, my predominant mind set was replete with indifference to my fate that was at times punctuated with a vague longing to sink down and go to sleep forever.

'I was thus dragging myself through the howling blizzard for what seemed an eternity to me, barely conscious but still setting one foot in front of the other automatically and without fail until, all of a sudden, I thought I saw a structure of a building a few metres away from me on the left. However, I almost immediately doubted my eyes, convincing myself that my current state of almost complete exhaustion was playing tricks with my senses and my mind. Wasn't that what happened to people who were dying from thirst in the desert? They would suddenly see a beautifully lush oasis with glittering water and large palm trees that promised to provide them with some shade. Being thus lured further along the way, they would eventually collapse and with them their fervent notion of life-saving water being within their reach. Being aware of such tricks of the mind, I averted my eyes from the spot where I believed to have seen the outline of a house and focused on the snow immediately in front of me, if focused was the right word for a state of near-unconsciousness during which I functioned only through the body's in-built memory of movement and life-sustaining activities.

'Nevertheless, my gaze returned to the left a few seconds later and I shuddered when I now saw a derelict barn barely two metres to my left. My hallucination seemed to grow, which I put down to an advanced stage of delirium that would inevitably lead to my death. Such a delirium would show a dying person what they needed most to survive the life-threatening situation they found themselves in such as conjure up a life-boat for a ship-wrecked person at high seas, or, in my case, present the image of shelter in the worst snowstorm ever experienced. Still, I felt drawn towards what might or might not exist to my left and if it was just to get some relief from the icy lashings of snow against my unprotected face. Just lying down somewhere peacefully and drifting off was all that I needed.

'Walking along the barn's old wall facing me, I soon found a door whose heavy cross-bar I lifted with the last vestiges of strength I could muster and pushed against it until I almost fell inside. The barn was real and not a figment of my imagination. And this was how I came to be here.

★

Lisa ended her narrative at this point. Her eyes were open, but mentally she had not returned to her current surroundings. She was still immersed in the moment during which she had entered the barn and the time that immediately followed:

She staggered to the other side of the barn and let herself glide down with her back to the wall until her bottom hit the floor where she collapsed and was ready to pass out. Already starting to drift off, she did not notice at first that she wasn't alone.

Only when a woman with flaming red hair and clad in purple stood in front of her and spoke to her did she regain her awareness of her surroundings. The woman must have spoken to her, as her golden-brown eyes were firmly fixed on her and bore a waiting, questioning expression. Lisa's confusion must have been plain to see, as she heard the woman speak to her again, presumably in order to repeat what she had just said before.

'Are you alright? Do you own this barn?' The voice was hoarse and slightly croaky, probably from the cold weather and from not having used it for a while.

Lisa slowly shook her head and hugged herself tightly, which she always found comforting when she was confronted by strangers and didn't know how to respond and felt scared.

'Have you been outside and come across the barn by chance?' the woman continued.

Lisa nodded quietly to which the woman merely said in a meanwhile less husky voice, 'So have I.'

Then she turned away and walked up and down the barn before sitting down herself. Suddenly, she appeared oblivious of Lisa's presence and stared straight in front of her as if someone had flicked a switch and let her become introspective and frown, drawing worry lines around her mouth and underneath her eyes. The latter lost any shine they had before and to Lisa it seemed as if a light had been extinguished and darkness spread around the woman. Lisa also had the image of a bright balloon in mind, which deflated in the span of a second, shrinking to near-nothingness.

'Here, take this!'

The voice was close to Lisa and when she looked up, she saw Leo standing in front of her with his right hand outstretched in an attempt to give her an item that she couldn't immediately identify. Trying to return to the here-and-now, she hesitantly took the item out of his hand and asked him, 'What is this?'

Leo responded, 'It's a kaleidoscope. I came across it just now, when I got up after your story ended and went for a quick walk around the barn.'

Lisa realised that she must have finished her story a few minutes before but had not noticed Leo get up and walk around.

Leo continued his explanation, 'It was lying next to the farming tools. I hadn't seen it earlier but just now my foot accidentally nudged it and it made strange sounds when it fell over so I checked what it was. It's odd to find this here. I wonder whether a child had been in here to play and then left it behind. That's the only explanation I can think of, as it doesn't belong amongst the gardening tools.' He paused, evidently puzzled by his find. Then he resumed, 'You have to hold it like this and then twist its body here.' He showed her how to handle it by simulating the appropriate movements.

Lisa, although at a loss as to why he gave her the kaleidoscope, nodded to signify her comprehension. She was vaguely familiar with kaleidoscopes, remembering how she had been given one at a children's party she had attended when she was still at primary school. She remembered looking through one end of it and seeing a colourful pattern at the other end, which magically changed its shapes and colour arrangement when she twisted the tubular object. She replicated this process now and saw how pink, red and yellow flowers unfolded quickly against a background of green and blue. Continuing to rotate the item, she was in awe of how the image changed again, this time to intricate mosaics with violet crescents.

'You make patterns as you move it and you can change what you see at any time.'

Lisa was now deeply immersed in what the kaleidoscope showed her.

Charles, in the meantime, had got up and noticed the ever-changing arrangement of ice flowers on the window-pane he had stepped towards. 'And they're changing as well,' he muttered. 'There hadn't been that many ice flowers earlier on and they had been far simpler and less intricate than the ones that are visible now.'

Karen, who had been paying close attention to Lisa's narrative and the other people's movements and words, nodded vigorously, casting a quick glance at Charles and Leo before turning to Lisa at her side.

'And this is exactly what you can do in your life, Lisa. You can make changes and transform your life. I'm sorry you have suffered and been in so much pain over the years, but I firmly believe that you can change direction and things can improve. Nothing is ever static in life, as you can see when you watch the expanding network of ice flowers that Charles had just pointed out. And you can influence the nature of some of the changes that come about through circumstance or at least carefully choose your response to them. Most importantly, you can bring about both small and big changes when you act with deliberation. Take control and steer the kaleidoscope of your life.'

Lisa looked up at Karen and pondered what the latter had said for a few moments before her face darkened and she replied with great sadness in her voice. 'How can I? I'm trapped. Even if life was comparable to a kaleidoscope, I wouldn't be able to give it a meaningful direction. When I use the kaleidoscope, I have no idea how the patterns and colours will change in advance. I can handle it but without any idea of what the outcome of my actions will be. What will happen is the outcome of chance and nothing else.'

Karen shook her head with determination before she retorted. 'No, it's not like this, Lisa. I haven't used a kaleidoscope for a while so feel free to correct me if I'm wrong, but I believe that even when operating a kaleidoscope, you'll learn after a while what kind of changes in the pattern you can expect when you turn it one way or the other, which is the same in life. Yes, you cannot foresee everything; there will still be elements that are not under your control, but you can influence outcomes by the actions you take to a much greater extent than you think, Lisa. The kaleidoscope might draw your attention more to the factor of chance or processes that are beyond your control, but never underestimate the impact of agency.'

Lisa, whilst listening to Karen attentively, remained sceptical. She tried to cling to some hope that might be offered her here if she just believed in what Karen was telling her. However, she struggled to see how positive change in her life could be brought about.

'I don't know what I can do to change anything much. The man I fell in love with is unavailable and it hurts so much that I don't know how to deal with it or ever get over it, as I believe that he'll be the only one for me and that I'll never meet anyone else who I can be happy with.'

She was starting to become breathless in her agitation, which had only been briefly relieved when she had been ensconced in the workings of the kaleidoscope.

'I'm now past my mid-thirties, have never been in a relationship and don't know whether I will ever fulfil my dream of meeting someone and starting a family. I think most likely not. And on top of it, I don't think I'm a person in my own right. I feel completely merged with my mother and I don't think I could exist without her. She knows everything about me now. My innermost thoughts, feelings and dreams have all been revealed to her since she found my notebook this morning. And not only that, they have all been trashed.' Lisa's voice was rising in pitch.

Leo, who had tried to distract Lisa from the sorrow and suffering that was so clearly expressed in her story by passing his new find to her, now turned towards her with something like sympathy and concern in his demeanour. Something in her despair had struck a chord in him. He addressed her calmly. 'We can't fix all of this at once, but I think you need to prioritise the goals that you are most likely to reach and that are the most important ones.'

He paused for a few seconds and, when he saw Lisa's pained expression, resumed. 'You might think that being with a particular person and having a family with him is your most ardent desire, but I believe that what you need first and foremost is to leave home and carve out a life for yourself. You'll need to become independent, Lisa, have your own space and then follow your dreams in what you want to do. Didn't you say that you would have loved to study literature?'

Lisa watched him and replied, 'English literature and creative writing.'

Before she could say anything else, he added almost triumphantly, 'There you see. You do have your goals and passions, reading and writing being chiefly amongst them.'

Lisa interrupted him. 'But I can't just move out and study. I don't earn that much with my job in the bookshop and will certainly not be in a position to pay for a university course! That is the reason why I haven't done it in the past.'

Leo resolutely but affably waved off her objections. 'I'm sure you can afford to rent a one-bedroom apartment nearby. Even I, with my patchy work history, am able to do this. I bet you haven't even checked out what is affordable in the area and the main reason for this isn't a financial one but your mother who has been putting pressure on you to stay with her. 'You're a grown woman, Lisa. You don't owe anything to your mother!'

Lisa was becoming more pensive. She was obviously starting to take on board what was being said.

Karen now made herself heard again: 'As for the costs of a university course, it might be feasible if you study part-time, maybe do some distance learning, and thus spread the cost over a longer period of time. And even if you're still short of money then, it can be done. I could cover some of the costs for you.' Karen didn't quite know where this suggestion she had just made came from, but whether it had been made on impulse or not, she knew that she meant it and that it hadn't merely been an empty gesture. She had recognised that Lisa could do with some practical help to get her started in implementing changes and, being a pragmatic person, she had reacted accordingly.

Lisa had turned to Karen and stared at her in astonishment. What was it that made Karen come up with that generous offer? Lisa wasn't used to being offered anything. What had just happened was incomprehensible to her.

Leo, once again, showed more perspicacity than the others would have thought him to be capable of when he remarked, 'It's not the practical details that pose the greatest challenge to your goals, but the emotional dependence on your mother and the doubt you harbour of what you are capable of. You'll need to become strong to do all this, but you can do this because you want to become free. Think of Lara in your story. Your most profound need is expressed in her free and independent lifestyle that focuses on what she truly wants both at work and in her free time. It's time to follow in Lara's footsteps, Lisa! She has set an example that you can emulate.'

Charles, who was visibly moved by Lisa's story, commented, 'Isn't it usually our emotional vulnerabilities that prevent us from taking a new and more constructive path in life? They niggle at us and hold us back.'

The others turned their attention to Charles.

The latter continued, 'And agency is not always positive by definition. It depends on the choices you have made. If your choices are the wrong ones, it is unlikely that your actions will be beneficial in nature.'

Leo's eyes narrowed as he was weighing the validity of Charles's statements. 'I don't know whether choices are always good or bad. Who is to say what is good or bad, after all?'

'The law in the first instance,' Karen interjected passionately. 'That's why we have it in the first place. But it goes further than that. There are instances that are not necessarily considered illegal but are often unethical, usually when another living being is harmed by certain actions.'

Leo watched her calmly before he resumed, 'The law has been made by men and what is considered ethical is also the product of judgements made by society.'

Karen was about to interrupt but Leo, noticing her intention, continued his argument undeterred. 'All I'm saying is that there is no real objective measurement for what is a good or bad decision. What we consider objective such as the law cannot be that if you take its origin into account. I don't necessarily reject the law, but we need to remain critical and acknowledge that some laws are better than others.'

Karen, feeling in her element when it came to legal matters, was ready to jump in again, but Leo didn't give her a chance to do so, saying, 'And anyway, you've only focused on actions just now, but Charles and I have also mentioned choices. They're not the same and can't be treated in the same way even if there's a causal relationship between them. Actions can lead to direct harm, choices can't. You may make the choice not to forgive someone for something they had done to you, but how you specifically act on this choice will be of real interest, as you can, for example, just ignore that person or seek retribution by killing them. I believe that choices are often quite broad and comprehensive but actions are specific and definite.'

Karen started to become visibly impatient. 'I'm not entirely sure whether I agree with that but let's not split hairs.' She didn't even notice the irony in this remark insofar as splitting hairs was very much part of her day-to-day job. However, she was tired, cold, hungry and thirsty and therefore didn't feel up to engaging in long-winded disputes. Instead, she moved her attention back to Charles.

'Charles, sorry. Leo and I have hijacked the conversation. Did you want to add anything else to what you have said previously?'

Charles shook his head. 'No, not really. I just meant to say that bringing about changes through our actions can at times be as damaging to ourselves and others as not doing anything.' He lowered his head and added in a barely audible voice, 'I have personal experience of it. I've messed things up so badly.'

Lisa, who had still been thinking about what Leo and Karen had said to her earlier whilst being busy with the kaleidoscope and therefore not paid much attention to the debate about choices and agency, focused on Charles again. Being aware of his, once again, increasing inner turmoil, she said sympathetically, 'What has happened, Charles? Do you want or need to talk about it? It might not be as bad as you believe it is.'

Charles's voice was about to break when he replied, 'But it is. It really is.'

Lisa couldn't bear his sorrow any longer. She stood up with the kaleidoscope still in her hand, walked over to Charles, knelt in front of him and lightly touched his arm without quite knowing where she got the confidence from.

'Please talk to us if you can. It doesn't matter how bad it might be what you have done. Just tell us about it. I think you're ready now. I promise you won't feel any the worse for it. You need to release whatever is troubling you from the box in your head. Having it all boxed up in there does you more harm than it could ever do if you shared it.'

Charles didn't reply immediately but finally nodded and said, 'Alright. If you're sure you really want to hear about it.'

Lisa affirmed that they did and Karen echoed this sentiment whilst Leo didn't say anything to the contrary.

Charles cleared his throat and then began to reveal in a raspy voice to them what was causing him so much distress.

Dashed Hopes

'I have betrayed Annie. I have hurt her repeatedly and destroyed a wonderful relationship through my actions. She didn't deserve this. Our relationship didn't deserve this. I have caused her pain and now she is dead – has been dead for a few years – and I can't make it up to her any longer. I can't undo what I have done and I just don't see the point in continuing any longer. I have lost the love of my life after destroying everything. There is nothing left for me now. Everything has become pointless. I'm ready to die now. My deepest wish is to be reunited with her again after my death. If that was still possible. If she still wants that. Wouldn't it be almost superhuman to want to be with the person who has caused you so much grief in the afterlife? Also, would I really be allowed to enter heaven and be welcomed there by God? There is no question that Annie has been there for a few years and that she has experienced something more beautiful and joyful than what I had given her during the last few years of her life. Or maybe I should rather say the lack of happiness I had caused in her life.

'I can see that you're looking at me with incomprehension and I realise that I owe you some background or explanation of what I have just told you, especially after having gone on about our romantic courtship in my first narrative. Telling you about the events leading up to my cowardly and ill-conceived actions won't excuse them at all, but you might then be able to understand how and why our relationship changed. I am picking up from where I left off earlier.

'Things between us didn't go awry immediately after the wedding. On the contrary, we went for a few days to Torquay to spend our honeymoon at the coast. We had not expected to be in a position to go on a honeymoon, but our relatives and friends had put some money together and made the trip a wedding present to us in addition to the usual things one is given when starting a household, such as kitchenware. The honeymoon was a lovely time. For the first and almost only time in our lives as a couple did we spend our time together without having to squeeze it between family and work commitments.

'We were booked in at a charming B&B whose breakfast room offered a sea view and whose owner was a warm-hearted lady who made recommendations of the most attractive places to visit and who also helped us with directions, providing us with local maps that we could take with us.

'The rooms were comfortable and the windows facing east let in the bright light of summer every morning. We didn't care that it often woke us up between four and five in the morning to the sound of screeching seagulls that were trying to find their next meal. We would get up and stand near one of the large windows that – like the breakfast room – had a sea view, our arms around each other, still a bit sleepy and also still a little chilly in the cool air just after dawn.

'It was a new experience for both of us to fall asleep curled up next to each other with our bodies touching and warming each other at night. There was something reassuring about it. During the day, we would go on long walks along the beach, walking hand in hand in blissful abandon before frequenting one of the many inviting cafés where we treated ourselves to a delicious lunch of freshly-prepared sandwiches or home-baked cakes with aromatic Earl Grey tea for Annie and a coffee for myself.

'In the afternoons, we would visit the extensive gardens there, spend a bit of time browsing the local shops or take the bus to small places nearby from where we could explore the coastline some more.

'In the evenings, after having sated our hunger with a hearty pub dinner, we would walk along the beach again and were rewarded with spectacular sunsets. After almost five days of exploring Torquay and its surroundings areas, of walking dozens of miles and breathing the invigorating sea air, we returned back home with tanned faces, arms, necks and calves and were dizzy with joy, light-heartedness and love for each other.

'Moving into a new home together and leaving the security of the parental home behind might have caused us anxieties or difficulties adjusting to the new situation but it didn't in the end, as we were both raised in a way that enabled us to stand on our own feet and we were optimistic young people who did not shy away from change. Moreover, we were devoted to each other so that we were looking forward to living together. After our families had helped us move into our new home, we therefore settled in very quickly. Having worked as a carpenter for a few years now, I made quite a few items of furniture for our little house and Annie decorated it with hand-made tapestries, rugs, blankets and other pretty items that – for the most part – the women in her family had created.

'Especially during the week, we were incredibly busy with our work and, in the evenings, with the projecting duties at the cinema in my case and with spending time with nephews and niece in the case of Annie. We were doing shorter Sunday excursions and sometimes went together with Annie's sisters and their families, as they wanted to take the children out, too, and Annie was reluctant to miss even a few hours of watching their physical, cognitive and emotional development. I would have sometimes liked to spend a bit more time with Annie alone rather than share her so much with the rest of her family, but I realised how vital her connection with James and the twins was to her so I didn't want to make demands on her.

'A year went by very quickly and during the weekend the twins turned one, we all went out to have a picnic in the hot summer sun. Patrick and Sara wore face paint that tried to make them look like a lion and a zebra respectively. They both wore dungarees – Patrick wore light brown ones and Sara wore black-and-white striped ones, both of which emphasised their respective animal look – and matching T-shirts. Both of them had just started walking without holding on to anything, and Annie took great delight in walking next to them to catch them before, or sometimes when, they fell into the soft grass and steer them back to the picnic blankets. Little James was, as a two-year old, already quite steady on his feet and took an increasing interest in his cousins, picking daisies for them or playing with them, throwing a small ball that they had to catch and fetch. Elaine and Marisa watched them smilingly, brimming with pride of their active, sociable and dexterous children.

'When Annie sat down again at some point to drink some lemonade, I heard her say to her sisters, "They're absolutely delightful! I can't wait to have my first one soon as well and then they will have another little cousin to play with!"

'However, another year went by without Annie becoming pregnant and her delightful anticipation on that summer's day on the twins' birthday gradually gave way to expressions of worry and bewilderment. Soon after that day of happy double birthday celebrations, her older brother and his wife announced that they were expecting a child.

'It was then that Annie could feel something inside her shift. Whilst her first reaction was still joy and excitement, which she expressed by hugging Matthew and Maria tightly and congratulating them with a big smile, the moment she held Maria close to her a sudden pain shot through her body and she nearly cried out. She had briefly imagined the developing life in Maria's body when the pain set in and she had to pull away from her sister-in-law, muttering something about acute back pain she had recently been suffering from, causing Maria to give her a puzzled look.

'For a long time, Annie didn't understand this pain, which from then on occurred more frequently, in fact, every time she learned about another pregnancy or birth in our small town. She couldn't comprehend why that pain increasingly encroached on the elation she experienced about such happy news. However, what she did know was that the unpleasant sensations she had would last for a while and – while diminishing in intensity after half an hour – leave her physically and mentally drained.

'When she described all this to me, I didn't have an explanation for what was happening to Annie either because I knew her as a very healthy young woman who delighted in other people's good news. I couldn't reconcile the pain Annie was experiencing and that started to have a crippling effect on her with the energetic person I knew. Eventually, I spoke to my mother about it, hoping that her experience as a nurse might give her an idea of what the problem was with Annie's body and what could be done about it.

'My mother watched me very attentively when I told her about all that and when I finished speaking, she continued glancing at me with her piercing, dark blue eyes. Eventually she said thoughtfully in her deep, resonant voice, "Annie is very attached to her family, isn't she?"

'When I confirmed this, she resumed. "You see, Annie defines herself hugely through family relationships. I guess all, or at least, most of us do so to some extent, but to Annie it's a huge part of her identity. This is not surprising, as we women have been taught – you could even say indoctrinated – to take our place in our adult lives as wives and mothers and be that first and foremost."

'I frowned and retorted, "I know you're critical of it. You don't approve of Annie valuing a big family and wanting to have one with me. You might want her to be a bit more like you in her wishes and aspirations."

'At this, my mother vigorously shook her head. "No, Charles," she said. "This is absolutely not true. I have come to love Annie very much for who she is. I'm merely trying to explain to you how social conventions and expectations form a person's outlook on life and Annie coming from a large, closely-knit family, has understandably an outlook on family life that puts the woman at the centre of the household in which she reigns as mother. Undeniably, there will most likely be a natural inclination on her part to become a mother that is not totally explained by customs and social norms, as I have come from a big family as well and never felt the same urge to have a big family that Annie has. It is therefore a combination of her natural propensity to value family and the environment she grew up in that makes her so intent on starting a family soon, I think. Whether we agree on that or not is maybe secondary although I outlined the connections that I can see so that you might be in a position to understand Annie better. The bottom line, though, is that Annie's longing for children is so overwhelming in its nature that she starts to manifest her emotional pain of being childless so far in the physical pain she experiences when she is reminded of it, usually by other people's announcements of their pregnancies.'

'I thought about what my mother had just said and objected. "But if other women are announcing their pregnancies, it's not about Annie," I said. "It's about them and their happiness at that moment. Isn't it selfish to then immediately think about yourself when you hear such news? Annie has always so easily been able to join in other people's happiness and feel it and she still smiles right after hearing such news. Is she changing now? Do you think she's becoming more selfish?"

'My mother answered calmly. "What is selfish?" she asked. "Is it selfish to think of your needs when they're not met? Is it selfish to acknowledge the pain? In fact, I believe Annie doesn't do that enough, which is why it expresses itself predominantly in physical symptoms. There is a danger of her becoming increasingly unwell if her perceptions and subsequently her feelings don't undergo any changes.

Eventually, she might become bitter and depressed. She needs to confront her thoughts, work through them and find another way of living a happy and fulfilling life."

'I recall how alarmed I felt and exclaimed, "But, Mum, we will have children! You talk as if you don't expect us to have any! I have heard that sometimes when people try very hard to have them, it doesn't happen very quickly. Isn't that true?"

'She told me, "Charles, I'm not saying that you definitely won't have any children. I certainly hope for you both that you will have some soon as Annie – and probably you as well – long for them. I merely mention the possibility to you that it might not happen and that I worry about Annie if this will be the case."

'After a brief pause she asked me earnestly, "How important is it to you, Charles, to have children? How do *you* feel about possibly not having any?"

'I was in some turmoil and confused at that stage so it took me a few moments to gather my thoughts. I said, "Well, I've never much thought about children either way before I met Annie. Not having had siblings, I'm used to my own company and that of other adults. However, I've started to enjoy the company of Annie's family members and – whilst not being as ecstatic as Annie – have grown fond of the babies in the family including the latest arrival, Penny, who is a real charmer. I therefore look forward to our own family. You ask me what it would be like for me if things turn out differently. I suppose I would be a bit sad, but as we see so much of Annie's nephews and nieces I wouldn't think of it as the end of the world. I'd still have enough exposure to children. Also, I'm so busy outside of my regular work with the projection work I do and so excited about it that I don't think that there will be any time to be too downhearted."

'After I had clarified my considerations and views on this matter, my apprehension that my mother had evoked by painting a future without children for Annie and me gave way to a sense of palpable relief. I had come to realise that, to me, it didn't matter all that much if we couldn't have children. At the same time, I still firmly believed at this point that it was only a matter of time before Annie became pregnant. In order to conclude the conversation, I remarked, "Okay, but at the moment it looks to me as if we will probably have children. Do you not think we should just keep trying or would you go and have a medical check-up if you were in Annie's place?"

'My mother shrugged her shoulders and said, "That's a possibility. I would say that both of you could go for a medical check-up, as it's a myth that fertility issues only occur in women, but of course it's typical of our patriarchal society to hold such a view."

'I flinched at the thought of someone examining my nether regions and quickly left the room to find my father to speak about business matters.

'I didn't quite know how to suggest a medical check-up to Annie but as my mother had convinced me that her difficulty in becoming pregnant was at the root of Annie's bouts of unspecific but intense physical pain, I was determined to tackle the issue even if I didn't feel comfortable with it. Therefore, one evening when we were both in our bedroom and getting ready to sleep, I said to her quietly, "Annie, I'm not sure how to say this, but do you think it might be a good idea if you had a medical examination to make sure everything is alright with you?" I added quickly, "You know, even if there was an issue, that would put you in a situation to seek treatment for it so that it can be sorted."

'Annie, who had just slipped into her white nightdress with the light blue borders, turned to me and looked at me questioningly for a couple of seconds before I detected some kind of recognition on her face. "Oh, you mean the bad pains I sometimes get, Charles? Yes, you're probably right. I have thought I should probably go to be examined, too. The problem is that they don't just affect my head but my entire body so it might be difficult for a doctor to know where to examine me first." Annie was laughing now, trying to make light of the matter.

'I took a deep breath, attempting to clear up the misunderstanding. "No, I mean it might be good to have an examination to find out why you haven't conceived yet.' The moment I had said it, I realised that it had not come out the way it was intended to.

'Unsurprisingly, Annie reacted accordingly. "What do you mean?" she said. Her normally happy and friendly face displayed strain, hurt and shock, and her tone was uncharacteristically defensive. "You're unhappy and impatient with me because of that!" Her question, which was more an exclamation, had a shrill edge to it.

'I cursed myself inwardly for having taken such a clumsy approach. "I'm sorry, Annie. I didn't mean it that way." I was about to say that I couldn't care less about that before I realised – just in time – that that statement, apart from not being entirely true, could also be misconstrued as me only going ahead with trying for a baby with her in order to do Annie a favour. Instead, I said: "I'm not impatient at all. I'd be happy if we were having a child soon, but I'm also happy for us to have one a few years further down the line and enjoy our currently busy, fulfilled lives as they are a little longer. There's no rush for me. I only suggest you might want to see a doctor soon because my impression is that you are unhappy not to have got pregnant yet and I believe your bodily pains reflect that sorrow."

'Annie, still looking somehow upset, evidently considered what I had just said, but then dismissed my suggestion with an uneasy laugh. "No, Charles, that's not necessary. I'm sure it will happen imminently."

'I suspect that she must have been aware of the cause of her bouts of pain but just refused to fully acknowledge it to herself and certainly did not attempt to discuss it with me. After having expressed her disinclination to undergo a physical examination, I felt I had done what I could and fell silent on the topic.

'Annie, however, maybe to convince herself of her impending pregnancy, told her nephews and niece that they would soon have a little cousin to play with. She repeated that announcement frequently without having a good reason to assume this would happen in the next few weeks, and I started to become even more concerned about her.

'Another five years passed. During that time Annie mentioned the prospect of having a baby soon less frequently to the children until she became completely silent about the topic. She saw more children being born into the family and rejoiced with her siblings about the new arrivals as much as she could: There was aforementioned Penny, Matthew and Maria's firstborn, who charmed everyone with her black hair, her unfathomable dark eyes and her simultaneously sweet and mischievous smile. Almost everyone was surprised by the darkness of her eyes and hair and by the contrast it formed to her porcelain-white skin. Whilst Maria's dark-brown hair and eye colour wasn't too far off from her daughter's, the former's skin was of a much darker shade than Penny's. Matthew didn't have such light skin either.

'Only Maria recognised as soon as the midwife had placed her baby daughter into her arms how closely she resembled both Maria's mother and grandmother, both of whom she had lost early in life. She clearly recalled the alabaster skin of the two women, which had been framed in stark black and how that combination had given them an air of exoticism and other-worldliness. She was proud to see these characteristics repeated in Penny as a visible reminder that the ancestral line continued with an aura of beauty and grace.

'Her brother Adam was born only a year later. He didn't have the same strange beauty that his sister exuded, but Maria and Matthew were pleasantly surprised by how closely he resembled Maria. His features were almost a small replica of hers and his many gurgling noises were delightful to everyone who met him. From the second he was born he seemed to have this great urge to produce sounds, which has continued throughout his life during which he appeared to float on the sound waves of music.

'Almost exactly halfway between Penny and Adam's births, Elaine gave birth to her second child, Martha. Her wiry red hair, which was hard to control and give any kind of shape to, made everyone smile the minute they saw her. Contrary to common belief that red-heads usually turned out to become real tomboys, little Martha was a rather quiet and contemplative, albeit not a timid, child who seemed to live in a world of her own. Similar to her livelier older brother, James, she could immerse herself in something for hours without interruptions, but unlike James, who would freely share his observations and thoughts with others, she wouldn't make a sound and it happened more than once that her concerned parents believed she had left the house without permission when she was quietly sitting somewhere inside, looking intently at an item of interest, which she more often than not explored with her hands. It was important to her to touch things in order to understand their nature. Whilst her brother's curiosity was more on an intellectual level, which expressed itself in a stream of questions that his poor parents were doing their best to answer or in extended spells of reading books, Martha truly learned about the world through her senses. She was attracted to warm and earthy colours and her greatest excitement was to touch her grandmother's large array of textiles. She would look at them for an instant before gently stroking the different fabrics until she felt she knew them. It didn't take long until she demanded to be shown how to make many of the items she admired and she was barely five when her grandmother introduced her to such crafts.

'Annie continued to spend much of her time outside of work in the presence of her nephews and nieces and often, like in the first two years after James's birth, became absorbed in their company: She was part of the twins' wild games and seemed to match them in their seemingly never-ceasing energy. Marisa and Andrew were always grateful when Annie was around to give them some relief from childcare. Other family members never really wondered how these two had turned out to be such exuberant, boisterous children who never sat still, as they remembered vividly that Marisa had been the same as a child.

'Annie knew how to manage Penny when she was wilful and used her unusual female beauty and charm, which she became aware of quite early in life, to get her way. They would play with the light grey cat, Simba, which Matthew and Maria had recently acquired, and try to teach her some tricks. When Annie spent time with Adam, she indulged his passion for music by bringing along children's song books and teaching him all her favourite songs. It helped that Annie had a good voice herself and absolutely loved to sing.

'When she was at Elaine's, she and James read books about science, nature, art and other fields of knowledge, and she and Martha delighted in dressing up in clothes in a range of colours and materials that they found in their respective wardrobes and that they combined and recombined with careless abandon. They laughed a lot whilst doing so, and it was during these moments that little Martha abandoned her usual reserve.

'Despite all these many merry scenes and times, it happened not infrequently that Annie suddenly paused in the middle of something and it was as if a shadow darkened her face for a while before she resumed whatever she was doing with visibly less energy than before. At home, Annie was generally quieter than she used to be and her episodes of pain, which utterly exhausted her by the time they came to the end, continued to occur unabated.

'And then the day came when Annie changed her mind about not seeing a doctor for her childlessness. It was the outcome of a conversation she had with my mother on that same day. It was a Saturday. I was still finishing off with my father before closing the carpenter's shop for the day, which only amounted to half a day on a Saturday. Annie had already finished her shift at the hairdresser's where she was scheduled to work on a Saturday morning once a month. We were going to have lunch together at my parents' before I would head off to work with Tobias at the cinema and Annie would go over to her sister-in-law, Maria's, to keep her company whilst Matthew was working on the farm with his dad, and to give her some relief from looking after the children. Annie enjoyed these afternoons, which not only involved being in the company of her niece and nephew but also an extended chat with Maria, who was easy to talk with and who Annie considered to be another sister.

'Annie and my mother were busy laying the table for lunch when my mother noticed Annie slow down in her movements, looking pensive and as if she was about to say something but didn't quite know how to start. My mother watched her closely for a minute before she addressed her. "Annie, is everything alright? You seem a bit thoughtful today. Do you want to talk about anything that is on your mind?"

'Annie looked up from the cutlery she had been arranging nicely around the plate, hesitated for a moment, but then decided to speak whilst holding my mother's direct gaze. "Yes. I was wondering if I could ask you something. You know, you being a nurse..." She faltered at this point.

'My mother watched her intently now, put the glass jug quickly down on the table, and took a few steps towards Annie before she pulled her down on a chair whilst taking a seat on the one next to her. "We're done with setting the table now so we do have time to talk. Annie, what is it you wish to ask me? Are you unwell? Have these episodes of exhaustion and pain increased in frequency and strength?"

'Annie had occasionally mentioned the episodes to my mother in passing without making a big thing of them. She shook her head now and replied slowly whilst feeling my mother's eyes on her: "No, it's not that," she said. "I have a different question." Again, she paused before resuming with more determination. "Do you meet many women, Ellen, at your work who don't fall pregnant for the first few years of their marriages until it just happens naturally?" Not giving my mother much of a chance to respond, she added "Or at least some women?" Annie's face had now assumed a worried expression and a frown emerged on her forehead.

'My mother looked at her steadily before she put her hand gently on Annie's forearm, a gesture she often used to comfort patients And said, "Annie, I thought you might be worrying about this." She pondered something for a second before she replied, "It can happen, but most of the time there is a physiological reason for it."

'Annie's face darkened when she heard these words.

'My mother continued, "Only a thorough medical investigation will give you an answer to that but we might be able to rule out a few things if I ask you some questions. Have you ever had any abdominal illnesses or operations?"

'Annie shook her head. "No, I always used to be very healthy and robust before these pains started that I mentioned. Apart from chickenpox and tonsillitis, which I had when I was a young child I've remained free from illnesses otherwise."

'My mother asked, "What about appendicitis? Have you ever had an inflamed appendix?"

'Annie thought about the question before exclaiming, "Oh, yes, I did. I tend to forget about this because I was still so little that I barely remember anything of it, just tiny snippets and what my parents told me about it. I was only three years old and apparently in a lot of pain, but the doctor I saw first didn't diagnose it correctly. He thought that I suffered from colic, as so many young children do, and sent me and my parents home with a few instructions on how to best treat it. But apparently one night I became so poorly that I wouldn't stop crying and ran a high fever. This was when my parents rushed me to hospital where the doctors diagnosed a highly inflamed appendix that had burst. They rushed me to theatre and had to perform emergency surgery. They said that had my parents brought me in any later, I would have died. My parents must have been truly shocked when they heard this and told me that it's hard to describe the relief they felt when I finally recovered."

'My mother nodded knowingly. "Annie, it can happen that a burst appendix will affect your fallopian tubes by blocking them. I have seen this more than once in my practice. It would be advisable to get them checked out to get some clarity."

'Annie's green eyes looked solemn as they returned my mother's gaze. Eventually, she nodded, being newly convinced that a medical check-up might be useful after all.

'I distinctly recall the day of Annie's hospital appointment. I knew the importance of the appointment to her especially and how much she needed my support in those circumstances. I had therefore asked my father to be given the day off so that I could accompany Annie to the hospital and be with her during the consultation that followed the examinations.

'My father knew that I hardly ever asked for any time off work and had thus readily agreed to it. "Go with her, my boy. I hope it all goes well."

'It was a long wait for me, as Annie was in the scanning room for a very long time. When she finally came out, there was another longish wait ahead of us until we were finally called into the consulting room. I held Annie's left hand, which was damp with sweat. Her face displayed the strain she was under.

'The consultant's facial expression gave nothing away when he shook our hands, asked us to step in and take a seat before he closed the door. He looked at the papers on the desk in front of him before he got up again and walked towards a lit-up panel to which a couple of scans were attached. "I'm cutting straight to the chase. You wanted us to check whether we can find a physiological reason why Mrs Doyle hasn't become pregnant since you married seven years ago." He paused for a second to look at Annie and me out of his steel-grey eyes, which were in complete harmony with his salt-and-pepper hair. "We have identified what we believe to be the reason for it." He turned to the scans and pointed at a certain spot. "I don't know whether you are able to see it from there, but these are Annie's fallopian tubes." He now made a circling movement with his right index finger.

'I guess he could have told us that the image showed an elephant and we would have believed it. We – or at least I – were unable to make out anything on this scan, especially from a few metres away. We had to take his word for it.

"There is some clear blockage in both tubes and we can say with a high degree of certainty that this is the result of Annie's burst appendix when she was a child, which you have previously told me about."

'There was a pause as we took in the diagnosis, which mother had already mentioned as a possibility. We were now both waiting for the consultant to suggest an action plan or a particular treatment approach to us. When he remained silent and sat down again on his chair behind the desk, I therefore asked him directly, "What does that mean? How can we move forward from here? How can Annie be treated?"

'The consultant, who – I now noticed – looked still quite young despite his grey hair, answered my question calmly. "I'm afraid at the current state of medicine, we don't really have any treatments that are tested and established enough in order for me to recommend them."

'Annie swallowed hard next to me and then said in a barely audible voice, "Am I infertile then and will I not be able to have children in the future?"

'It broke my heart to see her well up with tears.

'The consultant replied, "Unless there will be a medical breakthrough in treatments of tube occlusion in the next few years, I'm afraid it's unlikely you will have children."

'Seeing that these words now opened the gateway to a flood of tears on Annie's part, the consultant brought the consultation to a quick close, shook our hands and walked us out of the consulting room.

'Annie was shaking the entire way back home and I was at a loss as to how I could best console her. I eventually pointed out to her that we had such a close relationship with her nephews and nieces that it was almost as if we had children of our own, reminding her how dear they were to her. When she didn't respond, I added, "And isn't it even better that way? We don't have the sleepless nights that come along with young children. We have all the fun and enjoyment with them without having to shoulder all the responsibilities. Really, it's ideal, Annie."

'After I had said this, Annie looked at me in an almost accusing and very uncharacteristic fashion and said, virtually tonelessly, "You don't understand, Charles. You don't even seem that keen on having children. Of course, I would want all the responsibility that comes with having children. Being an auntie is different from being a mother! You can't compare the two. I love being an auntie, but this will never lessen my wish to become a mother."

'In hindsight, maybe it was my inability to fully appreciate Annie's grief of something she had never had in the first place and my apparently inadequate response to this grief that closed the door to any real conversations about the diagnosis she had received and what it meant to her or us from then on. Something started to change between us and although it might not have been immediately noticeable to others, it was obvious to me.

'What was apparent to everyone though was that Annie from then on started to withdraw from others and her immediate environment. She turned inward and practically became someone different: More often than not she stayed away from family gatherings and her zest for, and spark of, life were soon all but extinguished. These changes in Annie became increasingly pronounced over the years and came along with a steady decline in her health. The periods of pain and exhaustion she had suffered became more frequent and more intense and increasingly made her house- and bed-bound. Eventually, she could not hold her job any longer and had to stop working.

'However, whenever she was reasonably well, she threw herself into doing crafts. Whilst she had previously been happy enough to do some, it had never been a real passion of hers. She much preferred being physically active outside or in the dance hall than being cooped up with needlework, crocheting or similar activities that require a calm and sustained application. It was therefore a little surprising that she now started to work on elaborate tapestries and wall hangings and applied herself to these projects with such fervour that nothing around her seemed to exist any longer and as if her life depended on it. The large majority of her time was dedicated to them. Compared to the early years of our marriage, she saw less and less of her family. Only Martha, who loved working with materials, came regularly to learn more about making beautiful things from her aunt and to share the experience of creating something new with Annie. They would often sit there quietly, immersed in what they were doing, but still aware of and somehow reassured by the other person's presence.

'In the meantime, I spent the vast majority of my time when I wasn't doing my day job during the week with Tobias at the film theatre. He was becoming frailer over the years and had less energy than when I first met him. I was therefore soon doing the late hours that he couldn't do any longer and it was an uplifting experience to have gained his trust and do some of the projection work without direct supervision when he wasn't there. He started referring to me as his chosen and deserving successor. I tended to cut him short when he said this because I didn't want to think of him as retiring or not being there any longer and also because I wouldn't leave my father in the lurch with the carpentry business and intended to always work in that trade until I retired, which I made clear to him. I had promised as much to my father and also gained some satisfaction from the labour of the trade. Tobias accepted this but he made me promise him to never give up the projection work as it was clearly my passion and I was very good at it.

'I clearly remember him saying, "It is important to follow our passions, Charles. Don't you forget this. We only live once."

'Neither of us had any idea at this point that these words might take on a much less idealistic but a rather baser meaning in my future actions. Over the years, however, I have often thought about the irony of the intended encouragement to pursue what you truly believe in and the (self-) destructive path I started to tread on when I did give in to one of my passionate impulses. I'm not trying to justify my actions when I say that at the age of thirty I was at the height of my health, vigour and masculinity and wanted to expend my energy in the way most men my age did, namely through hard work, some fun and being with the woman I loved. The latter, however, became increasingly ghost-like and ethereal with the decline in her physical and mental health. Our lovemaking became more and more infrequent and didn't have the same sense of giddy abandon about it that it used to have during our early years together. I missed all this. I missed everything about Annie – her strong, youthful body and her bubbly personality.

'It felt to me that Annie, as I knew her, was vanishing and in the end, I couldn't compensate for that loss by immersing myself in work alone. Instead of trying to spend more time with her and providing her with more support and love to ease her pain and console her in her grief, I turned away from her and sought some light-hearted distraction in the arms of another woman – a woman whom I didn't love as I loved Annie but whom I kept visiting to remind myself that there were joy and laughter and an easy sexuality in this life to be had.

'The first time I met her was after Tobias and I had screened a romantic comedy at the end of a long and busy week. The times when Annie and I had gone to watch a film together and had gone dancing on Friday and Saturday evenings respectively was long gone although I did manage to watch a film with her occasionally when I wasn't projecting and she was well enough. Tobias saw how tired I looked that night and because I was scheduled to do a lot of projecting work with him over the next few days, he walked me to the door of our projectionist's room and told me firmly to go home and get some sleep while he would quickly tidy up there. I was too tired to protest as I should have done. Therefore, my feeble attempts at persuading Tobias to let me finish off didn't get me anywhere.

'As I stepped out in the foyer, my attention was drawn to two young women who were standing there chatting and laughing loudly and who were obviously in no hurry to go home. They both wore summer dresses in bold colours and patterns that formed a stark contrast to the usual flower-patterned or uniform dresses the majority of the women wore in town. Both women wore strong make-up and high heels and wore their hair in graduated bobs that framed their oval-shaped faces perfectly. Just when I was about to step through the cinema's front door, the young blonde woman in a red-and-white dress saw me and shouted out, "Hello! Where do you come from? I haven't seen you earlier during the film."

'I was a little taken aback by this direct address, unsure of what she wanted from me. I turned back hesitantly and responded, "No, you wouldn't have. I'm the assistant projectionist here so I wouldn't sit in the cinema but do the work behind the scenes. May I help you with anything?"

'The blonde woman responded with a giggle and turned towards her friend whose bright yellow dress and shoes shone like the sun, with the dress's swirly pattern of different shades of yellow adding a dynamic element to her appearance. "Isn't that sweet, Tina? Such a polite gentleman – asking us whether he can help us," she said mockingly.

'I must have frowned and shown my displeasure about being laughed at and was just about to leave the cinema once again, when the blonde woman positioned herself in front of me and stretched out her hand, presumably as a peace offering.

'"I'm sorry," she said. "I didn't mean any harm. It's just so rare to meet a gentleman these days. You must think me so rude. My name is Lucy."

'As she said this, her blue eyes shone warmly and a smile emerged on her face that I can only call bewitching and seductive and that took me completely by surprise. I felt disarmed and the anger I had felt earlier vanished in an instant. "I'm Charles," I mumbled.

'She then signalled to her friend to join us, introduced her to me and added, "We were just thinking of going for a drink at the pub around the corner. Would you like to join us, Charles?"

'I slowly and automatically shook my head as I would never go for drinks without letting Annie know about it, particularly not with two young ladies I had only just met and whom Annie knew nothing about. I knew my responsibilities as a married man and certainly didn't want to give the girls the wrong impression. I said, "No, I can't. I need to go home and besides I'm too tired to be good company tonight anyway."

'Lucy evidently did not take no for an answer however. She exclaimed, "Oh, come on, Charles. It will be so much fun! You can tell us what your job entails and what films you like most. And you can order coffee if you're really so very tired. That will wake you up!"

'Her friend, Tina, started to look a bit embarrassed about her friend's insistent demeanour towards me whilst I was about to walk off after having my wishes ignored. But then I made the mistake of letting my eyes rest once more on her face, and the smile she gave me was even more dazzling than before and was devoid of any of her previously-employed mockery. Something else inside me, probably an animal instinct, took over and I said meekly, "Okay, I suppose I can come along for a short while for a drink and a chat."

'And this was how we went to the pub together for the first time with her friend. There, I learned that she and her friend lived at the other end of town and usually went to the neighbouring town where they worked, shopped and also occasionally went to the cinema rather than going out here. That certainly explained why I hadn't met them before. They, especially Lucy, weren't women I would have easily forgotten. They were too conspicuous and, in many ways, formed a strong contrast to their surroundings. Their ideas and ambitions clearly exceeded what our region could offer them: Both of them were shop assistants in one of the bigger department stores where they sold and advised on clothes and fashion in the women's section. They found the range of fashion they dealt with very limited however, which I immediately believed just by looking at their outfits that they had acquired on a trip to London. Fashion and design were at the centre of their mental world but they were longing to find a better outlet for their passion.

'I listened with interest to their big plans of one day opening a store in Paris with their self-designed clothes. They dreamt of the lifestyle there, picturing themselves sitting outside a street café with their newly coiffured hair with long, elegant cigarette holders in their hands. Right then, they embodied these ambitions by smoking cigarettes in a simultaneously staged and carefree-looking manner, tucking strands of hair behind their ears on a regular basis even though their hair was perfectly arranged.

'I suggested to them to go on some training course if they wanted to pursue this but they replied that they had already learned skills such as tailoring and seamstressing, which was all that was available to them, as fashion design was not something that was being taught in what they called the backwater they lived in.

'We talked about films for a long time and I was pleasantly surprised that Lucy and Tina were more knowledgeable with regards to foreign films than most other people I met and spoke to. In particular, they knew about many French and Italian actors and quizzed me about the latest releases they might be interested in. Their outlook was so much wider than what I expected from the local population that I thought they would probably appreciate having a chat with Tobias as well, as these were the kinds of conversations I was having with him. In fact, they seemed to notice things, for example cultural idiosyncrasies, that I had never picked up on when I had watched the same films. Their cosmopolitanism was both baffling and alluring due to its largely alien nature to me.

'Even though I had been very tired when we set off to the pub, I felt animated and very much alive during the time we spent in the pub and did not notice how two hours had quickly gone by until last orders were announced. None of us were inclined to leave just yet and while the women got themselves more gin-and-tonics after having refused my offer to buy them drinks, which was probably due to their emancipated attitude, I got myself a beer. I wasn't much used to drinking. Apart from the odd beer with my father after work sometimes or a beer or a glass of wine with Annie's or my family for Sunday lunch, I didn't normally drink alcohol and certainly not more than two drinks on any one occasion. On that evening, I must have had at least three and I felt definitely tipsy when we finally left the pub and had to concentrate hard in order to walk straight.

'When I was about to say good-bye to the two women by offering my right hand for a handshake, Lucy laughed in a way that reminded me of the ringing of tiny bells and before I quite realised what she was up to, she had already hugged me and placed a kiss on each of my cheeks.

'"There you are," she laughed. "Aren't we friends now, Charles? This is the French way of greeting and saying good-bye to each other. Don't you think it's so much nicer than our stiff English handshakes?"

'Her friend Tina and I were now placed in a position in which we felt we had to follow suit and awkwardly hugged each other albeit we didn't place kisses on our cheeks but merely mimed the action.

'When I arrived home late, I felt the pangs of conscience about having been out for so long without letting Annie know that I would return late. She knew that even if I had spent quite a bit of time tidying up and having a chat with Tobias, I would have normally come home much earlier, as I had informed her of the film screening times that night. When I came in, I found Annie in the living-room with her crocheting. She would normally have been in bed by this time on a weekday evening but she had evidently waited up for me.

'When I stepped into the living-room, Annie looked up at me and the relief and worry about my late arrival was written all over her face, which made me feel even worse. I stepped towards her, swallowed hard with discomfort and said, "Annie, I'm so sorry it's got so late. I didn't want you to worry and stay up for me. You need to rest." The realisation that she had spent some of the evening agonising over my wellbeing whilst I hadn't given her a thought during the time I spent in animated conversation with Lucy and Tina in the pub made me flinch.

"What happened?," she asked. "You normally call me if you're coming back later than usual.' There wasn't any accusation in her tone of voice, just confusion and puzzlement.

'I replied, "I came across some friendly cinema-goers at the end of the film, we started talking and they insisted on me joining them for a drink in the pub."

'Annie frowned in surprise. She wasn't a clingy or controlling person and since she had been unwell so frequently she had, if anything, become rather aloof. Her frown was clearly not disapproval of me for having had an evening out without her, but that I had failed to communicate with her about my intentions even when that decision had been made on the spur of the moment. In a way, her reaction made me hopeful, as it showed me that our relationship was still important to her, which I had – I have to admit shamefully – at times doubted in recent times.

'"Anyone I know? Any of the regulars?" Annie enquired.

'This was a justified assumption, as we knew most of the people in town who attended cinema performances, at least fleetingly.

'I shook my head, still feeling awkward and said, "No, I've never met them before. They live at the other end of town and usually go to the cinema in the neighbouring town."

'"A married couple?" Annie probed further.

'I could feel the blood rise to my head and blush, suspecting that my face was now probably of a deep crimson colour. However, I couldn't lie to Annie at that moment so I told her that I had gone out with two young women. Simultaneously, I tried hard to convince myself that there was nothing untoward about doing a bit of socialising with some people I hadn't encountered before and who might become new friends. I knew though that I was lying to myself if I viewed my evening from that perspective. I was aware that the seeds of betrayal had been sown.

'Annie looked at me for a few seconds before averting her gaze. She got up from her armchair and merely said, "I need to go to bed now, Charles." With these words, she ended our conversation and left me behind in the living-room with the lingering feeling of guilt, unable to gauge what she was really thinking.

'Two weeks passed before I saw Lucy and Tina again at the cinema. Although I didn't want to, I couldn't stop myself from thinking about Lucy and her unconventional attitude. Her coquettish demeanour was appealing and I started looking out for her between screenings, trying to spot her golden hair and her eyes that were the colour of the cloudless summer sky. When I finally did catch sight of her again, I was bedazzled by the smile she gave me when she detected me. That evening, we went for drinks again in the same pub but this time without her friend Tina, who claimed that she had to go home to do something important although I strongly suspected that that was just a pretext – probably suggested by Lucy – to give Lucy and myself some time together. This time, I did phone Annie though from the phone in the projectionist room to inform her that I would be returning late because I wanted to sort our film reels and check some of the technical equipment.

'Tobias gave me a long and meaningful look when I said this. I guess he must have overheard my conversation with the two young women earlier through the partially open door. He turned to me when I had finished my conversation with Annie and asked, "Charles, is everything alright with you and Annie?" He was fond of Annie and saw a lot of her at the beginning of our marriage when she often picked me up after work or walked me to my workplace before the start of my shift. He knew about the decline in her health and spirits and I had at one point mentioned the suspected cause, her childlessness, to him. He hadn't said much at the time but had quietly listened. When I hesitantly denied that things weren't right between Annie and myself, he said seriously, "Charles, be careful, please. I know that your marriage is not as easy-going and joyful as it was at the beginning in view of the changes Annie has undergone. But she is your wife and a lovely person who just needs a bit more emotional support right now. Please don't endanger your marriage to her. It's easy to get carried away if things are not all happy and temptation comes our way. But think of what you have in Annie."

'I mumbled something along the lines of not knowing what he meant, but I'd never been good at pretending and avoided looking at Tobias when he said this. I made a quick exit, but in times to come his words would echo in my mind.

'That evening in the pub, similarly to the pub evening two weeks earlier, time just flew by and, if anything, I became even more intrigued by Lucy. Her modern, feminist views reminded me of my mother's. The latter had always been ahead of her time. Still, my mother had found a way of being a respected part of our small town by settling down here, marrying and having a child, whilst Lucy had no such intentions. She didn't want to compromise on her beliefs and she was convinced that her cosmopolitanism could not be reconciled with the limitations of life where we lived. Marriage, to her, was and had always been a patriarchal arrangement that was unequal and had the subjugation of women as its foundation.

'Even though I personally didn't feel that passionate about issues of feminism – although I agreed with the concept of gender equality – I was hooked on every word Lucy said. It was the way she spoke with such animation about something she cared about, and her confidently radiating beauty that really had me in her thrall. I was like a captive who had been hypnotised and seemed to be lacking in reason and who did not have a will of his own.

'It probably wasn't surprising that our farewell turned out to be different from the previous one, which – not being used to having my cheeks fleetingly kissed by a stranger – I had already considered quite daring. She had walked to the cinema earlier, but as it was now late and dark, there wasn't a bus running in the next half hour and it was a fairly long walk, I decided to walk her home, pushing my bicycle, which I usually came to work with. I had expected a protest on Lucy's part to the effect that she was able to walk home by herself, but interestingly, she just gave me an inscrutable look and replied that if I wanted to accompany her, that was fine with her.

'Unexpectedly, she waited for me to reaffirm my resolution, which I did. In hindsight, I think she knew that me taking her home implied a lot more and was the next step that would lead to a long-standing affair. I believe that she waited for confirmation of my offer because she didn't want to coerce or lead me to anything that I didn't really want to do. Outside, it had started raining and I held her umbrella over her head with one hand whilst pushing the bike with the other hand. This proved to be a very wobbly enterprise as I found it hard to control both the umbrella and the bike. Lucy just laughed, telling me that it must look to others as if we were two drunks staggering along and finally took my arm to steady me a bit. I loved her laughter. It was contagious and soon I found myself laughing along with her and we didn't stop until we reached her street and found ourselves standing outside her flat.

'"Here we are," Lucy said light-heartedly. "Thanks for the company."

'I nodded but didn't say anything. We looked at each other for a few long moments before I felt the need to finally break the silence. "I enjoyed the evening," I murmured.

'Then Lucy gently put her arms around me.

'At first, I thought she would just give me the usual hug with a suggestion of kisses on the cheeks in the way Europeans would greet and say good-bye to each other.

'However, she paused at the end of the ritual with her face being only inches away from my own. It was then that I lost control over my impulses and instincts: Driven by an urge that was greater than my will, I came forward and met her bright red lips with mine before nudging them open to let our tongues explore each other. We stood there for quite some time kissing, which only left us wanting for more. I experienced such a rush of hormones inside me that I might have stumbled and fallen with the dizzy excitement and exhilaration of it all had we not held each other so closely that I felt her warm body pressed against mine with all its curves and soft and firm parts. By now, my manhood was highly aroused and I had to do something about it. I almost moaned, "What now? What now, Lucy?"

'Lucy gave me a fervent look and retorted, "It's up to you, Charles. You can go home or you can come upstairs with me. It's your decision."

'Again, she was giving me a choice, probably to make it clear that she wouldn't want to be held responsible for whatever might happen to my marriage if we became intimate. At the time though, it didn't feel like much of a choice. Instead, I felt at the mercy of uncontrollable forces being hard at work inside me.

'"Let's go up," I whispered in her ear.

'Once we entered her one-bedroom flat, I was struck by the bright colours that greeted me: The sofa was a bright red colour, the living-room curtains were in a matching cream-and-red pattern and there were vases and other decorative items on display in a range of colours. There were unusual pictures on the walls of women dressed in a style I hadn't come across before with short, sparkling dresses and feathers in their hair, carrying long cigarette-holders in their slender hands.

'When Lucy noticed my gaze resting on these women she laughed and explained that this was art deco style. Her hand was lightly placed on my upper arm and she gave me an exquisite smile when she asked, "A drink, Charles?"

'A drink was not what was on my mind at that moment though and, besides, I had certainly had enough to drink in the pub. All I wanted then was to hold her, touch her and feel her. Shaking my head, I drew her close to me again before she pulled me into the adjoining bedroom, which was fairly small being just about able to fit in a wardrobe with a mirror at its front, a chest of drawers, a small bedside table and a double bed with minimal floor space around it. Despite being relatively small, the room was unmistakably Lucy's, displaying a very similar style to that in the living-room: The walls were painted in bright yellow and there were feathers and feather-fans pinned to them, which reminded me of the feathers that the women in the pictures that I had previously looked at wore. The pillow cases and duvet cover were made of a cool, smooth, satin material and looked extravagant in their ruby red colour with an elaborate, dark border. I had truly entered a different world.

'However, I didn't spend much time dwelling on the setting I found myself in. Lucy and I fell onto the double bed at the same moment, pulling each other onto it. From there, things happened incredibly fast. We took off our clothes in seconds, our hands were stroking each other's bodies firmly until only a few minutes later I was inside Lucy. I had never lasted as long as I did with Lucy. Eventually, we both came at the same time with cries of fulfilment and relief and lay next to each other, spent but happy. It felt natural and there was a perfect synchronicity to it all, I thought at the time. I felt deliriously dizzy and elated and just wanted to lie there with Lucy forever. I lost all sense of time and place at that point and must have finally drifted off, as I was woken up by an involuntary nudge Lucy gave me when she rolled to the side and got up from bed to go to the toilet, as she explained when I gave her a puzzled look.

'After she had left the bedroom, I looked at my metal wristwatch, which I had put on the floor next to me. When I saw that the time was just past two in the morning, a sharp electric current ran through my brain and body, which dispelled any vestiges of either sleepiness or even the previously experienced ecstatic light-headedness. It was the middle of the night and I was not at home with Annie! This was the first time in the last few hours that I actually thought of home. My upper body shot to an upright position like a bolt of lightning and I realised what I had done. Earlier on, I had been so intoxicated that I had managed to push the reality of my married life out of the realm of my awareness. It had just vanished from my mental horizon and thus seemingly ceased to exist.

'I recall clearly how I broke into a sweat and hurriedly put my clothes back on and merely muttered to Lucy when she re-entered the bedroom that I really had to leave now and ran out of her flat. I barely took in any more how her initially disappointed facial expression changed to one of understanding of what was going on inside me and only caught a fleeting glimpse of a light nod on her part.

'Later on, I wondered when Lucy had realised that I was a married man and was surprised when she told me, when I did eventually ask her about it, that she had been aware of it since our very first pub visit together with her friend Tina, as she had quickly spotted my wedding ring. I questioned her then why she had started an affair with me in those circumstances, as this could hardly be described as ethical conduct. Lucy's stance was that I tried to put the blame on her for something that we both clearly wanted and were ready to embark on and that by doing so I denied my own needs and inclinations. She added that she had never put any pressure on me and did not force me into anything that I was not willing to do. Moreover, I hadn't been particularly transparent with her either about my marriage, she argued, having never mentioned it once before or even on that night when I broke my marriage vows. I saw that she had a point and whilst not abdicating her from responsibility for her part in the adultery, especially when she knew I was a married man, I knew that I could not seriously deny my own wrongdoing.

'Despite that painful insight, that night just turned out to be the beginning of my betrayal, which was fed by lies. I vividly recollect Annie's startled expression when I quietly sneaked into the bedroom like a thief at night and woke her up, despite my best efforts not to. I also recall my clumsy lies and excuses for coming back that late, claiming I had got carried away with the film reels, having tried to fix all the damaged ones and then playing them to check whether they worked again.

'Annie didn't respond to my awkward explanations in any way. She just turned to the other side and tried to go back to sleep again.

'I thought she would discuss the incident with me but she didn't mention it at all nor did she talk about it in the days, weeks and months that followed. Relations between us appeared to continue in the same way as they had been before that night. At least that's what I made myself believe. I guess I could have noticed changes in our relationship following that event had I been perceptive enough at the time and willing to face reality. Only much later did I become aware of how it was about then that she began to withdraw even further from me and kept communication to a minimum. I blamed another deterioration in her health for her silence and inwardness but of course I could have reflected on the reason for the continued decline in her health. As it was, her silence gave me a convenient excuse for meeting with Lucy again and again, telling myself that it was indifference towards our marriage that made her act like that.

'Did Lucy give me what was lacking at home – joy, comfort, happiness and a sense of being wanted and loved? Probably, but that cannot excuse my actions. I had experienced all of the above with Annie before and could not deal with the changes in our relationship.

'I didn't really talk about Lucy to Tobias, but he knew what was going on and struggled not to interfere too much, telling me off on occasions when Lucy was mentioned and sometimes being abrupt with me when we were working together. Our warm relationship suffered somewhat. And then Tobias died. Whilst he had become frailer in recent years and had developed a chronic cough, he had still been able to work for many hours during the week and I was not expecting his death.

'It therefore came as a shock when my mother came to the workshop one fine Sunday morning and asked me to take an urgent phone call. When I took the call inside the house, Tobias's neighbour identified himself in a grave voice so I was immediately on the alert, as I knew that he would only contact me if something serious had happened. Like Tobias, he was an elderly man and didn't have many visitors or people who looked after him. Sometimes, his daughter would see him but she didn't live locally so he saw much less of her than he would have liked. He had also suffered two heart attacks and was only just about able to live on his own. After having lived in the same house, but separate flats, for twenty years and having gradually extended short chats to longer conversations, they trusted each other enough to give the other a spare key to their flats in case something might happen and looked out for each other.

'On that morning, the neighbour knew that something was wrong with Tobias, as all the blinds in the flat were still lowered by ten o' clock and Tobias never failed to get up before seven o'clock in the morning. After having repeatedly knocked at Tobias's door and rang the doorbell without getting an answer, he had fetched the key to Tobias's flat, let himself in and found Tobias lying motionlessly in bed in his pyjamas. He was already cold to the touch and the neighbour phoned an ambulance straight away. Immediately afterwards, he contacted me.

'I trembled when he told me all this over the phone, felt hot tears running down my face and almost choked on my words when I thanked him for letting me know. I admired his composure: Despite being clearly distressed, he had the presence of mind to do all the right things and somehow keep it together. I, on the other hand, slid down on the wall behind me until my mother found me sitting on the floor in the corridor in deep misery and comforted me in silence by putting her arms around me and holding me close as a mother would do with a young child that was distressed.

'The aftermath of Tobias's death was awful: Having found temporary staff covering his shifts, I missed his bent figure and his shuffling gait as well as his clear, all-knowing eyes so much that it hurt. More than once did I have to run out of the projectionist's room in a hurry to rush to the toilet where I gave free reign to my tempestuous tears. The only comfort – if I can call it that – was that Annie and I took in Tobias's old cat Pete. It was Annie in particular who formed a strong bond with him: She spoke to him and established a closer rapport with him over the following three years until his death than she had with many people.

'The grief over losing Tobias should have brought Annie and me closer again, rekindling our former bond, but this did not happen. Although I was now in a position to relate to Annie's grief more through my own, I refused to dwell on it or talk much about it and instead tried to fill that new hole in my life by going wild in my continued affair with Lucy. Thus, our secret relationship carried on until something completely unexpected happened a year later that served as a sharp reprimand of our careless behaviour.

'It was a glorious day in mid-June and the sun still shone brightly albeit with a warmer glow and a less blinding intensity than it had done during the day when I finished my work for the day at the cinema at nine o'clock and cycled to Lucy's place as I regularly did on a Friday evening. I felt happy after we'd had a good turnout for the screening of that night's film and I loved the warm summer weather. I was looking forward to sharing the lightness and joy with Lucy and pressed the doorbell with a smile of expectation on my face.

'However, that smile was quickly wiped off my face after I had entered the flat, surprised that I wasn't welcomed at the door as I usually was, and found Lucy sitting in a slightly hunched manner on the red sofa. Her posture struck me instantly as incongruous with her personality and her customary demeanour: Lucy had always struck me as someone who carried her head high whilst standing or walking in the most upright position one can fathom. Her posture always expressed a great presence and oozed with confidence, poise and determination. In contrast, the crumpled figure on the sofa seemed down-hearted and dejected. I was even more alarmed when Lucy looked up at me for a few moments and I detected signs that she had cried a short while earlier. Her cheeks were damp, her mascara was smeared around her eyes and the foundation she used was forming blotches. Moreover, her clear blue eyes that normally shone with mischief, playfulness and coquettish cheekiness had lost their shine and were almost dull now.

'I stood still for a few seconds, unsure what to do or how to react to this untypical scenario until my instincts guided me towards Lucy and I sat down on the sofa next to her and put my arm around her shoulders. "Lucy, what on earth is the matter? What happened?"

'She didn't immediately reply. Instead, my question was greeted with a silence that I would never have associated with Lucy. I was just about to repeat my question when she said, in a raspy voice so unlike her normally high and clear one that I had to look at her to ascertain that it was in fact her who was speaking, "I'm pregnant, Charles."

'She delivered that sentence in such a matter-of-fact, almost toneless voice that the importance of the message was at first lost on me. When it did eventually sink in and I became aware of the seriousness of it, I was stunned and unable to respond in any way. The golden light of the sun, which now started to take on an orange tint, stood in all its beauty in stark contrast to the dark shadow that had suddenly descended over our affair. Our conversation that evening was halting and for the first time since I started coming to Lucy's flat, we were not intimate with each other. All thought of that was gone for the moment in the face of the repercussion of our previous intimacies. We held each other, though, trying to figure out what to do next.

'"I'll be getting an abortion, of course," Lucy said, and I could hear the apprehension of undergoing the procedure in her voice.

'Having grown up with Christian values that upheld the sanctity of all life, which therefore must be protected and cherished including the lives of the unborn, I was aghast at the thought of Lucy having an abortion. I expressed my feelings about the matter to her, but Lucy just looked at me sadly and retorted, "But what would be the alternative, Charles? If I had the baby, the latter would be visible proof of your infidelity, which also contravenes Christian values and, if your family learned about it, there would be even more woe and suffering. Can you not see that there is no sense in bringing this baby into the world? And what would I do with a baby? I have no maternal inclinations and can definitely not see myself raising a child. It wouldn't be me. Besides, what would become of all my plans?"

'I could see how a baby would further complicate the situation I was in, as a married man who was having a secret affair. However, hearing Lucy's open declaration that she was not the maternal type, which she seemed to employ not just as another excuse but in fact as a staunch justification for not having a child in general, and not the child she was pregnant with in particular, surprised me in its audacity at a time when most women would unquestioningly adopt the role of mother when the opportunity arose. It might have required courage and a fair amount of independent thinking to put one's individual ambitions or career plans before the pursuit of founding a family, but I couldn't appreciate these attributes in this context. Just then I thought of Lucy as incredibly selfish for saying all these things.

'I didn't stay much longer as any further discussions about the matter would not have been constructive that night. Our feelings were too raw, our positions on the issue too different and I knew that I needed some time and space to form a clear view, as my current position was ambiguous even if I was leaning towards Lucy having the child.

'On my way home, I regarded the descending, deepening darkness as a reflection of the enormous upset that had suddenly entered our lives. I'm not normally a superstitious person but in this instance, I was convinced the universe was holding up a mirror to our private catastrophe. It was a strange echo of Annie's superstitious trepidation at our wedding when nobody caught the bridal bouquet. At the time, I had thought of her fear as silly and unfounded. However, all the sadness and ill-health that had occurred since Annie's desperate longing for a child had been confounded could maybe be seen as the ill-luck predicted by that sign – as she saw it – at our wedding after all. I didn't know whether that was the case. I wasn't sure of anything any longer. All my certainties were called into question and I felt in danger of being crushed by the weight of the descending debris of my shattered soul.

'Simultaneously, rage was rising inside me about Lucy regarding a life in the making begotten by me as a disaster and an upset. I couldn't quite believe that I was close to becoming a father to a son or a daughter but Lucy would have none of it. There was a visceral response to this on my part that made my body tremble. What a bitter irony it was that I had fathered a child accidentally with a woman who did not want one rather than with my wife who so badly longed for, but could not have, one!

'When I reached home, Annie was still up. I had noticed with relief that she made use of the long, bright summer evenings by keeping busy with her tapestries for whose creation she strongly favoured natural daylight. She had virtually abandoned her previous habit, from the winter months, of going to bed early in the evenings and spending much of her time there during the day. She was just drawing the heavy, floor-length living-room curtains and Martha, who had kept her company for the last few hours, was packing up her own materials and work. They both turned to me when they caught sight of me, and Martha's startled expression told me that I was not successfully concealing my shock about what I had learned earlier at all.

'Martha asked anxiously, "Uncle Charles, what is the matter? Has anything terrible happened?"

'I quickly tried to conceal my agitation and ventured a smile instead but guessed that it was far from convincing. "No, no, Martha, everything is fine." And as if to prove to myself that things were indeed as they should be, I reiterated, "All is good." Then, trying to deflect her and Annie's attention away from my mental state, I asked them in an attempt at cheerfulness, "How have you two got on with your work? Have you worked on the two tapestries in the making with their beautiful colours again?"

'Martha still studied me quietly. She was a perceptive child and not easily fooled when someone pretended something was the case and it wasn't, but although not reassured by my pronouncements, she chose to comply with my distraction technique. "Yes, we have. We got quite a lot done. Do you want to see it?"

'I nodded, relieved that her attention had moved to other matters. She pulled out her tapestry again and unfolded it. Even though it was only half-done, it looked stunning and I could see a beautiful autumnal scene in which the trees showed off their stunningly colourful autumn foliage and the people who walked amongst them held brightly coloured umbrellas to find shelter from the steady drizzle that fell from the dark clouds. It was a scene you could easily step into, in your imagination, and lose yourself in. I was impressed by my niece's ability to conjure up a setting and a scene through her craft that looked so realistic and was so detailed, especially when considering her young age. For a few moments, I almost forgot my worries and just became immersed in what was in front of me in a way that all good storytelling takes you to other places. It was then that I realised that my young niece wasn't only very talented but a storyteller at heart and therefore a truly kindred soul. I smiled for the first time in many hours and said that I would like to join the walkers but would need a brightly-coloured umbrella as well.

'Martha laughed when she heard me say this and promised that I would get a bright orange umbrella that blended in with the leaves. Then she hugged Annie to say good-bye and I took her back home, as it was well past her usual bedtime and her parents had already been very generous when they let her stay at ours until the sunset.

'Coming back home after I had delivered Martha safely at her family's place, my fear and anger returned but Annie didn't probe further into my mental state after I had told her I was alright in response to her question whether I wasn't feeling well. I'm sure she knew that I wasn't honest. You might want to ask why she didn't insist on finding out what bothered me. Did she sense and possibly fear my anger? Did she suspect my infidelity and link it to my present mood but by not enquiring any further protect herself from the pain the confirmation of my affair was likely to cause her? This was not a consideration I had at the time but one that I have adopted fairly recently with the benefit of hindsight. Then, again, I took the absence of questions for indifference on her part and for a sign of the decline in our marriage relations. Today I am certain that whilst Annie had to some extent distanced herself from human interactions, she remained silent for reasons of self-preservation. She had probably reached an emotional threshold to which she needed to pay attention, if she didn't want to completely disintegrate.

'The following week brought no relief to my frenzied state of mind. I didn't see or hear anything from Lucy until the telephone rang at lunchtime on Saturday. It was – I thought at first – a lucky coincidence that I was in and took the phone rather than Annie although thinking back now, it maybe wasn't. Lucy knew when I finished work with my father on a Saturday and what time I would leave again for the cinema. Besides, Annie rarely picked up the phone any longer even when she was the only one at home, which was difficult to understand for her parents and siblings and which they sometimes lamented in my presence. When I then heard Lucy's voice on the phone, my anger welled up again and before she had time to say much, I cut her short and almost shouted at her never to call me at home again and put down the receiver. The only thing she had a chance to say before I ended the call so quickly and abruptly was that we had to talk, with some obvious urgency in her voice. I didn't recognise myself in my behaviour. It was as if I had changed into someone else and that this change was definitely for the worse and felt entirely alienating to me.

'The weeks passed in the blink of an eye as I filled my already busy days even more, going out with my bicycle after work in the evenings to expend all my surplus energy, which was a product of my inner turmoil, until I came home exhausted, fell into bed and was asleep shortly afterwards. I couldn't bring myself to confront Lucy's pregnancy again and, instead, did everything to take my attention off it, maybe subconsciously harbouring the irrational hope that it would then just go away. Of course, I noticed nevertheless that Lucy had stopped her regular cinema visits and it was hard work to ignore her absence.

'However, there came a point when I couldn't ignore the situation any longer after I had repeatedly had nightmares of Lucy undergoing an abortion during which not just the unborn child, but Lucy herself, died, bleeding to death as a result of a botched job. I had heard enough of such procedures that ended tragically to be alarmed and worried. I hoped that Lucy was more sensible than to go to any unregistered abortionist as I call them, who performed abortions illegally. When I found out from my mother that it was not necessarily that easy to get an abortion despite the – at the time – recently introduced Abortion Act I wondered whether Lucy had in fact much choice in how to get an abortion if she was determined to go through with it. If Lucy couldn't make the point that either her own life or the life of the unborn child were in danger or at least were likely to be harmed, there wouldn't be a way for her to get this done with legal means.

'I couldn't extract more information from my mother without arousing her suspicions as my pretext of trying to educate myself a bit more in our legal history would not have been convincing. My anger and shock had by now almost completely given way to fear, not just for the baby but also of losing Lucy and of maybe already having lost her.

'One day, therefore, after finishing my shift at the picture house, I took my bicycle and cycled to Lucy's flat at a fast speed. I barely took time to lock my bike to the fence around the house's front garden before I pressed the bell to her flat with such an urgency that I didn't let go of it for probably about a minute. Despite my impatient action, nothing happened. Seconds lengthened into minutes without receiving an answer. I was just about to ring the doorbell again when the front door opened and Lucy's elderly female neighbour from across the landing appeared. They knew each other by sight and had on the odd occasion engaged in some small talk. She looked at me wide-eyed, saying that she had heard the bell ring opposite with such insistence that she felt she should check whether there was an emergency. I'm sure curiosity played a big part in it, too, but of course I didn't comment on this observation.

'She said, "I saw Lucy come in earlier. I don't know why she wouldn't answer the doorbell."

'I know that she thought of me as Lucy's boyfriend and always looked a bit baffled by how secretive we were about our relationship, letting go of each other's hands when we noticed her and retreating into Lucy's flat as quickly as possible. She must have thought of our behaviour as incongruous with Lucy's personality but maybe she thought we believed her to be old-fashioned about a young couple spending long evenings at the girl's place on their own before the wedding had taken place. I'm sure that right at that moment she suspected that we had had a lovers' tiff and I was here to make up with her. I didn't bother to explain anything – the less she knew the better – and merely nodded at her, walked past her up the stairs and then knocked loudly on Lucy's door. I was about to identify myself and shout out that she had to open the door as we needed to talk when the door to the flat suddenly opened a few inches and I saw Lucy emerge in the door and got a shock at the sight of her. She was in a creased satin nightdress, her usually immaculately styled hair was dishevelled and unwashed, and her make-up-free face was blotchy and barely recognisable. Instead of a woman who placed great emphasis on her looks, I faced one who was neglecting herself. The transformation was stark and to some extent it reminded me of Annie when she was at her worst. I quickly pushed the thought of Annie aside, addressing Lucy in a tone of alarm once we were in the flat and the door was closed. "What on earth is happening, Lucy? What have you done?"

'It seemed that some of my worst fears had come true. My mind was racing whilst Lucy slumped down on the red sofa: She must have had an illegally obtained abortion and the shock about the whole process had now caught up with her. Considering how ill she looked, she might actually be suffering from an infection as a result of a terribly executed procedure and probably needed urgent medical attention.

'Lucy's voice was almost without inflection and so raspy that I had to strain my ears to understand what she was saying. "Is that all you have to say? Is that all you want to know? What have *I* done?" She laughed bitterly and grimaced in disdain. 'What have *you* done, Charles? You cut me off on the phone when we should have talked, you haven't come around once since I told you the news about my pregnancy and by doing that you have basically done what men tend to do – run way if there are issues to be resolved and let the woman deal with them on her own."

'I swallowed and once again felt anger join the fear that had gripped me for some time now. I only just about managed not to burst out that she, in fact, normally liked dealing with things on her own and had made it quite clear to me that she should be the one who decided on that life inside her, given the fact that it was her body it was growing in. Although I managed to suppress a comment to that effect, I was bristling. Something dark took possession of me and I burst out whilst towering over Lucy, "So you killed my child. You did manage to take the life of an innocent, helpless baby, which was my flesh and blood! You aren't just careless and selfish, you are a murderer as well!" I hurled these words at Lucy and they must have hit her like bullets fired from a powerful gun.

'For a few moments, she stared at me and remained on the sofa without moving, as if paralysed, before she rose from it with tremors running through her body. She gave me the coldest of stares I had ever encountered and that I wouldn't have believed her lively, sparkling eyes to be capable of and said in a steely voice that sent shivers down my spine, "Leave! Leave my place immediately! How dare you! How dare you say such things to me!"

'I was walking backwards and about to open the door to her flat when she added, "And for your information, I lost the baby! I had a miscarriage less than a week ago and it was awful."

'I stopped and looked at her as I was trying to take in what she had said but she opened the door, pushed me out and screamed, "Go! And stay away from me, Charles!"

'I was reeling when I made my way down the staircase and was fortunate enough not to encounter Lucy's curious neighbour again.

'Although Lucy and I gradually resumed our affair over the next year because the attraction was still there between us and did not want to be denied, something had changed between us since the events of Lucy's pregnancy and miscarriage. It was hard to put my finger on what it exactly was. Maybe our relations were less carefree, maybe there was a relative lack of trust between us now. At some point, I discovered that I had stopped being the only man in Lucy's life and confronted her with it, but Lucy only replied that she was not the only woman in my life either, pointing out that I had absolutely no right to question her about her polygamy, adding that she was of the opinion that monogamy was vastly overrated and led more often than not to boredom and frustration.

'Moreover, Tobias's old cat Pete died during that period, which wasn't merely another sad event, it also was a big blow to Annie, who had regarded him as her closest companion. This did, of course, nothing to improve her frail health and made me worry even more about her.

'Work, especially my job at the cinema, was the only thing then that made me truly forget my worries and concerns and I was lucky that Tobias's successor was a man I got on well with and was happy for me to take ownership of some tasks, in this way demonstrating his confidence in my abilities. That being said, we kept our relationship on a purely professional level and I did miss the friendship I had established with Tobias.

'Finally, ten years after Lucy and I had begun our affair, the day arrived when Lucy left our rather quiet and picturesque part of the world and moved to London. I guess it had always been on the cards considering Lucy's cosmopolitan way of thinking, her bohemian lifestyle and her keen interest in fashion. In some ways, I was surprised it had taken her so long to leave. I had sometimes nudged her over the years that she was not doing anything with her ambitions and talents and that she should try harder to realise her dreams. What I didn't see at the time was that she was afraid to make that big leap of trying to establish herself professionally by moving to London on her own, guessing that she would possibly at least initially struggle with paying her rent and would have to budget very carefully. It wouldn't cross my mind during our time together that Lucy was anything but daring, confident, strong and independent although I should have realised at the time of her pregnancy and miscarriage that she had a vulnerable side to her. It's easy to observe only a person's most prevalent characteristics and form an image of the person in our minds based on these, but we rarely become aware of how reductive that image is.

'I knew that she initially moved in with her cousin who had lived in London all her life. The few letters we exchanged after her move mentioned how she started to contact some designers and began to put a portfolio together with what she had done so far. Simultaneously, she was looking into applying for a fashion and design course once she had earned enough money from the waitressing and shop work she had found herself in London to pay for it. She told me in her letters that it was hard to get into what she wanted to do without already having a name in the field or connections. I was glad for her, though, that she had made the leap and worked hard towards becoming a designer. I had never seen her truly apply herself to something even when she had talked about her interests.

'Our communication ended about two months after she had moved. She just didn't respond to my letters any longer. In the end, I think it was better that way. Our affair had already lasted too long and I hoped for her sake that she was happy with her new life in the capital.

'I have, however, often thought back to our last meeting at her place. We were sitting amongst her packed boxes and there was a sombre mood between us. I don't know what I expected but I seemed to be looking for an answer – answers to our affair, what it was we had between us, what we were looking for in the other person and what we maybe didn't get. In my search for answers to these questions I asked Lucy point-blank, "Lucy, what did you see in me that you wanted or needed during all these years?"

'She looked at me in surprise and swept a loose strand of hair back behind her ear before producing her crystal clear, melodious laughter that I had always been so fond of. "Isn't that obvious, Charles? Sex, of course."

'I had long since stopped being shocked by statements like this one by Lucy and responded unperturbed, "You had that with other men, too, and you didn't have such a long…" I was searching for the right term. "…affair, relationship or whatever you want to call it with them. So what else attracted you to me? What else did you need from me?"

'Lucy smiled but had to pause and think for a moment before she said, "I guess I found you cute. Maybe I liked your innocence."

'I frowned at this and replied, "And now you're making fun of me. Be serious for once."

'She replied, "Oh, you wouldn't want me to be serious, Charles." And then she resumed with a perspicacity that I hadn't suspected her capable of, "You relished the light-hearted banter and play we had together because there wasn't enough of that in your home life and you were craving joy like a drowning man was yearning fervently for a rescue team to arrive. I guess I was also searching for my opposite in you to achieve some kind of balance. It might surprise you but I saw –

despite being unfaithful to your wife – a steadiness and rootedness in you that I never had."

'"So we've looked for what we couldn't find in ourselves in the other person to complement us?" I pondered.

'Lucy retorted quietly, "I wouldn't use the word complement, as I believe we are whole people as we are and can find in ourselves what we're looking for if we look long and hard enough. Sometimes that's hard though and then we're searching for what we need or want externally – usually in other people, as we have done.'

'When I thought about her words occasionally in the years that followed, I came to the conclusion that she had a point.

'After Lucy had moved away, I found myself spending much more time at home with Annie in the evenings, time that I would have previously spent with Lucy. Also, advances in technology that involved amongst other things the decrease in film reels that had to be handled by us projectionists left me with additional time on my hands. Being around Annie more brought us a little bit closer again. It was a sense of comfortable familiarity that we shared rather than times of dizzying rapture and excitement and I guess this was something to be valued as well. After all, I realised that I couldn't really expect to rekindle what we had in the early days or years of our relationship and marriage, especially because Annie's health was not improving. Whilst she was generally unwell, I most feared the periods of severe ill health when she was in so much pain and so distraught that she only managed to briefly get out of bed with my or someone else's help. It was heart-breaking and disturbing to see this happening.

'The years passed in this vein. We sometimes saw her family, but her nieces and nephews were growing up and lived their own lives and Annie had let contact with them slip, as I guess – apart from her illness being a factor that contributed to her being aloof – she didn't always want to be reminded of her siblings delighting in their children when we had none of our own. Martha was the only one who kept coming regularly to us and with whom she truly connected.

'Martha, unsurprisingly, got into the sewing and tailoring trade and started working locally at first. However, her talent and dexterity with fabrics could not be fully exploited at her workplace in our small town. In this way, she resembled Lucy. Like Lucy, she also hesitated to leave and move away, but in Martha's case it was mostly her strong bond with her family and to some extent her rootedness in the place she grew up in and less the fear of financial hardship in a big city that made it difficult for her to start somewhere else.

'Nevertheless, she did go to Exeter in her mid-twenties where she had successfully applied at a store that produced most of its own fabric goods, from clothes to blankets and wall hangings by employing talented staff who made them with much care and skill. Martha was amazed when she was hired there, as she had not done all the training and courses that most of the other applicants had completed. In fact, when her mother had told her about the vacancy, which she had spotted when she was in Exeter to do some errands, and pointed out how suited she would be for the position, she had initially just shaken her head and informed her mother that she barely met the essential – not to speak of the desirable – person specifications. She didn't even have a portfolio, which was absolutely key to the role. Elaine and the rest of the family, Annie and myself included, did not allow her to see this as an insurmountable obstacle that would stop her from applying for it. After convincing her that she had done all the work required to create a portfolio, she did indeed compile one and took her chance, and we were delighted for her when we heard that she was offered the position. The samples she had shown the senior staff at the interview must have truly impressed them. Of course, we had expected nothing less from them.

'Although Martha thrived, in some ways, on using more of her skills and talents at work, feeding off other talented colleagues' ideas and work, attending numerous professional development courses that were paid for by her workplace as they were directly relevant to her work, she found the transition to Exeter challenging. For a long time, she suffered from terrible homesickness and she came home whenever she was not at work even when she had to study for her courses. Rarely did she not manage to come over to see us for a visit on these occasions and she always told Annie in detail what she was currently working on and what she was learning. Annie gave her her fullest attention even when she was in pain. I think she almost forgot her pain when she was raptly listening to Martha. There was an acute keenness in Annie to learn to create what Martha described and showed her. It was strange to see that the roles from the past were now reversed and that it was now Martha who had taken on the role of the teacher and Annie that of the pupil. What truly pleased me was how deep the women's bond was and how alive Annie became when it came to their shared interest.

Her depression always lifted when she and Martha talked about, and were immersed in, their handiwork. Her curiosity and ability to enjoy something truly gained the upper hand then and I loved to see her like this.

'These lighter times Annie enjoyed were harder to sustain and became more infrequent when Martha met a young man at the age of thirty. He had recently started working at the store and after having had some interactions with each other, he asked her out. Martha was a very attractive young woman, but her quiet and reserved nature, which only became more animated when she was around family members, had unintentionally discouraged men from making any advances, probably out of fear that they might be rejected. However, this man was unafraid of a possible rejection on her part and they found that they got on very well and he made Martha laugh.

'We met him occasionally when Martha came for a visit with him and we liked him well enough. He was charming, engaging and funny and it wasn't hard to see what Martha saw in him. Unfortunately – albeit understandably – Martha came around to see us much less frequently now, as the couple spent more time together in Exeter during most of their days off.

'I worried what the impact of the decrease in the number of her visits would be on Annie. As I expected, I saw some decline in her well-being, but it wasn't as pronounced as I initially feared. I think the reason for that was that Annie was still driven to create more by implementing more of the skills and techniques she had learned from her niece. That motivation carried and sustained her.

'Nevertheless, I was glad when Martha continued to come regularly again when her relationship ended after two years. I know it sounds selfish and of course I was sorry for Martha that the relationship hadn't worked out, but Annie's welfare and our home life took priority for me. Martha never really let on what the reason for the break-up had been – at least I hadn't been informed – and it was not my place to pry. All I can say is that their work with fabrics in each other's company had a therapeutic effect on both of them.

'Watching Martha and Annie over the years, I became aware of my own need to become deeply involved in something I felt passionate about. Yes, I loved my projectionist's work but, as indicated earlier, the work hours I got there had diminished and sometimes I didn't quite know what to do with myself on a Sunday when Martha often spent a few hours with Annie. I became restless and was looking for a project but without a clear idea of what it might be that I would find.

'It was at this time that I became more aware of the changes in our neighbourhood. I could detect more signs of social deprivation, which was likely to be the result of the diminishing presence of certain trades and industries that made it hard for people to earn a living with the skills they had. Another cause for this plight was the decreasing importance of the institution of marriage and the erosion of family values, which manifested themselves in an increase in divorces, more single-parent families and the stress and emotional burden that went along with these developments. I started seeing more children hanging around outside who – due to boredom and frustration – turned on others, got into petty theft and were generally regarded as a nuisance at best and a waste of space at worst. They presented an image of a lost youth and every time I passed them I thought how regrettable this was.

'It wasn't until one day we showed a film at the cinema that was met with particular excitement by our audience who talked about it intently when walking through the foyer – while I briefly passed through – towards the exit that an idea formed in my mind: If it was this passion for and involvement in a particular story that was so rewarding for people and gave such meaning to their lives, why not draw the children and young people in my neighbourhood into this world to give them some perspective, to enrich their lives and to show them that there was beauty and meaning to be found? With that thought, I found a new and vital project.

'I made the decision to build an extension to our home, which I would then use as a small, private cinema or screening space. I used my manual skills to challenge myself in doing the work as much as possible by myself. I was pleased when I succeeded in adding the extension in a relatively short timeframe. Getting the equipment also proved less problematic than I had at first anticipated, as we had some older equipment at the picture house that we barely used any longer and that I could take, and the few items that I had to buy were affordable thanks to my boss giving me special deals. Although he had been worried that my project would keep customers away from our picture house screenings when I first told him about my plan, he was quickly reassured that this would not happen when I explained that these children and youths would not come to the cinema in the first place due to their lack of money. I would offer them something for free, which they would otherwise not be in a position to enjoy.

'As my boss liked to do the Sunday afternoon screenings and it was now sufficient to have just one person doing them, I decided to start off my 'private' screenings on Sunday afternoons. I had partly bought, partly been given, some film reels – many older but also a few relatively new ones – that covered different genres and subjects and that I was determined to put to good use. The main obstacle now was to entice the youths to come to the screenings. They never seemed willing to engage in any non-confrontational conversations with an adult. When I described the dilemma to Annie and Martha one Sunday afternoon when we were all sitting together in the living-room, the women busily working away on their fabrics, they both agreed that I needed some colourful leaflets to attract their attention to the proposed screenings, ideally with some slogans promising adventures and excitement. We worked on them together until we had produced a small pile of leaflets, each unique as they were hand-drawn and – written, unconventional and – even if not professional in their appearance and finish – fun to look at: The colours and motifs were bright and the slogans sassy and curiosity-arousing.

'I was pleased with them and used the next opportunity I had to hand them out, thus inviting the young people in my neighbourhood to the first screening a few days later. I didn't get too much of a reaction after distributing them, but at least the youngsters stopped whatever they were doing to inspect the unusual invitation. Some of the teenagers sounded dismissive about what they said would just amount to be a 'kiddie thing', thus trying to maintain their cool and ostentatious superiority; others were suspicious of my motives behind the invitation, which made me sad to see, as it appeared that to these youngsters every action was based on a selfish, possibly harmful intent on the part of the person who carried it out. I had to leave it at that and hoped that curiosity got the better of at least some of them who would turn up on the day.

'I had been warned by my boss and Annie that it was a risk to invite these adolescents who could be rather challenging and who didn't shy away from criminality, as there was the possibility of them going wild and destroying my meticulously-assembled equipment. Whilst I understood these concerns, I reassured them that I would establish ground rules right from the beginning and maintained that it was a risk worth taking.

'When the time of the screening came on Sunday afternoon, nobody was waiting outside the extension. I had set up all my equipment inside and chosen an adventure film that I believed would be the most likely one to capture the attention of an audience that was not known to sit still for any length of time, playing truant more often than not and shouting over each other. I hadn't anticipated big numbers but I had hoped that a few of the youngsters would show up. I waited for a few minutes until I saw a small boy in rather scruffy clothes and unkempt ginger hair, who hadn't seemed to make recent contact with a shower or bath, shuffle up to me hesitantly, clearly unsure whether he should approach further or retreat.

'"Hey!" I called out to him and gave him a smile.

'He didn't show any reaction and now stood stock still, his facial expression assuming an even more guarded look.

'"Are you coming to watch a film?"

'The boy hesitated again before he nodded.

'"That's fantastic. You can come closer. I'm Charles. I'm the projectionist."

'His confused look prompted me to explain further, "I'm the one who shows you the film."

'The red-haired boy nodded in understanding but still didn't say anything so I said, "What's your name? It's nicer to know each other's names if we're going to share an experience such as watching this film together."

'"Anton," he at last responded.

'"You mean Anthony?" I enquired.

'"No, Anton."

'"Are your parents German?"

'"No. They just liked the name."

'I pondered this for a second before I commented, "I understand. It is, after all, a fine name." Then I added, "Where are your friends? Did they not want to come and watch a movie, too?"

'Anton shrugged his shoulders so I said, "Well, it seems to be just you and me then, Anton. Do you want to come inside and make yourself comfortable?"

'He was seriously considering this when I saw a handful of children approach us. They were much more forthcoming than Anton had been, asking immediately about that film that I had mentioned to them.

'I told them that we were just about to start and that I wouldn't let any latecomers in once the film had started as I would be busy then and if others opened the door for anyone who was late I had no control over who came in. The children looked a little puzzled. They had obviously not grown up being taught the idea of timekeeping and apparently thought it only existed in connection with school, which they didn't always attend anyway.

'Before we went in, I introduced myself to them as I had done to Anton earlier, made them introduce themselves and then I explained the ground rules of what they could and couldn't do in the small film theatre after welcoming them. And they observed them on the whole, watching the film excitedly but reigning themselves in when they were about to become too loud and I made shushing sounds. They also managed to watch the movie from start to finish without running around. In fact, after the end of the film, they remained seated on the wooden benches that I had put in there as if waiting for more to come. They had clearly been absorbed in the plot. I asked them how they found the film and encouraged them to articulate what they liked and didn't like about it. They clearly weren't used to being asked for their opinions or about their preferences so it took a little while until I elicited some responses from them. Eventually, they left and I felt they looked brighter, having a glow in their eyes that I hadn't seen before.

'In the evening, I told Annie that I was happy about how it had gone. Half a dozen children was not too bad a start for the first screening. I had hoped that I would also attract some adolescents to the screenings in the future. I also voiced my concern over Anton appearing particularly neglected and also quite isolated.

'Annie smiled after she had listened to my impressions of the afternoon as well as to my concerns. She smiled much more these days. It was obvious how happy she was working away on her fabrics and sharing this creative time with her niece and she was well enough to delight in me pursuing a project in which I wholeheartedly believed. Her eyes beamed as they used to in the early days of our relationship as she told me she was positive that Anton would turn out just fine, especially now that I could keep an eye on his well-being and development, and that the older boys and girls would attend screenings as well soon.

'And Annie was right. The children who had attended the first screening came back and in the course of a few weeks some of the adolescents started to join them after listening to marvellous tales of films the former had watched. Initially, there were some behavioural issues with some of the young people but I managed to get through their protective layer of rebellion and cool play not just by setting boundaries and reiterating the rules whenever needed, but also by showing them that I was glad they were here, that I valued their views and that they were important. Anton often stayed behind for a chat with me and I formed a particularly close and trusting relationship with him. The withdrawn and timid child started to blossom. He still wore his old clothes, but Annie had taken it upon herself to wash and mend them and he had started to wash himself and his hair after I had complimented him on his fine skin and beautiful hair, telling him that I would love to see more of them after he had undergone a proper wash and had shampooed his hair. And a fine lad he looked after he had started to take his personal hygiene more seriously: His hair shone like the rays of the setting sun and was contrasted by his clear, milky-white skin that was interspersed with playful, little freckles.

'I achieved what I had set out to achieve: The young people who I saw regularly at my Sunday film screenings developed in new and wonderful ways. They came to love the tales they saw on screen and understood the beauty of imaginary worlds and plots. They were less aggressive and confrontational and more hopeful, gradually gaining a better perspective on things. I saw many of the children and teenagers eventually get into a trade and make something of themselves despite their difficult upbringing and this made me incredibly happy.

'Little Anton started work at a printer's shop where he learned everything about the printing business. Since he had been introduced to storytelling through film, he found he was too impatient to wait for another film a week later so he brought me some picture books and I taught him how to read properly. He made rapid progress, applying himself to master this new skill because he realised that he would unlock more stories, which were the only true treasures to him. He quickly moved from picture books with very little and simple text to books that only consisted of text and that at times contained long and complex sentences. As printed paper was the medium through which he learned about these stories, paper and print attained a special status for him. Soon he had made the resolution that he wanted to be instrumental to the process of printing and this was how he chose his trade.

'For seventeen years my life continued happily in this vein, seeing children and adolescents come and go, enjoying the screenings with them, the talks and the laughter and feeling generally fulfilled. Annie, on the whole, remained animated; severe bouts of pain and depression were rarer even if her health was still fragile. I rarely thought of Lucy any longer.

'Then life suddenly took a catastrophic turn, a turn from which I have been unable to recover to this day. I was seventy-two and enjoyed my retirement, which I took a few years ago. This might come as a surprise considering how much work I had done over the decades, not just in my father's carpentry business that I had eventually taken over when father became too old to work any longer with the support of a newly hired carpenter, but also at the cinema in town and the screenings at the annexe. However, energy reserves decline with advancing age and eventually one needs more and longer periods of rest. Saying that, I still did some work at the cinema and I now did private screenings for the youngsters in the neighbourhood on both Saturdays and Sundays. I spent much of the extra time I had with Annie. We watched many films at home and listened to radio programmes and even if Annie didn't always pay full attention to what was shown or broadcast because she more often than not concentrated on her fabric work, I enjoyed the companionship we shared.

'When the weather was sunny and warm we drove out into the countryside, taking a blanket and a picnic basket with us, and relished the undulating landscape. We thus finally savoured again what we had loved doing on a regular basis when we first started dating – being out in nature, just the two of us. Now we were getting old and had been married to each other for so many years, we were both less exuberant and less shy around each other, treasuring our time together in the open air in a different but not in a lesser way I dare say.

'When Annie first displayed signs that something was seriously wrong I didn't recognise them as I didn't know what they meant and put them down to Annie's general poor health, knowing that even the times when she was quite well were interspersed with bad episodes. I'm sure my mother would have recognised the symptoms and identified the condition behind it, but she had died ten years ago, a few years after my father had passed away, and could not alert us to the seriousness of it. It started with a persistent cough as well as breathlessness, both of which were accompanied with pain. The tiredness that came along with the symptoms was not unusual for Annie's bad episodes. To me and her, it looked as if she had caught a nasty virus or bacterial infection that even made her cough up blood after a while.

'Later on, I would blame myself for not recognising its true nature, telling myself that she might then have been saved. Everyone I spoke to about this, which were her family members and the medical staff at the hospital after she had finally seen her GP and been sent there for tests, reassured me that this would have most likely not made a difference to the final outcome of the disease progression. After all, lung cancer was an often deadly disease and symptoms tended to present themselves when the cancer had already spread to other parts of the body and nothing could be done any more but to treat the person affected by it palliatively.

'When the diagnosis and prognosis were given to us many weeks after Annie started suffering from the symptoms of the condition, we were in complete shock. The doctors gave her less than three months to live. After trying to take in and digest what she had been told, Annie was insistent that she didn't want to be hospitalised but stay at home and die there if I was alright with it. It was heart-breaking to hear her speak like that and I reassured her that of course she would stay at home.

'When we explained her wishes to the doctors, however, they cautioned us not to get too fixated on this plan, highlighting the importance of palliative care as her condition progressed and that this care could not adequately be given at home. Annie was upset and had tears in her eyes when she heard this and started begging me with terrible desperation in her voice that she wanted to die at home and that I was not to take her to hospital. I didn't know what to do other than give her a hug, knowing better than to clarify to her at that moment that medical staff at the hospital would try their best to lessen her suffering. It was not the right time for that, as she was too tormented to see sense and besides I sympathised with her wish to end her days at home. When Annie had already left the consulting room after having received the devastating news, I briefly turned back to the doctor, who looked at me gravely, and said in a choked voice that we would reassess things as time passed.

'Annie's family was devastated when they learned the news. The only saving grace was that neither of our parents were alive any longer and were therefore spared the shock and pain the rest of us suffered. Helen and Jacob McKenzie had died fifteen and sixteen years earlier respectively and fortunately their deaths had been quick and devoid of pain. Both of them had died peacefully in their sleep and I guess you don't get a much better way to leave this Earth.

'I was grateful that my own parents didn't suffer for long either after a heart attack had struck down my father and my mother had had a severe stroke from which she never woke up. Like Annie's parents, they had been relatively healthy and independent until the end.

'I was a bit concerned when Annie's siblings, in particular, and also her nieces and nephews started pouring into our home in the following weeks, offering their support and company and any practical help we might need. Although I appreciated the gesture and was grateful for the assistance and the company in the face of Annie's deteriorating condition, I knew also how much Annie had needed her alone-time and, whilst loving her family, had also struggled with the fact that there was an ever-expanding family circle to whose expansion she did not contribute and whose individual family units she could only bear to be with for a very limited period of time.

'However, my concerns proved to be unfounded. Annie started to relish her relatives' company almost, if not as much, as she had done as a young girl and woman. I don't know where that change came from. Certainly, she had been better and more contented in previous years but that could hardly be the sole reason for this marked departure in her attitude, feelings and needs. Her bitterness, resentment and frustration which – as I had eventually understood – she had partly hidden under the cloak of pain, suddenly fell away from her. Where was the lingering, deep depression that lay at the root of all that and that even when it lightened up, as it had done in recent years, was never far from the surface? I had expected and dreaded Annie to fall into a very dark emotional hole.

'In the immediate aftermath of her diagnosis, it certainly looked as if Annie was going down that route, but once her shock and terror had eased off a little and we had informed her relatives and they started visiting every day, a kind of serene joy radiated from her that I couldn't account for but that was very much welcomed by me. Annie showed a renewed, genuine interest in the lives of the different family members: She asked Seb, who had taken over the family farm, how the farm work was progressing and how his two adult sons, who had followed in their father's footsteps, were getting on with the implementation of new machines and systems to enhance workflows as they had once explained to us in a kind of business jargon that was new to us but that they had obviously picked up somewhere.

'She joked with her brother, Joe, whose energy never seemed to cease and who showed no signs of retiring from his mechanical and engineering business, what machine he had given the breath of life that week, to the delight of its owner.

'From Marisa, she wanted to get the latest updates on the welfare of the animals that lived in their house or the surrounding grounds. Since she and Andrew had retired from their work at the vets' surgery, they had increased the number of dogs and cats at home and built a chicken coop outside with the help of their son Patrick, who was a builder. Animals were important to them and Annie was tickled every time Marisa told her that they had acquired a new animal but that this would now definitely be their last one, reminding her that there were likely to be young ones after a while.

'She asked Adam to sing to her in his beautiful tenor voice, relishing what his pupils at the local school, where he worked as a music teacher, were able to enjoy on a regular basis, and she delighted in Sara's depictions of the flowers and plants that were currently in bloom and that she was monitoring and tending to in her vocation as a horticulturalist.

'She pressed her rather vain niece Penny, who worked as a beautician in the neighbouring town, for any beauty treatments for her wrinkly skin, adding mischievously whether a mud mask or a slug treatment would be the preferred application in her case, thus ever so slightly poking fun at the beauty industry and some of its bizarre manifestations and putting it in its place.

'She smiled when she encountered James's puzzlement about the new trend of young boys wanting to all have a new toy, a small tabby cat that could miaow and walk and generally move in the most feline of ways when you pressed a button, which they had just started to sell in the local toy store where he was the manager.

'I was amazed at Annie's transformation, unsure whether I could trust it to last, but I willed myself not to think too far ahead and to stay in the moment. I realised that this was exactly what Annie was doing – she lived every moment as if it were her last, which was something she had often not been able to do over the years, instead wishing her life had taken a different course and dwelling on what she perceived as lacking in it.

'Her family also took great pleasure in Annie's attitude even if they could not fully account for it either. They were pleasantly surprised by it, especially as they saw her health steadily decline further and watched her body succumb to the ravages of the cancer cells.

'Elaine took Annie's illness particularly badly. She had always been extremely fond of Annie. When they grew up, Annie's liveliness and vivacity complemented her own, more careful and considered approach to life very well, and Elaine loved the innocent, child-like spark in her sister that had been an integral part of her until her illness and disappointment changed her. Even then, Elaine tried to be a steady presence in our lives although she had to eventually accept that Annie had put a wall up between her and others and, through her illness, was not able to keep the kind of regular contact Elaine had hoped to maintain with her. It was a comfort then to Elaine that her daughter Martha had formed such a close bond with her sister, which made her to some extent still feel close to Annie by extension. Yet, there were times when she had the impression that she had lost her sister – lost her to what life had dealt to her. The prospect of losing Annie caused her regret about their more distant relationship over the decades even if she had done everything she could, not to let it cool off. And whilst it hadn't exactly done that, she sometimes felt almost alienated from her sister as if she didn't truly know her any longer. She knew that neither of them was to blame so she started to resent fate, what some people would call life's circumstances and conditions. It saddened me to see Elaine so tormented every time she came, but I didn't have the energy or resources to comfort her, as I was struggling too much with what was happening myself.

'It was Martha who eventually took her mother aside and reminded her of how important it was to make these last few weeks of Annie's life as happy for her as they possibly could, rather than drown in grief – a grief that was so deep that it was clearly written in Elaine's face. Elaine understood her daughter's plea, but couldn't just put on a happy and smiling face and explained to her daughter her thoughts and feelings and Martha, listening carefully, calmed her agitated mother down.

'It was one of the last few days of her life, which she had to spend in hospital in the end to provide her with adequate analgesia and a more dignified way of dying, that Annie said to Elaine in a feeble voice, "Elaine. Please take care of yourself." It took her a lot of effort to continue speaking. "I – I'm sorry we haven't had the kind of close sisterly relationship for many years now that we had when we were younger. I know you would have liked to have had that."

'Elaine couldn't suppress her tears any longer then, hugged her sister's weakened body and placed a tender kiss on her forehead. She wasn't able to reply in any other way, but that was enough.

'It was also after Annie had finally agreed to be admitted to hospital, that I tried at last to be honest with her about my adultery in the past because I felt that I owed it to her. Or maybe I just wanted to be absolved from the guilt that was chipping away at my soul. I held her bony, cold hand and almost whispered, "Annie, I need to tell you something. I've done something terrible and I'm so very sorry about it." I barely managed to hold back my tears at this stage. "Years ago, decades ago in fact, when you started to become ill and were so sad about the fact that we couldn't have a child together, I met…".I swallowed hard but before I could resume, Annie interrupted me. "Shhhh, Charles. Don't. Don't explain anything!"

'Her voice was barely audible as she was clearly lacking in strength, but I leaned in closely so I could make out what she said. "I know. I thought that this was what had happened. Don't explain. Don't talk about it and don't feel guilty. I was not available to you at the time. I had withdrawn inside myself and you were lonely. You felt helpless about what was going on and searched for a distraction and happiness."

'I was startled by Annie's words. I had had no idea that she had known about, or at least suspected, my infidelity, as I had assumed she was so wrapped up in her grief that she was barely aware of my absence or presence at home. She had been a lot more perceptive than what I had given her credit for and her empathy with me left me speechless.

'She then said, "Charles, please don't fret. We had a wonderful time together despite the difficulties and the darkness surrounding me at times, which you had to witness."

'My tears began to fall now. "Annie, I want you to know something. I love you and I've never stopped loving you even during our rocky times. I didn't manage to express this as I should have done and made mistakes!"

'Annie shook her head almost imperceptibly. "No, Charles, it's fine. I know that you've loved me. Neither of us has ever stopped loving the other person and that's a great thing we should value and be grateful for." Her teary eyes shone with joy that was underlined by one of her most beautiful smiles.

'I knew that no more needed to be said and that all was good and forgiven between us.

'I had dreaded the day of Annie's death more than anything else I had ever feared. When the day finally came less than three months after she had received her diagnosis, everything was a lot more peaceful and less agonising than anticipated – not that one can truly anticipate such an event – although still heart-breaking, of course. I had been called in to hospital at night because Annie's vital signs were becoming weaker and the doctors indicated that she would not last many more hours. Fortunately, Annie's hospital wasn't the big one all the way down in Exeter but a small one in the neighbouring town that had amongst its many wards one for end-stage cancer patients. I hurried and was lucky in hindsight that there was no traffic on the streets as I didn't drive very safely that night.

'When I arrived at the hospital and entered Annie's room together with the doctor who had called me, I was struck by how pale Annie looked and turned to the doctor in alarm, thinking that I had come too late. The doctor indicated however that Annie was still alive by making me look at the monitors that displayed Annie's vital signs. She wore an oxygen mask to ease her breathing. She had started wearing one over the last few days so that the sight of her with the mask attached didn't shock me. All the machines around her made some whirring sounds, interrupting the silence of the room in a way that I found unnerving. I sat down and took Annie's cool hand in both of mine and didn't let it go. I asked the nurse to contact her siblings for me, which she did promptly and it wasn't long until they all arrived. We spoke to Annie quietly, sometimes in whispers, reminding her of happy or funny incidents from the past, especially from the siblings' shared childhood. We also talked about our current activities and plans, which Annie had been so keen to hear about when she was still a little bit better. Between these short narratives were silences during which we held Annie tenderly. We weren't sure to what extent Annie took in what we said to her, but we knew that she was aware of our presence. She half-opened her eyes a couple of times and once breathed my name. There was also a barely noticeable tightening of her hand a few times whilst I held it, which to me amounted to an acknowledgement of me and an appreciation of my support and company. This comforted me at the time. It was important for me to be with her on her last journey in this world.

'In the early morning hours, her breath became more shallow and more irregular but fortunately she had slipped into unconsciousness or at least near-unconsciousness at that stage so that the terrifying death struggles filled with fear and panic that I had dreaded never happened. At one point, she just didn't take another breath and the surrounding machines went silent. We also remained silent and quite still for what seemed an eternity after that and I see that now as an honouring of her life. Soon the silence was broken by tears and commiserations during which we held each other and started the process of mourning. Most of all, though, I treasured the preceding moments of silence during which we still tried to understand what had happened. We felt emotionally united in our grief on a very deep level and it was Annie who had brought this about.

'We also shared our grief at Annie's funeral, which took place on a dark, chilly day in November on which the heavens opened and wept alongside us. Elaine and I both had to be supported at times when our legs nearly gave way and we were close to fainting. Everything around me seemed to happen in a haze: The music and the pastor's words sounded far away and muffled and I felt as if I was in a cocoon that – albeit having transparent walls that weren't sound-proof – couldn't be fully penetrated.

'This happened three years ago and since then I've had the most difficult time in my life. I gave up my private projection sessions at the weekends after Annie had been diagnosed with cancer and have never resumed them since. This meant that there has been nothing to break up the monotony and darkness of my days. One day follows another and I can't distinguish between them. Yes, Annie's family sometimes comes around, but otherwise I'm just alone with my grief, my loss and an overwhelming sense of despair. And there's the guilt that is eating me up. I know I've said that Annie forgave me and that everything was resolved between us, but despite of that, guilt has come back for me like a thief in the night except that it refused to go away.

'Many of my mornings start with me waking up and wondering why I couldn't have just died during the night. I know many people would consider such thought a sin against God and the precious life he has given us, but I'm not certain of my faith any longer and I can't help regarding my life as pointless and futile now. There is nothing more for me to do. I can't undo the mistakes I made in the past and I am tired of the oppressive black cloud of despair that weighs down on me every day. This is not a life any longer. This morning, I decided that I couldn't bear any more days like this and left the house without a clear plan except for the resolution not to come back. I took a bus that would take me out of town and hoped to be closer to Annie when I was exposed to the elements outside, as that is what she has returned to. I walked around in the increasingly fierce snowstorm, calling for Annie and I believe that I heard her answer in the end. The last thing I remember from earlier today was that I eventually sank into the snow and had this overarching sensation of deep relief that the pain and struggles would now finally end and I would be reunited with Annie.'

★ ★ ★

The barn was almost completely silent. Only some breathing was just about audible in the deep darkness and silence surrounding the four people who had been sitting on the cold stone floor throughout Charles's narrative, barely moving.

Now their limbs felt stiff and they started to stretch them and wriggle their fingers and toes to make the blood circulate better. The difficulty they experienced in making their bodies move again and obey their commands indicated how long Charles's narrative must have lasted. They had forgotten almost everything else around them and delved into the world Charles had depicted, had seen Annie's transformation in front of their eyes and had felt Charles's helplessness in the face of it, his need for solace in another woman's arms and had experienced the overwhelming pain after Annie had died. They had been transported powerfully into that world, and the silence was a sign that they struggled to return to the here and now.

When Charles gradually became aware of the others' presence again, it hit him not only how much time he had taken to tell his story but how many intimate details including those of the time with his lover he had revealed. This was unlike him, but he hadn't been fully conscious of anyone whilst telling that story. He had merely followed an urge to release all his emotions that had been building up inside him by speaking about the events that were at their source.

Leo and Lisa had managed to get back on their feet almost simultaneously and were stiffly walking over to the window behind Charles, which was now so densely covered with multiple layers of ice crystals that their intricate patterns almost merged into one white surface.

Karen stretched her legs while still sitting and Charles slowly rubbed his arms that felt as if they were being pricked by hundreds of pins and needles.

Lisa turned back to Charles and said pensively, 'Your private film screenings sound fantastic. I think you should really take them up again. Have you still got the extension where you did them? Have you still got the films?'

Both Karen and Leo liked this idea and smiled in approval.

Karen commented, 'Lisa, you're right.' And turning to Charles, she added, 'Charles, I'm sorry and deeply moved by your loss. I think what is most important now is that you don't remain mired in this feeling of guilt that you have been carrying with you for so long. You said yourself that Annie has forgiven you. You're human and I fully appreciate how difficult circumstances had been and how hard it was for you to find more constructive ways of dealing with Annie's disappointments and her illness. Don't be so hard on yourself, Charles. From what I gathered you and Annie shared many beautiful moments as well and you became closer again to each other after the affair was over and even more so when you retired. Hold on to this, Charles, but also look ahead. It hurts me to see that you have decided that your life is now over. The fact is that it isn't, Charles. It doesn't have to be the way you think about your life at the moment. You still have so much to give. Think of all the wonderful things that you have done, some of which you can take up again any time you want to. Like Lisa, I too think that these private screenings for children from socially deprived backgrounds in your neighbourhood were wonderful and I wonder whether you cannot host them again. It would give you such a sense of purpose and it's something you truly believe in.'

Karen had worked herself into an impassioned speech, but decided to stop there to give Charles a chance to respond.

Charles remained silent but Karen had the feeling that he was thinking about her words. At last he said, 'I feel out of touch. I don't know the children in the neighbourhood any longer. I've just kept myself to myself. If I had at least one child or a small group of children to start with, then it would be easier to attract the attention of others. It's too much hard work for me otherwise, as I haven't got the same light and playful spirit I still had to some extent when I first started this screening project in the neighbourhood.'

Leo had a sudden idea. He turned away from the window and sat down next to Charles. 'I think I might have your first private cinema-goer for you.' He smiled and his eyes lit up. 'I think my sister would love to come to such screenings. She loves watching films and she and I have frequently been to the cinema, but I can't take her often these days.'

It took them less than a minute to establish that although they didn't live in the same town, they only lived a bus ride away from each other and that it would certainly be feasible for Leo to bring his sister over for an afternoon without too much hassle. Once she was comfortable, his sister, who did not live with Leo, could probably take the bus on her own and attend Charles's screenings.

Charles's attention was now captured by the prospect of meeting Leo's sister and projecting films for her that she might enjoy. 'Please, tell me more about your sister, Leo. I want to know more about her. I want to know what she likes and dislikes, what makes her happy and what makes her sad.'

Leo nodded and said. 'I can tell you about her, but...' and here he hesitated.

The others waited.

'I'm worried about my sister. She's in an impossible situation and I need to find a way of getting her out of it.' His gaze was insistent, almost pleading.

Charles looked at Leo seriously, 'What do you mean, Leo?'

Leo cleared his throat. He didn't like revealing gaps in his knowledge or asking someone for advice. At the same time, the context in which they interacted had become supportive and encouraging, something that Leo had rarely encountered before during his life. Suddenly, it wasn't all about confrontation and competition any longer.

'You see, I don't really care about my own life any longer. It might be impossible for me to have any kind of life that is not chaotic, destructive or out-of-control. And I don't care about whether the world around me slowly but surely destroys itself and whether people behave like complete morons or not, as that is their business.' His voice had taken on an angry and more scornful tone again. 'But somehow I can't stop thinking about my sister's predicament.'

His voice softened again. 'If I don't make it out of here alive, it doesn't matter with regards to my own fate, but if I could find a solution that would make things better for my sister, I would have some peace of mind.'

Charles was completely focused on Leo now. 'Tell us, Leo. Tell us more.'

Lisa remained quiet but, anticipating Leo's story, went back to where she had sat before, and waited for him to tell his story.

Karen did the same.

And so Leo began to tell them about his and his family's lives.

Falling Apart

'I might need to tell you a bit more about my family background so that you can understand why my sister is in her current situation. Much of it is related to my mother's life trajectory.

'My mother comes from a simple and quite poor background and as is so often the case in such a context, the family made up for the lack of money by having more than the average number of children even at that time. There were six of them and my mother was the youngest by quite a few years. It seems that she had mainly been brought up by her siblings rather than by her parents who left the children mostly to their own devices. Her siblings, who were often wild and full of mischief, involved little Carla in their games, some naughtier than others. Sometimes they teased her or played tricks on her but, maybe surprisingly for such unruly children, they were never mean or nasty to her. And there was a reason for that. Carla was an unbelievably cute child: Her silver blonde hair fell in pretty ringlets around her face and shoulders, her light blue eyes, which looked straight at others when she spoke to them, were the colour of the sky on a beautiful summer's day and the curved lines of her lips were simultaneously tantalisingly appealing and innocent-looking in their smallness.

'Later in life, it would be the sensual appeal of her lips men responded to quickly whilst any remnants of innocence would soon vanish. Moreover, she was a slight child and her size sent signals of vulnerability and the need for protection to others. As an adult, the wrong kinds of men would exploit her physique and demand submission from her. As a child though, her appearance triggered a protective, gentle, caring attitude on her four brothers' and one sister's part that let her enjoy a predominantly carefree and joyful childhood.

'If I were critical of anything about her kind of upbringing, apart from the relative lack of parental involvement and her siblings' dodgy misdemeanours at times that could amount to brushes with the law, it would be that her siblings were rather overprotective of her. They regarded her as their little princess and, as a result, did not let her fend for herself outside their home environment out of fear that she might get hurt. This did not equip her to stand up for herself in later life in a recognisable way, which caused all kinds of problems. It also prevented her from being cognisant of the dangers of the world around her. Unlike her siblings and many other children and young people from her background she didn't become streetwise until she was a grown-up and even then, I don't know whether streetwise is the right word for how she behaved.

'Her siblings started to work as soon as they had finished compulsory schooling. In her family and their neighbourhood, boys traditionally worked in stores and girls cleaned wherever someone required them for cleaning. Her brothers and sister followed this path set by previous generations unquestioningly, but still lived at home for a while due to the low wages they brought home. It was only after a few years when she herself finished school that her four older brothers were in a position to move out and found a couple of small places to rent, each of which was shared by two of them.

'It was then that my parents met for the first time. My mother had just started a cleaning job at the local primary school which my father was called to whenever there was an engineering maintenance job to be done – or, more precisely, he or whoever was free at his small but well-established engineering company would be called.

'During the week my mother started her new job, it was my father who came to the school to fix a couple of radiators that did not work properly any longer. Carla's cleaning duties started early in the day before anyone else was in so that she would not be 'in the way' when the pupils and teachers arrived, ready to swarm into the corridors. My father, Archie – he always hated that name but preferred it to Archibald – also came in early on that day for the same reason and also because he had other work assignments to do later on. He was a cheerful, friendly young man, who was committed to his work but interested in so many things above and beyond what he did. He was about ten years older than Carla who was still a very young girl, but on the cusp of womanhood. When he saw her in her plain, dark-blue cleaner's outfit, which was hugging her slender body, with her curly, light hair tied up with a hairband into a tight knot at the top of her head and deeply focused on her work, he couldn't help but smile at her. He wished her a warm 'good morning', which made her jump, as she had been so much in her zone that she had not heard him approach. My father told me years later how he was bewitched by her the moment her startled eyes met his and that he knew then that he wanted to be with her.

'Their courtship was relatively slow in view of that immediate certainty he had about her, but that was the case due to her young age of only fifteen. He was initially concerned about what her parents would think of him dating their youngest and with such an age gap between them, but he soon discovered that her parents didn't mind that at all. On the contrary, they were relieved to soon have an empty nest and more time and space for inviting cousins and friends over to stay with them. They also liked the fact that Carla would marry young and probably then have a large family like they had. They wanted grandchildren and thought that Archie was an excellent match for their daughter. As a result, they were more than happy to see their daughter get married to him at the age of sixteen.

'Carla took to married life quite easily. At home, she and her sister used to do most household chores, which her parents had assigned to them and – to some extent – to her brothers and they made sure the chores were done even if they didn't involve themselves otherwise in their children's lives. Similarly, she had a good idea of how to bring up children, as so many of their relatives and neighbours came around with their babies and toddlers. On these occasions, she had ample opportunity to watch mother-child interactions from breastfeeding to nappy changing. Often, the mothers were quite tough with their babies when they didn't stop crying or they misbehaved in another way: If they didn't ignore them, they might shake them or give them a slap so that they 'would come to their senses' as they claimed. My mother, having from time to time experienced a similar treatment from her parents before they lost interest in the upbringing of their children, unsurprisingly came to regard this as the way to raise children, which was one of the reasons why she would later allow things to happen that absolutely should not have happened. But I'm getting ahead of myself here.

'Carla was happy in her new home with Archie and fell pregnant only a few months after their wedding, which she and my father were very happy about although I was later told that they both would have quite liked to spend more time together just as a married couple before having children. However, Carla had been brought up to see having children early as a matter of course so that wanting to spend more quality time alone with her husband could only be regarded as an idle fancy which she had no right to hold onto.

'After I was born my mother was ill for many months. When she told me about it later, it took me a while to figure out what had been wrong with her, as she did not explain much. In fact, I believe that she didn't know exactly what ailed her either, as her poorliness expressed itself in ongoing exhaustion, irritability and bouts of helpless crying, all of which were atypical of her nature.

'When I was younger and she mentioned this to me, I asked her whether it had been a long, difficult birth with complications, which might have involved an ensuing infection on her part, but she denied that. Now, of course, I realise that she was suffering from post-natal depression. I was too little to remember any of it, but it couldn't have been an easy time. My father, who was a knowledgeable and insightful man, recognised it for what it was and spoke to both the health visitor and then the doctor whom he called in, trying to find a way forward.

'The doctor prescribed her an antidepressant, which didn't work on her though, and then they had to change her medication slowly, which meant that months passed until she was on the full dose of a different antidepressant, which eventually showed an effect. During this time, it was almost impossible for her to take proper care of me and they could only make it work by having the health visitor in for a while on a daily basis to help her with me. Also, my dad's sister, who worked part-time and had two children of her own, came over on a regular basis and helped to get me washed, changed and fed and, if her own two kids gave her the chance, tried to keep the household going at least on a minimal level.

'I don't know whether it's true what is said, namely that if a mother doesn't create a close bond with her baby in the first few weeks of the latter's life, it will negatively affect the future relationship between mother and child in a way that true closeness cannot be achieved any longer. This might have happened, but I still recall some happy times we had as a small family once my mother felt better again. At weekends, we often went on walks together. My father especially enjoyed woodland and was prepared to drive for a while to take us on walks in the forest. On the walk, he would show me the different trees and ferns and tell me their names, and he would point out different types of mushrooms and explain how to distinguish between them, especially with regard to which ones were edible and which ones weren't. He did the same when it came to the different kinds of berries. I remember how I loved these trips. Like my father, I was inquisitive and was keen to absorb new information and my dad always gave me some time to explore on my own as well.

'My mother would laugh and smile when we ventured out and played games together such as hide-and-seek between the trees. I suspect she found walks themselves rather boring and a bit pointless, but if they were interspersed with fun, games and adventures, she was more than happy to come along. After all, she was used to getting her fair share of action and excitement from the time she had grown up with her older siblings, who had involved her in many of their schemes and ventures. She was surprised by, but also pleased about, how lovingly and patiently my father treated me and how much time he spent with me. This was a new experience for her and very different from her parents' distant child-rearing approach and the harsh treatment of children by their parents in our neighbourhood.

'When we were all together, she emulated his way of interacting with me, but when my mother and I were alone she fell back on a tougher stance, which had in the past always been presented to her as the only productive manner of bringing up children. She would then have a short fuse, shout at me when I was annoying and sometimes slap me when she was really angry with me. Although she played with me for a while when I was little, she soon stopped doing that at least when my father wasn't around, as this was what her parents had done as well and it turned out that their questionable parenting behaviour over so many years, probably unsurprisingly, had a greater influence on her approach to mothering than my father's. I guess she didn't regard my dad's relationship with me as a viable alternative for long, but she indulged him because she was happy on the whole and not out for a confrontation.

'Surprisingly, I did not have any siblings during the years we were all still together as a family and I never learned the reason for that. When my dad was at work and I was expected to entertain myself, I discovered my love of music. My parents both enjoyed music but their tastes were very different, which ensured that we had a wide range of

CDs at home to choose from, which I was allowed to borrow as long as I took care not to damage them, not to turn up the music too loudly or wear headphones and to return the CDs to the place where I had found them.

'I had my own CD and radio player from an early age – partly because my dad wanted me to discover and appreciate the delights of music in my own time and partly because my mother did then not have to engage with me quite as much. For someone who had always been very playful herself and had barely left her own teenage years behind it was, in a way, remarkable that she wouldn't try – or enjoy – playing with me much more, but I guess she had internalised the family roles she had experienced too much for that. My mother's CDs covered some pop, a lot of rock music and some heavy metal. Her brothers had played these genres all the time when she grew up and she had soon started to happily move along to the loud and fast rhythms and beats. She also had techno, house and drum'n'bass music in her repertoire, genres that would become some of my favourites, too, although I hate to admit that my mother and I shared anything even if it was just a predilection for a particular kind of music. But then I shouldn't use the word 'just' in this context, as music has been central to my life and I would like to regard myself as a musician. I'd also like to remind myself that I discovered other kinds of music like indie, too, so that I can at least say that my listening habits weren't identical to my mum's.

'My father's CD collection was very different: Whilst he did enjoy some rock music as well, he was passionate about classical music and jazz and had acquired an unbelievable number of pieces over time. He also tried to get hold of concert tickets when he found out that some jazz bands or classical ensembles were scheduled to perform somewhere that wasn't too far away. Initially, he took my mother along to them, but he soon noticed that she was bored during these concerts and didn't enjoy them at all so that he eventually went there with his friends or by himself. I was still too small to join him on these occasions, but I recall attending one live jazz event when I was six, which was a fairly low-key, relaxed afternoon affair that I thoroughly enjoyed. I remember sitting in a tent with my parents and some other families and couples moving my feet along to the ground beats of the drums.

Although I loved the steady rhythm of the drums, it was another instrument that wholly captured my attention and intrigued me and that was the electronic guitar, which would become my instrument in the years to come. I spoke to my father about how much I would love to have one of my own and learn how to play it and my father smiled at me, delighted by my interest, and told me to wait a little while, but that I would be getting a guitar. He, himself, had dabbled with it when he was an adolescent and played the oboe for a while in a youth orchestra. For one reason or another that he couldn't clearly remember any longer he gave up playing music altogether and now regretted it. He thought sometimes about digging out his old oboe and checking whether he would remember how to play it, but in the end, he never did. He always found one excuse or another for not trying, for example that my mother would not appreciate it. At the same time, some of his enthusiasm for playing an instrument had been re-awoken and on my seventh birthday I received the best present I had ever been given by someone – a beautiful, shiny, classical guitar.

When my father presented me with it, it was still wrapped in big sheets of shiny, red paper that were held together with Sellotape. He must have used several rolls of wrapping paper to get it all covered. I knew immediately what it must be, as the shape of the present was a big give-away. My dad told me later how happy he was when he saw the joyful anticipation in my eyes before I started to tear the clumsily wrapped paper off. When it was revealed in front of me in all its elegance, I was awe-struck and my father, who had watched me closely, played things down a little to hide his embarrassment and said to me, 'It's not an electric guitar, but it will get you started. It's good to learn the ropes on a classical guitar and you can move on to an electric guitar later.'

He also gave me a couple of guitar-lesson books that contained some easy practice pieces. In addition, he located some CDs that contained what could be called mood pieces that were performed on a classical guitar and handed them to me, too. They were part of his own CD collection but I had somehow never seen them. I asked him why he had never played them recently and he explained that he had, but that he had to be on his own when he listened to them. When I put them on, it didn't take me long to understand why that was. The music was soulful, melancholy in places, and possessed the power to carry you far away, to a place of magic and wonder that was filled with an alien beauty and allure. Whenever I listened to it during the years to come, I made sure that I was on my own so that nobody could break the spell I was under and dissolve its enchantment.

I learned how to play the guitar easily and quickly, teaching myself with my father's books but also receiving lessons from my father, who came alive then and rediscovered the joy of holding the instrument and extracting some beautiful melodies from it. He told me that I was a natural and I took pride in his praise. There wasn't a day on which I didn't play from the day I got the guitar until my dad's death six months later.

'It is hard to describe the shock my mother and I experienced when we learned of my father's death for which we were totally unprepared. My father wasn't even in his mid-thirties, healthy, sportive and full of life. I still clearly remember the knock on the front door one evening, my mother opening it with myself just behind her to find out who was outside and then finding a couple of police officers outside whose serious facial expressions left us in no doubt that something disastrous had happened. After my mother had asked them inside on their request, they took off the helmets of their uniforms and one of them said quietly, "I'm afraid we bring you bad news. Your husband was involved in a car accident."

'He paused then and my mother's eyes widened with fear. "'An acc-ccident," she stammered, as if she had never heard the word before. "How serious is it?" she insisted to know and her voice nearly broke.

'The police officers merely shook their heads in response and I knew immediately – despite my young age – what that meant, but when my mother kept staring at them, still waiting for a more explicit answer, the verbal confirmation of what I had already gathered came and felt sharp like a slab of ice on the skin. "I'm afraid it was a fatal accident." And when my mother still showed no reaction, he added, "Your husband died in it."

"It was I who reacted to the terrible announcement, whilst my mother had still not seemed to take it in, by howling piteously before running to my room and slamming the door shut behind me.

'The aftermath of my father's death was tremendous. One would have expected this to hit us hard, but my mother became completely derailed and never found a way back to a life that was not completely dominated by chaos and turmoil. I maintain that part of the reason for that was that she was simply ill-prepared to fend for herself having always had someone – first her older brothers and sister, then her husband – who would guide and protect her. Moreover, the way many people interacted with each other in the neighbourhood she grew up in did not set a good example of how she could live a constructive life.

'In the absence of other adults who could guide her now, she fell back on what she had seen people do since she was young. Grief and adversity were mainly drowned in alcohol in the community she lived in and the alcohol seemed to soothe or at least muffle the inner pain and turmoil. So far, she had never taken much to alcohol, as she found spirits too sharp and even beer, which she had sometimes drunk with Archie, not particularly palatable as it was too bitter for her. Archie, who had liked a range of alcoholic drinks but was a very moderate drinker, called her his sweet-toothed girl due to her predilection for lemonade and other fizzy drinks. Now that he was dead however my mother seemed to have made a resolve to overcome her relative dislike of most alcoholic drinks in the hope of experiencing the desired numbing effect they could have on the brain. Ironic as this may sound, my mother therefore gritted her teeth and soon downed an alcoholic drink on a daily basis.

'My mother's pay, as a cleaner, was of course not enough to sustain us so she claimed benefits not long after my dad's funeral with the little inheritance money having been spent quickly on necessities and a few indulgences on my mother's part such as pretty clothes, jewellery and a large makeup kit. However, even with benefits we struggled and were now much poorer even if not downright destitute. There was nobody else there to help us, as my father had lost his parents a few years earlier and my mother's parents and brothers did not have any money to spare and even if they had, they wouldn't have been willing to offer financial support, I suspect.

'There were many aspects about poverty that didn't bother me whilst they appeared hugely problematic to many other people without money: I didn't care about clothes as a young boy nor was I focused on gadgets or expensive toys. As long as I could play my guitar, listen to music and get some sheet music from the public library I was happy. Eventually I would become desperate for an electronic guitar and my own proper, highly-developed sound system and would get into trouble in my attempt to get hold of this equipment but that wouldn't happen for a few more years.

'My mother, in the meantime, tried to obtain support and protection in places where it was unlikely for her to find them, which changed our lives profoundly. I recall her telling me how it all started.

'It was a very rainy late afternoon. I had gone to the home of one of my classmates, which I sometimes did when my mother was on a late shift and wouldn't always finish work on time to pick me up or when she had to work overtime. The parents of a couple of other boys were very good at having me over on such occasions and my mother had arranged that afternoon's stay with the other family in advance. At the time, she wasn't bad at organising and making sure I was looked after, especially because she felt sorry for me to have lost my father so early in life.

'I bet if it hadn't been for my father's death, she would have had no compunction in letting me be on my own at home for a few hours at the age of seven, having seen her parents take such an approach. In fact, it took her less than eighteen months until she did exactly that, possibly forgetting that in contrast to her when she was a child, I didn't have any siblings who took me under their wings. On that day though I was still looked after by another adult who kept an eye on her son and me whilst we first watched a children's programme on the telly that I found rather silly and then played a card game whilst hearing the rain lash forcefully against the window-panes.

'Meanwhile, my mother was completely caught up in the downpour. It had started a while earlier so that she had hoped that by the time she finished work, it would have eased, but when she left the school she saw immediately that her hopes had been in vain. She had resumed her work at the local primary school once I started pre-school, which of course was well after her maternity leave had come to an end. She had been lucky that a position had become available again there when she had been looking for work, and the staff at the school had remembered her as someone reliable and trustworthy, which meant that they had been happy to take her back on. Mother, on her part, liked the friendly atmosphere of the school and was glad to spend a few hours a day there.

'Stepping into the pouring rain with one hand holding her flimsy umbrella, which was immediately caught up in a gust of wind and turned inside out when she opened it, she briefly considered going back to the school to wait for the worst of the weather to pass, but dismissed the idea very quickly: She had to pick me up from my classmate's house after all and nobody knew how long the almost monsoon-like conditions would last. It was a twenty-minute walk from the school, which was also the school I attended, to my classmate's house.

'When I first started school a couple of years earlier – pre-school had been at a different location – it appeared very convenient that the school was also my mother's workplace and, at first, she made use of the advantages this offered such as letting me stay on at the school when she had to work late or taking me in early with her on her early morning shifts. A few months ago, however, a new principal started at my school who would not allow me to stay at school outside of normal school hours, explaining that it was against school policy and a health-and-safety hazard as well and that my mother's insistence on me being with her was neither here nor there. He pointed out that even if there weren't any breaches in policy or rules, my mother would hardly be able to supervise me whilst she was working. We therefore had to make arrangements with other parents much of the time now.

'After ten minutes of hurrying down the streets in the heavy downpour, Carla was completely drenched. Rain was running down her flushed face and her hair was dripping with water, as she didn't have a hat she could wear and some of the spokes of her umbrella had now broken after another attempt at using it.

'When she saw one of the local pubs, the Rose & Crown, a few metres in front of her, she determinedly steered towards it and, a few seconds later, stepped inside. "Just a few minutes," she said to herself, "to let the worst of the weather front pass." She was greeted by a low-key hum in the bar area, which was typical of a pub before the majority of its customers entered to get some drinks later in the evening when it became considerably louder. The hum consisted of the voices of the few customers who were already there, the sounds of drinks being prepared and some very quiet, almost inaudible music in the background, probably coming from the kitchen.

'Carla, who had been here before a few times with Archie, headed straight towards the toilets to dry herself as much as she could. She let the hot air of the dryer blast her hands and lower arms before lowering herself down to put her head underneath it, hoping it would at least stop her hair from dripping water down her neck and face. She also took her heavy coat off, which had absorbed much of the rain. Even though it was only early October, there was a chill in the air and most people had started wearing their warmer clothes.

'After a few moments of hesitation during which she thought of the small, but nevertheless, additional expense she would incur – the reality of having no money again since Archie's small inheritance had been spent and relying to a large extent on benefits made her temporarily extremely cautious about spending anything on more than the bare essentials – she let her broken umbrella fall into the bin underneath the sink. When she returned to the bar area she found that more people had come into the pub to find refuge from the rain and strong wind.

'She had thought of checking whether the weather had improved and she could now resume her journey, but when she saw a man, who looked like a workman in his mid-thirties, enter the pub with water running down his navy-blue anorak and with raindrops on his bald head, she decided that there wouldn't be any point in this. Instead, she tentatively walked towards the bar before gingerly climbing on a barstool at one end. She would have a tea whilst waiting for the weather to improve. Before the barman had come over to her to take her drink order, she heard a voice from a couple of metres away say "'What weather! Were you caught up in the deluge as well?"

She turned her head and saw that it was the man who had just come in who had addressed her and who was wiping his wet face with a handkerchief. She nodded but her attention was quickly diverted when the barman asked her what he could get her. She had only just ordered her tea when the man next to her jumped in and said, "A tea? Surely you want something stronger than that to warm you up inside," and without waiting for her response waved the barman back, ordering him to get a whiskey for the lady.

'Carla started to remonstrate that she couldn't have a whiskey now, thinking that it was only late afternoon. She had so far stuck to a deal she had made with herself to only have a drink in the evenings in order to function properly and not end up like some of the women in the neighbourhood she grew up in, who had been in a near-constant stupor and whose lives had clearly fallen completely apart. Moreover, Carla knew that she still had to pick me up as soon as the weather allowed and she was not inclined to go to my classmate's house, whose parents were above her in status anyway, reeking of alcohol.

'Although they had never given her any indication that they looked down on her and found her inferior and wanting, she believed that they would most definitely do so if she gave them only the smallest of reasons, and being drunk and late when picking up her child might not be considered such a small reason. In fact, that reminded her to give them a ring to tell them that she would be late. She explained something to that effect to the man who had pulled his bar stool next to hers and just then pushed a glass of amber-coloured liquid in front of her whilst she was digging in her bag for her phone. She jumped when the man put his strong hand with its rough skin on hers to make her stop in her search, as she had not expected to be touched by him.

'The man laughed at her reaction, but his voice was reassuring and friendly. "Don't worry. I won't do you any harm. I just think you should stop worrying, sit back and relax for a little while. I'm sure the people your son stays with realise that you want to wait for the rain to stop before picking him up. Anyone with a bit of common sense would think that."

'He then stretched out his hand, which she automatically took without thinking. "I'm Marcus. I live just a few streets further down and work as a builder. What's your name?"

'Carla introduced herself, feeling herself surrender to his persuasiveness. She let him lead the conversation and found she enjoyed it. He loved to talk and obviously liked the sound of his own voice, but that didn't bother her: He was funny and she had to laugh at his jokes. Moreover, he was clear to understand and follow and his views on people and politics were refreshingly one-dimensional, which was a pleasant contrast to Archie's conversations that had been replete with a range of perspectives that he had presented for debate and whose thirst for knowledge and information she had initially found endearing but ultimately exhausting. She felt light, carefree and happy for the first time since Archie's death and it was only when her phone rang and she saw that two hours had passed since she entered the pub that she stopped smiling and laughing and answered the call, which was made by my classmate's mother to enquire where she was and at what time she could expect her to pick me up.

'Pangs of conscience hit Carla when she became aware of having forgotten about me during her long chat and banter with Marcus although they were somehow muffled in intensity due to the effect the alcohol had taken on her. She had barely noticed how a second glass of whiskey had appeared in front of her whilst she had been listening to Marcus and talking to him, and wasn't quite sure now whether she hadn't even had more drinks after that. What she did know though was that her head was spinning crazily when she slid off the bar stool and that she would have lost her balance and fallen over had Marcus not caught her just in time. He laughed again – not so much at her expense but in a good-natured way – and asked her when she would be back here again and when she didn't answer put a piece of paper with his phone number into her hand.

"'It's been a pleasure,' he said rather suavely and added, "call me when you're free. We're good together."

'Carla's nod was almost imperceptible as she hurriedly left the pub to pick me up shortly afterwards. She struggled for the remainder of the day to hide her inebriated state but she couldn't fool me.

'It didn't take her long to call Marcus. He was just what she needed, she thought, to lift her out of her widow's grief and to take her mind off her financial worries. Things then happened quickly. I believe she went home with him on their second encounter and from then on, they were at each other's places a lot and I remember that time as being replete with laughter, sex and alcohol.

'Marcus had a very strong sex drive and when they were in our flat in the evening or at night, they would go on for hours. I could hear the rhythmical creaks the bed made, the panting and the shrieks of ecstasy, which at first made me storm into their bedroom because I thought that something untoward had happened. I was mortified to learn what had truly been going on. Whilst my parents had always been quite discreet about their sexual lives, Marcus and my mother did nothing to hide their rabid sexuality from me, and it didn't take long until they were openly making love on the sofa in the living-room where I could just walk in on them.

'Their complete lack of discretion and their disregard for what was generally considered appropriate for a child of my age to watch were partly the result of their high alcohol consumption. Gone were the days and weeks following my father's death when my mother started drinking but restricted herself to one drink a day in the evening. Marcus loved his drinks and always encouraged my mother to partake of them, too. My mother, being easily led, did not need many invitations, especially because she appreciated the soothing effect alcohol had on her mind, dispersing her concerns and anxieties, and I suspect it enabled her to keep up with Marcus's sexual stamina. Alcohol then transported my mother elsewhere, which had in turn the effect that she forgot about and neglected me. I was left to my own devices.

'When I wasn't out and about with my friends and classmates to play games outside or – when the adults were distracted – to do some mischief, I was in my room listening to and playing some music. It was the best way to drown out the sounds and grunts my mother and Marcus were making, which I had no desire to listen to. After I had turned the music up a little bit too much a few times, my enraged mother insisted on me wearing headphones and even gave me a pair, which I was surprised by, as she hardly spent any money on me, even on inexpensive things. I guess though it was for her own benefit, as she would then have a quiet home in which the only noise made would be hers and Marcus's. I had loved the acoustics when the room was filled with the music I put on and played on the stereo, but I discovered that having the music transmitted so close to my head was a fantastic experience, too.

'When my mother and Marcus were not in the bedroom but watched telly in the living-room, I tended to play the guitar my father had given me on my seventh birthday. Usually, my mother didn't protest about that even when I played some louder pieces as she closed the living-room door and turned the volume on the T.V. up so high that she couldn't hear me any longer.

'There had been a few weeks, directly after my father's death, when I didn't pick up the guitar, as I was so distressed by his death, my feelings being so raw that I couldn't expose myself to the strong memories of my father teaching me to play the guitar, which would have undoubtedly surfaced had I played the instrument then. When I started playing again after my mother had started seeing Marcus, and I used the music to separate myself from their shenanigans, I found not only that I could cope with the memories and mental images thus evoked, but that the music had in fact a cathartic effect on me. Through the music I could express and release my feelings of anger, helplessness, frustration, sadness and even, at times, despair. Over the following years, I started composing my own music, experimented and eventually also wrote song lyrics, which I then performed for myself.

I was able to spend an increasing amount of time on this, as my mother and Marcus barely acknowledged me, or only when it suited them.

'Marcus wasn't antagonistic towards me. He was, as he said, "just not very good with children" and therefore rarely exchanged more than a few words with me. I didn't care, especially as I was not that keen on his company either. He meant nothing to me other than that my mother paid me very little attention since they had started that relationship. Therefore, if I had any feelings towards him at all, they were tinged with resentment, but mostly, the resentment was directed towards my mother. She should have known better than to just ignore me.

'Later I would hanker back for that time that gave me the freedom to be as creative as I wanted to be, as by that time I realised that there are worse things than being ignored.

'Marcus's lack of affection for children finally terminated their relationship and destabilised my mother further. This came about when she fell pregnant less than three months into their relationship. Although my mother wasn't great with children herself and not overly keen on them either, she had been raised believing that children were just what you had – a part of life, and that you wouldn't question what she had been taught to be the natural order of things.

'She had been quite lucky really to have been granted a break, which was longer than a decade, between giving birth to me and falling pregnant again. Of course, it hadn't really been a matter of luck as I learned later that my mother didn't get pregnant again for so long but had come down to the use of contraception. My father had been happy to wait for a bit before having a second child, as he quite enjoyed the time spent with just my mother and me, and Marcus was adamant about doing anything he could so that he could have sex but simultaneously not impregnate my mother.

'In other words, Marcus – from the start – wanted his cake and eat it, and that was exactly what he did. As soon as he learned about my mother's pregnancy after she had made sure that she was indeed pregnant despite the precautions they had taken and had plucked up her courage and told him, he bolted. He literally ran off after refusing to discuss the matter and my mother didn't see him again – or only when she accidentally ran into him in our small town – but on these occasions, he pretended not to see her.

'I was worried for my mother when that happened. I knew she wasn't a strong person when she was on her own and there was the very real danger that she would fall apart. And in some way, that was what happened albeit in a slightly different way from what you would expect. She did get one reprieve if that is what you want to call it: She miscarried shortly after Marcus had left her. At least she didn't have to worry about having to deal with another child, not to speak of the additional financial pressures. From then on, my mother's trust in men went into sharp decline. However, her lack of faith in them did not result in her keeping her distance from them but had the opposite effect. She was ready to use them for whatever fleeting pleasures they could give her, and she was very much used by them in return.

'Life at home became absolutely terrible. Men came and went in rapid succession and they were the worst of their kind. Any kind of conversation was now replaced by shouts and yells, which consisted for the most part of curses and vulgarities. Where I had previously been exposed to voluble sex noises, I now heard sounds that were barely human emanating from the bedroom, which scared the hell out of me and which were, as I soon discovered, the result of the intermingling of sex and crude violence. When I first detected injuries on my mother's face in the form of bruises, a swollen eye and a split lip the morning after such a terrible row had occurred, I was shocked.

'After I stared at my mother for a while without her taking any notice of it, I finally asked her quietly, "Mum, what happened? What happened to your face? Did he beat you?"

'My mother then looked at me for a long moment and it was clear that she didn't know how to answer that question. I saw her hesitate as if she would have liked to unburden herself by giving voice to whatever terrors had happened during the night just gone. It was a watershed moment, which could have brought us closer again and could have somehow pulled her back from the abyss she was hurtling towards by focusing on our relationship rather than throwing herself into wildly dangerous liaisons. However, the moment passed and – whether it was from a feeling that it would be inappropriate for her to speak to her not-even-eleven-year-old son about domestic abuse or from shame – she chose to brush off my concern and worry by responding abruptly with a fake laugh. "What on earth are you talking about, Leo? Nobody has beaten me."

'When I kept gazing at her, now in obvious disbelief at the veracity of her words, she said more forcefully but, in my opinion, unconvincingly, "Nobody beats me. I fell and hit the corner of the bed and then the floor. It can happen." Then she added in an almost friendly tone as she must have noticed how frightened I looked, "Now, don't concern yourself about me or my health and do something fun instead. Aren't you going to meet some of your friends after breakfast? – Let's get ready for them," she added in a forced attempt at cheerfulness. I wasn't sure how to reply, so let it go for the moment.

'However, I made another attempt at speaking to her about the matter in the evening when we were both alone in the kitchen. Unfortunately, the conversation quickly took an unexpected turn, which would put me off from ever again seriously trying to make her speak to me about incidents of violence. I think my mother realised that my unhappiness and fear about what I had seen could easily be picked up on at school where I might be questioned about it and reveal everything, which in turn, might result in visits from the police and social services. Her brothers, who had not infrequently had encounters with the local police force, had taught her that the police could not be trusted. She was therefore determined to make sure I wouldn't let on about the domestic situation and was at her most intimidating when she bent down so that we were now eye-to-eye.

'Her voice turned almost into a hiss as she said, "Listen, Leo. Do not get involved in your mother's business. Never ever. Do you hear?"

'Her eyes were blazing now, which made me involuntarily want to take a step back but my mother held my arms in a firm grip, which did not allow me to budge. It was surprising how much strength she had despite her petite stature. "And do not even dream of coming into my bedroom when I'm there with someone," she continued in an even sharper tone of voice.

'I had, in fact, considered knocking on her bedroom door the night before, when the sounds emanating from there had become almost unbearable. However, I hadn't done so in the end because I knew that any knocks on the door would almost certainly not have been audible inside, and I was too terrified to just walk in. At the same time, I knew that I should have first knocked and then walked in and protected my mother. After all, I wasn't such a small boy any longer at almost eleven. All day, I had felt deeply uncomfortable at my impotence. My father would have done everything in his power to ensure that my mother was alright but I had failed her when she most needed me. In my father's absence, it should have been me who looked after her. At least that's how I berated myself at the time. Was I turning into one of these weak men like Marcus, who close their eyes or even run away from the first difficulty they encountered?

'She added, "Even when I'm in my bedroom on my own, Leo, you are not supposed to just walk in. In that situation you can knock, but you will only enter when I call you in. Is that clear?"

'Her eyes were piercing through me but I managed not to flinch or avert my gaze. I didn't respond though and my mother demanded, "Promise this to me and also promise that you won't tell anyone anything about our home life!"

'My mother's hold on me grew firmer and it was apparent that she wouldn't let go of me until I had made my promise, so promise I did, but I was worried and scared.

'As it turned out, I had good reason for alarm, as all the men my mother brought home seemed to have a penchant for violence. The violence was usually aimed at my mother, but sometimes I inadvertently stepped into the firing line and was shouted at, slapped or beaten as well. When my mother protested against my treatment after I had suffered a particularly vicious beating, she would be battered in return and eventually and unsurprisingly stopped intervening. Quite possibly, she stopped caring about anything much soon enough.

'It didn't take long until she lost her job, as she stopped going there regularly and more than once was very hung over or even drunk when she did get there. She had taken to drinking a lot. All restraint, which she had shown in the past, had gone and she was only able to get through the pain and pointlessness of her days by numbing herself sufficiently, which meant drinking herself into a stupor. She would start shortly after waking up and finish late at night when she passed out wherever she happened to sit or lie, leaving a trail of bottles, beer cans and unwashed crockery behind her, which nobody would clear away and wash if I didn't do it and I would get fed up doing that as time went on.

'When I was sixteen, I started getting into trouble. Until then I had managed to plod along. I had long since stopped trying to rescue my mother from her men or from herself: Not only had she made it crystal clear to me that she didn't want me to get involved in matters she regarded as only concerning her – and I had, as I mentioned, felt the pain when I even unintentionally crossed paths with one of her blokes – I knew my mother well enough to recognise that she would not listen to me anyway. The tough part of herself, which had been shaped by her brothers' example – even if they pampered her – had metamorphosed into something aggressive in nature, which she didn't hesitate to expose me to whenever she was not semi-unconscious.

'Being continuously either treated like vermin or ignored had dispelled my scruples about not fulfilling my filial duties. After all, she had long since stopped discharging any maternal obligations towards me. I guess I toughened up during my teens and stopped caring or worrying so much. I spent most of my time outside of school listening to but also increasingly composing and playing songs and found some like-minded people who I went to play with and, at the age of fourteen, formed a band with them. Whilst we initially just practised in the garage of one of my band-mates' parents, we managed to promote ourselves and soon got some slots for pub gig evenings. All this kept me relatively sane, but it could still not prevent things from sliding rapidly just after I had sat my GCSEs.

'I don't think it was exam pressure that made things go pear-shaped. There wasn't really any pressure to speak of. My mother wasn't even aware of my exams and I didn't care about them. Like many adolescents, I wasn't massively interested in school except for the odd topic here and there in different subjects that caught my attention. Mostly, though, I wasn't disinclined to learn, but I disapproved of the educational system, which fed us nothing but 'facts', which we were then expected to reel off at the numerous exams we were expected to sit. We were not encouraged to think for ourselves or use our creativity. I had been tempted to hand in some of the GCSE exam papers with the word 'nonsense' written in capital letters across them, but refrained from doing so in the end. I would leave school in the summer and then just dedicate all my time to my music and, if that didn't bring our band enough money in soon, I would just look for a job somewhere as well to keep me going. I wasn't fussed what job it would be, as it would merely be a means to the end of concentrating on my music. I wasn't worried about the future or – at least – I wasn't conscious of any worries.

'There was one life event though, which I consider having contributed to my loss of control over my life and that was the birth of my half-sister. It might be a sad thing to say but I wasn't sure who the father of this new baby was. In my opinion, there were at least two men to choose from, maybe even more. To be honest, I had stopped paying attention to who came to our flat. When I was at home, I kept to my room and avoided any potential encounters with guys in our flat whenever possible. I was appalled when I learned about my mother's pregnancy, not so much because teenage boys would often be mortified by their mothers' pregnancies as they regard them as an embarrassing reminder of their 'old' parents being sexually active – after all, my mother wasn't even middle-aged yet and I only knew her as a sexually active mother – but because the prospect of a child being born into such a chaotic, dissolute household horrified me. What kind of childhood would that child have? There wouldn't be any kind of upbringing. What kind of life would it have? I found it bad enough, but at least I had had a few fairly happy years before my father died. The child wouldn't even have that. It would grow up amongst violent men and an alcoholic mother.

'I have to admit that I prayed for my mother to miscarry again for the sake of everyone, especially because she did not stop her drinking once she learned that she was pregnant or even noticeably slow it down. I could only imagine what her alcohol consumption did to her unborn child. However, despite my hopes to the contrary and a scare in the third month of her pregnancy, my mother did not suffer a miscarriage this time and gave birth to a baby daughter, albeit prematurely. Jenny was six weeks early and absolutely tiny when she first laid eyes on the outside world. It was almost certain that my mother's alcoholism had caused her to go into labour prematurely and it had indeed caused fetal alcohol syndrome.

'As soon as my sister was born, she was inadvertently on withdrawal, she cried a lot, she was too small and weighed too little and had to go into an incubator for a few weeks. She had a terrible start in life. My fears had turned out to be well-founded: During her first year of life, she got one infection after another, which seemed to be proof of a severely compromised immune system. She also was, according to my mother, hyperactive and found it hard to concentrate on anything. Her teachers, once she started school, raised their suspicion that she might have learning difficulties, which wouldn't have been an unexpected outcome of high alcohol exposure in utero, but I believe that this wasn't the case. But this would happen later.

'During the summer when my sister was lying in her incubator fighting for her life, I derailed completely. I didn't know what was happening but my mood suddenly changed from worry and fear about my sister's future to manic activism and a sense of exhilaration which did not have an identifiable cause. My energy levels were unusually elevated and tried to find an outlet. I went on long pub crawls with my mates, which ended more often than not in me getting blind drunk, shouting and hollering in and outside the bars and pulling a girl here or there.

'My sexuality was now awoken as well. Whilst I had previously only had one or two fairly innocent, romantic encounters, which couldn't be called relationships, I didn't feel I could or wanted to rein in my sexual needs. In fact, it got to a stage where I had sex with a girl in a night-club. We were right next to the dance floor and in plain view when I thrust myself inside her and the girl's moans and shrieks were barely drowned by the thumping music surrounding us. Of course, the security staff intervened. They also called the police who gave me a warning and let me go after having made sure that at least the sex had been consensual and no coercion or rape had been involved.

'My turbulent, feverish state of mind sought other outlets as well though and showed no signs of calming down. After I left the bars and on the occasions when I wasn't with a girl, I roamed the neighbourhoods, and when I came to the richer areas, I started to throw stones or rocks that I had picked up on my way in people's gardens, at their garage doors and their front doors. Finally, one of the big stones broke the window-pane of one of the houses and I was insane and drunk enough to shout out full of joy, "There you are, you motherfuckers with your privileged backgrounds. Does a broken window upset you? If it does, you're just wimps and deserve no better. You have no idea what we, who only live a few streets away from you, are going through and you clearly don't care. As long as you are comfortable, you are smug and would probably prefer it if we didn't exist. But this is a reminder that we won't simply go away and that we are here to stay!"

'Even if the breaking of the window-pane had not woken people up in the neighbourhood, my shouting in the silence of the night, most definitely did. The owners of the house whose window I had just shattered as well as some of their neighbours stormed outside and descended on me like vultures. I knocked two of them down to the ground in fury when they got hold of me, but I still didn't get very far when I was trying to run off as the police, who must have been just around the corner and must have received an urgent call by one of the neighbours, stopped me in my tracks and took me to the police station. I was interrogated there and this time I did not get away with a warning. I was kept at the station overnight and told that a court might impose a fine. The next morning, I returned home and, not having any keys with me, had to wait for a long time until my dopey mother finally opened the door to me. Despite her clearly intoxicated state, she must have guessed by just having taken one look at me that I had got myself into some serious trouble.

'When she was somewhat more sober a few hours later, she told me off in no uncertain terms. Actually, 'told me off' is an understatement. 'She gave me hell' is a more apt description of what she did, telling me that I was absolutely useless and caused nothing but trouble, that I was a parasite at home, sponging off the little money we had. Her words hurt even though I was aware of the injustice of her allegations and could have said to her that it was her after all who spent the little benefit money they received on alcohol and that I never got any money from her and had been barely fed over the last few years. Although it wouldn't have been incorrect to mention this, I refrained from doing so for two reasons: I, myself, had recently stolen some money from her, which had allowed me to go on my drinking sprees and, so I reasoned, would make her drink less. I know this sounds like a perverse logic, but I felt that it was working. She did appear more sober during the day and managed to my amazement to visit my baby sister on the neonatal unit most days. There must have been some maternal instincts left in her after all and I did not want to risk destroying them by being argumentative, which was the second reason for keeping my mouth shut. Instead, I promised her to pay back the fine the officer had asked me to pay and that I couldn't pay myself and my mother could barely afford. This was actually true; I didn't want to owe that fine and I also was sick of being financially dependent and wanted to start looking for a job seriously now.

'However, I didn't proceed with that plan of finding work as soon as possible, which would hopefully have entailed me moving away from home, as shortly after the incident with the police and the broken window-pane, I crashed down from a dizzying high to a deep low, which reversed my speed and energy levels completely. I remember waking up one morning with a head so fuzzy and unfocused that it felt as if it had been stuffed with cotton wool. This was not a symptom of a hangover from another excessive, drunken night.

'In fact, I hadn't even gone out the previous night, which was most unusual, but I had felt tired and nursed a headache. I had therefore gone to my room early with just one bottle of beer and played the classical guitar mood pieces that my father had given me what seemed a lifetime ago. I hadn't listened to that music for a while, usually putting on the thumping, noisy beats of high-energy rhythms played by an electric guitar – I, myself, had acquired an electric guitar less than three years earlier, too – and other instruments, but today it felt right to get lost in the soothing tones of my father's music. I fell asleep whilst the music was still on, but it wasn't a deep sleep but one that was disturbed by nightmares. I had alternating sensations of heat and coldness throughout the night, normally an indication that I had contracted the flu or a severe cold.

'When I woke up in the morning with a numb head and felt extremely tired and lethargic, I was convinced that I had come down with something. It was strange though that I experienced no other symptoms such as a sore throat or blocked sinuses, but brushed it off by thinking of it as a specific kind of head cold. During that time, I was mainly in bed, dozed a lot, but got no quality sleep. I was listless and didn't want to face the world, as doing anything seemed pointless.

'Days turned into weeks and all I did was vegetate in my room. I didn't even go to hospital any longer to see how my sister was developing, which I had done every few days after she was born despite telling myself that she was my mother's problem and that I had stopped long ago to have anything to do with her affairs.

'However, since I first saw my sister in her little incubator there had been something inside me that refused to genuinely regard her as a problem. It was not her but the environment she would grow up in that was the problem. I was touched by her from the start even though I had decided I would remain indifferent. Certainly, had I remained indifferent, things would have been easier and I might not have developed such extreme mood swings and mental states.

'This does not mean that I'm blaming my sister. Not at all. I'd just found that caring for someone comes along with its own difficulties, especially when you want to help them and lighten their lot but you can't or don't know how to. But we can't seem to just switch off caring for someone even if we decide to do so. We can just try to take our minds off any concerns and I had attempted that in many different ways with a life of excess including the use of alcohol with its dampening effect.

'During these weeks when I shut myself into my room, not visiting my sister was also a way of trying to distract myself from worrying about her although I wasn't conscious of that at the time. Back then, I had barely enough energy to drag myself to the corner shop every few days to buy some alcohol. The bottles and unwashed glasses accumulated and turned my room into a right tip. Add to that some unwashed plates – although I ate very little then – and you get an idea of how disgusting my room was becoming. I had always been someone who cleaned up after myself, as I didn't want to turn into my mother, who I at first had cleaned after as well before abandoning that venture as hopeless.

'It was only thanks to a couple of friends who were also in my band and who kept pestering me and refused to be sent away, that I finally, on their insistence, went to my GP's and had myself checked out. The GP immediately diagnosed me with depression but when I described my earlier hyperactive state to show him what a contrast it was to what I had been like in the period leading up to that slump, he revised his diagnosis to bipolar or manic-depressive disorder as it was still most frequently called then. He prescribed me some medication but warned me that the tablets would not cure me but could help me to manage the symptoms better. He advised me to see a therapist as well, a suggestion which I resolutely and instantly rejected. I had no desire whatsoever to let a shrink in on my life with my thoughts and emotions. The latter were my own and for me to deal with. Besides, what could a shrink do anyway other than sit down and listen as if you went to confession? At least this was the impression I got when I heard other people speak about therapy.

'I did try the medication though. Generally, I liked any substances that altered my mind in more pleasurable ways, which was why I liked alcohol in all its varieties and I had also dabbled with some of the softer drugs, although I wasn't a regular user as I was determined not to become dependent on them and thus ruin my life. New and even prescribed substances that directly targeted the brain were therefore more than welcome. And they did help. I would say that they took the edge off things. Two weeks after I had started taking them, I began to feel more like a human being again rather than like a vegetable. My mind became clearer, my energy wasn't quite so low any longer and the overarching thought of how pointless life was receded into the background. At the same time, there seemed to be a kind of barrier present that blocked the strength of some of the feelings like anger and frustration that had been so prominent in the past. Instead, joyful emotions rushed through me in waves.

'There was something else my GP had been spot on with, apart from the ameliorating effect of the tablets on my mind: They did not cure me. From then on, I have struggled to this day with what the doctor would call manic and depressive episodes respectively and whilst the medication didn't let things slip too far on the whole, there were times when my medication needed to be adjusted and everything became quite bad again in much the same way I have just outlined.

'I found some work once I was in a functioning state again. The jobs I did were not great jobs, but I didn't expect them to be. After all, I didn't have A-levels or anything equivalent to show to employers, many of whom expected such qualifications even for relatively simple jobs. As I had no desire to undergo further education or vocational training, I didn't care that my first job was a very monotonous one in a warehouse, which consisted of unloading crates from delivery vans, emptying them of their contents and stacking them in a corner of the warehouse where they would be picked up again. I can't even recall what the contents of the crates were. Other jobs included a short spell as a telephone operator in a call centre, which I truly hated and therefore quickly left behind, working as a store assistant in an IT shop and serving as a waiter in a restaurant-café. I deliberately didn't ask about bar work, as the danger was too high to once again abuse alcohol there after a shift, the free and price-reduced drinks I would get making that possibility even more likely.

'Finally, at the age of twenty, I found a job in a record shop and realised that for the first time I actually liked a job. Not only did I enjoy the continuous background music – we took turns in deciding what would be played – that mainly consisted of the latest releases, I took pleasure in finding some music pieces for our customers. Some of them would ask for a particular CD, band or musician, whilst others were much vaguer, indicating that they liked some quiet music or some jazzy tunes or any pop music from the 1960s. As you have probably realised, I was well-versed in a range of musical genres –

albeit by no means in all of them – and my knowledge and love of music served me well in this job. I prided myself in normally locating a specific album or single at no time whatsoever and liked the challenge of finding something appropriate for those customers who were vague by trying to figure out who they were and what made them tick and matching the image thus created of them to the music they needed. I knew how important it was for people to find 'their' music and what a change it could make to their lives. It made life so much more bearable.

'The work in the shop also had the benefit of introducing me to both genres and artists I knew nothing or very little about, which broadened my horizon. This was the first job where I didn't frequently turn up late and where I did not take a single day of sick leave during my six-months' probation period. On the contrary, I stayed longer than I had to, when I didn't meet my mates for band practice or had a gig to perform. I guess I knew that if I had a shorter evening, I had less time to drink. Drinking was less of a problem then, probably partly because I was happy in my work, which was acknowledged by my manager who gave me a pay rise and a few more responsibilities once my probation period had finished, and also because the medication kept me on a more even keel. In addition, I knew that I wanted to keep up playing my music in the much more limited time I now had available so that I fitted that in most evenings and then listened to music until I fell asleep.

'The band was going well, we were promoting ourselves much better and, as a result, were invited to more well-known venues. It also brought in a little more money. I would describe this as one of the better times in my life when I had the energy to be proactive and even managed to rent a small, one-bedroom flat and move out of home where I had had such a miserable time for so long. Today, in my current frame of mind, I can only wonder how I managed to make such a decisive change in my life. I don't seem to be able to make any changes these days even though some action should be taken. But I'm digressing.

'However, the years after my sister had been born unfortunately turned out how I had dreaded they would. My mother, in her dissolute lifestyle, was barely capable of looking after Jenny. There were a few occasions on which I was readying myself to alert social services despite the promise I had made to my mother a few years earlier not to do so, but as if she'd guessed it, my mother would just then always look after her better. To be fair to her, she had much reduced her drinking in the first one or two years after Jenny's birth and there were far fewer men around. Even though she didn't like children much, she still had a sense of responsibility and had no desire for social services to become involved in our lives. I think that she could not see anything worthwhile in her life any longer and she almost certainly could not envision any kind of future for herself.

'Carla felt dismal every day. It had been like this for a long time if she was honest with herself. How did she get herself into the situation she was in – a single mother of a teenager and a new-born whose father's identity she wasn't quite certain about. She felt trapped with the new baby. Why on earth had she not been more careful or had plucked up the courage to get rid of it once she learned about the pregnancy?

'She vaguely recalled how she had felt awful after my own birth as well, but this was different. Sixteen years ago, she had been ill and had been diagnosed with postnatal depression. This time, she didn't feel unwell in the same way. She just knew that this was not a life she wanted to have but thought quite rationally about it and concluded that there was nothing she could do about it. She knew that it was not only that she wasn't particularly fond of children and hated having to bring another one up as a single parent that made her feel trapped, but that having not worked for a few years and met other people outside and having let alcohol and men rule her aimless life contributed to her sensation of being caged and not in control. She had messed up but she had no idea how to get back on the straight and narrow. All she could do was to try to do better on her daughter than she done on her son with whom she hardly had a relationship to speak of.

'She went through the motions of feeding and washing the baby, of changing her nappies and taking her to the doctor when she was ill, which was the case more frequently than her being well. Jenny's infections were sometimes treated with antibiotics and a range of other medication, all of which Carla imagined must have taken their toll on her feeble little body. The GP tried to reassure her and said that her immune system would gradually improve, but that we had to be patient, as she hadn't had the best start in life. It was clear what he was referring to, as it was all in the patient record she assumed. At least he wasn't judgemental like the other GP in the shared practice who she had seen first. She recalled how that one had looked at her very sharply when he had read the baby's notes on the computer and had commented loudly, "Fetal alcohol syndrome. You drank heavily during your pregnancy." It had been more than a factual statement. There had been an obvious reproach in his voice. "Well, her sickly state now isn't surprising considering what she had to go through before she was even born and being a premature baby obviously didn't help."

'She swallowed but said nothing. She was waiting for him to suggest treatment. Instead, he asked her whether she was breastfeeding and what her alcohol intake was like now. She shook her head and explained that she had been told that her baby had to be formula-fed so she did that, ignoring the second part of his question. He pulled out a leaflet on alcohol consumption with addresses of advice and support groups on the back, which he pushed towards her. She stared at the leaflet, unable to fathom how talking about her drinking in front of a group of strangers could possibly help. It might be that he was trying to be helpful but his whole demeanour was patronising in her opinion and she felt deeply resentful when she left the surgery. Who was he to judge her, after all! He had no right to do so. In his idyllic world that most probably came with a big house and garden, a flashy car, a few holidays abroad every year and a perfect family, he wouldn't know what it meant to be all by herself, having sole responsibility of first one and now two children and feeling aimless and so lonely that it hurt. Add financial worries to the mix and her situation looked bleak indeed.

'Was it a surprise, then, when she tried to calm the worries and soften her isolation through the muffling, soothing effect of drink? Yes, it was true, she supposed, that she overdid it: She didn't experience the lightness that comes with tipsiness any longer, as she drank so much so quickly that she knocked herself almost or fully unconscious and then continued to be in a heavy daze. It was good to forget problems at least temporarily, though, and if oblivion was achieved by the trickle of sharp liquid down her throat so be it. And who could begrudge her meeting men? She was single, still relatively young and with a life to be lived. She deserved a bit of fun, comfort and some light relief in someone else's arms. Except that there was no relief if she was honest. At least not from the men she met. Even sex was just rough but not exciting or even arousing for the most part. In her view, she was treated like a doll and, as a result, felt lifeless and without a will of her own, being there simply to serve other people's needs whilst her own were not taken into account. There was no real, pleasurable distraction to be had from her sexual encounters and entanglements any longer as one man after the other turned to violence that she was exposed to, but she found herself unable to be on her own with just the kids so that she put up with it. Arguing with them or putting forward her plea to stop the use of force had no effect she soon found out and was, if anything, counter-productive.

'How did everything go so wrong in her life? She remembered her years with Archie during which everything had been lighter. They hadn't been the perfect couple: She would have probably preferred someone who was less inquisitive or keen on discussing a range of topics, but she had felt loved, held, protected and secure around him. Now she was in a completely different situation in which nobody protected her, or her children for that matter, and dangers seemed to be lurking everywhere. She was not in control of much in her life and she decided that all there was to do was to get through each day without too much harm being done.

'It could be questioned whether my mother had ever been in control of her life, but this wasn't really my problem as I kept reminding myself. Moving out of home, which hadn't been a home at all as you would want or expect it to be, proved to be predictably liberating at first. The flat might have been small and a bit cramped, particularly with all the music equipment in it, but to me it felt as if my world had expanded.

'Before I moved, my world had really been restricted to my bedroom. Venturing out to the kitchen or bathroom came along with the risk of bumping into one of the violent men who were so often in the house and being at the receiving end of their temper. I had avoided the living-room altogether for a long time even when I knew that nobody but my mother, sister and I were at home. The reason for that was that I couldn't face my mother being in an inebriated state, which highlighted the fact that she didn't take enough responsibility of my sister and struggled to fulfil her duty of care, which made me really angry.

'I know I had mentioned earlier that she tried harder and wasn't constantly drunk or hungover any longer, but by the time I left she had fallen back into drinking more heavily and bringing men home again, and even if things had not quite deteriorated to the same level as before Jenny was born, it was just not good enough and I thought that I was not prepared to cut her any slack any longer.

'Jenny was a small child who deserved better. At that point, I probably should have informed the authorities, as I had left my teens behind during which previously uttered warnings or threats had served as a deterrent and I had been too afraid as well as suspicious of officials to approach them. However, was it still fear that kept me from intervening at the age of twenty and has done so until now? I'm not sure. I'm afraid it probably had more to do with choosing the path of least resistance and not be exposed to the volatility of home life any longer. I didn't believe I would be able to deal with police officers and social workers very well and the prospect of making statements that would be recorded somehow sent shivers down my spine. Neither did I trust people in charge to do the right thing nor could I face the turmoil and upheaval it would cause me. At best, you can use the argument of self-preservation, which I frequently employed in a number of self-talks, but I realise that there is a high degree of selfishness involved in me not taking action.

What I did make sure of, though, was that I saw my sister at least once a week even during busy weeks with lots of band practice and gigs and my daytime job and, at least initially, I adhered to this plan of mine. It was the least I could do for her. It allowed me to enjoy some quality sibling time with Jenny, but more importantly, it would enable me to some extent to observe whether Jenny coped or whether the situation at home deteriorated further, which would undoubtedly show in my sister's behaviour, I reasoned. Seeing her and picking her up required some contact and communication with my mother, but I soon learned that I could keep that down to a minimum, as Jenny was usually at home when she wasn't at pre-school and my mother was probably relieved when she got 'a break' at home although I doubt that she paid much attention to her in the first place at this point.

'Whether I wanted to or not, I became deeply involved in my sister's life. You might have expected me, a young bloke then who had hardly outgrown his teens, to be bored or unnerved in the regular company of a small child, but somehow this was not the case. I might have merely had protective feelings towards my sister at the beginning with a strong desire to shelter her from my mother, her men and the chaotic life at home, but I soon became fond of her as the person she was. Like my mother, her teachers at preschool considered her hyperactive and mildly complained that she was unable to sit still and focus, and that she was wild and unruly, and would run into trouble at school if things didn't change. I didn't share their view. I knew that my mother's alcohol consumption during her pregnancy was to blame for my sister's fidgety and unfocused nature but I believed that my sister had potential and noticed all the improvements she had made since she was born and had been so poorly. The times when she had suffered a long series of infections were over. Her immune system made a recovery that was even surprising to the doctors. Moreover, she gained enough weight to be considered healthy, albeit merely on the lower end of the scale. She wasn't much – if at all – behind other children in her developmental milestones. Yes, I do admit I read up on child development because it was important for me to see my sister grow up in a good way and help her if she required assistance with anything.

'Mostly, we just had a nice time together. We went outside together a lot where she could expend her energy as much as she wanted. She loved going to the parks with their playgrounds and she couldn't get enough of the climbing frames there. She went up there like a flash and I realised how nimble she was when I was going after her, trying to keep up. She would laugh at me and my slowness as well as at my reminders that she needed to be careful if she didn't want to fall. Her movements were confident and assured though. There was no hesitation or wobble when she made her way up the frame. She had the agility of a monkey. We also played catch if I remembered to take a ball with me or we would play tag, sometimes asking other children on the playground to join us to increase the fun factor. Jenny loved playing these games. Being cooped up indoors most of the time, it was obvious that being active outdoors with me and, at times, others as well gave her a sense of freedom. It was a pleasure to observe how her pale complexion acquired a more healthy-looking colouring and I could not help but smile when I watched her slight figure whizz past me with her ash-blonde hair trailing behind her in the wind, laughing with abandon and with a shine in her light blue eyes.

'In the autumn, we collected conkers and played with them for hours at a time until all the conkers had turned to mush and we laughed our hearts out. We also saved some of them and made little figures, landscapes, houses and animals with them using toothpicks, match-sticks and cotton wool for our conker creations. In the end, I picked up a wooden board on which we arranged what we had made until we had a lovely little farmhouse and farm display, which we were both quite proud of. When we worked on our items, there was no indication that Jenny was clinically hyperactive with major difficulties concentrating. It is true that when we just stayed at my place on a rainy day and did something quietly, she was rushing and her mind flitted from one thing to the next, but if she had a substantial amount of exercise first, her fidgetiness was almost gone and she wholeheartedly applied herself to pursuits that she enjoyed.

'The first winter after I had left home was also great fun for both of us. It was a very cold winter with a lot of snow although without heavy snowstorms such as the one we're experiencing at the moment. Jenny and I were out every week, going on walks in the snow, having snowball fights and building snowmen. We even managed to build a small igloo together even if it didn't last very long before it collapsed. I might not be very dexterous in that respect, but then I hadn't been trained as a builder and at least we tried and enjoyed crawling inside and sheltering there whilst it was still standing. These times reminded me of my early childhood when my father was still around and played in the snow with me before these joys came to a premature end with his untimely death.

'What Jenny loved most of all was throwing herself into the snow and playing snow angels, which is what she had seen some other children do in pre-school. She would lie on the ground in her light-blue ski suit with its matching anorak – I was surprised that my mother had got her something so pretty and matching – and move her arms and legs up and down in synchronicity with a big smirk and some wisps of hair across her face. She would then jump up and delight in the form of an angel with its wings spread wide that was imprinted on the sparkling, diamond-studded snow. Everything around her appeared enchanted and, somehow, she enabled me to share this sense of enchantment through her eyes.

'When we were back home at my place – usually after having had another snowball fight – we rubbed ourselves dry and warm before putting on some clean and fresh clothes, me always making sure I took an extra set of clothes for Jenny with me when I picked her up at our mother's. I would then make hot chocolate for both of us in my small kitchen and I was quite proud of the fact that I made what I call the proper stuff rather than a ready-made, artificial mixture that only required you to pour hot water over it before you could drink it. No, I took a saucepan out of the cupboard and poured cold milk into it, which I heated on the cooker until clouds of steam rose up. Then I would spoon pure cocoa powder into the hot milk and stir it at a reduced heat level. I would also add a bit of sugar but not too much, as I loved to drink the cocoa in its slightly bitter, milky state. When I poured the thick liquid into the two mugs I had set aside, I made sure to add some more sugar into Jenny's mug for her to enjoy the drink fully. We would then take our mugs over to the small sofa where we sat down and held the hot mugs in our hands to warm the latter before taking small but appreciative sips. It was cosy and I guess the only thing that was missing was a crackling, open fire but when I mentioned that to Jenny she pointed out that we could just think of a fire instead. She was so young and already she had grasped the power of the mind. We would then watch a cartoon or a children's film that I would enjoy as well on my small telly until it was time for me to take her back home with a heavy heart.

'During that first year in my new place I really felt more like an agent in my own life rather than a spectator who was being pushed and pulled in all directions at a whim and was unable to do anything about it. There was this great need to define my life in a new way that constituted a complete break with how things had been at home: One example of how this need was expressed was that I started exploring other, more ethical and thoughtful approaches to being in the world. I tried to reduce the environmental impact I had on the planet by buying less packaging and focusing more on organic produce, simultaneously giving up all meat and cutting down on my dairy consumption with the goal to eventually become vegan, which I didn't quite manage but considered to be the way forward.

'All this stood in stark contrast to my mother's thoughtless consumption of convenience food which I had grown up with, and taken part in, for so long. This drastic change in lifestyle went hand in hand with, and was facilitated by, my increasing awareness of the conditions of the world around me, which to a large extent I learned about by reading articles and books and watching documentaries and other educational programmes. I now pursued knowledge deliberately, partly because I found myself to be – to my own surprise – curious about things, which had become clear to me and my colleagues in the music shop, but also to a large extent because I refused to be trapped in the low socio-economic, low educational background cycle. By that I don't necessarily mean that I set my heart on finding higher-paid work through getting more formal educational qualifications, but rather that I wanted to expand my horizon instead of being content with the limitations circumstances had imposed on it. I longed to be a self-made man albeit not necessarily in the profit-seeking, capitalist way the American dream has promised people to become if they pursued a certain path.

'In order to get more understanding and insight into society and various aspects of the world I wanted to learn more about, I got myself a library card and borrowed piles of books, usually the maximum number I was entitled to borrow. I wanted to understand poverty and social inequality and therefore borrowed, at first, non-fiction bestsellers dealing with these issues and then more difficult, groundbreaking works that tried to provide a theoretical framework with which to understand these social phenomena and processes. Equally, I was driven to comprehend the role of the state in this context, investigating its functions in our own society to start with but soon looking into different political systems with their different methods of governing the people.

'Never having been much of a reader when I was younger either at school or at home where there were virtually no books after my father had died because my mother had disposed of them, I now read voraciously, absorbing Max Weber's ideas and comparing them to Durkheim's before going on to read about Marx and Lenin's communism, interspersing my reading of these texts with John Stuart Mill's famous essay *On Liberty*, his work *Utilitarianism* and other works on utilitarianism such as those written by Mill's predecessor Jeremy Bentham.

'I believe I was on a quest, trying to find out how our systematically flawed society could be made better, what alternatives there were and how to bring them about. Whilst I soon developed socialist and utilitarian leanings, I also quickly identified the drawbacks and pitfalls each of these approaches had, if not always in theory, then in their practical implementation especially if the latter turned out to be a distortion of the underlying, original ideas. You only have to look at the abuse of power under socialist or communist regimes in Russia and the former Soviet Union, in the GDR in post-war Germany and, of course, most famously, in China where it reached its brutal climax in the Cultural Revolution in the 1960s and 1970s.

'A sense of disillusionment coupled with a growing cynicism came upon me, which was when I started to turn to speculative fiction, initially to the hopefulness and idealism of utopias before directing my attention the gloomy visions outlined in dystopias such as Orwell's *1984*, Huxley's *Brave New World*, Margaret Atwood's *The Handmaid's Tale* or Joseph Heller's *Catch 22* and many other classics of the genre as well as newer publications in it.

'I don't know whether it is coincidental or not that just as I focused on the darker manifestations of power in societies, my mental health declined again. Maybe it was belated proof of me not coping when living on my own, but I like to think that this is not the case. It didn't help that a couple of my band members moved away and although we tried to keep the band going, both rehearsals and performances decreased steadily in number until we disbanded two years later. Not being part of the band any longer affected me more than I admitted at the time. There had been a camaraderie, the shared joy of doing something together that was important to us, the deeper understanding of each other that comes from this experience of sharing a passion and the pride in playing in front of people who appreciated our music.

'The two guys who moved away were less and less in touch as they became increasingly wrapped up in their new lives elsewhere and the other, remaining band member focused on his career in business, which seemed to take up almost every single minute he had. As a result, I was suddenly a lot more isolated and if I wanted to go out I went out on my own, which meant that I ended up in bars drinking. Probably unsurprisingly, I experienced another major manic episode of a kind I hadn't gone through since just after my sister was born, which was closely followed by the black dog of depression whose jaws bore down on my neck in an attempt to suffocate me.

'I went to the doctor's on my own accord this time because – despite my dislike of seeing a doctor about my mood swings – I felt that I had too much to lose if things escalated and by that I mean both my job, which I thoroughly enjoyed, and access to my sister. Maybe it was the awareness of having more responsibilities that I didn't want to simply discard than when I had my first breakdown, maybe it was the adjustment of my medication, probably it were both these factors that allowed me not to fall quite so deeply. But it was deep enough:

'In fact, the last six years have been an almost continuous struggle to keep everything together with very few and all too brief periods of respite. I even tried, against my conviction, counselling at one point, but I didn't stick with that for very long. I reckon if you are highly critical of and sceptical about its benefits, you are unlikely to see any of them. I'm sure that the counsellor I saw disliked me because I saw through her and knew how her mind was programmed and said so to her. That might not have been wise on my part, but at least it was honest. It was obvious how she functioned in her job: Every time I said something, she tried to categorise it, identifying it as a symptom that could be linked to a condition and then potentially tackled by talking about it. I hated her knowing smile of satisfaction when she thought she had successfully used her knowledge to label me or something about me.

'Maybe I shouldn't have been surprised about it. After all, this was exactly how doctors worked as well when dealing with the physical body of a person. More than that, this is how we resolve problems and challenges on a daily basis; we identify an issue and then we work on it by resorting to our knowledge we have acquired through learning and practice. Why should it be any different with professionals of the mind? I guess though that I have always firmly believed that nobody can have quite the same insight into a person's mind than that person themselves, because only they are aware of the exact strength and nature of their feelings and of their entire personal history that had given rise to these feelings, certain thoughts and behaviours.

'Professionals might be able to recognise certain mechanisms between these, but they will always be at a disadvantage because they can only learn snippets about the person they talk to and will therefore never be in a position to see the whole picture. And the whole picture is crucial to arrive at as the human mind is complex – even if it sometimes seems very simple as in my mother's – and her men's – cases, and cannot be treated by taking one part out of context and working on that part as we would when being faced with a flat car tyre. Therapy must therefore be precarious and problematic by its very nature. I knew what was good for me and didn't need a counsellor to tell me that; I just needed to act on my insight.

'Work turned from something I loved into something I struggled through. Maybe that needs moderating or at least explaining a bit more. I still very much enjoyed advising our customers and being at the music store but my increased alcohol consumption, and nights during which I got very little sleep, made getting to the shop and staying there in a reasonably alert state almost impossible or at least turned it into a major challenge. Somehow, I mastered it on most days through sheer willpower and determination because I knew very well that losing this job might mean losing everything; my flat and thus my newly-found freedom and unless I moved back in with my mother, a possibility I considered disastrous in its likely impact on me, access to my sister. I had to hold on to this job if I wanted to avoid a fall all the way down the abyss.

'However, despite keeping my sick leave reasonably low, my behaviour at the store changed enough to prompt initially some frowns and eventually questions from the manager. In hindsight, I'm not surprised that my sometimes near-catatonic state in which I barely reacted to anything, and occasionally fell asleep, drew attention to me, especially because these low times were sharply contrasted by other times during which I couldn't sit still, spoke twice as fast as usual and adopted an overfamiliar attitude towards customers that was considered inappropriate.

'Eventually I had to explain my mental battles to my manager, as I considered that the only way not to get fired. Of course, I hated speaking about it but my boss was one of the few people I didn't want to disappoint as he had given me all these developmental opportunities by promoting me and had always been very good with me. Fortunately, he was able to make the imaginative leap that allowed him to come close to stepping into my shoes.

'He therefore didn't consider me a freak but showed some understanding and even thanked me for having been so open with him. Moreover, he asked me how he could best support me and urged me to get all the specialist help I was entitled to. I just nodded to his plea instead of telling him what I really thought about specialist help, namely what I had told you earlier. Although I'm not a person who hides his true opinions and thoughts as you have probably noticed, revealing them in this context might actually have cost me the job there and then, as my attitude towards therapy might have been interpreted as a refusal to try everything in my power to get better and thus perform excellently at work again in a consistent manner. How could I hope for my employer's continued support if I gave him the impression that I made no effort to get into a better place? How could he trust me and rely on my professionalism if my behaviour became increasingly unpredictable? Therefore, I lied to him when he sometimes asked me whether the specialist help was working for me, saying that it was useful but that it would take time until I was back to how I had been at the time of my promotion and he accepted that. I found it hard to lie, as it wasn't part of my nature, but it was done in a spirit of self-preservation.

'I managed to carry on like this at work until about a year ago when I was sliding further down the hole and was forced to take extensive sick leave for the better part of six months. Even then, my boss was as understanding as I could have wished for when I returned to work but suggested, which was completely understandable, to relieve me of some of the duties I had taken on when I was promoted and basically offered me the job that I had when I first started work at the music store. I shocked myself when I felt close to tears and struggled to hold them back, which was the last thing I had intended to happen.

'My manager must have seen what was going on inside me and one day said gently, "Leo, please don't take this the wrong way. You're a very talented person with a real interest in, and a passion for, music and I am convinced you can achieve anything you set your mind to. I'm not taking responsibilities away from you because I don't have confidence in your abilities. I do, but I want to give you a better chance to truly recover after the tough time you had during the previous few months. You also owe it to yourself to slowly ease yourself back into work. I'm glad you're back, Leo, but I want you to be back and well rather than struggling and although I partly say this with our business in mind, I also say this because I care about your wellbeing."

'I took a deep breath to calm the storm of emotions that had surged up before I nodded in acquiescence. "Of course," was all I uttered before I busied myself with work.

'It wasn't that I didn't believe my manager when he said that he had my wellbeing at heart or thought his actions unreasonable. On the contrary, it was precisely because he showed concern and solicitude towards me and, because of my knowledge, that I had let him and the store down that I – in the end resigned – less than two weeks after returning to work and having had this conversation.

'I remember how taken aback and how worried he was when I couldn't answer his question about what I would be doing next, but I brushed his reaction aside because – in my experience – not many people had truly cared about me for a sustained period of time, which made me think that in a few days' time he would be relieved to be in a position to employ a more reliable and stable person and not waste a thought on me. I don't know whether this was an accurate appraisal of him and his attitude towards my resignation, but maybe that doesn't matter any longer because the fact is that I left that job six months ago and have not tried to go back or find work anywhere else.

'During these last six months of upheaval and agitation I still saw my sister fairly regularly but merely by using every ounce of willpower and determination. I realised early on how disappointed she was on the occasions I cancelled our meetings because I was too unwell to either get up and leave the house or to look after her in a responsible manner or both. Her disappointment stirred something inside me that was hard to bear, which was what gave me the strength to get out of bed during my severely depressive episodes and stay away from the bars during my manic phases on the days I had promised to pick her up.

'It was because of her that I kept going even if the effort of doing so took its toll and caused me extreme exhaustion. And I only just managed to see her in a reasonably presentable state most weeks. What I couldn't, and didn't, do any longer was take her home to my flat, as my energy and willpower certainly didn't extend to cleaning and tidying what had turned into a chaotic, stinking mess filled with the reek of stale cigarette smoke and the sharp vapours of spirits that seemed to use up all the air's oxygen. I was responsible enough not to expose her to the evidence of my dissolute lifestyle.

'She saw enough of that at home and I certainly wanted to avoid her going back to our mother and telling her about the kind of life I lived. Not that it was likely that our mother would have been interested in that and forbidden her contact with me. It was far more likely that she would not have taken any notice in view of her deteriorating life and health, but I would not run any risks. My sister was too precious to me and I dreaded to think what might happen to her if I didn't keep an eye on her.

'Initially, Jenny would ask why we didn't go home to my flat any longer, especially when it was pouring down with rain outside, but she eventually stopped doing so when I kept insisting that I spent far too much time indoors, and so did she, and that it was important to get some fresh air, or, in the case of rain, at least have a change of scene. The walks and physical activities we had so keenly participated in before were curbed by me as I didn't have the physical energy for them any longer but I still encouraged my sister to do all the things she wanted to do in the playground. The fresh air must nevertheless have done me some good as I felt a bit better at the end of the day, despite the lingering tiredness and exhaustion, and if it was just that my mood had been lifted a little. Breathing fresh air for a few hours must have had some positive effect on my lungs and head as well, particularly when considering how much I exposed them to harmful conditions.

'When it rained, I took Jenny to the cinema, which she loved, and then to a nice café where I bought her a hot chocolate and whatever cake she fancied on the day, which mostly turned out to be date and walnut cake. She loved everything about going to the café that we usually visited: the waiter or waitress greeting us warmly when we entered and taking us to a free table, the comfortable, nicely upholstered chairs on which we took our seats, the square mahogany tables with a pretty albeit artificial carnation in a small, shapely white vase on top of them, the large mirrors on all the walls with their shiny messing frames, the display counters with some magnificent-looking pastries and cakes behind glass, the way our table was nicely laid and the cream-coloured cups and saucers and plates that were made of what looked like fine china. She wasn't used to any of that at home. Our mother certainly never bothered any longer with setting the table and when she gave Jenny something to eat, it was either carelessly dumped on an unclean plate or a serviette and tended to consist of greasy fast food, bread or some burnt porridge.

'It was a pleasure to see therefore how much Jenny relished our visits to cafés, even if I had to teach her how to use her fork properly in order not to draw unwanted attention to herself. She was used to either eating with her hands or to clumsily using a spoon. Fortunately, she enjoyed learning how to use cutlery properly and was proud to show off her newly acquired skills in front of the waitresses and café owners. The serious and concentrated facial expression she then adopted made me smile.

'Often, she would tell me about what she had been up to at school, most of all what they had done in their P.E. lessons. Whilst I had never cared much about sports or sports lessons myself when I was still at school, I was in fact glad that she was so much into sports and good at it, as this meant that she was more readily integrated into friendship circles that formed – even if they were superficial and transient in nature – and not bullied. Initially, we had to work on her coordination for ball games and some other sports, which I believe was a bit skewed as a result of her previous alcohol exposure when she was still inside our mother. But she loved physical activity so much and obviously needed it and was keen to get things right that she asked me to show her how to do the sports properly, which I did even if I wasn't very sportive myself.

'I enjoyed watching her improve and being proud of her achievements. I made sure she could join the school's netball team when parental permission was sought for it and our mother didn't react one way or another to her begging to be part of the team. I had to intervene and explain to our mother why this was important for Jenny until she shrugged her shoulders and agreed to pay the minimal contribution that was required. Jenny soon started meeting up with some of the other girls from her netball team outside their training sessions to play some more at the playing fields that had the equipment they needed. In addition, they played other games and I saw my sister blossom in the company of, and acceptance by, her peers.

'There were occasions though when I became painfully aware that not everyone shared my regard for my sister: Her teachers didn't think very highly of her cognitive abilities and, like her teachers at pre-school, considered her too unfocused and restless. I found unopened letters to our mother at home in which the school asked her to come in for a meeting and a talk with them.

'It took me a while but I eventually responded and went to Jenny's school to talk about her educational progress. I explained the circumstances of Jenny's upbringing to those teachers who weren't aware of them and the challenges they posed. Moreover, I described how inquisitive she was, highlighting her thirst to learn, and that she certainly did not have any real cognitive deficits. When her teachers remained sceptical, I decided that I had to prove them wrong, reaching out to them half-way when I promised to study with her. I used my newly-found eloquence from my self-study of books and other information sources to get my point across more convincingly.

'And so I learnt together with Jenny after letting her engage in some physical activity first and it went well. I made sure that I kept each learning interval short, engaging and interactive and found that this really worked for my sister. Although this wasn't the most important part of it all, it was satisfying to see her marks improve and read comments of praise under some of her school work now. I had proven my sister to be intellectually capable and the teachers even started to take on board my comments about Jenny requiring slightly different teaching and learning methods to reach her full potential. They made more attempts to do justice to her and presumably some other children who required adapted ways of teaching even if their implementation of a greater range of teaching methods that catered for more diverse learning needs wasn't always perfect.

'Despite all these positive developments in her life, there were still the challenges of a highly problematic, volatile home environment to contend with for her, which deteriorated further over the years. It was hard to see how her surroundings at home would not offset the moments of joy she experienced outside of it.

'If there was any specific event that decisively tipped the balance and brought on worrying changes in her it was the moving in of our mother's latest bloke, Dan. He really was the worst of the worst. Not only was he the most violent and intemperate bloke my mother had had – and considering her track record of men that was quite an achievement – he was also the most misogynistic and lewd beast I've come across in real life. I had only met him a few times in passing when I either picked Jenny up or brought her home after an afternoon out, but each time he gave me the creeps with his butcher's face and stocky stature that had adopted a battle stance. At one point, he even bared his teeth like a rabid dog and I half-expected to feel those teeth dig into my arm and maul it to pulp. I had nightmares after that and refused from then on to set foot inside the house and arranged with Jenny to meet me outside.

'I repeatedly thought of reporting him, having seen more bruises on my mother's skin, but I was too afraid that they would take Jenny away and none of us would have any contact with her, and there was always the possibility that she would be mistreated in her new home. Once again, I decided that I couldn't risk that, but I know that there was a lot of selfishness that went into that decision. I did ask my sister about Dan though and whether he beat her or behaved horribly towards her. My sister would always shake her head and then quickly change the topic and because I didn't see any unusual bruises or injuries on her, I believed her. Or rather, I wanted to believe her. It was easier not to dig deeper.

'However, I noticed how she became increasingly body-conscious before she even reached the age of nine. I knew that this was not unusual for adolescent girls, having noticed this development in girls I went to school with, but was suspicious that my sister started to focus on aspects of appearance at such a young age, especially because she had not previously shown any signs of being overly worried about her looks and body image and had always shown a healthy appetite and relished the allegedly pleasant physical sensations gained from exercise.

'When I now took her to a café, she would order herbal tea instead of hot chocolate and make sure that they served her a thinly-cut slice of cake. When I asked her about these changes in her, she said to me to my astonishment that she had to watch her weight. I quizzed her why she thought this and eventually she replied that Dan had told her that she had a finely-shaped arse but that she had to watch it so that it didn't become too fat and have it groped by all the men, who would not be as gentle and nice as he was being to her at the time. A nasty laugh followed his statement before he added that she might actually enjoy that kind of thing.

'I nearly spat out my coffee when I heard this and demanded in a fit of rage that she told me what he meant by that and whether he had touched her. I could see Jenny squirm on her chair in the café and guessed that she was afraid to say anything negative about our mother or Dan in case they found out and took it out on her. I clearly remember my own fear when my mother told me as a child not to reveal anything about our home life under any circumstances. If they had warned my sister in a similar way, I wouldn't have been surprised. She could see my anger clearly though and, feeling safe with me, she told me more. "He slapped my bottom and then stroked it and laughed and I didn't like it."

'My face was reddening with chagrin and my breathing became faster. Jenny instinctively tried to reassure me and calm me down by emphasising that he normally didn't do anything like that and certainly didn't do anything else. I felt a bit sick at the thought that Jenny might already have knowledge of what something else might be.

'I spoke very seriously to her, which made Jenny fall quiet and listen carefully to me. I said to her that Dan had absolutely no right to touch her and that she had to promise to tell me instantly if it happened again. Moreover, I reassured her that she could and should eat properly, which included all the food she really enjoyed having, and that she certainly wasn't about to become overweight or had to 'watch it' as Dan had expressed it. I asked her insistently whether she had understood what I had said and whether she believed me and thought I was an honest person.

'She didn't react immediately but nodded in the end. Nonetheless, this wasn't the end of it. I was convinced that Jenny was still calorie counting even if she tried to hide it from me. I caught her more than once throwing away a big part of her fast food when she thought I wasn't watching her and there were other worrying signs: Over the last nine months she had adopted a hunched posture as if she wanted to hide her body or even disappear and wore oversized, loose shirts that hid the shape of her torso. This change occurred at about the time when she visibly began to develop into a teenager and she started growing small breasts and her body became slightly more rounded. She was still slender though. She just wasn't the tiny thing that she had been as a baby and toddler when she had struggled to gain enough weight to stay healthy. A cheap, calorie-rich diet and a sound appetite had ensured that this was not the case any longer even with her relatively recent tendency to watch her calorie intake.

'Picking up on my sister's self-consciousness, I wondered about how she regarded herself. I had read accounts of young girls who battled with eating issues and had seen programmes on distorted body perceptions. Amongst them were many girls with completely normal body shape who were disgusted by what they saw as the fatness of their bodies. As a result, they purged themselves after every meal they had and developed bulimia or anorexia, with girls who developed the latter ending sometimes up in hospital and being force-fed. I was shocked and highly alarmed by these programmes. Even though I did not think that my sister was in the same position these girls were in, I was very concerned that she might end up like them if she wasn't careful.

'I strongly suspected that Dan's influence showed itself in the behaviour she exhibited and I was determined to find out whether he was bothering her. I therefore ignored her attempts at staving off my questions and insisted on receiving an answer.

'Once again, she spoke to me at last. She replied that Dan had not touched her again but that she disliked the way he stared at her, letting his eyes glide down her body from head to foot and lingering on her chest with what I would call a lascivious leer.

'I balled my hands into fists but didn't know how to respond so I said nothing and decided to mull over what could be done.

'Jenny also became more shy and unsure of herself and I soon learned that some of the other children at school had now in fact started to bully her, something I had always worried about. She was losing some of her spark for life, her energy and passion.

'The last few months have been extremely difficult. Everything that was worrying me came together. My mental health was spiralling out of control, I'd left my job and had to fill in application forms for benefits which I could barely concentrate on and Jenny was becoming more and more quiet, withdrawn and absent-minded. When I picked her up on a weekend afternoon, I was often late, barely dressed and, more often than not, unwashed, my teeth unbrushed and my hair uncombed and extremely dishevelled. I was also growing a stubble, which I disliked, but I couldn't find the energy to shave any longer.

'When Jenny started complaining that I smelled, I washed out my mouth by gurgling with mouthwash, put a Polo in my mouth before I left my place and sprayed eau do toilette all over me in the hope that it might cover my mouth and body odours. I'm not convinced that it worked as Jenny kept a distance between us.

'We now mainly went to the cinema as I didn't have the strength to go on walks and dreaded to see more signs of her eating issues if we went to a café. In hindsight, I'm surprised that the cinema employees even let me in, as I must have started to resemble a homeless person.

'I highly doubt that I was much – if any – good to my sister during that time apart from giving her a break from our mother and Dan. I hope that she still enjoyed seeing me and treasured the bond we had, but I think that even that must have become a strain on her, as she must have been alarmed by my self-neglect and decline, which was impossible to hide from her. She didn't comment on my transformation after she had told me that I smelled, but I caught her watching me from the corner of her eye sometimes when she thought I wasn't looking at her and her face showed concern and worry before it changed into an expressionless mask once she noticed my gaze rest on her. The last thing I wanted to do was to cause her additional anxiety and sorrow.

'It became quite clear to me though that that was exactly what was happening when I picked her up yesterday and went to the park with her to enjoy an invigorating walk in the winter sunshine. We hadn't done this for a long time now, but in the last few days I had been pleasantly surprised by a slight lift in my mood and a small elevation of my energy levels. I was determined to make up to Jenny by giving her the opportunity to do some exercise outside which she so loved and needed and take her to our favourite café again afterwards and just chat with her. Besides, I knew that some more sunlight and fresh air was likely to improve my state of mind further, too.

'Jenny was far less enthusiastic about my plans than I had hoped though. She simply nodded and walked next to me but didn't make an attempt at running or engaging in any other vigorous exercise. Maybe she just didn't think it was cool to do this now that she was a teenager. So many young teenage girls stopped exercising because they became self-conscious and didn't like the way their body looked when exercising. I partly sympathised with that, as I had more often than not felt clumsy and foolish during many PE classes at school. I wasn't going to quiz Jenny about it at the time though and instead relished the fact that we were about to spend more quality time together that allowed us to engage more with each other again.

'However, Jenny answered all my questions about school or netball in a very monosyllabic way and seemed absent-minded despite making an effort to smile when she heard me say something vaguely funny. Just before we entered the café, she turned to me, looked at me directly and asked me, "Are you feeling better then, Leo?"

'The question took me by surprise. It could have been uttered by a doctor or a nurse or the kind of solicitous mother I had never had, but I didn't expect my kid sister to come out with that. Her question was clear proof that she had been fully aware of how much I had been struggling. I stopped in my tracks outside the café's entrance, returned her gaze and, holding her upper arm, said seriously, "I'm fine, Jenny. Don't you worry about me. Everything is well."

'She gave me a look of disbelief, but I continued regardless. "I need to know that *you* are alright. You're unusually quiet these days and your energy and enthusiasm seem to have gone." I now couldn't help myself any longer but had to raise my concerns. "You look so downcast, Jenny, and you keep worrying about food and how you look and, as I have told you before, all this is completely unnecessary. There's nothing more I wish for than to see you happy and fully alive again. If there is anything – anything at all – that I can do to help with that, please tell me."

'I must have looked very worried now and my words had been spoken in an imploring tone of voice. What alarmed me the most was Jenny's reaction to my plea: She burst into tears and suddenly started shaking badly.

"'I'm sorry, I'm sorry, Leo," she sobbed, an apology she must have uttered a million times at home to deflect our mother's and Dan's anger, but which she now made not out of fear of an angry or even violent reaction from me as a result of her weeping as she knew she had nothing to fear from me but out of trepidation of the emotional burden her tears and sorrow would have on me, which became clear when she added, "I know that you struggle as well, Leo. It won't help if I tell you all about what is going on."

'Naturally, this statement of hers only alarmed me more. At the same time, I was amazed at Jenny's maturity, her ability to empathise and her love and concern for me that she put before her own emotional needs such as the one to be listened to. I wasn't sure how she had managed to develop in this way in a home environment like hers. It seemed like a miracle at first, but then maybe it wasn't. Had I not always been convinced that Jenny was special? Her quiet concern also worried me though as it wasn't hard to see how this could be exploited by callous and selfish people and it wouldn't do her any favours at home. I was determined to make Jenny speak about anything that was on her mind and listen properly and help whenever I deemed it feasible.

"'Jenny,' I said hoarsely, working hard to hide my agitation, 'I want you to tell me anything that worries you. As I said, I'm fine. I want and need to hear about you," I urged, raising my voice at the end to add emphasis to my words.

'Jenny nodded slowly before she said that she needed to sit down. Only then did I realise that we were still standing in the cold outside the café, with customers entering and leaving it by pushing past us, as we almost blocked the entrance.

"'Of course," I replied and led Jenny into the welcoming warmth of the café's interior.

"Once we were seated and had placed and received our orders, she spoke quietly to me of how some of the other kids at school kept taking her things and were hiding them so that she spent almost all of her breaks searching for her gloves, her pens or pencils or other things that seemed to have vanished. Although she usually found them somewhere in the classroom, the toilet or the courtyard in the end, these incidents upset her, especially because they were usually accompanied by her classmates' broad grins.

'Even her netball team didn't offer her the kind of respite that allowed her to recharge any longer as the other girls had started to become very focused on clothes and accessories, proudly showing them off with some well-known brands on display and looking down on her cheap, plain clothes from the supermarket. The fact that she was sportive and competitive was no longer enough to let her fully be part of the group. Instead, the other girls either ignored her or hurled cutting remarks at her that reflected their scorn.

'As if all this wasn't bad enough, Jenny – albeit used to it to a large extent – could not help but worry about our mother's now near-constant stupor, which sometimes looked comatose and which scared Jenny so much that she had been on the verge of calling an ambulance on a couple of occasions when she had not been certain whether her mother was dying right in front of her or had already died when she couldn't rouse her. Each time, her mother had stirred right after Jenny had picked up the phone to make the 999 call.

'Moreover, Dan kept staring at her and had suggested measuring her 'nicely-growing breasts' so that he could get her some nice bras to keep them in check and save her thus from too many gropes by horny men although that plan might backfire if he got her some padded ones. When he said these things to her, she willed the earth to swallow her up and drown his mean laughter by replacing it with a comforting silence.

'Finally, she added that she disliked her body and thought that it was largely her body's fault that Dan came out with these things. If she could get rid of any curves and just be straight and thin, things would be a bit better. She lamented that she unfortunately didn't have enough willpower to achieve this and it made her miserable and hate herself.

'When Jenny had finished talking, I was overwhelmed by a crushing melancholy, deep emotional pain and a roaring rage all at the same time. I felt tears forming in my eyes and I could only just in time make my excuse of needing to visit the loo urgently before my face turned wet with rapid streams running down my cheeks. I stayed in the toilet for a few minutes until the torrent of tears had abated in its flow, washed my face and presented myself to my sister again if not in a calm, then at least in a more collected manner.

'Jenny looked worried when I sat back down at the table, possibly regretting her outpouring of grief. I didn't give her a chance to say anything to that effect however and spoke with a determination and a sense of resolve that I had rarely shown. "Listen, Jenny. I'm so sorry you're feeling terrible and life is so hard at the moment. I promise you that things will get better and that I'm going to help you!"

'After this exclamation, I saw her doubtful facial expression, which was punctuated by faint glimmers of hope. On an impulse, I took my phone out of the pocket, did a quick search and then announced almost triumphantly, "Let's get the bill and go to the cinema. You might get home a bit later today, but surely that will be fine. There is an excellent new comedy on release and I can't wait to go and see it. Do you want to watch it?"

'Excited by my idea and relieved by my enthusiasm and ostensibly happy mood, Jenny eagerly agreed and a few minutes later we left our table with the barely half-eaten cake on Jenny's plate and made our way to the movies.

'It was much later in the evening, long after I had dropped Jenny off at home after we had enjoyed a light-hearted, perfectly pitched comedy, that it hit me forcefully that what I had promised Jenny would be impossible to fulfil for all the reasons that I have mentioned earlier and that had kept me from taking any decisive action to truly change things for her, particularly with regards to her life at home. I agonised over this for hours last night, tossing and turning whilst the scenes she had described to me unfolded like a film in front of my eyes. I had never considered myself an empathetic person and still don't think of me in that way, but I think last night I came close to vicariously experiencing situations my sister had been in and seeing things through her eyes and all I can say about that is that it was terrible and almost unbearable. I can't see how anyone can sustain an empathetic attitude over a longer period of time and remain sane. It's torture. I only fell asleep in the early hours of the morning and that sleep was short and disrupted; I felt dreadful when I woke up. The thought of lying in bed any longer, though, tormenting myself with my restless, harrowing thoughts and dreams was much worse than getting out of bed having had hardly any sleep.

'Staggering out of bed, I nearly fell flat on my nose due to dizziness and faintness. In the bathroom, I splashed my face and neck with cold water, which helped a little to steady myself. Then I went to the kitchen to make myself a cup of strong, black, instant coffee, but managed to spill boiling water over my left hand as I was pouring it from the kettle because my hands were shaking as if I was under the influence of alcohol, although I wasn't. I cursed and held my hand under running cold water from the tap. My composure had now completely vanished and, once again, like yesterday, tears formed and were not to be stopped any longer. By then I was sobbing and intermittently even howling.

'I lowered myself on the kitchen chair and buried my head in my forearms on the small kitchen table, giving my emotions free rein. I don't know how long I was sitting like that without feeling much relief and battling with oppressive thoughts that insistently revolved in my head. Eventually, I decided to go outside, hoping that being outdoors would provide me with some distraction and thus ease my pain. I took a quick, cold shower in an attempt to cool down my feverish mind, threw some clothes on, grabbed my keys and jacket and hurried outside.

'It was snowing steadily and a freezing wind was blowing when I stepped outside, and I hugged my suede jacket with its woollen lining closer around my body. Although it felt as if the chill in the air hurt my lungs, it felt good to be outside. It was probably the combination of the openness of the outdoors and the whiteness and brightness of the snow that had an uplifting effect on me. I was still extremely agitated but I was glad for the small improvement I experienced. I had often found that walking was conducive to letting the mind come up with ideas or solutions that it wouldn't necessarily have if I just sat down and thought hard about a matter. If I wanted to create a new song or just think of a different tune I could play on the guitar and in the past share with my band members I would often go on a walk. If I wasn't low on energy, I would sometimes walk for a long time and when I returned home play something new and different, which excited me.

'Circumstances now called for another extensive walk. In fact, I was determined not to go back home until I had found a viable solution to my sister's demise. If I didn't find an answer, there was no point in going back and continuing as I had before, as it was crystal clear that this didn't change anything fundamentally for my sister and was completely insufficient. I didn't care much about my own life. I felt and still feel that I have wasted it. The world is probably better off without me if I'm incapable of bringing about positive change even only for the person I feel closest to. If I perished in the increasingly bracing conditions outside, it didn't really matter and I say this not out of self-pity but out of conviction. At the same time, I kept thinking about a way forward for my sister while I walked briskly across the fields, leaving the distractions of the small town behind and hoping that in the vastness of the barren, white, flat winter landscape my mind would provide me with an answer to my question what I could and should do. How can the experience of solitude in nature not suggest new possibilities begging to be explored? You can see that I was torn between feelings of resignation and notions of idealistic hope.

'I'm not sure how far I walked, as I had neither put on a watch nor had I grabbed my phone in my hurried departure from home earlier, but I guess it must have been quite some distance, as it felt as if the hours were passing. The snowfall had soon become dense and the earlier windy conditions had now transformed into a fully-fledged storm that made walking a challenge, especially as I was soon exposed to the gale blowing straight at me.

'Whilst I had initially been able to scan the flat landscape, which was interspersed by a few settlements here and there and stretched out in front of me to the horizon, I soon could barely see two metres in front of me. Walking had now turned into a major physical battle as the snow whipped sharply against my face, hitting me almost horizontally. I didn't care about the discomfort: I was thinking hard about how to best provide Jenny with a better life than the one she was leading now. The one thing I was certain of was that my mother and Dan were beyond hope and would not change.

'Therefore, the only solution was to remove Jenny from the environment she lived in. Once again, I got stuck at this point, as I didn't trust the authorities to allow me as much access to her as I had now, once they became aware of my circumstances. After all, who would grant a jobless, bipolar addict who can't even look after himself close contact with his younger sister? If you consider the mere facts, I couldn't blame anyone for arriving at the conviction that I was a terrible influence on Jenny. Even though I knew that this wasn't true, how could I expect strangers to understand the close bond we have? Besides, as I said earlier, I had inadvertently started to worry Jenny by not being able to properly conceal my poor mental health. Authorities would pick up on this quickly and naturally feel confirmed in their negative views of me.

'As I was struggling against the force of the wind I had an idea that had never occurred to me before and that was properly both risky and crazy simultaneously: Maybe I could take Jenny in and let her live with me! I didn't anticipate much resistance from our mother and Dan, as they would have one responsibility less, a responsibility which they couldn't even remotely fulfil at their best of times. And the authorities didn't need to know about the change in Jenny's circumstances.

'However, as soon as these thoughts entered my mind, I realised that this would be a totally unrealistic and unfeasible venture. Not only did I have little space, I couldn't even keep my place in a state that did not resemble a junkyard with some terrible smells emanating from it and, when I was undergoing a bad patch – as I had done for the last six months – I was just not able to clean and tidy and keep everything in a decent enough state. Nor did I trust myself to be in control of my excesses – be that alcohol or picking up women – or not to lie in bed for days and weeks observing not even the bare minimum of personal hygiene. This was no place for Jenny to be, let alone live in.

'Suddenly, I stumbled over something uneven in the ground and during my fall I banged my head against something heavy in front of me. I went down on my knees, dazed by the knock on my head and uncertain whether I could or should get up again. When I looked up, I was taken aback by discovering that I was right outside an old building which – as far as I could make out in these low visibility conditions – stood abandoned and uninhabited in the snow-covered landscape.

'Although I didn't care much about myself or my comfort any longer – if I had ever done so – I was instinctively drawn towards the prospect of finding some shelter and giving my body a rest from the exposure to the relentless blizzard that was hurting and exhausting it in equal measure. I therefore grabbed the door latch in front of me and after a few pushes managed to open it and stagger inside where I found you, Karen and Lisa, although I didn't know your names at the time.

⋆ ★ ⋆

'I'm dehydrated,' Leo moaned. Having finished his story, he was acutely aware again of the other people's presence and tried to cover up his feelings of mild embarrassment about having divulged so much information about himself by diverting their attention to other matters. He muttered to himself, 'Let's see whether there is some water left in the canister.' Picking up the canister next to him, he drank from it, simultaneously trying to think of some other diversionary techniques he could use.

There was silence. It was a silence during which everyone contemplated what Leo had just told them.

They heard Leo say, 'Does anyone need to go for a pee or a poo? Just to warn you – conditions are likely to be still the same out there.'

The change in register on Leo's part to a more basic, childlike one was blatantly obvious and a defence mechanism to keep any emotionally involved comments on his story at bay. This didn't mean though that he could stop them from responding to his narrative altogether: It was Lisa this time who spoke first.

'Leo,' Lisa began, but then paused. She felt that she had to say something. Leo, despite his apparent anger and frustration, had taken enough of an interest in her life story to talk to her about a way forward. Not to return that kindness and interest would amount to ingratitude. Besides, she found it hard to be exposed to other people's hopelessness and despair and, as a result, to experience these mental states herself to some extent, coping barely with her own. Despite having made herself heard earlier, her anxiety resurfaced about whether she would be listened to, or ignored, or maybe even laughed at for trying to overcome her insecurities and venture some advice or at least make some constructive suggestions. After all, what advice could she possibly give? Her life had been sheltered and in many ways very different from Leo's who was, at about ten years her junior, far more streetwise and au fait with the ways of the world. What could she possibly tell him that he didn't already know? Moreover, she was convinced that her fear of other people was always reflected in the tone of her voice. All these concerns had prevented her from saying more.

However, she now reminded herself of how she had previously encouraged the others to speak about what was on their minds, to tell everyone in the barn their stories and how she had actually been listened to. If anything, everybody had been very supportive of her and her woes. Leo, who had appeared very scary at first, was really mainly furious with himself and of course with his mother and Dan, but previous signs of aggression and annoyance in the barn had not been truly directed at any of them. They were his way of releasing some of his accumulated fury. And he certainly had been increasingly kind to her. She therefore convinced herself to go on.

'Leo, you know that things can become better. *You* can turn this around.' Her voice had been unsteady, but it began to assume greater assurance as she resumed. 'You and Karen have spoken about taking charge of one's own destiny earlier and how I can make important changes in my own life. If this is true, you will certainly be in a position to make them. You have achieved so much already, which I can only dream of, such as having moved out of a damaging home environment.'

She was now steadfastly looking to her right where Leo was sitting. 'You can find a job you love again, Leo. You have held your previous job for years, which was no mean feat given what you told us. And you can do more with your music again, which could mean finding aspiring amateur musicians who also want to play in a band. You must have enough contacts by now.'

For a few moments, nobody said anything before Leo remarked calmly, 'I don't know how this would work. There's my condition – I hate the term but I use it anyway – to consider. There might always be times when I can't control myself any longer and just go wild and then there are the lows during which I can barely get up. I'm tired. I'm spent. I can't do this any longer!'

The last few words were almost shouted and Leo's angst was clear for everyone to detect in his voice.

Karen stirred. 'Where's your fighting spirit, Leo? Are you giving up? How disappointing, but maybe I shouldn't expect anything else from you.'

Leo scowled at her which, naturally, Karen couldn't see due to the lack of light. Did she belittle him and his life and make light of what he had told them? Did she think he was a mere weakling? He bristled with anger.

Karen intuited his fury and smiled inwardly. Her strategy was working. If she could only rouse him from his downcast mood, which was replete with resignation, then there was something to work with. In Leo's case, this regularly meant replacing the latter with arrogance, but Karen knew that this involved an increase in energy that could be channelled into something more constructive.

'Okay then. Let's do this differently. I bet you aren't able to do what Lisa has just suggested. Shall we have a proper bet, Leo? If you prove to me that you can get yourself back to where you were in the past by which I mean get a job again and engage in your music I will give you £100 as a result of losing the bet. I challenge you to it.'

Leo looked confused. 'How can we have a bet if I don't believe I can do it either? I'm of the same conviction.'

Karen responded unperturbed: 'Don't you want to prove me wrong, Leo? Come on, you'd love to win a bet against me, admit it. If you lose the bet and nothing changes with regards to finding a job and making more music in the next three months, you will be at my place at weekends for a month and be put on cleaning and gardening duties.'

She had to grin when Leo took the bait and emitted sounds of disgust before protesting, 'You must be fucking joking. I'm not going to clean your fucking house.'

Leo's sudden use of swear words reassured Karen that she was getting him where she wanted him to be. Slowly but surely.

'Then prove me wrong, Leo. How much satisfaction would it give you to show a university-educated, successful career woman that you know better than her what you can achieve?'

She was in her element now. In some way, she was surprised that Leo, critical and bright as he was, didn't see through her scheme, but he was obviously tired and too overwhelmed by the burdens in his life to think clearly. 'Besides, the money surely would come in handy. You could treat yourself to some new CDs and you can take your sister out for a nice treat.'

He had been about to add that he had no intention to enter a bet he didn't believe in, but the mention of his sister took the edge off his irritation and he decided that he didn't have the energy to argue further with Karen and that it was easiest to acquiesce instead.

'Fine, Karen. Have your bet. We probably won't get out of here alive anyway so there is no point in having such bets. Also, me taking a job and playing more music again, doesn't address the main issue of my sister's welfare. There's no solution to that.'

Karen, in the meantime, had walked over to where Leo was sitting and now knelt down in front of him. 'We will address that in a moment, but first I need you to shake hands with me that the bet is on.'

Before she finished the sentence, she had already stretched out her hand, which Leo – with a resigned headshake –took rather lamely just to have his hand shaken firmly by Karen in return. Karen then remained where she was and spoke with conviction.

'As to Jenny, there is a solution, Leo, and I can help you with it.'

Leo frowned suspiciously at her. What on earth was she going to suggest next after she had already expounded her crazy bet? He started to revise his idea of her as a rational, clear-sighted individual.

Karen faced him calmly as she explained, 'There are legal ways of allowing your sister to live in a more secure and nourishing environment that do not necessarily remove you from her life. You're probably the person your sister feels closest to and trusts and confides in. It's crucial to show the important role you play in Jenny's life to the authorities. I'm more than happy to liaise with some social workers on your and Jenny's behalf, as I have useful connections and know who in the area would be best suited to take on Jenny's case.'

Leo looked at her thoughtfully, being torn between scepticism and hope. Hope was hard to fully embrace: After all, during the last few years Jenny's life at home had merely got worse and nothing had changed for the better. How could there possibly be a way forward in the form of a satisfying solution to what he regarded as an impasse? He couldn't fail but notice Karen's tone of conviction, which also turned professional. He could easily imagine her dealing with her clients, outlining their options by giving them a better insight into how the law applied and could be utilised in their individual situations.

Sensing Leo's inner struggle between wanting to believe her and finding it hard to do so, Karen added, 'Believe me, Leo, I know what I'm talking about. Trust me. I know it's a lot to ask for, as the people who should have proven to be trustworthy in your life have turned out not to be so, but it's really important.'

She paused for a second before she carried on, 'And I want you to get some more support for yourself, Leo. If you really can't face counselling – although I believe you should give it another, and this time a proper, go – you could and should join a support group.'

Leo frowned, which Karen could see as she was within reach of him. She didn't give him time to raise any objections. 'Leo, these are groups where people with similar issues and difficulties come together and have the opportunity to voice whatever would otherwise just be bottled up, lodged deep in their minds and ready to erupt uncontrollably at any moment. Many people find talking about what they are going through in front of a small group of non-judgemental, understanding individuals incredibly helpful. It provides them more often than not with a feeling of being held and affords them some instant relief. It might be daunting to start with to open up in front of strangers, but these people will soon not be strangers to you any longer. I urge you to give it a go. There are a number of such support groups in this area and even if they are not in the town you live in, you can easily and quickly get there from wherever you live.'

Leo didn't respond to this. He didn't know what to think or believe any longer, whether there was still any point in making plans at all or not.

Charles, who was sitting close to Leo, looked at the latter's silhouette next to him. He was filled with sympathy and an urge he hadn't felt for a long time and that he hadn't thought he would strongly experience again – the urge to make someone's life better and happier. Although possibly not visible to the others, his eyes had started to lose their dullness that had barely masked his despair and had now a warm shine in them. He didn't even hesitate before he made a decision and announced with a calm determination in his voice that the others had not had occasion to observe in him before.

'Leo, you are right. Your sister shall be my first cinema attendee when we get out of here and I will host screenings again. I will select the films carefully for your sister. In fact, I can't wait to meet her.'

Leo was deeply moved by Charles's words. He gave him a brief nod of acknowledgement.

Intensely grateful as he was for all these declarations of support, there was still a part in Leo that resisted such help and emotions of warmth and solidarity, as he had long been suspicious of them. Some of the sarcasm he had used earlier that day made a comeback. He whistled, which made everyone turn towards him to find out the reason for this. They didn't have to wait for long.

'Wow, this is the first time today that one of us actually warms to a plan that involves the continuation of their lives outside of this barn.'

This left the others puzzled. Karen's voice had a sharp note in it. 'What on earth do you mean by that?'

Leo looked at her outline across from him and retorted, 'Do you really not know what I'm talking about, Karen? I'm sure you are observant enough to know. You probably just don't want to face certain facts.'

Karen had to suppress a swear word that came to her mind. Leo brought out this desire in her to relieve her irritation in this way when he was combative. It was hard to believe that he had just received an honest and generous offer of professional help from her. The way he behaved, this might just not have happened at all.

In the meantime, Leo continued undeterred: 'It can't have escaped your attention that none of us have made any serious efforts to get out of here or talked about what we plan to do if we leave this place behind. Suddenly, Charles wants to do film screenings and go back home. That's quite a change.'

Karen responded quickly, '*You* suggested this and involved yourself in this plan by proposing to take your sister to the screenings in the first place!'

When Leo didn't reply to that, she resumed, 'Just because we don't speak of our plans for when we get home doesn't mean that we don't want to go back. There's no inevitable logical conclusion to be drawn from that.' Her analytical brain was rarely at rest.

Leo objected. 'Why then has nobody checked whether one of us carries a mobile phone that we can use to at least try to call for help? We might not get any network coverage but if we really wanted to end our stay in this barn we would have tried, wouldn't we? It's a bit odd not to check for the presence of phones in such a situation in the twenty-first century.'

The others had to admit to themselves that there was some logic in Leo's argument and did not comment.

Leo was in an argumentative mood again so that he didn't let things rest here. He addressed Karen directly again: 'You strike me as someone eminently sensible.'

Hearing this from Leo in his current mood immediately suggested a certain amount of mockery to Karen, which made her frown.

Leo picked up on it and persevered, 'No, really, Karen. For someone who is bright and not without common sense, it's quite astounding not to have raised the matter of phones or any other practicalities that could help us to get back home safely. Don't you agree?' He didn't give Karen much of a chance to reply. 'This, of course, leads me to the conclusion that you are not exactly keen on getting back to your life outside – no more than anyone else in here. We have heard three different accounts of why life as we know it can just become too much. And I think you might have such an account to give us as well, Karen.'

Karen looked at him in surprise and became even more angry for being put on the spot. She could feel herself blush and was grateful for the near-darkness they were surrounded by, as she hated for others to see her embarrassment, as it made her feel and probably appear weak in the eyes of others.

She quickly fought down the sensation and snapped at Leo. 'What is this? An interrogation? What gives you the right to ask me to give you an account of my life?'

Leo held up his hands in mock surrender. 'Calm down. There's no need to be so angry.'

Karen just snorted at this statement, muttering, 'Says who!'

It struck the others that Karen could certainly match Leo's sarcasm and that there was some irony in the fact that she frequently employed a way of communication with Leo that ostensibly riled her when it was used by him.

Lisa clenched her fingers. She did not cope well when the mood around her turned tense and antagonistic. It reminded her too much of her mother's mood swings and her own anxiety and helplessness in the face of it. Being trapped in a confined space on such an occasion made it all a lot worse. However, she used all her willpower and reason to calm herself down by telling herself that this was not comparable to her situation at home, that it was normal for people to argue, that there wouldn't be an escalation and that she was safe. She was still not confident in her powers to make a difference despite her earlier success at calming Charles down by making him focus on something that made him happy thus starting off the storytelling amongst them and then encouraging him to unburden himself by letting him put into words what weighed on his mind.

Despite these lingering self-doubts, she felt that she still had to try to defuse the situation. After all, these people around her were not her mother and so far, they had reacted differently to how her mother would have behaved in the same situation. She turned to Karen on her left and said quietly to her, 'Nobody has to do anything that they don't want to do. So far talking about things hasn't done any of us any harm. On the contrary, it feels as if some of the heavy load weighing me down has lifted and I can breathe a little more easily. You can tell us whatever *you* want to talk about, Karen; you don't have to though,' she added quickly.

Karen didn't react for a few moments but eventually said after some further consideration, 'Right, I see your point, Lisa. I don't owe anyone anything, but as we're trapped here and – yes, I admit this, Leo

– all of us seem to struggle one way or another I might just as well tell you what has brought me here on this snowy last day of the year. It seems fair.'

She paused but sensed that she had her listeners' attention. 'However, before I start, shall we first check whether one of us has a phone with them and then we can still discuss whether we want to make a phone call and, if so, who we want to call.' Karen avoided looking in Leo's direction when she said this. 'For my part, I left home quite quickly this morning and only just managed to think of grabbing my purse and my keys' – she patted the pockets of her purple ski anorak – 'before I departed.'

The others confirmed that they had been in similar situations, which made it clear that nobody would have been able to call anyone for help. Karen couldn't help but glance at Leo with a small sense of triumph although she hadn't exactly scored any points. Then she looked at the ground in front of her to gather her thoughts, cleared her voice and commenced.

The Call for Justice

'My previous story has already shown you that I was an adventurous, daring youngster who didn't shy away from challenges and dangers. Unfortunately, it was my adventurous spirit that inadvertently set in motion a train of events whose final outcome was nothing short of disastrous. Everything that followed in my life – from my choice of career to how my personal life has panned out – can be traced back to it.

'I was always an outdoor person when I was young and loved nothing more than playing and exploring outside with my friends. The earlier story about the dare that involved swimming across a tidal river portrayed my nature quite succinctly. I was also in the Girl Guides where I was in my element and made many good friends.

'My parents appreciated my strong need for the outdoors, physical activity and the company of my peers and let me roam outdoors as long as I came back at a previously agreed time and would let them know if, for one reason or another, it would get later than that. At the time and place I grew up parents had far fewer safety concerns and it was normal to let us young teenagers go where we wanted unsupervised.

'Also, my parents were very liberal. My mother, being a PA to the director of the local college, was well aware of how important peers were for young people. Both she and my father, who worked in the marketing department of a small company, were very much at ease with other people and enjoyed mingling socially. They hence formed and welcomed my sociable nature and equally warmly welcomed my friends when I brought them home after having played outside. They made it clear that as long as I did my schoolwork I could enjoy my free time in the way I wanted to, knowing that I was reliable and would not get involved in any criminal activities.

'Keeping my side of the bargain wasn't difficult: I enjoyed learning and absorbed information quickly so that I was a good pupil even without having to make much of an effort. In fact, had I spent more than the minimum amount of time on studying at home I would have probably achieved the highest grades. Good grades were sufficient though for my parents and me, and I didn't yet have to study for important exams such as O-levels.

I had my first boyfriend early – well, I guess these days – thirteen-and-a-half, would be an average age in that respect. He was called Fabio and was one of the boys in my friendship group and we were fully savouring the excitements of our young love discovering our sexuality and celebrating it. We had got together in late autumn and in the following spring and summer we searched for secret hiding places where we had sex, which heightened the thrill of it all. Although we both had open and liberal parents and they knew Fabio and me, neither of us felt that our parents would have been comfortable with knowing that we were already sexually active, which meant finding locations outside of our homes where we could enjoy each other freely.

'Some of these locations were anything but comfortable but we didn't care and were in fact rather tickled by the inconveniences. My parents were used to me coming home with some bruises, as I had done this since I was a child and run around everywhere, climbed or jumped. They therefore didn't pay much attention to the fact that I came home with new ones on a continuous basis. Moreover, they knew that I bruised easily for one reason or another.

'Unfortunately, there were other people who took notice of my bruises and misconstrued their origin and context in a way I didn't foresee. I only learned about this after they must have detected an injury on me that alarmed them and that prompted them to take action. I remember clearly how it happened:

'Fabio and I had ventured out far into the nearby woods one Sunday near midsummer. As you know, there isn't much woodland in this area so we were quite pleased to explore the little we found. We soon discovered a tree house and were absolutely thrilled. Fabio and I looked at each other excitedly and had the same thought, which made us climb up the ladder in a hurry. Once we were at the top we fell laughingly into each other's arms and after brushing off any concerns that we might be seen as one of the walls was missing, we stripped quickly and lowered ourselves onto the wooden slats. I climbed on top of Fabio and tried to arouse him further before Fabio couldn't take it any longer, grabbed my body firmly, lifted me up and turned me on my back next to him with the intention of reversing our positions. However, what neither of us had seen was the wooden beam that was lying on the ground and that my arm, shoulder and part of the right side of my body hit with full force. I must have screamed as I felt the sharp pain shoot through my body and consume me.

'Fabio, knowing that I was tough and wouldn't shout out like this unless there was a very good reason for it, stopped in his tracks and looked at me in shock as I tried to roll over to my left, unhurt side in vain. Due to the shock of what was happening, I later on couldn't recall everything clearly, but Fabio told me that I went completely pale and that I was sick when he gently helped me to sit up. We didn't know what to do. My arm might or might not have been broken and surely the safest thing would have been to call an ambulance and get it checked as soon as possible but we weren't keen on having the circumstances of the accident revealed to our parents so we decided to wait and see whether the pain would lessen.

'Fabio placed me in as comfortable a position as he could and made me drink water at regular intervals. Fortunately, the pain did decrease noticeably quite soon, which gave us hope that the arm was possibly not broken but would probably soon look badly bruised. It also gave us confidence in me being able to make the long way back home without having to call for a lift. In fact, during the time we spent in the tree house we eventually even made love together after the accident had initially prevented us from doing so.

'Fabio was worried about hurting my arm further, but I said nonchalantly that now that we had made it all the way up there we should enjoy what we most wanted to do. Also, it might make me feel much better, as I explained to Fabio. And so we took pleasure in our bodies joining each other, this time in a gentle, careful way rather than in the wild and tempestuous manner that was characteristic of our love-making.

'At the end of the day, we were able to walk home alright and I was able to manage the pain. I didn't say anything to my parents upon my arrival about what had happened and just quietly took a couple of Paracetamol with a glass of water before going to bed. I didn't have a great night as I still felt quite a lot of pain during the course of it, especially when I turned. On waking up in the morning though, my usual positive energy made me think that I could now firmly put the accident of the previous day behind me and resume life as I knew it. How wrong I was about that.

'A couple of days later, my arm and shoulder were covered in large bruises and, as it was summer, I didn't seriously contemplate covering my arm up once I had taken off the school blazer. In P.E. I always wore a sleeveless top and I didn't change that habit this time. Some of my classmates commented on the bruising, half-jokingly as they knew that I got up to all kinds of adventures and was rarely without a bruise but also with some concern in their voices, as it became apparent that I couldn't use my arm to best effect at basketball.

'At the end of the lesson the teacher told me to stay behind and then asked me in the then-empty sports hall what had happened to my arm and shoulder and why I hadn't got the injury seen to instead of ignoring it and participating in the sports session as usual although it clearly impeded me in my movements and quite possibly caused me pain.

'I said that I had a fall when I was out on Sunday when I stumbled over a big branch on the ground that I didn't see. I figured that this was probably closest to what had really happened with regards to the outcome, i.e. the injuries sustained from the impact in either case. When the teacher pressed me to explain why I hadn't seen a doctor, who would have certainly signed me off P.E. lessons and treated my arm, I responded that I wasn't squeamish, loved sports and that – as I had established that my arm wasn't broken – I didn't think it was necessary to say anything. My P.E. teacher still didn't appear satisfied. She looked at me solemnly and wanted to know whether my parents were happy with me not giving my arm a chance to heal. I hesitated, which my teacher observed and interpreted in her own way, before I replied more quietly than usual, as I felt interrogated and put on the spot, "I didn't mention it to them."

'When my teacher's eyes bored into me, I felt forced to add, "I didn't think it was necessary to worry them. It might not look great, but it's something that heals quickly on its own accord."

'My explanation met with silence on my teacher's part, which was broken by her words, "Karen, is there anything you want to tell me? You know that you can speak in confidence to me or someone else in the school if you prefer. Everything you tell us will be dealt with the utmost discretion."

'I was confused by my P.E. teacher's words. I didn't understand what she was getting at so I didn't respond. After what seemed an eternity of silence she let me go but not before adding, "I would encourage you to talk to someone about it, Karen. We're here for you."

'Two days later my form teacher pulled me aside and had a similar conversation with me. I was still at a loss as to what all this meant. I had put my P.E. teacher's interaction with me behind me and had put it down to her having an off day. Experiencing now a repeat of it meant that I couldn't simply explain such behaviour away like this again. I therefore decided to get some clarity about it by asking, "Why are you asking me these questions? People have accidents sometimes. As it didn't happen here at school, I don't have to complete an accident report form, which means it's unnecessary for me to report on every detail of the accident." I'd never had a problem about addressing a matter directly with anyone.

'My form teacher was obviously reluctant though to give me an unequivocal answer. She only went as far as asking me, "Are things alright at home, Karen? Are there any problems or issues we should know about?"

'I recall becoming rather impatient when my teacher, after prompting her again, refused to be any more specific. Later on, I realised how my subsequent, somehow defiant declaration, "No, everything is perfectly fine at home. Stop asking me about it," and my swift departure convinced my teacher that the opposite was the case and that I was merely unwilling to talk about it.

'On the following Monday, I immediately noticed that something was wrong when I returned home in the evening after having spent some time out with Fabio after school. My parents were both sitting on the sofa in the living-room and were deeply engaged in conversation. Neither the radio nor the CD player were on, which was unusual.

'When I came into the living-room my parents fell silent for a second before asking me in a very serious tone of voice to sit down. This had hardly ever happened before so you can imagine my surprise. I didn't even ask a question but sat down in the opposite armchair waiting for what they had to say and fleetingly thinking that hopefully it wasn't about anything I had done. My parents didn't say anything immediately, which highlighted the seriousness of what they were about to impart to me.

'My father finally cleared his throat and explained. "Karen, we were visited by a social worker when you were out."

'I blinked, attempting to grasp the import of these words but failing to do so. I therefore asked, "A social worker? Why? I don't understand."

My parents exchanged meaningful glances before my father resumed. "She wanted to speak to you as well, but we told her that you weren't in. She said that she will meet you for a chat in the next few days and would like you to give her a call. This is her number. She said she's happy to meet you at home, at school or a neutral place – wherever you prefer or feel most comfortable at."

'My puzzlement did not decrease one iota after listening to this message. "Why on earth should I want to contact a social worker!" I exclaimed.

'My mother picked up the thread now. "The school has contacted social services, Karen." I could tell that she forced her voice to remain calm and steady. Despite her efforts, I could still make out a tremble in it. "The social worker mentioned an injury that your teachers couldn't fail but notice. We told her that we knew nothing about it, but she did not seem to believe us and pointed out that your arm and shoulder were badly hurt and certainly not in good shape." My mother displayed a seriousness in her demeanour that I had rarely seen before. "Karen, is she referring to the bruises on your arm that developed after you fell over a branch in the woodland that you told us about when we noticed them?'

'I swallowed. "I don't know, Mum, what she's referring to.' I paused for a second before something came to my mind. "Both my P.E. teacher and my form teacher asked me about my injury and I did think at the time that they asked me very strange questions. It must have been them who contacted social services. But then why would they do that?"

'My mother struggled to keep her composure. "Karen, it looks as if they believe that we have beaten you or have used some other form of violence against you."

'I gasped in sheer disbelief, but then things started to fall into place. Of course. Now I saw where all these strange questions by my teachers had led to. How could I not realise what was going on earlier? But then, these assumptions were completely outrageous and absurd and blatantly untrue. Nobody who had ever met my parents could believe them to be capable of such a thing, surely. My form teacher had met my mother, though, so how could she reach such conclusions?

'Both my parents now had tears in their eyes, which shocked me, as my parents weren't people who cried easily. I could feel helpless rage rise inside myself and cried out, "How dare they! How dare they make such accusations!"

'My father held up his hand thus signalling to me to contain my emotions and listen to him. "I know, Karen. We are as shocked by it all as you are, but we need to stay calm now. The social worker mentioned that your teacher had voiced their concerns that this was not an isolated – albeit more severe – incident but that you have repeatedly come to school over the years with bruises."

'"But…" I interjected, but was cut off by my father.

'"Of course, we all know that you are a very active and adventurous person who would inevitably experience some stumbles and falls and that you also bruise easily and we did try to convey this to the social worker. She responded that this was what the teachers used to believe as well but that this latest injury of your arm was unlikely to have originated from a stumble outdoors. Your behaviour suggests otherwise in their opinion."

'My eyes widened. "My behaviour? What on earth does that mean! How have I behaved!"

'My dad continued as calmly as he could. "Well, in their opinion, it is odd if not suspicious that you wouldn't immediately tell us about an injury of that magnitude and also wouldn't go to the doctor's to get it seen to."

'I interjected in a loud voice, "But it's not broken and I didn't want to worry anyone unduly."

'My father nodded. "I, or we, realise that, Karen, although I think you should really have said something about your arm if it has been sore. Being tough and resilient is great, but sometimes it's better to ask for some help.'

'When I was about to retort something, my father didn't let me, as it was obvious that he needed to get something off his chest.

"Be that as it may, Karen, we now have to deal with what we are facing. We're facing social services and possibly an investigation started by the school authorities. All we can do is to be composed and honest, showing them that they are making a huge mistake. I'm sure we'll get through this together, Karen, even if the next few weeks might turn out to be hard."

'I admired my parents' bravery in the face of a shock of such gigantic proportions, their ability to still plan how we could best get through this together and their capability to remain strong and stable. I was speechless, unable to stop my tears from flowing. In the end, we were all lying in each other's arms, hugging each other tightly for a very long time.

'The next few weeks were a nightmare. Suddenly social workers and solicitors became part of our lives and school life became increasingly strange. I wasn't given to paranoid thinking but I now started wondering what my teachers might be thinking about me at any given point during the school day and began to second-guess their thoughts. I could feel their eyes linger on me when I was quiet for a while. To me, it seemed that no matter what I did, they would misinterpret everything about me anyway. I had no trust in them and, for the first time ever, I dreaded school and thought of how I could avoid it, but of course I knew that I wouldn't get away with it so that I stuck it out with gritted teeth.

'My friends and Fabio were pillars of support during this difficult, insecure time. Most of my classmates didn't know what was going on and I was content with this, as we were thus able to chat about other things together, which took my mind off the matter at hand. My close friends and Fabio were supportive, listening to me describe what was happening, sharing the sense of insanity pertaining to it but also just engaging in our usual shared activities when I needed to get mentally away from it all, which was most of the time.

'I will spare you the excruciating encounters and conversations my parents and I had, particularly with the social workers. Don't get me wrong – I believe that most of the time social workers do an incredibly important job in helping secure a child or a vulnerable person's welfare in adverse conditions. We need them and the profession is of real importance. However, in my case, due to some gross misperceptions on their part planted by my teachers, they did an awful lot of harm. The bottom line was that not long after that first visit by a social worker I was taken into care and my upbringing became the responsibility of the state. I wasn't yet fifteen years old and was stunned by the outcome and the inability of our legal representatives to convince the school authorities and their lawyers of the truth. My parents were no less overwhelmed with shock. We all had in the end trusted that the truth would win. Instead, we faced a miscarriage of justice on a devastating scale that left us reeling and at a loss as to how to deal with and come to terms with the new reality of our lives now.

'For the next seven and a half months I was in a children and young people's home in a town more than three quarters of an hour by bus away from home. There was an injunction in place forbidding any contact between my parents and me. Trips to my home town were strictly monitored by a member of staff who would accompany me there, which spoilt the enjoyment I got from seeing Fabio and my friends again. I therefore asked them to visit me at the home when they could where we were free to roam the grounds without a member of staff following our every step. I still didn't see my friends often enough and it became very difficult to continue my relationship with Fabio – also because there wasn't much of an opportunity any longer to be intimate with each other. I was a person who relished and thrived on freedom and suddenly I felt like a caged bird that was prevented from spreading its wings to take off and fly. Moreover, I felt monitored in a way that I considered entirely inappropriate for my age. It was ludicrous to think that all this was done to protect me from my parents who had been nothing but loving towards me all my life.

'I tried my best not to think about it when I wasn't arguing and fighting my case in vain with the authorities, as I would have become insane otherwise. However, it was hard to fill my free time with enough distractions now that I didn't see my friends every day. Quite a few of the other young people in the home had many personal issues and were considered behaviourally problematic by staff. Making friends with them therefore didn't turn out to be straightforward. When some of them tried to bully me soon after my arrival, I made it clear to them that I wasn't having any of it and that I could stand up for myself very well despite being traumatised by recent events and being generally more sedate as a result. I guess one's instinctive response nevertheless kicks in in such situations even if one doesn't feel at one's best.

'After a while, the others got the message and left me in peace and whilst I didn't feel close or on a similar wavelength with many of the other pupils I socialised with some of them, particularly in the context of team sports. I wouldn't tell the others much about the reason I was here though and they came to respect my privacy. I spent the remainder of my free time pursuing individual sports like swimming, my all-time favourite sport, running and cycling. I guess I could have started thinking about training up for triathlons but I wasn't really aware of them at the time. Being a competitive person I was always happy to participate in competitions, but I also got quite a lot out of training independently: It kept me not just physically but also mentally strong, shifted my focus away from the oppressive, new reality I lived in and it ensured that I was so exhausted at the end of the day that I would fall asleep quickly instead of ruminating about what had happened.

'Finally, a couple in their mid-fifties came and chose me as their foster child. This involved a move to another small town, which was even further away from my home town and a new school again after the summer that I moved in with them. Whilst I did make new friends quite quickly there, I know I was behaving in a more cautious manner around them and other people I met for the first time. My hitherto carefree nature was taking on an element of aloofness. This was partly because I still fought to return to my parents regarding the situation I was in as merely temporary. Another reason for this change in me was that I had started to lose trust in people. If I kept my cards close to my chest I might suffer fewer disappointments.

'Of course, deep down I knew that my thinking was flawed. The reason why I was separated from my parents wasn't that I had revealed too many things about myself to others but were the false assumptions others had made on their own accord. Still, I believe when we have suffered disappointments of one nature or another, our inclination is to withdraw into ourselves.

'My foster parents were alright. They were a couple who had wanted to give a child a home for a long time. When they were younger they hadn't been in a rush to have a child, enjoying their lives as they were, and when they were finally ready for children, they discovered that they had left it too late. They didn't mind that too much though, as both of them were great proponents of social justice and equal opportunities and could see the appeal in adopting a child whose biological parents would not be able to keep it. Somehow, they had not been selected as adoptive parents for years even though they had the financial means including a large house that would have made it unproblematic to raise a child in a good environment. The results of the background checks on them were impeccable.

"'Sometimes it's hard to explain why things happen the way they do," my foster mother once said to me when she spoke to me about their many attempts to adopt a child. "In hindsight though, you can see how some unexpected, but equally beautiful things can occur instead of what you had hoped for in the first place. In this case, it has been you, Karen."

'I remember how I recoiled when she said this. How did she dare to claim that my placement into her and her husband's care was a beautiful thing when it had been the shocking outcome of my enforced separation from my parents, which left our world in tatters and which was based on terrible falsehoods? It was wrong to say such a thing and I strongly dissociated myself from such a view and I made this clear to her by being stroppy and uncooperative around her and her husband until a social worker had a word with me about my behaviour. She told me that I had been known for being one of the least complicated and burdened young people in the home, which they had proudly mentioned to my foster parents when the latter considered fostering as another option for having a child in their lives. They had already been informed that there were currently no young children available that could be taken into foster care, which meant that they already had to say farewell to their hope of sharing and facilitating the journey of a child as it grows up, goes through its teenage years and eventually reaches adulthood. The least I could do now was to live up to the image of me that was presented to my foster parents of being untroubled on the whole and easy to deal with.

'As you have probably guessed, the previous sentence wasn't the social worker's but my cynical attempt to provide the gist of her message to me. Her words me made me feel like a commodity whose features were described in words of praise and that must turn out to be and do exactly as previously proclaimed. However, the social worker was correct insofar as being stroppy and antagonistic normally hardly featured in my personality. I was also sensible and rational enough to eventually tell myself that what had happened was not my foster parents' fault and that they should at least be treated civilly.

'And this was what I did after spending a few months putting up a resistance to what they called my new home. I started to treat my foster parents politely, helped them with chores and did my best to engage in conversations at meal times even if I didn't feel like talking to them about my day or other things.

'In the meantime, my relationship with Fabio didn't survive the distance and fizzled out and I also saw fewer of my friends from where I grew up and the ones that I saw I met less frequently. It was nobody's fault but time and distance had turned into obstacles to maintaining these social relationships and we were all still young and went with the flow.

'I clearly remember the day that proved to be another turning-point in my life giving me a new focus that I have not lost since. It is therefore no exaggeration to describe the impact of that day's event as profound and life-changing.

'It was around the time of my O-level exams that my school scheduled a careers day. Some of my classmates decided not to attend, as it was inconveniently scheduled between exams, and to revise instead. Besides, most of us wanted to go on to sixth form and do A-levels so that we still had two years to decide what we wanted to do in the future. We therefore regarded attendance of the event as low priority even if our teachers explained that there wouldn't just be advice available on apprenticeships and career paths post-O-level but also on professions that required A-level or similar qualifications and subsequent degree courses. The teachers further emphasised that our presence on the day was compulsory, but this announcement didn't make those classmates who had already planned to stay at home or go elsewhere to study reconsider.

'I decided to listen to the different talks and presentations, not because I was overly keen but because I needed a break from the never-ending revision, which made me feel simultaneously bored and fidgety.

'I attended a range of talks that shed a light on some very different occupations from medicine to business. Some of them, like broadcast journalism, sounded interesting and might have been a possibility, but none of the career options presented on the day really called out to me. At least that was the case until I attended the last talk of the day, which was held by a couple of solicitors. They briefly touched on what embarking on a law course entailed before showcasing a couple of areas qualified lawyers could work in, which were corporate law and family law.

'When the female solicitor spoke about her area of family law and the custody disputes that had to be settled with the child's best interest at the heart of it, something fell into place for me. Her mention of the rights of the child and the parents and the duty of the state made me prick up my ears. Her part was over far too soon and left me with many questions I wanted to get answers to. In fact, at the end of the talk I walked up to her and put many of my questions to her that concerned the state's intervention in family matters, particularly the appropriateness of taking children or young people into custody. I realised that there was an expert who was not involved in my or my parents' case but who might be able to speak objectively about rights in this context and by this I mainly meant parental and children's rights. She answered my questions as best as she could, but at times she emphasised that she would require the specific context of a case to give me a more detailed response. She and her colleague also had to leave at some point, which meant that I couldn't continue the conversation indefinitely.

'Before she left, she gave me her card, though, letting me know that I was welcome to contact her if I had any more questions. Most importantly, she left me with something else, namely the conviction that knowledge is power.

'From then on, I assiduously applied myself to my studies showing a dedication that was new. I now had a long-term goal, i.e. to become a family solicitor, and I knew that I would do everything I could to reach it. I began to channel my tenacity and energy, which have always been amongst my most noticeable characteristics, into the pursuit of what I would describe as my calling.

'I studied hard in sixth form, only making time for breaks that involved exercise, particularly swimming, and some meetings with friends, which occurred much less frequently though. I wanted to get the grades that would allow me to choose the university where I was going to embark on my law course. When I achieved this objective, leaving school with straight As in my chosen subjects, I was overjoyed. I accepted a place at Glasgow University and moved to the other end of the country with an anxiously beating heart but full of resolve and excitement.

'My foster parents, whilst delighted about my career ambitions, were disappointed by, and sad about, my decision to move so far away from them and suspected that they would not have much regular contact with me once I lived in Scotland. With my coming of age a few months before doing my A-levels, they were legally not responsible for me any longer and not required to support me financially or otherwise although the fostering agency had a scheme in place that allowed me and others in my situation to continue and finish school whilst remaining in the same family. My foster parents made it clear to me that they considered me their daughter and that I would not lose this status with them now or in the future.

'They weren't the only ones who felt dejected about my imminent move: My parents voiced similar feelings and I couldn't blame them after having missed out on being around me for a big chunk of my adolescent life. Having not been allowed any contact for the last three years, the experience of being in touch again proved to be overwhelming for all of us, however, which was one factor in my decision to go to Glasgow.

'When all our attempts at being reunited again had failed, there was the prospect of my eighteenth birthday to look forward to when we could finally reconnect. I recall giving my parents a ring first thing on the morning of my birthday. Our phones had been monitored and it was possible that some monitoring – albeit of our re-established contact rather than of our absence of communication, which the monitoring initially set out to ensure – would remain in place if authorities decided to categorise me as a vulnerable adult who still needed some protection. We hadn't been told about this yet but would undoubtedly be informed shortly. All we knew was that contact between us was allowed again. When my mother heard my voice on the phone we both choked up and could not speak for an eternity. My mother merely managed to say my name. Eventually I said through my tears, 'Mum, it's my birthday today. I want to come and see you and dad after school. Will you be around?'

'She answered me whilst simultaneously laughing and crying and I could just about understand her words. "Yes, of course, darling, of course. Your dad and I will be waiting for you." She then recalled what I had just said about what day it was.

"Happy birthday, darling. Happy, happy birthday."

'I remember that reunion in the evening vividly. I didn't tell my foster parents that I had made contact with my parents again and planned to go and see them, letting them believe I would go out with my friends and celebrate with them until late. My foster parents had always believed in the 'truth' of my parents having been abusive towards me – understandably, as how else would they have been able to justify fostering me – and would most likely have tried to talk me out of re-establishing the relationship.

'When I got off the bus and walked to my parents' house in the early evening of that day, I couldn't believe that this was happening and when I rang their doorbell it still seemed unreal. When my parents opened the front door a second afterwards, we simply stood there and looked at each other for a while before I stepped towards them and hugged them tightly.

'It's hard to describe the strength and complexity of our feelings that evening. There was, of course, a feeling of exuberance, but also of disbelief and of pain and grief about the years we had lost and about the injustice of our enforced separation. My mother had done some shopping and had prepared a delicious three-course meal of my favourite food, which consisted of a minestrone, a spaghetti Bolognese and apple pie with custard. I was touched by it but struggled to eat much, as the excitement of it all had taken away my appetite. I could tell that it was the same for my parents. They had aged a lot during the last three years: Their faces were more deeply lined and their hair was greyer than when I had last seen them.

'The conversation was halting. We couldn't possibly summarise what had happened since we last met, but we didn't need to. It was enough that we were all together again. I stayed until quite late before my parents drove me back, as the next day was a school day. They had given me vouchers for a department store chain so that I could buy myself whatever I wanted or needed.

'In the next few months I went to see them almost every weekend, sometimes taking my exam revision materials with me. For logistical reasons, we agreed that I would stay with my foster family until I completed my A-levels. However, whilst we relished our time together, we found it hard to manage the emotional pain that descended on us every time we were together. We hadn't expected it to be like that. I guess we had tried to push the pain aside over the years and focus on other things but now that we saw each other again that was not possible any longer and we often felt that we were reliving the trauma of how we were separated from each other.

'Whether I judged it well or not, I decided in the end that it wasn't good for any of us to suffer again and thought that moving far away for my studies might actually do us some good, as I couldn't bear my mother's tearful eyes and shaky voice every time I saw her any more, especially since she had never been like that when I grew up.

'You might wonder why I couldn't get any financial support from my parents for my course but I worked many long hours in a bar in Glasgow, which didn't leave me much study time. In fact, my parents immediately offered to help me finance my course once they learned about my plans, but I politely but firmly declined their offer telling them a white lie, namely that I had saved some money from part-time jobs and that I would be fine with a few hours of work per week, which would be good for my CV anyway and it would also offer me a break from studying. I didn't want them to spend much money on me after they reluctantly revealed how much money they had spent on legal fees in a conversation about their legal fight to get me back.

'My parents were earning comfortable middle incomes, we lived in a fairly spacious house and there had always been some money in the savings account for any extras. I quickly picked up that the latter was not the case any longer and that my parents had to budget very carefully to cover all the costs they had. Although they were not exactly destitute, it was heart-breaking to see them in this much tighter financial position. I think there was relief on their part when I declared that I didn't need any money, and I tried my best to dispel any vestiges of guilt I could discern in them.

'I didn't accept much money from my foster parents either. Although they offered me financial support for my studies, I only took a modest amount of money as a one-off payment from them and rejected all further offers of help, having decided to take out a student loan and work as many hours as I could once I had secured a part-time job.

'So far, I had mainly helped other pupils by giving them some private tuition, but I was prepared to do almost any kind of job for the duration of my course. My decision to only accept a one-off payment from my foster parents can be explained by my resolve to sever all ties with them. They had been good to me, but that was secondary. I should never have been removed from my parents and my foster parents were a constant reminder of what shouldn't have happened.

'And restricting contact with them was what I did. I soon only sent them a Christmas card. With my parents, I kept in regular contact but couldn't bring myself to call them more than once or twice a fortnight, worrying about the emotional turmoil the conversations might continue to cause us.

'The next few years turned out to be the busiest of my life so far. During the day, I attended lectures and studied in the library whenever there was a break. In the evenings, I waitressed and served in one of the city centre bars until late and, after closing time, walked the rather long way back to my student accommodation to save money on fares.

'There wasn't really any time to do anything else but, somehow, I managed to squeeze a swim at the nearby pool in on a few mornings and at weekends went for a longer swim and fitted in the gym or a run before devoting the rest of the day to my studies. It was a crazy time and I don't know how I did it but I was driven and used every ounce of energy I possessed. In the end, it all paid off I guess. I got a first-class degree and a recommendation from my lecturers for my knowledge of and dedication to the discipline of law. Whilst I took nothing for granted, I was confident that I could get the job I really wanted as long as I continued to apply myself long and hard enough. The years of financial hardship would come to an end eventually, which was a pleasant prospect even if not the main goal in my endeavours.

'Shortly after finishing my studies, I started a job at a family solicitors' practice in Glasgow as a junior employee, which I absolutely loved.

'Having moved out of shared accommodation, I now rented a small place in a quieter neighbourhood, which was much more conducive to studying and sleeping at night. In the student place I had shared I had basically had to wear earplugs all the time. Although my degree course had finished, studying was far from over and necessary without doubt if I wanted to have a career in law. After work, I would not only review what I had learned and done in practice during the day, I would also read up on professional matters that had come up and read beyond what I absolutely had to know at that moment in time.

'Having had a manically busy schedule during my course with my part-time job, which had almost been a full-time job, I didn't find it too hard to do a full day's work and then still put in a few hours of study. I didn't need my part-time evening job any longer but still put a few hours in at weekends in order to pay off my student loan more quickly. I also made some friends at the law firm I worked in and at the local swimming club which I joined after I had moved to my new neighbourhood. I sometimes went to a bar, party or, especially with the swimming club friends, on a walk, run or picnic and enjoyed having a little bit more of a social life again than in previous years during which I had foregone the thrills and excesses of student life to dedicate myself to my goal. At the same time, even during the years I worked at the Glasgow practice I prioritised work and studies and couldn't have been suspected of living a wild life. I'm pretty sure that if I hadn't been taken from my parents and, as a result, discovered the strong calling to have a positive impact on the lives of children as a family solicitor, I would have continued acting as the tempestuous social creature I had been and used almost every opportunity to socialise at parties or elsewhere.

'Whilst I met first boys and later young men and had flings and a couple of relationships, the latter were of a fairly short-lived nature. I got the feeling that they were intimidated by my fierce determination to pursue whatever I set my mind to, the independence I showed and by the sharpness of my mind and occasionally of my tongue when I was under a lot of stress or thought someone didn't treat me right, which I was increasingly reluctant to put up with.

'Although I was initially sad and disappointed that my relationships didn't last long, I soon shrugged it all off and reminded myself how this allowed me to invest my time even more in my legal endeavour although I had already limited the time I spent with my boyfriends carefully and strategically, which was – I suspect – another reason why my boyfriends might have got a bit fed up with the relationships. Gone were the days when Fabio and I roamed the countryside often from morning until it got dark.

'Due to my efforts and single-mindedness, I climbed up to higher positions in the same legal practice I had started at, being soon promoted to a senior solicitor position and then to one that also gave me joint management responsibilities with the person who had previously been head of the practice. I enjoyed the journey I undertook in the practice but when the time came that I felt that I couldn't develop any further there, I moved to London to take up positions in the Temple area.

'I was only in my late twenties when I embarked on this exciting new life in the city and it didn't take long until I started to make a name for myself in my field, which involved regular appearances with my clients at the High Court. I became respected by my colleagues and my name was dropped when they weren't able to take on a particular case but wanted that person to receive the best legal representation they could possibly get in family-related matters.

'In the last few years I additionally took on a High Court judge's duties albeit part-time on a needs basis. I loved the challenge and responsibility in a different way I enjoyed my work as a solicitor. Whilst I loved the advocacy and the time I spent working with and defending a client, I was intrigued by the power a judge could wield. Don't get me wrong: I wasn't interested in power for power's sake but for the greater impact I could thus have on people's lives. I knew that at some point soon I would have to decide whether I would want to go into it full-time and embrace it without having the solicitor's work to think about at the same time but I wasn't ready to make a decision on this yet.

'During the one and a half decades I spent in London I visited my parents sometimes and we spoke on the phone probably a bit more regularly than when I was in Glasgow. I guess the reason for having closer contact with them again was that time helped us all to deal better with what had happened and our grief became less raw, which made being in touch less emotional and less painful. I wouldn't however say that the wounds that had been inflicted on us, at least on my parents' part, ever properly healed. Had they done so I would have had even more contact with them. We were all aware of our scars that would from time to time redden and even partially open up again and start to bleed. I blame these emotional injuries for my parents' health problems and deaths.

'My parents had always been very healthy and robust people, but a few years after I moved to Glasgow my father developed an unexpected and serious chronic heart condition, which required him to be regularly checked up on, to be put on strong medication and also to be taken into hospital a few times as an emergency. He had to take early retirement in the end and was restricted in the activities he could do. He died less than five years ago of a massive heart attack.

'It was then that I knew I had to move back to Devon to support my mother who had asthma and a couple of other lung conditions, none of which she had had before I was taken into care. I therefore bought a place near my mother's so that I could look after her whenever I was not at work, and started a position at a solicitor's office in Exeter to which I commuted every day.

'Did I miss my more high-profile jobs and my busy life in London? To some extent, yes, but the practice in Exeter had an excellent reputation, too, and I was very busy so that I didn't have much time to dwell on what I might have lost. With regards to the people I knew in London, I realised that they had mostly been acquaintances rather than friends, as I had invested hardly any time in pursuing friendships there. Similarly, in Exeter, I quickly made good and affable contacts, but having to commute back didn't allow for much socialising beyond the actual work context.

'Three years ago, I received a major blow when my mother died out of the blue having suffered a major brain haemorrhage. When I found her in her home on the day she died and neither I nor the ambulance staff I called managed to resuscitate her, I was heartbroken and could not console myself for a long time. The weeks after her funeral I was just numb and recall having gone through the process of clearing the house and sorting out the legal matters in a daze.

'However, I soon threw myself with renewed effort into my work in Exeter and even took on some jobs in London that came up including some more appearances as a judge convincing myself that work, once again, would help to alleviate the pain by distracting my mind and shifting my focus. This time it proved harder to do so though. I have increasingly suffered periods of what I would call – for a want of a better expression – disorientation if not confusion, which have become increasingly difficult to ignore. They could set in at any time no matter whether I was in the office, at home or standing in the aisle of a supermarket. The sensation was that of being hit by a strong force such as a bolt of lightning. Everything around me then faded into the background until I was hardly aware of my environment any longer. Instead, a voice inside me urged me to answer her questions: "What are you doing here? Why are you doing what you do? Where are you going with it?"

'Whenever this inner voice made itself heard I felt shaken and it took a while to silence its echo, which was reverberating in my head. Once I had escaped its spell, I still couldn't understand the reason for its emergence and still can't fully do so now although I believe I begin to comprehend it a bit more.

'My usual thoughts after such an episode tended to revolve around my strong drive to do something good for others in my work, which is a conviction I have not lost. I was still goal-orientated and determined and would not have swapped my path in life for another. What was the point of the internal voice then? Maybe I should have dug a bit deeper and examined my life a bit more closely, as it might have saved me from these sudden episodes during which I was overwhelmed by existential questions that refused to go away and during which I wasn't fully aware of my surroundings any longer. But then I wasn't given to introspection and extensive soul searching and I'm not sure whether I would have been able to avoid this morning's experience had I done some self-analysis previously.

'I guess it hit me almost the second I got up and went to the kitchen to make breakfast: The deep silence in the house, which I normally treasured after long days at work where I have had plenty of interaction with others heavily descended on me like a weighted blanket that threatened to immobilise me underneath it. It wasn't the silence alone though, which had this effect. It was the combination of the lack of any sound with the realisation that it was New Year's Eve and I had nowhere to go or anyone to celebrate it with but not enough urgent work for the next couple of days that would warrant burying myself in my work instead.

'Maybe it was odd that this realisation had such an impact on me. After all, there had been a few occasions in previous years when I hadn't been at a party, at my parents' house or with one or more friends either so it wasn't an entirely new albeit fairly rare experience. Previously I hadn't given it much thought and was quite happy to either catch up with some non-urgent work or just read some new publications in my area of work to ensure that I was definitely up-to-speed.

'I could have done the same this morning except that I was strangely lacking in motivation to do so. A sense of futility came over me, which then morphed into something graver, which I would call despair and panic. Through my initial listlessness the internal voice that I mentioned earlier made itself heard loudly and clearly as it had never done before, saying "Karen, what are you doing there all alone in your house on the last day of the year with nobody to celebrate the end of the old year and the beginning of the new one? You have suppressed your need to socialise and to build close relationships and now you are all by yourself although I know you would deep down have loved to be at a social gathering and talk, laugh and dance. You have neglected this social part of yourself and now you feel lonely and isolated."

'I could see the truth of these words. My work this morning didn't feel like the sole important thing to concentrate on any longer. I craved company. I was past my mid-forties, without a partner, without children or the prospect of still having any and without even a network of close friends!

'This realisation was painful and I wondered for a few moments how an extremely successful person like myself could end up in such a position. But then the reasons were clear, as the voice in my head reminded me, if I looked back in time to the point when my parents and I were forcibly separated. There had been something bigger at stake and I knew that I had to put the fight for justice above everything else. Whilst I was fighting for children's welfare and their right to have positive relationships in their lives, I neglected significant bonds I could have had with others over the years and I guess it didn't help that I regarded human bonds as something fragile ever since I had to leave my home as a teenager. Trust in others can easily be eroded. At the time, I did trust lawyers – if not some more discerning social workers – to put things right if I told them that the accusations against my parents had been wrong. I believed then that I had formed a bond of trust to the lawyer I spoke to, but this has proven to be false.

'Things started to unravel fast from here. I felt utterly lost in the world, a sensation I had last experienced with such force in the face of the miscarriage of justice that I had described earlier. All my single-minded determination seemed to have evaporated. I couldn't stop the voice inside from nagging me: "What are you doing? Where are you going? You are so alone. You have no-one. Who are you important to? Who is important to you? You have isolated yourself and now you feel it. Loneliness is tough. It's hard to bear. It's weighing you down. You don't know how to lift the weight off you. Yes, it's painful. This is your life now. This is the life you have created. Can you carry its burden? Or will it crush you? You, who had considered yourself strong! You, who had thought you could deal with anything! Where is your strength now? Where is your resilience when you most need it? Tell me, where is it?"

'The words came fast and the tone of voice had become both louder and more insistent as it went on. I put my hands over my ears in a futile attempt to drown it out. By now I was shaking, tears were running down my face and I started to sob and gasp for air. Panicking about what was happening, I dashed to the phone to call an ambulance. By the time I had dialled 999 and heard the calm, reassuring voice at the other end, my breathing had slowed down a bit and I realised that

I was having a panic attack – something quite alien to me – and that I didn't need medical attention but just had to calm myself down. I therefore put the receiver down again and forced myself to breathe deeply and regularly, which helped. Once I felt somewhat less fearful I grabbed my purple winter anorak, slipped into my snow boots, snatched the key from the key ring near the front door and hurried out of the house. I needed fresh air not just to bring my breathing back to normal but also to clear my head if that was at all possible. I couldn't bear to be alone in the house any longer with that internal voice refusing to be quiet but instead mocking me cruelly.

'When I stepped outside, it was snowing steadily. I wasn't completely aware of my surroundings or where I was walking to; I was just following the urge to move – to move away from everything, from my home, from my life and hopefully from my thoughts and emotions. Eventually, I saw the bus station ahead of me and had an idea: Why not get on a bus, which would take me away from home further and more quickly than if I kept walking?

'I fumbled with the zipper of the outer pocket of my anorak and found some change. I always try to carry some change with me, as it often comes in handy. At the bus stop, I entered the first bus that stopped, merely said 'Final stop' to the driver without checking where it was going, paid the fare and took a seat at the back of the bus. I was in a peculiar state by then: On the one hand, there were still the remnants of the previous agitation that had culminated in my panic attack; on the other hand, tiredness coupled with a lack of engagement in my surroundings spread through me. The way I experienced these opposing sensations almost amounted to a mind-body split: My body was still ready to move forward, my muscles still being tensed, but my mind was almost shutting down, as I assume the vehemence of my previous thoughts and feelings had been too much for it to deal with for a longer period of time. I stared out of the window at the passing houses and scenery, the latter turning whiter by the minute.

'I didn't pay too much attention to the large snowflakes that came down from the sky at increasing speed, but stared at the trees we passed. I've always loved trees but now they seemed to try to make their presence felt even more with me. I gazed at their bare winter branches, which were devoid of any decoration, barren and colourless and seemingly without life. The season of death was expressed so aptly in them.

'And yet, they weren't dead. Each of these trees had a solid enough trunk to carry its other parts; each of them had so far successfully weathered the wind that was now turning into a storm. I wanted to hold these tree trunks, I wanted to hug them and I wanted to merge with them. I kept looking at them until they were out of my field of vision, which was when I refocused on some other trees ahead of us. I had lost all feeling for time and didn't think to check it so I had no idea how much later it was when the bus came to a standstill and the driver shouted, 'Final stop,' and another passenger and I alighted.

'The wind had picked up sharply and was whipping the snowflakes against my face and nearly took my breath away. I didn't really care though. My body needed to move, and move I did. I didn't know where exactly I was but it was clear that I had soon reached the very outskirts of a small town, which bordered on open fields, which were interspersed with some snow-covered hedges and the odd tree here and there.

'I ran towards the first tree that caught my eye, which was standing tall and straight next to the last couple of houses on the estate, and hugged the tree trunk firmly. I took off my gloves, which I had put on after I got off the bus, put them back into the anorak where they normally were when I didn't wear them and touched the bark of the tree with my bare hands once I had penetrated the layer of snow that covered it. The cold of the snow around my fingers sent shivers down my spine, but I tried to ignore the sharp sensation of pain and instead concentrated on the uneven, rough surface structure of the bark. And then I could feel it: A stream of warmth was running through my fingers, hands, arms and then through my entire body as a result of touching the tree. The latter might be leafless and bare, but there was a life force running through it. It was an intoxicating experience, which revived my weary and downcast mind. I felt lightheaded with joy and almost ran to the trees further out in the field to see whether it was possible to communicate with them in this way as well. Yes, I did regard what I experienced here as a communication. The tree had been trying to tell me something.

'The next tree I embraced was even bigger and I stood next to it for what I think must have been a very long time and let its internal current suffuse me. Eventually though the snowfall had become so steady and the wind so powerful that the warmth inside me started to ebb away and I began to shiver. My face became wet and painful with the icy sensation of the snowflakes whipping against my face. My body commanded me to move again if I didn't want to freeze to death there.

'Although some part of me would have been happy to stay in close union with the tree, another part of me, which asked me to follow my instinct to get moving again, won out in the end. Thus, I walked on across the fields, still trying to focus on the trees I encountered on my way, but soon finding that this became impossible with the snow coming down so densely that I could barely make out what was one or two metres in front of me. I now staggered through the snow like a drunk, struggling to keep my balance and not be hurled into the freezing snow covering the ground.

'I jumped when, out of the blue, I became aware of something emerging right in front of me, which I only just managed to stop myself from walking into. After a few seconds during which I walked alongside it, I discovered that it was an old and seemingly abandoned barn in the middle of nowhere. When I found its entrance, I tumbled inside before letting myself glide down to the floor, grateful for the drier and less freezing conditions in here. My previous agitation and the adrenaline that had kept me going had dissipated and a deep weariness and sadness came over me and replaced the last vestiges of the joy and exuberance I felt when I was holding on to the trees. This is how I remained until Lisa and then the rest of you entered the barn separately.

'Now you know how I came to be here on this day.

★

The silence in the barn weighed heavily on her after she had ended her narrative. Whilst having given a voice to the events of her past and, more particularly, to what had been going on inside her this morning – but without letting the nagging, spiteful voice inside her head do the talking – was liberating in a way, the dawning awareness of how much she had revealed about herself to practically strangers made her uncomfortable now. She wasn't used to either having to deal with or to speaking about emotions of real distress that she had experienced herself. Whenever such emotions had tried to manifest themselves, she had shown them what she believed their place should be by deliberately redirecting her attention to matters she could confidently handle.

She shifted uncomfortably on the floor, waiting for someone to say something, as she – for once – was unsure about what to say. When nobody said anything, she got up and walked to the window near Charles.

Charles got up from the floor with difficulty, stiffly took the few steps that separated them from each other and then joined her looking at the white window pane.

'You can barely make out any ice crystals any longer,' he commented.

Karen laughed in surprise. It wasn't laughter at his expense, but it was laughter that was the result of her nervous embarrassment about having shown the others in the barn the tumultuous feelings she had encountered earlier this morning. It was part of her defensive stance when she retorted with unnecessary sharpness.

'Barely? The window-pane is completely white now. You would be a magician if you were able to show us any ice crystals on it, Charles.'

Charles was unperturbed by her exclamation and responded, 'There are still some though. You can spot them if you look very closely. The patterns are dense and faint, but I can still see them.'

Karen looked at the window-pane sceptically. She was still not able to see the crystals. However, what was the point of arguing about ice crystals? She shrugged her shoulders, letting the topic drop, but was unable to come up with another one to divert her and the others' attention away from everything that she had just told them.

To her surprise it was Leo who took up the topic in a calm, thoughtful voice when he addressed her now:

'Karen, why do you not directly work with children?'

When she was about to retort something, he didn't give her a chance. 'I know your work involves children and fighting for their rights, but you are always at one remove from them and what I gather you need most of all is social interaction with both adults and children, forms of interaction that go beyond the strict confines of your legal role.'

Karen had turned around and was looking in his direction. She was slowly shaking her head. 'No, I don't think I can, or want to, give up my profession and do something else. My profession is more to me than just a job; it's been a calling.'

338

Leo's voice remained calm but determined. 'Yeah, I get that, Karen. The importance of your work has shone through your narrative, crystal clear. I'm not suggesting you stop working in the capacity you are in now but that you add other elements to your life that you are obviously missing.'

Karen became more pensive and said feebly, 'Where shall I find the time for that from? It's normally extremely busy as it is, and that's a good thing. You can see that it's only because I have nothing urgent to do at the moment that things have got on top of me. Besides, even if I had time to spare, I would need to retrain to work in a very different kind of job.'

'Not necessarily,' Leo retorted. 'People are always needed, for example to help children with their homework or just to give them a little bit of their time to talk and play. You don't need to be trained for this. I think a children's home would be the perfect place for you. You lived in a home yourself for a while as a young person and, by your own admission, it was sometimes a rough environment. The state might try to do the best for young people who have nowhere else to go by providing these homes for them, but a home – in the true sense of the word – they are not. And not every child will be as confident as you are and refuse to be bullied. Anything that makes these children's lives better would be beneficial. You can ask at the nearest children's home to where you live what volunteering opportunities they have. I'm sure there will be something for you.

'With regards to commitments and the limited time you have available, volunteers are often taken on no matter what amount of time they can spend on the work they have volunteered for. Employers tend to be quite flexible when it comes to volunteers. Also, you could probably do with cutting the hours of your job a bit and deliberately make room for something else. That must be possible, as I gather that you work well beyond your contracted hours, and your judging duties in London are on top of your full-time position in Exeter.'

Karen was surprised at how much thought Leo expended on her situation. His interested, almost caring, demeanour, which she had regarded as a blip when he had shown it earlier, formed such a stark contrast to the provocative and confrontational attitude he had frequently shown since they had all been in this barn together and that had gained the upper hand again before she started her story. Similarly, she couldn't fail but notice the apparent change in register and language, from him employing vulgar and coarse expressions to more sophisticated speech patterns. By now it was obvious to her that there was more to Leo than one would initially think when merely being greeted by his brusque manner and sometimes downright rudeness. She thought about Leo's suggestion carefully.

Leo noticed this and decided to add, 'You would also most likely make new friends amongst the adult staff and have conversations that do not involve your legal work.' He sensed that his ideas would have a higher chance of being implemented if he stopped talking about it now and let his words sink in with Karen.

Charles shuffled back to his place and nearly lost his balance when he was trying to sit down, as he was too fatigued now to have his limbs under full control. He then became aware of Lisa diagonally across from him. The last time she had said anything was before Karen had begun her story. He saw how she was – although still in a sitting position – nearly falling asleep. He said, 'We're all exhausted now. We should rest and maybe try to get some sleep again. We will probably feel better when we wake up.'

Karen, although not as tired as Charles and Lisa acquiesced, walked back to her previous spot and tried to assume a lying down position on the hard floor that she could bear being in for a while.

Leo had not stirred from the spot near Charles's that he had moved to previously. He and Charles were now curling up on the ground in close proximity of each other.

Had they been a little less dazed from tiredness, hunger, thirst as well as emotional exhaustion and been aware of the time, they might have wondered how odd it was to go to sleep at half past nine on New Year's Eve, being surrounded by strangers in a desolate location they had never been to.

★ ★ ★

The dark grey clouds hung low and looked as if they were ready to release their heavy load at any minute, which made her hurry along a busy street in central London even faster. She wasn't exactly running late for the court hearing, but having left her umbrella at home, she knew she would need to factor in quite a bit of extra time to dry herself – especially her thick hair – if she got soaked in a sudden downpour and she didn't want to madly rush around before she even entered the courtroom.

Just as she reached some traffic lights and pressed the button to stop the noisy traffic around her, something utterly strange and unexpected happened: Everything came to a sudden standstill. It wasn't so much that the cars and other vehicles on the street slowed down and eventually stopped. They completely stopped moving from one second to the next as a machine stops working when you hit the 'off' button or switch.

Was it a coincidence that she had pressed the button to cross the road just then? It must have been. She blinked. Cars and bicycles were simply standing in the middle of the street but did not form a proper queue yet in front of the traffic lights as they had not got as far as the lights. Both the cyclists and the pedestrians around her and on the other side of the road were frozen in time, mid-movement, which looked incredibly odd.

Some people had one of their feet lifted off the ground, their mouths open as if they had been in the middle of a conversation and their phones firmly pressed to their ears. A small child holding its mother's hand grimaced and had seemingly started to cry, its tears having been halted on its cheeks were looking now like transparent gems that were glued on in an artistic and decorative manner. A pigeon was captured in mid-flight, hovering not far above people's heads but not yet low enough to make them duck as so often happens when pigeons fly past and consider a landing. Everywhere she turned, all she saw were still images capturing street scenes at a particular instant. At the same time, the din in the streets had evaporated and a profound silence descended in its place.

It took her a short while to become fully aware of her being the only living being who could still move. She had turned around a couple of times to take in the unusual scenario around her and, unlike everyone else, she did not experience any difficulties in her movements. Just as she was about to step into the street, the silence surrounding her was broken by the sound of horses' hooves clapping along the same street from the left and she watched in amazement as a gleaming white carriage drawn by a couple of muscular but graceful horses rolled towards her at a steady pace.

Was there a special event scheduled today? She wouldn't have been surprised if it had escaped her notice as she could get so mired in her work that she sometimes just missed news about non-work-related happenings. Her astonishment reached new heights when the horses stopped just in front of her and the carriage door opened and discharged a little girl. It was hard to guess her age as she had a very young face, which suggested that she might only just have reached school age but had the average height of a ten-year old. She wore a white satin dress with a myriad of small, golden stars against its light background. Her hair was of an intense red colour. It was straight around her scalp but curled at the end where it fell softly over her shoulders. The girl's amber eyes emitted a warm shine and were full of life.

A flash of recognition went through her and she stared at the girl wide-eyed. She was even more baffled when the girl stepped towards her, took her by the hand and gently but determinedly led her into the carriage where she beckoned her to take a seat on the upholstered white bench in the back. The girl took a seat opposite her, stuck her head out of the window, clicked her fingers and made a sharp whistling sound. That was obviously a signal for the horses to start moving, which they did promptly without so much as a moment's hesitation. She watched her surroundings in astonishment as they made their way through the eerily silent London streets where every sound and movement had completely stopped and people, animals and vehicles had become part of a still life. Only the horses' breath and their hooves hitting the street could be heard. The girl turned back from the window and towards her. She gave her a wide smile that radiated sheer happiness.

What did this girl want? Where was she taking her? Was this an abduction? She was confused but not genuinely worried, she realised. In fact, she felt oddly at peace with this determined, smiling girl sitting across from her. Somehow, she sensed that the girl had her best interests at heart.

It didn't take long until they were in the open countryside and just as they were leaving the city behind them, the darkness of the day lifted and gave way to sunlight that was so bright that she had to close her eyes for a second.

When she opened them again, her eyes slowly adjusted to the dazzling sunshine that steeped the green fields and meadows into a glorious light. When she returned her gaze to the young girl opposite her, the girl's eyes were still fixed on her, quietly watching her absorption in the beauty of the landscape and her delight in now hearing bird song and sheep bleating in the distance. They smiled at each other and it was then that she understood why she was here.

They were in a clearing of the forest. The warm glow of the autumnal afternoon light illuminated the earth, moss, tree trunks and leaves as if trying to create a stage for them on which to perform. They laughed and danced with abandon to the music of string instruments that seemed to come out of nowhere. Whilst they had started to move slowly and hesitantly when they heard the first sounds of the invisible violins, they picked up the pace once the instruments started to play faster and twirled around the glade in tandem with the leaves on the ground that were inexplicably swept up by it all as well.

Suddenly silence fell and hushed all the sounds. He and his sister stopped their dance in disappointment. Miraculous as the unexpected onset of music had been, it had only lasted for such a short duration that they were now wondering whether they had merely – improbable as this seemed – imagined it all.

At this moment, something else happened that was entirely extraordinary. A guitar floated down from the sky, descending towards him. When it was just above him, he saw to his astonishment that it was his first guitar. He grabbed it from the air and began to play, at first melancholy and thoughtful tunes but then louder and more powerful music. It did not take Jenny long until she started to move in new and different ways and he joined in as much as his guitar play allowed him to. White petals were falling from the sky now. Children and young people entered the clearing from behind the trees. They were dressed in a strange assortment of colourful patchwork clothes and were moving wildly to the now-dissonant music, sometimes dancing with Jenny, at other times with him or each other. There were many variations in the formations of dancers. Often, they danced on their own but it nevertheless felt that there was a kind of invisible band that held them together. Colourful petals were dancing around them. There was a new radiance on his and Jenny's faces that lent them an aura of exuberance.

She didn't know how she had got to the door that she was now opening with determination. Nor did she know where she was. However, it didn't seem to matter, as she felt a force inside her that compelled her to step inside and close the door behind her and there was, strangely enough, no question about resisting that force and pondering the options she had. Instead, she was completely swept up by the force.

Once inside the room, she discovered that she was in a classroom like the ones she used to spend time in when she still attended school with its small tables for two students each arranged in rows from near the front to the back of the room. She was about to go down the central aisle to find a seat at the back of the room when she noticed that all the chairs were already taken. It wasn't a huge classroom but she still felt herself blush when the gaze of all the people in that space was directed towards her. The attention she received didn't end there: She now heard the people around her, who were all adults at different ages, say almost in unison, 'Good evening, Ms Jamieson.'

For a moment, she stood in front of them feeling stunned and didn't know what to do next. Her eyes fell on the papers she carried with her and then everything started to make sense. The top sheet showed a number-letter combination and the heading 'Creative Writing' with her name listed as tutor underneath. Before she could worry about this discovery, she once again felt led by this force that she had experienced earlier. It now propelled her to take her place behind the teacher's desk, look at the notes in front of her before taking a deep breath and, feeling reassured by the friendly and encouraging smiles on her students' part, start the lesson.

Had she stopped and thought about the situation she found herself in, she would have completely frozen, telling herself that she would never have the confidence to teach a group of people.

However, the energy that coursed inside her pushed her on and did not give her pause to let her self-doubts fully come to the surface. Instead, she calmly introduced herself and the aims and objectives of the course and gave them prompts so that they could do their first writing exercises. Whilst they were working on them, she walked around the room and individually supported each student by answering their questions and helping them when they got stuck. She felt animated and not at all shy when they talked about their approaches to the exercises and read out what they had all written. In fact, she was in a state of flow when she engaged with her eager students and offered advice and feedback, which carried on when she talked to them about structure in creative writing.

Her students listened to her with genuine interest and, when the class came to an end, all too quickly they stood up and walked past her desk with huge smiles on their faces, thanking her for the session and telling her that they were looking forward to the next one. A wave of warmth went through her and suffused her whole being. She knew then that she had arrived where she wanted and needed to be.

He stood in solemn meditation in front of her grave, which was how his visits to the cemetery usually started before his mood rapidly deteriorated and a sense of deep despair came over him.

Just before this process could set in today though something extraordinary happened. The middle of the gravestone suddenly lit up and a moment later a bright beam of light shone directly on his face, increasing quickly in brightness until he threw himself down on the ground with a shriek of pain. It felt as if his eyes had been pierced with a sharp instrument. Kneeling on the ground on all fours, he squeezed his eyes shut until the pain eased. Before he opened them again he made sure he shuffled a couple of metres to his right so that he wouldn't be directly in front of her gravestone any longer and would not have a repeat experience of the pain whose vestiges still coursed through the neurons of his brain.

He now turned carefully to his left ensuring first that the beam of light would this time not directly hit his eyes. Following its direction, he could see that its beam pointed towards the cemetery's front gate. He could not fathom what that meant or how this light beam could be emitted from Annie's gravestone. Right then, he clearly experienced the sensation of his right upper arm being squeezed gently. He turned around to identify the person who had just touched him, but found that there was nobody near him. How strange!

The soft grip on his arm did not go away though, which made him wonder whether his body played some tricks on him, toying with his mind. What he experienced as another human being's touch wasn't unpleasant though. In fact, there was something reassuring about it, which made it possible for him not to be unduly alarmed by this unprecedented occurrence. There was now a sense of him being nudged into a standing, upright position just by the way pressure was applied to his arm. Once he was in a vertical position again, he felt how he was guided by the invisible hand on his arm to walk next to the bright light beam and follow it all the way to its end. He didn't even take a proper farewell from Annie's grave as he usually did before leaving the cemetery. However, it didn't feel as if he was betraying her memory by not saying 'good-bye' this time. Rather, it seemed as if Annie was with him in a new and different way as he exited the cemetery and looked at the street scene in front of him that was illuminated by the light beam, which ended here.

On the street, which was a lot wider than how he remembered it, a group of children were deeply engaged in some sort of activity. On his approach to them, he was greeted and smiled at by every passer-by, some of whom he recognised and some of whom he had never seen before. When he stopped near the kerb, he saw what the children were doing.

Some of them were creating patterns by arranging glass marbles on the street, marbles which themselves had swirly patterns inside the otherwise translucent glass. A few of the arrangements showed recognisable figures and objects; many displayed abstract patterns. Other children were using coloured chalk to draw shapes and even scenes. They were all working from just below the kerb on both sides of the road as well as from the right and left towards the centre, which they seemed to know how to reach simultaneously. The effect this had was that of a huge mosaic in the making or even that of an intricate mandala.

He was drawn towards them and could still feel the invisible hand on his arm, which steered him towards a spot where a few colourful chalks lay on the ground. He picked up a red one, knelt down in the road not far from some other children and joined them as he began to paint the pavement, uncertain of what might emerge but at the same time not worried about it. He let himself be swept up by the flow he soon started to experience, as the children did, whilst all the time he stayed warm and reassured, still feeling the presence of the invisible hand albeit he was less conscious of it now.

⋆ ★ ⋆

The temperature in the barn had quickly dropped after they had all gone to sleep. Shivering with cold, one after another of them woke up and hugged themselves in order to get some warmth back into their bodies. Karen groaned with discomfort but made herself get up, mustering all her willpower because she knew that moving was essential to keep the blood circulation going and to stave off frost bite and hypothermia. Her body ached a lot and she needed two attempts to get back on her feet. She walked around Charles and Leo, who were partly lying, partly sitting, and stepped towards the window, which was covered in dense ice, wondering whether even Charles would now still make the claim that he could detect patterns of ice flowers on its pane. She was looking down at her watch, which she had been completely oblivious to all day. She couldn't even remember putting it on that morning, but she must have done out of habit. It was a simple watch, which would not have helped her with navigation or anything else that could be considered useful out here in the countryside. Looking at its face now, she saw that the watch was still working when it became clear that the hand indicating the passing seconds still moved steadily around. It was twenty to twelve. Karen made this twenty to midnight. It struck her that the New Year was almost upon them.

It didn't take long until she was joined by Leo, who rubbed his hands against each other and blew on them in an attempt to lessen the sensation of his sore fingers dropping off like icicles from a drainpipe.

'I now start to understand what it means when people die from the cold and we're not even outside. The extremities hurt like hell and become increasingly rigid and eventually the cold will probably immobilise the entire body. At least that's what I can sense is going to happen. Imagine the fear people experience when being thus trapped and their bodies have become coffins harbouring a rapidly dying flame that flickers ever so faintly.'

Karen turned towards Leo, giving him a glance that reflected her astonishment at the sophistication and poetry in his words although she should by now probably have been used to his abrupt changes in register that indicated the possibility of transcending the circumstances he had grown up in. She could have said that fear soon receded into the background in such situations, as people dying from the cold normally drifted off after a while losing consciousness and therefore the awareness of their impending death. However, she decided not to discuss this rather grim prospect any further. Instead, she rubbed her arms and walked on the spot before she went over to the other two who still did not move much and asked them whether they were alright.

They nodded and Charles added, 'It's just so very cold.'

Karen acknowledged this and stressed the importance of moving.

'You'll need to get back on your feet and go for a wander. We'll all need to warm up a bit at least, otherwise we'll be in danger.' She didn't elaborate on the danger she was referring to, but she didn't have to. Everyone was cognisant of what was likely to happen if they were overcome by the cold. Nevertheless, they were reluctant to get up from the floor as their legs felt stiff and achy. Every move they made proved painful.

Karen was firm enough though in her determination to make them stand up and move around, reaching out to Charles to help him up from his seated position. When she struggled with that, she called out to Leo, 'Leo, come here and give me a hand! They can't stay like that.'

Leo saw immediately what she meant and helped her with Charles before assisting Lisa to get into a vertical position.

Karen urged them to do some exercises. After briefly checking her watch, she turned back towards them.

'It's nearly midnight, folks. I'm not sure whether the weather will allow us to welcome the New Year properly by going outside but I think, as we should check the weather conditions again anyway, we could just as well give it a go.'

With these words, she pulled open the door with great determination, ignoring the somehow impaired mobility of her fingers due to the cold. To her surprise, she wasn't greeted by a strong gust of wind that whipped snowflakes into her face as she had half-expected to be. When she stepped outside, she realised that the storm had not merely abated but ceased. In fact, it was completely calm now, which was hard to believe when one considered the vehemence of the storm earlier. Looking up to the sky she saw that the dense cloud cover was partially broken and gave her a glimpse of the black night sky.

She called out to the others to come and join her and when they did she pointed at the surrounding landscape and said, 'The storm has passed.'

Just as she added, 'Look at the sky. Its cloud cover has broken,' and the other three were directing their gaze upwards, something miraculous happened: The remaining clouds dissipated within seconds, as if someone had pulled a curtain aside, and gave way to a night sky full of glittering stars that were gleaming up there like jewels and other precious stones. It was a sight to behold. They stood there in awe of the spectacle that nature presented them with, barely blinking in order not to lose that view for even a fraction of a second.

Suddenly, Karen thought she could hear the sound of church bells even though she was quite certain that that was impossible, as she did not believe that the nearest church was close enough. Nevertheless, she knew that midnight had arrived and the New Year was being rung in. She didn't bother checking her watch before she announced solemnly, 'A new year has begun.'

The others didn't respond but kept watching the night sky. They felt strangely transformed. Only after a long time had passed did Charles break the spell when he stated that he would go back inside the barn until daybreak. When the others looked at him, they saw how much he shivered.

After a while Karen stated, 'How insignificant our problems and concerns appear against the immensity of the universe of which we only catch a tiny glimpse even now that everything above and around us seems vast.' She paused briefly before resuming. 'This puts things in perspective. We should probably do this every time we are overwhelmed with something: pause to contemplate the night sky in all its splendour.'

It took about a minute until Leo commented, 'It can remove us from the urgency of our emotions, I agree. At the same time, it doesn't mean that our feelings and thoughts are nothing. We still have to live our lives in the small world we find ourselves in.'

Lisa nodded sadly. 'Yes, unfortunately. We need to hold onto our ability to transcend our reality through the power of our minds.' Something else entered her thoughts. 'And maybe…' She was thinking aloud but didn't dare to finish her sentence, as she had never been able to fully believe in the veracity of it.

It was as though Leo had come up with the same thought and now finished the sentence for her, 'Maybe we'll be able to change our lives enough to deal better with what is thrown at us.'

Karen reacted to this with a nod and then went back inside the barn, leaving Lisa and Leo to their stargazing activities.

'I had this dream,' Lisa said, 'that I was teaching creative writing to adults. It almost made me think that I could do this. It was like a wonderful prospect.' She fell silent before she said so quietly that Leo would have missed it had he not been standing so close to her, 'But maybe this is just an illusion. Someone or something is probably mocking me through this dream.' Her voice faltered.

Leo shook his head. 'That's just your self-doubt speaking here, Lisa. I get that because I woke up from a dream with the conviction that my sister and I can find a happier and easier way of living that liberates us, but only seconds later I became dubious about that notion and dismissed it as being merely part of a dream.'

Lisa replied pensively, 'It's funny that you say this. It was you, after all, who urged me earlier to believe in my dreams and pursue them. I guess you meant conscious dreams, which reflect our wishes and aspirations, rather than the dreams we have when we are asleep.'

Leo pondered this. 'Yes, I guess I did. These dreams are different in nature. We don't normally let ourselves be guided by our nightly dreams.'

Lisa responded. 'Maybe not very much, but I wonder whether we should be. Are these two kinds of dreams not merely two sides of the same coin, one side being dominated by our consciousness whereas the other side is controlled by the unconscious? Our unconscious does a lot of important things. It digests and transforms events that occurred and impressions that the mind formed during the day; it brings our feelings and instincts that we often suppress to the surface and it shows us how transformation is possible. In all this, the unconscious guides us but we choose not to listen because we think it's of no importance.'

Leo added in agreement, 'Because we think it's reason, which is part of our consciousness, that should rule the world.'

Lisa nodded. 'We neglect our unconscious at our hazard. That's what the Gothic period amply illustrated.'

Leo smiled at Lisa's flight into a historical and literary epoch to illustrate her point. He often found people's displays of learnedness pretentious – not least due to his own underprivileged background – but Lisa seemed so completely unaware of it and anything but pretentious that he found her historical references rather endearing.

Lisa resumed, 'We would be pursuing a new kind of wholeness if we took carefully into account what the different parts of our minds are trying to tell us and reconcile them with each other.'

'I guess,' Leo remarked. Then he turned to Lisa so that, for the first time, since he had stepped outside the barn he was facing her fully. 'To wholeness, Lisa!'

Had they been holding glasses of Prosecco, this exclamation would have been clearly identified as a toast to the New Year. As it was, Leo and Lisa stood somehow clumsily opposite each other, not quite sure how to add emphasis to what was being said. Leo made a move that suggested that he was about to hug Lisa, but when she didn't react in any way he thought better of it and touched her gently on her upper arm. His touch was reassuring and Lisa did not draw back.

'We should go back inside,' Leo declared. 'We could do with some sleep before sunrise.'

When they re-entered the barn, they saw that Charles was asleep again. Karen was sitting on the ground a couple of metres away from him and made small circular movements with her feet and hands so that she wouldn't lose sensation in them altogether. She nodded at Leo and Lisa when they came in. The latter almost returned to the spaces they had previously occupied but not quite – they had moved slightly closer to each other and further into the centre of the barn where they were also a shorter distance away from Karen and Charles.

When they had stood outside, they hadn't felt particularly tired any longer possibly because they were too enraptured by the starry sky. Now, however, it only took them a few minutes after they settled down on the floor before they fell into a deep and, this time, dreamless sleep.

The morning came and brought along some daylight so that the barn was now steeped in a kind of twilight. The four people inside ascertained that even though far from being well, they were at least all still alive and just about able to move. Despite feeling weakened and incredibly cold, they smiled at each other and all experienced relief and serenity that a new day had begun.

They helped each other get up from the floor, making their stiff legs obey their minds' commands. Charles unsteadily made his way over to the window that was still covered in snow and ice and stood there in silent contemplation. Just as Karen was about to open the door of the barn, he muttered happily, 'They're still there, you see. Look at the ice crystals.'

The others stepped towards the window and this time they all saw the dense, intricate patterns the ice crystals had created on the window-pane and smiled.

Then Karen walked back towards the door and pulled it open. She took a step back when she was greeted by bright sunlight that hurt her eyes after the many hours spent in darkness. The light suffused the interior of the barn and for the first time since the previous afternoon they saw each other clearly and made out more than just each other's silhouettes. In fact, even on the previous day – due to the muffled light of the snow cloud covered sky – they had not perceived each other's features as distinctly as they did now. Whilst tiredness and exhaustion was written on their faces, there was a luminosity and lightness about each of them that had not been there before. Once their eyes adjusted to the brightness around them, they stepped outside without hesitation. They were greeted by a bright blue sky and the gentle winter morning sun that shone on the deep white snow surrounding the barn and made it sparkle like diamonds.

The four people standing outside the barn inhaled the cold, clear air eagerly until their lungs were filled with it to the point of nearly bursting. They were surrounded by that white landscape that stretched out around them for what could have been miles. The flat land was interrupted by trees here and there and in one direction there were some dark, indistinct dots in the distance. Were these other barns or even houses in a nearby village?

Karen called out to direct the others' attention towards them. The others nodded when they followed the direction of her pointing hand and saw the dots on the far horizon. Between the dots and them was a thick blanket of knee-deep snow.

They turned towards each other again and smiled. There was no need for words. Then, as if following an inaudible command, they turned towards the warming rays of the sun and closed their eyes.

A new year had begun.

Printed in Great Britain
by Amazon